PRAISE FOR WAR UNDER THE MANGO TREE

"Loaded with plenty of whiskey-tango-foxtrot moments, War Under the Mango Tree *is a thoroughly entertaining lampoon of the US military machine via a fictionalized mission in an equally fictional Central African country. Author Voelz delivers realistic characters and sharp, witty dialog that will leave you alternating between feeling genuinely sorry for the Army officers, who are constantly played by their third-world hosts, and hysterical fits of laughter. Not since Catch 22 has a novel this brilliant come along.* **Five cheeky stars!***"*

—David Edlund,

USA Today bestselling author of "Guarding Savage"

". . . a brilliant satire of the hypocrisy, bureaucracy, banality, and ineptitude of the military—as well as the sinister agendas and left-handed ways of the profit-hungry companies that work with them. Like the classic film Dr. Strangelove, War Under the Mango Tree *is scathingly funny and often feels absurd—yet other times, all too real."*

—David Aretha,

editor of multiple award-winning military books

WAR UNDER THE MANGO TREE

A NOVEL

GLENN VOELZ

War Under the Mango Tree, a novel
by Glenn Voelz

Copyright © 2019 by Glenn Voelz
All rights reserved.
First Edition © 2019

Published by

FSP First Steps Publishing
     PO Box 571
FIRST STEPS Gleneden Beach, OR 97388
PUBLISHING

Interior layout, cover design by Suzanne Parrott
Cover Art, "War Under the Mango Tree", ©2019 / Suzanne Fyhrie Parrott

Library of Congress Control Number: 2019940597
Genre: *dark humor, political satire, military fiction, war*

ISBN: 978-1-937333-96-6 (hb)
ISBN: 978-1-937333-94-2 (pb)
ISBN: 978-1-937333-95-9 (epub)

10 9 8 7 6 5 4 3 2 1

Printed in the United States of America.

WAR UNDER THE MANGO TREE

A NOVEL

GLENN VOELZ

FSP
FIRST STEPS
PUBLISHING

For the Author Seeking
a Solid Foundation

ACKNOWLEDGMENTS

Thank you to Jonathan and Laura for your time and thoughtful suggestions as this project evolved.

To Susan.
For your love, support, and patient editing

One who shakes the tree
expects some fruit to fall his way.
–Swahili proverb

CHAPTER ONE

US MILITARY FORWARD OPERATING BASE,
DEMOCRATIC REPUBLIC OF GISAWI (DROG)

The men in camouflage sat around the conference room table staring blankly at a checkerboard array of televisions mounted on the wall. Muted images from several international news networks showed live footage of an unfolding drama involving a baby elephant mired in a monsoon-swollen river.

The air in the room was thick with humidity and the funk of perspiration. Steel bars and black curtains covered the windows, giving no hint of the time outside. Along one wall, a bank of computer terminals glowed in the dim light, screens flickering with weather forecasts and intelligence reports from around the globe. The conference table was littered with evidence of the day's labor, briefing slides filled with cryptic military symbology and topographic maps covered in doctrinal graffiti and yellow Post-It notes.

The men watched impassively as a band of good Samaritans on the screen struggled to free the miniature pachyderm from a swirling eddy. Suddenly, the digital chirping of the entry control system pierced the silence. Heads turned with choreographed precision at the steel-reinforced door as Colonel Ed Kittredge, commander of Operation Righteous Protector, entered the room. His gaunt frame and arthritic gait gave the impression of a man whose years of service to the Army were felt with every step.

The colonel lowered himself stiffly into the seat at the head of the table, then glanced up at the time-zone clock dangling from the ceiling.

Washington DC: 1550
Stuttgart Germany: 2150
Democratic Republic of Gisawi (DRoG): 2250

"The general will be dialing in from Germany any minute. Let's run through this one more time. I don't want any fuck-ups in front of the boss. Intel update first," Kittredge said, looking down the table at Major Pete "Sid" Sidwell.

The heavyset officer was blessed and cursed with a mild disposition and the sluggish metabolism of a tree sloth. He wore his hair in an old-fashioned flattop, neatly trimmed and waxed to geometric perfection. Sid glanced nervously down at his notes through bookish, half-rim glasses and began his briefing.

"Good evening, sir. No change to the enemy situation here in DRoG. The Gisawi Liberation Army continues conducting low-level attacks in the western region. We believe that GLA leader Daniel Odoki remains somewhere in the safe-haven zone just across the border where the Gisawian Defense Forces can't touch him due to tensions with the neighboring regime."

"Got it, Sid. Old news. Cut to the chase. What are we looking at for tonight's mission?" Colonel Kittredge said, glancing impatiently up at the clock.

"Based on the recent information provided by our Gisawian counterparts, tonight we're looking at an area of about fifty square kilometers northeast of the border. They believe some GLA cells have recently been staging there between their operations."

"What have we got for overhead surveillance?"

"Unfortunately, not much. We've been allocated a few hours from an unmanned platform that's diverting down from another mission up north. At best that'll give us about ninety minutes over our target area."

"Ninety minutes! Are you kidding me? We're talking about an area the size of Manhattan. Most of it jungle!" Kittredge fumed. "The general's gonna flip his lid when he finds out that's all we got."

"Sir, we're doing our best to optimize," Sid stammered. "We've narrowed down the search area to a few spots where the Gisawians think Odoki's men are active. Hopefully, we'll have enough time overhead to confirm or deny their presence."

"How's the weather?"

"A few scattered clouds but generally favorable. If Odoki's men are out there tonight, we should have an OK chance of picking them up on the infrared camera."

The colonel's face puckered. "Really? We haven't seen or heard them in months. We're not getting any useful information from the Gisawians."

Sid shrugged apologetically. "We don't know what to make of it, sir. The Gisawians are claiming that their sources on the ground dried up. That's why we haven't been able to pinpoint Odoki's whereabouts."

Kittredge shook his head in frustration. "So, you're telling me that he's just disappeared into thin air? We have the most sophisticated intelligence apparatus of any military on the planet, and we can't even track down a few hundred guys wandering around out in the jungle?"

Sid shifted uncomfortably in his chair, having been through the same conversation dozens of times before.

"Sir, the GLA fighters aren't stupid. They know we're watching from above, so they lay low at night. They've stopped lighting campfires. They park their trucks far from where they sleep since they know our cameras can pick up engine heat. They've stopped talking on the radios unless they're about to hit a target. The same goes for cell phones. Even when we get lucky and pick up some chatter, it's all just code words and gibberish in local dialects. Our translators can't make heads or tails of it."

"What are they saying over at the Gisawian Ministry of Defense? Does MoD have any clue about what Odoki might be up to?"

"They have a few theories, but I'm not sure I'd put money on any of them. Our contacts over at MoD keep insisting that Odoki is planning something big, but we never seem to get any details about what it might be."

"For god's sakes, it's their damn country! Don't they have any idea what's going on out there?"

Sid paused, giving the colonel a moment to simmer down.

"Sir, if Odoki is really planning a major operation, then there's a chance we might pick up some activity during tonight's surveillance. Our sensor package has foliage-penetrating radar. It's pretty good for seeing through the tree cover."

"And that's going to give us something actionable? Something we can hit with the strike teams?"

"Probably not," Sid conceded. "We just don't have the assets to cover such a large area. Even with our advanced sensors the analysts still have a hard time telling the difference between a GLA training camp and hundreds of little villages that don't even show up on our maps. Not to mention the occasional tourist safari or geologic survey team passing through the area. There's just no way to tell the difference between them and a patrol of GLA fighters. From ten thousand feet, it all looks the same."

"If that's the case, then what the hell are we looking for out there?"

"Basically, anything that seems unusual…," Sid offered sheepishly.

"All right let's just move on," the colonel said, rubbing his temples in frustration. "General Foster will be on any minute. What's the status of the bird?"

"The platform entered the engagement zone approximately twenty minutes ago. It should already be passing data back to the analysts up in Germany. If they see anything interesting, they'll let us know so we can point the strike teams in the right direction. That's all I've got for now."

"OK, thanks, Sid. Let's go to operations next," the colonel said, turning to the other end of the table. "Jorgs, what's the status of the strike teams?"

Master Sergeant Jorgenson looked up from his laptop, pausing dramatically before setting his elbows down firmly on the table. The sleeves of his uniform pulled snugly over meaty biceps, which accentuated a chiseled physique. Sandy blond hair perfectly coiffed in bold defiance of the sub-Saharan humidity and military regulation. He carried himself with the deceptive physicality of a Komodo Dragon, with a hair-trigger reserve of kinetic energy that could arc from comatose to neck-snapping violence in the blink of an eye.

When he had the room's undivided attention, Jorgenson tapped at the keys of his laptop, bringing up a live-action map on the screen at the front of the room. Animated icons showed the position of three airborne assault teams moving in separate helicopters. Another slower-moving icon traced the path of the surveillance drone as it circled over the engagement area. Finally, Jorgenson looked up to address his audience.

"Sir, earlier this evening I conducted a pre-mission briefing with our team leaders embedded with the Gisawian Ranger platoons. Because of the large area for tonight's mission, we decided to break the unit down into three, separate assault teams. That will give us the flexibility to run simultaneous raids against multiple targets if required."

Kittredge nodded. "We have an American advisor onboard each of those helicopters?"

"Roger, sir, as per our standard operating procedure. We'll be right there with the Gisawians every step of the way," Jorgenson said, unconsciously flexing his biceps back and forth like a sinewy metronome. "You can see on the map where we've got the three teams in a holding pattern above the target area. If the drone picks up something interesting on the ground, we can vector them to any location inside that box in under twelve minutes."

"Are the Gisawians ready?"

Jorgenson nodded. "We've been training them hard for the last three weeks. The boys are ready. Now, all we need is some good intel to point them in the right direction."

"OK, Jorgs, sounds good," the colonel replied. "We're almost out of time so let's finish up with Public Affairs. Burke, you've got sixty seconds."

Captain Stephen J. Burke III straightened in his seat, having waited impatiently for his moment to speak. He looked obliquely at the colonel, accentuating his Romanesque features, giving the impression of someone sitting for a portrait. Even in his wrinkled camouflage uniform, Burke carried himself with an air of patrician entitlement. Seeming indifferent to his company and circumstances, merely tolerating the inconvenience as a way station to bigger and better things.

"Sir, the approved media scripts have been prepared," Burke began. "If we make positive contact tonight we're ready to move across all messaging streams, conventional and social media. Our standard talking points remain the same. We focus on Odoki's reign of terror and US actions to counter his destabilization of western DRoG," he said, annunciating the country's acronym as a twangy *Deee-Rog*. An affection borrowed more from his shallow roots in northwestern Pennsylvania than his formative years at Phillips Exeter.

"Any change to our bottom line?"

"No, sir. Key takeaways remain the same. We are highlighting the unprecedented successes of the three-year US advisory mission in DRoG aimed at bringing peace and stability to a valued American ally to secure vital American security interests across the region."

Just as Captain Burke finished speaking, Colonel Kittredge noticed a flurry of activity up on the screen. At the other end of the video teleconference, an entourage of officers scurried into the room, followed by Major General William G. Foster. He moved into the frame like a boxer entering the ring, bald head buffed to a high gloss finish, uniform pressed as stiff as plywood. The gaggle of subalterns stood rigidly at attention while Foster bobbed and weaved to his seat then jabbed a thick thumb at the microphone button.

"Gentlemen! Good evening from Germany," Foster's voice boomed through the speakers. "I've just been briefed by our intelligence section. They tell me we've identified two potential targets of interest. The drone picked up some indications of new vehicle traffic in a remote area without known settlements. We've already passed the coordinates directly to our advisors onboard the aircraft with Gisawian rangers. How do you copy?"

Colonel Kittredge glanced anxiously at Master Sergeant Jorgenson, waiting for him to verify the general's information. After a few seconds, Jorgenson glanced up from his laptop, nodding coolly.

"Affirmative, sir. We're pulling up the coordinates now," Kittredge told the general before covering the microphone and turning back to Jorgenson. "How long until the assault teams are in position?"

"Nine minutes until the first team is over the target area. The choppers have enough fuel to remain overhead for another thirty-five. After that, they'll need to pull back for refueling. I'm moving the last bird into a holding pattern between the two targets in case either team needs backup."

The colonel nodded and uncovered the microphone.

"General Foster, we're tracking the assault teams about ten minutes out from the targets. Standard rules of engagement apply. The Gisawians Rangers will have the lead once the teams hit the ground. Our advisors will remain at a safe distance while monitoring the operation."

"Thank you, Colonel. We'll be watching things from our end," the general said, flipping his microphone to mute and conferring with his staff.

Everyone stared blankly up at the screen, waiting anxiously for updates. On one side of the display was the muted image of General Foster involved in an animated discussion with his staff. On the other half, the live digital map showed the icons for the assault teams inching toward their targets. Periodically Master Sergeant Jorgenson broke the silence to read off updates sent via secure text messaging from the advisors onboard the aircraft.

2259: Team one beginning insertion

2304: Team one on the ground approximately 500 meters from the target...

2306: Team two preparing for insertion...

As the teams moved into position, General Foster abruptly ended the private conversation with his staff and turned his attention back to the map. A few minutes later Jorgenson read off another status report from the Rangers.

*Team one reports negative contact on the ground. I re-
peat, negative contact. The team leader says it looks like
an abandoned safari camp. No signs of GLA activity...*

General Foster shook his head, fists clenched on the
table. A minute later, Jorgenson glanced up from his laptop
with an update from the second team.

*Team two has identified several structures on the ground
at their target site. The Gisawians are moving into position and preparing to clear the buildings...*

Five minutes passed without any word, then suddenly
the silence was broken by the electronic chime of a new text
message popping into Jorgenson's laptop. His eyes focused
on the screen, reading the message to himself before looking
up at Colonel Kittredge.

*Team two reports negative contact. The camp is empty.
An initial sweep showed signs of recent GLA presence.
Possibly within the last twelve hours. Looks like we just
missed them, again...*

Kittredge exhaled and sunk into his chair before reaching
over and flipping open the mic.

"General Foster, I assume you just heard the same thing
we did. No joy on either target. Per SOP, our advisors will
walk the Gisawians through the site exploitation protocol.
We'll be sure they gather up anything of intel value. We may
be able to pull some DNA samples or fingerprints from the

camp and run them against our database of known GLA fighters."

The general nodded, then turned to speak with one of his aides. The microphone was still on mute but his frustration was obvious. A moment later he flipped open the intercom and looked straight into the camera.

"Gentlemen, I'm not going to tell you that I'm not disappointed. This isn't the first time we've been here, and it may not be the last. But each time, you've got up next morning and went back at it. I expect nothing less this time. You are the best damn soldiers in the world. The backbone of the most powerful fighting force in the history of mankind. And don't you forget it!" Foster growled, jabbing his thick index finger into the camera at the unseen audience.

"Colonel Kittredge, you and your team down there are making the best of a challenging situation. For that, the American people owe you an unmeasurable debt of gratitude," Foster said, pausing dramatically, rubbing at the stubble on his chin.

"Unfortunately, most of our fellow citizens will wake up tomorrow morning oblivious to that fact. They will go about their business without giving a second thought to the sacrifices necessary to protect and preserve their self-indulgent, morally debased existence. Sadly, such ignorance is the price we pay for freedom. But as defenders of this birthright, you deserve better. Better than a bunch of pointy-headed politicians, who don't know their asses from a hole in the ground, giving you an impossible mission without the resources to accomplish it. But I promise you, come hell or high water, we are going to track down this son-of-a-bitch and finish the job we were sent here to do. We are going home winners! You have my word on it," Foster said, leveling a steely-eyed glare straight into the camera.

"Now, if I could kindly ask you all to clear out the room, I have some business to discuss privately with Colonel Kittredge."

The audience at both ends of teleconference snapped to attention, saluted, and dutifully shuffled out the door. Once the room was empty, Kittredge flashed a thumbs-up into the camera and braced himself for what was coming.

"Goddamn it, Kittredge! How many times are we going to replay this goat screw?" the general bellowed into the microphone. Over thousands of miles of satellite links and fiber optic cables, Kittredge could see the splotchy red patches rising above the general's collar.

"What the bloody hell is going on down there? We've been at this for almost three years now, stumbling around like Keystone Cops in that godforsaken jungle. And all that time we haven't come up with anything more than piles of warm shit and empty beer bottles!"

Kittredge waited until the general's rant seemed exhausted before venturing a response.

"Sir, with all due respect, we're fighting with our hands tied behind our backs. We've got no intel on the ground. These tips we're getting from the Gisawians aren't leading anywhere. On top of that, we're only getting a few hours of drone time each month. That's nowhere near enough to track these guys down. We need dedicated assets. Otherwise, it's just going to be more of the same."

The general closed his eyes and took a deep breath, suggesting some herculean effort of self-regulation.

"Listen, Ed. We go way back. Afghanistan. Iraq. Now this little shithole. I'm gonna be straight with you. This thing is coming to a head. Last week I had a delegation of staffers from the Armed Services committee in my office. You want to know what I learned?"

Kittredge nodded hesitantly.

"I learned that you and I have somehow achieved the impossible. We have created a rare moment of bipartisan consensus in DC, with both sides of the aisle in full agreement that this mission is a complete pile of shit. The Republicans want out because it's costing a crapload of taxpayer money without killing or capturing a single big-name bad guy. Meanwhile, the bleeding-heart Democrats are whining about DRoG's human rights record ever since President Namono threatened to run for a seventh term. I'm telling you, Ed, this thing is turning into a perfect fucking storm. Nobody back in DC wants to hear anything more about Daniel Odoki or the goddamn GLA! They just want out of there as soon as possible."

Kittredge shook his head but didn't seem surprised. "Well, boss, I know the Gisawians aren't perfect, but they seem happy to have us around. This is the first place I've been in fifteen years where the locals weren't trying to kill me. Doesn't that count for something?"

"Apparently not. Here's the bottom line, Ed. We're about to get an eviction notice. It's low-hanging fruit. The average American couldn't find DRoG on a map if it was tattooed across their ass. No one gives a damn about Odoki anymore. Even the Jesus freaks have forgotten about him claiming to be the Messiah. This thing has just become one big liability with no end in sight."

"How much time do have?"

"Not much. The president won't risk blowback by crawling away with his tail between his legs right before the primaries. I'm guessing his plan is to let the budget committees quietly kill it off in the next appropriation. That way he can still pretend to give a crap about Africa while pinning the blame on Congress for yanking the money. So, here's the bottom line. We've got maybe six months, tops. After that, this entire thing gets flushed down the toilet."

Kittredge let the news sink in. "OK, sir, then what's the call? You want me to slow-roll this thing? Just wait it out, then start packing up our bags once we get the official word?"

"Goddamn it, Ed, that's exactly what those peckerheads want us to do! They pull this trick every time they get themselves into a war that doesn't deliver a ticker-tape parade in less than ninety-six hours. The talk show clowns start hemming and hawing about 'quagmire' and 'exit strategies.'" The general made air quotes with his fingers. "They did it to my old man in Vietnam. They did it to you and me in Iraq. But not this time. I'm not going to let them. Until those little fuckers turn off the money, I'm still in charge."

"But sir, no one is going to second-guess you on this," Kittredge said. "You've done everything humanly possible to accomplish the mission. There's no shame in that."

"Spare me the flag-waving, Ed. The honest-to-god truth is, I don't give a flying fuck about Odoki. But I'm sure as hell not going to end my career by walking away from another mission just because some Beltway pencil-pusher decided to nickel and dime us out of winning. They'll be happy enough just declaring victory on Twitter, then moving on to the next bright, shiny object. Hell, they might even throw in a seventy-five-cent piece of ribbon to put on my chest at the retirement ceremony. That's how my old man went out and he never got over it. He carried that shit with him to his dying day. But I'm telling you, Ed, I'm not walking out that same door. No...fucking...way."

Kittredge nodded as he digested the general's words. "Sir, I get it, but I just don't see how this plays out any different."

"Ed, you're not hearing what I'm saying! We are not ending this thing with a two-line press release buried on page eighteen of the *Washington Post*. Not this time. I want Odoki. Or at least someone who smells a hell of a lot like him."

"Roger, sir. I'm with you," Kittredge replied. "But my hands are tied. I've got no leverage. No assets. No authorization for direct action. We need something more. Maybe you can give a call over to General Armstrong at special operations and ask him for..."

"Hell...fucking...no!" the general's voice blasted through the speakers. "Armstrong wouldn't give me a glass of warm piss if I was dying of thirst in the desert! The only way he'd help us get Odoki would be if he knew that he'd be the one walking away with all the glory. It's been that way ever since we were goddamn roommates at the Academy. The only reason we're even getting what we have now is because somebody at the Pentagon forced him to cough it up."

"What about getting our own drones down here?" Kittredge asked. "If we get authorization for a direct strike, we might actually have a chance of catching Odoki out in the open."

"Fat chance," the general sniffed. "Armstrong's got that game cornered. He's not about to let anyone else get a slice of his action. He's spent the last ten years on big game safari hunting down terrorists and getting his mug on the cover of *Vanity Fair. Vanity*...fucking...*Fair* for god sakes!" Foster shouted into the mic. "He should have been court-martialed for that alone! But no way. The guy is bulletproof. An Ivy League Ph.D., a full head of hair, and a direct line to the president. He just picks up the phone and gets anything he wants 24/7. But one thing's for sure, Ed. As long as I'm in charge, Armstrong will make damn sure that we won't get as much as a paper airplane and spitballs down there. That little fucker hasn't changed a bit in thirty years."

"Then where does that leave us, sir?" Kittredge interjected, hoping to steer the conversation to safer waters. "Just tell me what you want. I'll do my best to make it happen."

"Ed, you're a smart guy. Smart guys make options. I don't know the answer yet, but I do know that we've only got a few months to figure it out. Here's the bottom line. I'm not going home without a scalp. Your job is to figure out how to get me one. Is that clear enough guidance for you?"

Kittredge nodded. "Yes, sir. All clear. I just need some time to think on it. We've got a new executive officer coming in tonight. This will be his number one priority."

"New XO? What happened to the old guy? The one with the eye tick, right?"

"Sorry, sir. I thought you knew," Kittredge hesitated. "He came down with malaria. We evacuated him last month. It took a while to find a replacement."

"Malaria? Jesus. Don't they have you guys on meds down there?"

"Yes, sir. Apparently, they weren't mixing well with his antidepressants. He went off his prescription and got sick."

"All right. Just let me know what you and the new guy figure out. The clock's ticking," Foster said before the video link abruptly cut off.

Kittredge sat there staring at the pale blue screen, gathering his thoughts for a moment before calling the staff back into the room. Once everyone had reassembled, he ran down through his notes.

"OK, team. I know it's late, so I'll keep this short. I've got some new guidance from the boss. I'll be working through the details with the new XO once he gets settled in. Who's picking him up at the airport?"

Sid raised his hand. "His flight lands in about an hour. I'll drive over and pick him up at the passenger terminal."

"OK, good. Give him this when you see the new guy," Kittredge said, pushing a folded piece of notebook paper across the table. "It's his to-do list. I want to see him first thing in the morning."

Next Kittredge turned to Captain Burke, the public affairs officer.

"Burke, obviously there's not going to be a press release tonight, but I want you to call over to the Embassy. Have the operator contact Ambassador Roberts at home to let her know what happened. I'll give the defense attaché a full briefing in the morning if she wants any more details."

Burke nodded as Kittredge turned back to Sid, suddenly remembering something else. "Is Louie Bigome over in his office?"

"Yes, sir. His light is still on."

"Good. Fill him in too. No reason for him to stick around any longer. He can brief his boss over at MoD in the morning if they haven't already heard the news. What else am I forgetting?" Kittredge asked, looking once more around the table. "Captain Dodge. Didn't you have something for me?" he suddenly remembered, looking at the Civil Affairs officer who had been a silent spectator all evening.

"Yes, sir. The cattle vaccination program. We're kicking it off next week during the exercise."

"What? Now we're giving shots to cows? How the hell is that supposed to help us get Odoki?"

"Winning hearts and minds, sir?" Dodge offered uncertainly.

"Whose?"

"Hmm…"

"Can it wait until morning?" Kittredge said, cutting Dodge off before he could answer.

The captain nodded, sensing that the plan would brief better in the light of day.

"OK then, great. I'll see you in my office right after I meet with the new XO. Gentlemen, that's it for tonight. Get some sleep. We'll get back at it in the morning."

+++

An hour later Sid pulled a white Toyota Hilux pickup truck into an unpaved lot across the road from the international airport. He had a few minutes until the flight arrived, so Sid eased back into the seat and pulled a bag of pork rinds from his backpack, reminding himself of the diet he intended to start first thing in the morning. Munching on the fried lard, Sid watched the bustle of activity through the truck's dusty windshield. The terminal building was a boxy modernist relic of post-colonial ambition now fallen into disrepair from decades of neglect. In front of the structure was a large open-air plaza teeming with locals awaiting the last few flights of the evening.

Sid turned off the engine and rolled down the window, preferring the humidity over the burnt rubber smell of the truck's faltering air conditioning. After a few minutes, he spotted the aircraft's landing lights through the hazy horizon. The lumbering jet arched gently into the pattern, settling onto the airport's single runway before taxiing alongside a few other idle aircraft awaiting their morning departures back to Europe.

As the passengers disembarked onto the darkened runway, Sid got out of the truck and crossed the plaza toward the arrivals area. He maneuvered purposefully through the mass of humanity mingling outside the terminal. Tight circles of taxi drivers sat on cheap plastic chairs, sipping warm soda, playing cards, and waiting for the last fares of the evening. Wandering lady merchants in floral-patterned dresses with swaddled babies across their backs sold baggies of drinking water and boiled groundnuts. A few small-time entrepreneurs flashed thick wads of local currency, calling out black market rates just a stone's throw from the official airport FOREX booth. Other young men wandered through the crowd selling cheap Chinese flip phones and prepaid calling cards, using battered suitcases as impromptu storefronts.

Sid emerged from the other side of the carnival-like plaza and nodded respectfully at a pair of bored-looking DRoG soldiers stationed on either side of the door leading into the arrivals hall. Barely more than teenagers, they wore distinctive burgundy berets and Soviet-era automatic rifles casually slung across their chests. They halfheartedly scrutinized the crowd between bouts of thumbing at their phones, occasionally shooing away a taxi driver loitering too close to the doorway.

Inside, Sid found a place to stand at the edge of the crowd, hoping to avoid attention. However, it didn't take long before he attracted the curious stares of several nearby children. He ventured a friendly wave, then immediately regretted it when the children began playfully chanting the local slang term for "white guy" until scolded by their parents. Sid tried his best to ignore them while scanning the faces of the passengers streaming out of the customs zone.

Most appeared to be local Gisawians coming home from jobs or studies overseas. The returning diaspora resembled a modern-day caravan crossing the Sahara, pushing overburdened luggage carts piled high with nylon bundles containing gifts from faraway lands. However, the exotic turned familiar as Sid watched the tired travelers spotting friends and families among the crowd. The joyous reunions required no translation as friends embraced, lovers kissed, and children clung tightly to their parents.

While he waited, Sid passed the time by profiling passengers as they exited from the baggage area. Two decades earlier, fresh out of high school, he had enlisted in the Army and was assigned into counter-intelligence. Years later, he still found himself going through the memorized checklists for assessing sources that he had learned during training, but now it was just a game to occupy his mind.

Sid focused his attention on the handful of white faces salted in among the African travelers. First through the door were two middle-aged men wearing pleated khaki trousers and blazers too heavy for the climate. At the front of the immigration queue, with carry-on only luggage, Sid presumed they must have been traveling in business class for only a short stay. One of them wore an expensive pair of silver-toed cowboy boots. Clearly on his first trip to DRoG given the inappropriate choice of footwear during rainy season when solid earth turned to bottomless mud in seconds. Both of them wore watches worth more than a year's salary for the average local. Sid scanned the room and quickly spotted a man whom he guessed was their driver: a local Gisawian sweating profusely under an ill-fitting gray polyester uniform and secondhand chauffeur's cap, holding a sign bearing the logo of a big multinational mining company.

Next through the door was a haggard-looking expat family, clearly exhausted from what was probably an extended journey stuffed back in coach. Clean-cut, self-assured travelers with enough luggage for a long stay. Sid marked them as new State Department arrivals. Perhaps a consular officer putting in a hardship tour hoping to land Bratislava or Bogota on the next assignment. Behind them were two more DRoG newbies clad in discount safari gear, sensible footwear and laboring under the weight of mountainous backpacks. They seemed insufficiently earnest and underdressed for LDS. Sid pegged them as new Peace Corps volunteers, bright-eyed and determined to rescue downtrodden Gisawians from the evils of split infinitives and traditional farming practices.

Next out among the sweaty masses was a group of euro backpackers enjoying a gap year or three, meandering along a sub-Saharan version of the hippie trail. The women appeared generically Scandinavian with dirty-blond dreadlocks bouncing over their shoulders and thong underwear visible through their thin muslin dresses. Trotting behind them were several male companions clad in surfer shorts and T-shirts, sporting scrappy goatees and plug earrings. The group floated effortlessly into their new environs. The jetsam of first-world privilege riding the currents of favorable exchange rates, cheap holiday bungalows, and rumors of good local weed.

Finally, Sid spotted his mark sticking out like a space alien among the braless, patchouli-oiled Scandinavian women. He looked like a lanky farm boy on his first trip away from home, with a high-and-tight haircut, Old Navy cargo pants, and a Kansas City Royals baseball cap pulled down low. Slung over his shoulder was a camouflage-patterned backpack adorned with Velcro patches of various military insignia and an American flag displayed prominently on the top flap. The entire ensemble gave the impression of someone determined to be the first passenger executed in the event of a terrorist hijacking.

Without moving from his spot, Sid casually raised his hat above his head, trying to catch the alien's attention. It didn't take long before his mark picked up the subtle signal from the only other white man standing in the arrivals area. He dragged his large duffel bag through the crowded room over to where Sid was standing.

"John Carson?" Sid inquired, offering out his hand.

"Yup," he answered.

"Pete Sidwell. But just call me Sid. You got all your shit?"

"Hope so."

"Good. The truck's parked out back. Don't worry about the crowds. This ain't Iraq. People actually like us here."

"Seems a good way to start," Carson said as he followed Sid through the doors into the mass of humanity outside the terminal.

Once inside the truck, Sid turned the ignition and backed out of the lot. Carson felt the blast of air conditioning against his skin as the truck's windows began fogging over in the humidity.

"Welcome to DRoG," Sid offered as he maneuvered the truck into the potholed road.

"Glad to be here."

"Sure. Whatever," Sid chuckled. "They must have tagged you on pretty short notice. The last guy has only been gone a few weeks."

"Yeah, the Army gave me ten days to pack my bags. My wife was pretty pissed when she realized I was going to miss my son's birthday for the third year in a row."

"Sorry to hear that," Sid said. "They couldn't find anyone else to take the bullet?"

"I wasn't really in a position to say no. I've got a promotion board is coming up. I need to get a good evaluation in my file just to be safe."

"I'm not sure this is the right place to make your mark, but if keep your nose clean while you're here you should be fine," Sid offered. "By the way, did you have to look DRoG up on a map when they told you where you were going?"

Carson hesitated for an instant before Sid smiled and put him at ease. "Don't worry. I'm supposed to be an intel officer and I still had to Google it when I got my orders."

"In that case, I guess I don't feel so bad. It's my first time in Africa."

"I'd say make the best of it while you can. If you believe the rumors, we may not be here much longer."

"Really? Then I wonder why they even bothered sending me over."

Sid shrugged. "Who knows? Of course, that could all change tomorrow so don't hold me to it. Anyway, the commander wants to see you first thing in the morning. He'll fill you in on all the details."

"Any words of advice?"

"About the colonel or just generally?"

"Either one, I guess."

"Nope, not really. You'll figure things out soon enough. The boss is a decent guy. Keeps to himself but he knows his business. As long as you're doing your job he's easy enough to get along with. Otherwise, just remember to take your meds."

"Meds?"

"Yeah, they gave you anti-malaria pills, didn't they?"

"Oh yeah, I've got them here in my bag."

"Good. That's what got the last guy. Don't forget to take them. Unless, of course, you're really itching to get home sooner. In that case, just throw them out the window."

"Right. So, any idea what I'll be doing?"

"Hard to say. I'm sure the colonel will fill you in tomorrow. He wants to see you in his office at 0800. Oh yeah, he told me to give you this."

Sid handed Carson a crumpled scrap of paper ripped from a spiral notebook. Carson flattened it over his knee and read it under the dim glow of the dashboard light. The title at the top of the page read "Priorities for the New XO." Underneath were three numbered bullets.

1. Fix coffee situation
2. New gym equipment???
3. Kill Odoki

"What the hell does this mean?" Carson asked. "Fixing the coffee is my top priority?"

Sid shrugged. "I have no idea. But the coffee could use some help. If I were you, I'd get some sleep and not worry about it until morning."

Carson shook his head and stuffed the paper into his pocket then turned to look out the window. It had been a long while since he had been on a stretch of road so dark. There wasn't a single street light or any other illumination beyond the moon. A few times he thought he saw something moving around in the shadows, leaving him wondering what kinds of things inhabited the night in this part of the world. After a while, he just assumed it was his jet-lagged mind playing tricks. He leaned his head against the window and closed his eyes, falling asleep for the rest of the drive to camp.

CHAPTER TWO

———

Carson woke the next morning shivering, having kicked off the bedsheet during a restless night. It took a moment to place himself, having to mentally retrace his journey from the day before. He remembered his kids crying when he said goodbye to them at the airport, unable to tell them how long he would be away this time. His wife had been more stoic. Steeling herself for another stretch of single parenthood. Resenting him or the army, or both.

When Carson's eyes adjusted to the light, he sat up on the flimsy mattress and surveyed his new home—a room about the size of a compact car with all the amenities of a low-security prison cell. Next to the squeaky metal-framed bed was a nightstand with a lamp, a wooden desk, and an empty trash can smelling of overripe fruit. The walls were made of reinforced plywood hastily covered in a thin coat of off-white paint. A small rectangular window provided the only source of natural light. Through the flimsy wall, he could hear someone, or something, shuffling around in the adjacent room.

Carson reached for the lamp, flipping the switch only to discover that it was missing a bulb. He fumbled around in semi-darkness, searching for his watch. For a moment he stared intently at the hands before finally grasping that it was still set to Eastern Standard Time. Working backward through the math he suddenly realized that he was about to be late for his appointment with the commander.

Carson leaped from the bed and flung back the curtain, his brain still groggy from lack of sleep. In a state of jet-lagged stupor, he couldn't remember the combination to the padlock on the duffel bag containing all his clothes. On the fourth attempt, he frantically dumped the contents on the floor and began digging through the pile in search of a clean uniform. After locating a matching top and bottom he paused and stared at the chalky-gray pixelated camouflage pattern, a color scheme utterly non-indigenous to the ecosystem outside. Resigned to the tactical faux pas Carson pulled on the wrinkled mess, reassuring himself that stealth would not be a driving concern of his appointed duties.

After a rushed effort with a razor and toothbrush, Carson ventured outside his room. Looking down the hallway, he saw several similar doors on either side of the corridor. The rectangular blockhouse had been sectioned off into a maze of container-sized sleeping quarters. He noticed that someone had already affixed a personalized name tag to his door identifying him as the cell's occupant.

He walked down the hallway looking at similar tags on all the other doors until eventually coming upon one labeled "Major Pete 'Sid' Sidwell." On the other side of the door, he heard the sound of muffled grunting. He was hesitant to disturb whatever activity might be taking place; however, with two minutes until his appointment and no idea where to go, there was no obvious choice but to knock and ask for help.

A second later Sid flung open the door, standing naked except for a ratty brown towel wrapped around his waist. He was flush and sweaty from some form of exertion being performed on a yoga mat crammed into the narrow space between his bed and desk.

"Hey! You're alive," Sid gasped, trying to catch his breath.

"I guess so."

"That jetlag is a bitch…"

Carson's gaze drifted involuntarily down to Sid's midsection where his ample gut bulged immodestly over the edge of the undersized towel.

"Sorry about that," Sid said, suddenly aware of the awkwardness. "I was getting in a little exercise before work. I promised my wife I would lose twenty pounds while I was here. You might not believe it, but I'm still a little behind. Maybe *really* behind if the rumors are true about us going home soon."

Carson averted his gaze, hoping to spare them both any further embarrassment. "Seems like a good place for a diet," he offered, looking for a charitable segue. "I can't imagine the food's that great."

"Yeah. I was doing OK for the first month or so. I had three solid weeks of the shits and was down almost fifteen pounds. Unfortunately, I kind of backtracked after that. I just need to get back into a routine. Or maybe get sick again…," Sid said as an afterthought, appearing to give the option serious consideration. "Anyway, I'm glad I caught you. Did you know that you're supposed to be over with the colonel right now?"

"Yeah. Thanks for the early warning," Carson shot back, slightly annoyed. "You mind telling me where I'm supposed to be going?"

"Oh yeah. Out the front door and straight across the dirt yard. You'll see a flag pole without a flag. The building behind that is where you want to be. The colonel will be there for sure. I'll come to get you afterward for a little tour of the compound. It won't take long. You can clear the entire place with a strong nine iron."

Carson nodded and moved quickly for the door, relieved to end the conversation. When he stepped outside the equatorial sun was low on the horizon, making it seem earlier than it was. The yard was strangely quiet except for the clucking of some scrawny-looking chickens pecking nervously in the dirt. All the buildings scattered around the camp seemed to share the same basic cinder block design. The weathered facades gave the feeling of another age, perhaps artifacts of the colonial era or a forgotten superpower proxy war.

As he crossed the yard, Carson heard the high-pitched whine of jet engines off in the distance. He couldn't identify the source but guessed that the camp must have been situated just on the other side of the airfield from where he had arrived the previous night.

Outside the door of the headquarters building, he glanced down at his watch, relieved to discover that he was only a few minutes late for his appointment. Inside of the front office, Carson noticed the colonel's name on a weathered placard hanging outside the door. He knocked, half expecting no one to be there, then heard a muffled yell coming from the other side.

Carson cracked open the door and saw someone sitting in front of a computer screen with his back turned to the door.

"Major John Carson reporting," he said, rendering an unseen salute.

"Right. Give me two minutes…," the figure replied without turning around. From across the room, Carson glanced over the colonel's shoulder and saw him scrolling through an inbox full of unread emails.

"There's coffee out front," the colonel said. "It's a day old, but you can heat it up in the microwave if you want some."

"No thanks, sir. I'm fine."

"Good choice. It's bad enough when it's fresh. Grab a seat. I'll just be a sec," the colonel said as he continued pecking away at the keyboard. A few minutes later, he turned around and extended his hand across the desk.

"Sorry about that," he said, shaking Carson's hand. "The general gets pissed if I'm not on top of his emails first thing in the morning. He shoots them out until all hours of the night, so I'm already swamped with taskings by the time I hit the office. Anyway, that's not your problem. Welcome to the DRoG."

"Thank you, sir. Glad to be here."

The colonel nodded, unmoved by the show of earnestness.

"So, what do you know about our mission here?"

"To be honest, sir, not much. I sort of remembered hearing something about it a few years ago but I didn't pay much attention at the time. I guess I just never figured I'd find myself here."

"Yeah, you and pretty much everybody else. Don't worry.

Nobody really follows this place except for a few policy wonks in DC who get paid to care about it. But you at least know some of the backstory on Odoki and GLA?"

"I'm no expert," Carson said with a shrug. "But when I got my orders I went back and read a few articles about Odoki and that massacre at the village. That's most of what I know."

The colonel nodded. "Right. That's the reason we're sitting here right now. Back when it happened, it was in the headlines for a few news cycles. The president made a big speech promising to bring fiery justice upon Odoki and his men. That was almost three years ago. Today, I seriously doubt anyone back home even remembers we're still here."

"Kind of fits the pattern," Carson observed.

The colonel nodded as he did a quick survey of Carson's uniform, scrutinizing the assortment of badges and patches that served as the Army's unofficial resume.

"Iraq?" he asked, noting the patch on Carson's shoulder.

"Yes, sir. I was up north just before we pulled out."

"Pretty quiet by then, as I recall," the colonel murmured.

Carson took his meaning without elaboration. "Yes, sir. Pretty quiet…"

"Still, I'm sure it was good experience. Nothing wrong with that. I kept learning even after my fifth time over there…," the colonel offered. "But that's neither here nor there. This is a different kettle of fish altogether. For starters, nobody's going to be shooting at you. The worst thing that's going to get you over here is diarrhea. Maybe malaria if you're a dumbass like the last guy and forget to take your meds. But don't even think about that," Kittredge said, pointing a finger at Carson's chest. "The general will have my ass if I go asking for another replacement."

"Yes, sir. Got it. Major Sidwell warned me last night when he picked me up. He also gave me your to-do list. To be honest, sir, I was a little confused. I was hoping you could fill in a few details."

Colonel's expression was blank.

"Sir, Sid gave me a piece of paper with three things on it...," Carson hinted. "He told me you'd explain it in the morning."

"Oh, right. Sorry," Kittredge said. "It was a late night. I didn't get much sleep. The note must have slipped my mind. Remind me again what was on it?"

"Coffee was number one.

"Oh yeah. Our support contractor runs a little java joint out behind the mess hall. Bottom line, the soldiers hate it."

"Really, that bad?"

"I don't know. Got an ulcer and don't touch the stuff anymore. But I'm sick of hearing them bitch about it. That's not helping my stomach any more than the coffee did. First things first. Get that fixed."

"Yes, sir. Will do."

"Good. OK, remind me what was next on the list."

"The gym."

"Yup, now I remember. The gym sucks too. There's nothing for the soldiers to do after work. If I don't keep them tired out, they'll be sneaking over the fence at night and getting drunk on the local palm wine. I don't need any more headaches with the Gisawian police. Get some new gym equipment so they can blow off steam after work. The stuff that's in there now is a health hazard."

"Yes, sir. I'll figure it out. Those two seem straightforward. It was the third thing that I didn't really understand."

"Hmm. What was it again?"

"It said, 'Kill Odoki.'"

"Oh yeah, right. So, here's the thing, Carson. We're really under the gun here. The general is on my ass to make something happen. I need your help with some ideas. Obviously, what we've been doing for the last few years isn't working. Now we're running out of time."

As he was speaking, Carson noticed the colonel's email queue already filling up with new messages. Kittredge glanced over his shoulder at the computer, shaking his head.

"Anyway, you've got plenty on your plate for now. Start working on the first two things."

"Yes, sir."

"Great. So, I won't keep you any longer. Sid will help you settle in and get the ball rolling on those projects. Any questions?"

"No, sir."

"OK. Good luck. My door is always open if you need anything," the colonel said, his attention already drifting back to his inbox.

Carson got up from the chair and showed himself to the door. Back out in the yard, the camp still seemed deserted. He stood for a moment, watching the stray chickens peck at the dirt until Sid appeared across the yard walking in his direction.

"Damn. It's already hot," Sid said, dabbing at his brow with a wrinkled handkerchief. "How was the first meeting with the boss?"

"Fine, I guess. I'm still not sure exactly what I'm supposed to be doing, but at least he confirmed the list. Coffee first. Gym second."

"Good to start with those. At least you have some chance of making progress," Sid offered.

"OK, so who do I need to see about the coffee?"

"Sammy is our local barista. But he's not the one calling the shots. Don Slyker is the guy you need to talk to. He runs the base support contract for ESP."

"ESP?"

"The firm in charge of running the base. I forget what it stands for. You can ask him when you meet. Basically, if you want something done around here, it's a safe bet that Don Slyker is the guy you need to see. But he's only here a few days each week. I'll check with his assistant to see when he'll be around."

Sid pulled out his phone and quickly tapped out a message. "So, how about a coffee?" he asked after sending off the text. "You should at least get a taste of what you're up against."

"Really that bad?"

"And then some. Last week a guy told me he found sawdust at the bottom of his cup."

"But you still drink it?"

"Yeah, I'm too lazy to make it myself. Come on. The café is around the corner," Sid said, pointing to a large mango tree rising above the cinder block huts.

The café was little more than a wooden hut, reminding Carson of the seasonal fruit stands that dotted the rural highways back home. Nailed across the top of the shack was a hand-painted sign with the words "Sujah Bean" written in bright tropical colors. Next to the hut, under the dense canopy of the mango tree, was a seating area with chairs and tables set inside a perimeter of miniature lemon trees planted in plastic buckets. The decor offered just enough ironic charm to be mistaken for a hipster hangout in some marginally gentrified neighborhood back home.

As they approached the hut, Sid and Carson spotted the barista behind the counter, a local Gisawian of indeterminate age who was busy refilling containers of sugar and nondairy creamer. The man was painfully thin, with slightly jaundiced eyes and a warm, welcoming smile. He waved as they walked into the garden and came over to meet them.

"Sammy!" Sid called out. "How are you, my good man?" he asked with mock formality.

"Very well, sir," the barista replied in deeply accented English.

"Sammy, we've got a newbie here," Sid explained, patting Carson on the shoulder. "I'd like you to meet Major John Carson."

Carson smiled awkwardly and reached out his hand, uncertain of the local protocol for greetings. He suddenly regretting not having read the "Gisawian Culture for Dummies" pamphlet in his government-issued travel packet. Instead, he had wasted the trip engrossed in a multi-part Steven Seagal biopic showing on the in-flight entertainment system.

"Welcome to my country, sir," Sammy said, taking Carson's hand in a calloused grip. "Please, be my guest."

Sammy held awkwardly onto Carson's hand and led them to a table. After sitting down, Sid nudged Carson and winked. "See! What did I tell you? Finally! A country where people are happy to see us," then turned to the barista.

"Sammy. We'll take two cups of your daily drip," Sid requested. "And please throw in some of those African doughnuts if you don't mind. Maybe a few extra for our new friend here."

Sammy smiled. "Yes, sir. Right away. Please, be comfortable," he said before disappearing back into the hut.

"Seems like a nice guy," Carson said, admiring the cafe's tidy garden and freshly raked dirt floor.

"Sure. Sammy's great. The shitty coffee isn't really his fault. Hopefully, you can sweet-talk Slyker into upgrading the offerings a bit..." Sid was interrupted by the buzzing of his cell phone. "Ah, speak of the devil," he said, scrolling through the message. "You're in luck. Slyker's coming in this afternoon on the flight from Nairobi."

"That's a good sign."

The phone buzzed with another message. "OK, it's confirmed. His assistant said he'll meet you here at 1800."

Sammy appeared at the table with two plastic cups of muddy coffee and a paper plate of fried dough balls. Sid picked up a fritter and popped it into his mouth.

"Although I don't care much for the coffee, these things are damn good," Sid said, chewing noisily on a fritter. "But do me a favor. After today, don't let me touch these again," he begged. "At the rate I'm going, I'll never get back to fighting weight."

After nibbling on one of the dough balls, Carson took a hesitant sip at the coffee, trying to gauge the scope of his challenge.

"So, what do you think?" Sid asked.

"You're right, it's pretty bad."

"Well, good luck getting it fixed. Slyker's a tough sell. It's all just the bottom line with him. Since you're new, perhaps he'll go easy on you."

"I'll do my best," Carson said, pushing the coffee aside.

The two of them sat there watching the camp slowly come to life while Sid munched through the entire plate of fried dough balls. Every now and then a few American soldiers wandered across the yard returning from morning exercise or on their way to the mess hall for breakfast. At the front gate, Carson spotted a group of Gisawian soldiers entering the compound. They were dressed in the same jungle-pattern camouflage he had seen the soldiers wearing at the airport— all except for one, who had a different colored beret and was carrying a leather briefcase rather than an AK-47.

The man was tall and thin, with the taut physique of a long-distance runner. He moved purposefully across the yard, giving the impression of someone who accounted for each minute of the day. Unlike the other soldiers who wore their uniforms like pajamas, his was pressed and fitted like a glove, as if he had been born to wear it.

When Sid saw him coming, he called out and waved him over to their table.

"Good timing," he said to Carson. "You need to meet Louie."

When he arrived at the table, Sid stood up and made introductions. "Louie, this is our new executive officer, Major John Carson."

"Nice to meet you," he said, taking his hand. "The name's John, but most people just call me Carson. I just got in last night."

"Welcome. I'm Major Bigombe—Lutalo Bigombe. However, since stepping foot on this camp, I've become known as Louie. For some reason, you Americans insist that everyone have a nickname," he said, winking at Sid.

"Come on, Louie. Would you rather everyone keep butchering Lutalo instead? We're Americans, for god's sake. We don't do foreign languages."

"Indulge me, Sid," Louie replied. "You promised to learn at least a few Gisawian words before going back home. I'm sorry to inform you that eating fried dough balls do not qualify as cultural immersion," he said, nodding at the empty plate on the table.

"Hey! Carson had a few too," Sid said defensively. "Join us for a coffee?"

"Thank you, but no," Louie said, glancing with mild disgust at the plastic cups on the table. "I have work to do. I'll just have some tea at the office."

"Jolly right, old chap!" Sid said in some poor affectation of an English accent. "As you might gather from his funny talking, Louie here is a cosmopolitan man of the world." Louie rolled his eyes as Sid continued. "Educated at Sandhurst among other venerable institutions. But more importantly, he is our liaison officer from the Gisawian Ministry of Defense. Louie keeps a desk here on camp when he's not downtown at MoD headquarters. If you want to know anything about what's going on outside the fence, Louie is the man to ask."

Carson nodded. "In that case, I guess we'll be seeing a lot of each other."

"Indeed. We usually meet at the café a few times each week to exchange notes. If you really want to know what's going on around here, the Sujah Bean is the place to find out. However, I recommend sticking with the tea…"

"I've noticed," Carson said, nodding at the unfinished cups on the table.

"So, gentlemen, my apologies for dashing off but I really do need to take care of a few things at the office," Louie said. "Perhaps we can meet later in the week?"

"No problem," Sid agreed. "I'll text you."

Louie nodded, then resumed his path across the yard toward his office.

"Seems like a good guy," Carson said once he was beyond earshot.

"Absolutely. What you see is what you get. Louie's a straight shooter, mostly."

"Mostly?"

"You'll see what I mean. His uncle is a bigwig at the Ministry of Defense. Sometimes I think he gets stuck in the middle between us and them. One thing you'll learn about working in the DRoG. One plus one does not always equal two."

"Thanks, I'll try to keep that in mind."

Sid finished the rest of his coffee in one gulp and then looked back to Carson. "How about I show you around. Then I'll take you over to the office and get you started with a fresh box of crayons."

"Sounds good. Just keep me moving so I can stay ahead of the jetlag."

"At least stay awake until your meeting with Slyker. You don't want to miss that. I guarantee it will be the most entertaining event of the day."

"How so?"

"I don't want to spoil the surprise. Let's just say that he's a bit eccentric."

+++

By six o'clock that evening, Carson was on the edge of exhaustion. He could barely keep his eyes open and regretted having made plans to meet with Slyker. The sun was low on the horizon when he arrived at the empty café, allowing Carson his pick of tables. As soon as he sat Sammy appeared beside him with a welcoming smile.

"Good evening, sir. You are back again!" the barista exclaimed.

"Yes, Sammy, back again," Carson said, stifling a yawn. "I have one last meeting if I can stay awake long enough."

"Will Mr. Sid be joining you? I saved him a few fried dough balls."

Carson chuckled. "No. Actually, I'm meeting with Mr. Slyker."

Sammy's eyes widened in surprise. "I didn't know Mr. Slyker was coming."

"He's on his way from the airport right now. He should be here any minute."

"Thank you, sir," Sammy stammered anxiously. "I must prepare. Will you be cupping this evening?"

"What? No, it's just a meeting," Carson said, uncertain what he was being asked.

"OK, very good, sir. Please excuse me," Sammy said before scurrying back to the hut.

A moment later, the garden was bathed in a pale glow of

Chinese lanterns woven through the branches of the mango tree. The sounds of mellow Afro-beats mood music began playing from speakers hidden inside the shrubbery. Carson felt himself being lulled to sleep in a leafy cocoon of hipster ambiance.

Carson waited another twenty minutes and was about to give up when he spotted a middle-aged white man walking through the camp's front gate. He was fit and well-mani-cured, wearing a tropical-weight linen suit, pale-blue silk shirt, and khaki suede shoes. He would not have looked a bit out of place strolling into a hip Miami beach bar with his two-day stubble and meticulously coiffed hair. The sol-diers waved him through without even bothering to check his identification, then made a beeline toward where Carson was waiting.

"Major Carson, I presume?" the gentleman said, offering out his hand, palm up.

"Correct. Mr. Don Slyker?"

"The one and only. Good to meet you," he said, slipping a thick bond business card into Carson's hand. Under the dim glow of the Chinese lanterns, Carson glanced down at the card.

Executive Support Providers (ESP)

"We know what you need before you do."

Don Slyker, *Esq*
Senior Vice President for
African Operations

"ESP. That's catchy," Carson said, stuffing the card into his pocket. "I don't think I've heard of you guys before," he said as they sat down at the table.

"I'm sure you're familiar with our parent firm, Techtron Industries. We're a boutique sub-unit operating as a partially owned foreign subsidiary. Mostly for accounting purposes," he added unnecessarily.

"Right. So anyway, thanks for seeing me on short notice."

"My pleasure. And please, call me Don. I prefer to keep things informal. My assistant said you're fresh off the boat."

"Yup. Still six hours short of a day."

"That trip is a killer. They drag me back to headquarters a few times each year for re-indoctrination. I swear it gets harder every time."

Carson's head bobbed with exhaustion.

"I can see you're fading. Maybe we should have a little pick-me-up. Can I interest you in some coffee?"

Carson shook his head. "No, thanks. I tried some this morning. In fact, that's one of the things I wanted to discuss."

"Great. It happens to be a passion of mine. But really, I insist you join me. I promise we'll have something different."

Sammy suddenly appeared beside the table, balancing a large tray of what looked like the implements of a high school chemistry lab.

"Mr. Slyker, welcome back, sir," Sammy said, as he gently placed the tray down on an adjacent table. "I did not know you were coming this evening, sir. The package arrived yesterday on the flight from Addis. Everything is just as you requested."

"Very good, Sammy. No difficulties, I hope."

"No, sir. The manager called and asked that you approve samples before he sends out the shipment."

"Excellent," Slyker said, before turning back to Carson. "So, you like coffee?"

"Sure, I'm in the Army."

"My apologies. An imprecise question. Do you know anything about coffee?"

"Hmm, sounds like a setup. I'll avoid the trap and just say no."

"Good answer. The wise man knows what he doesn't know. Watch Sammy and learn."

With that, the barista began setting up the mysterious equipment on the table. He lit a small butane stove, then cracked the seal on a bottle of imported spring water. Next, he measured out the liquid into a Pyrex beaker and placed it over the flame. Then he pulled two smoke-colored bottles from a shipping box and set them on the table. Slyker grabbed the first bottle and opened the lid, pressing his nose into the seal and taking in the aroma. He shook a few beans out into his hand and examined them before passing the bottle back to Sammy.

"Just roasted," Slyker explained, placing a few of the beans in Carson's hand. "It's Yirgacheffe. From the Sidamo region of southern Ethiopia. The birthplace of coffee. What you have there in your hand is an heirloom variety. Grown and picked the same way for centuries."

As the water came to a boil, Sammy proceeded to weigh out a small portion of the beans and pour them into a hand grinder.

"It's not ideal," Slyker said, nodding at the odd contraption. "However, intermittent power supply demands concessions to practicality. One lesson I've learned during my time in Africa, never leave home without extra cell phone batteries and a good hand grinder."

"I don't remember that from the Boy Scout manual," Carson joked.

Slyker ignored the comment, fully engrossed in his lecture. "So, we harvest these at high elevation. Over five thousand feet. There's nothing very modern about the process. All the fruit is picked by hand and then goes straight into water tanks for several days of fermentation before drying out. That gives it a nice, clean finish."

"Mr. Slyker. Sorry, I mean Don. You keep saying 'we.' I guess I'm a little confused. Is this part of ESP's operation here?"

"Hell no! It's just a little thing I have going on the side. I spent a lot of time in Ethiopia when I took over ESP's Africa portfolio. It was good money but involved a lot of weekends stuck in Addis drinking overpriced martinis in the hotel bar. To pass the time, I started taking trips down south to the coffee region. One day I came across a little family-run enterprise that was looking to expand. They needed investors and some legal advice to help take it to the next level."

"So, you represent the farm?"

"Managing partner. Since then we pulled in a few other local growers and formed a small co-op. We've professionalized the entire operation. All fully organic, fair trade production. We can't compete against the majors, but we've carved out a nice little niche among the usual suspects—urban hipsters, well-heeled suburbanites, pretentious African studies majors. It's all word-of-mouth advertising, which adds to the mystique. Now we're diversifying with a small B&B operation where guests can create their own individualized blends from start to finish. From picking fruit in the fields to roasting beans. Experiential tourism. It's the next big thing!"

While Slyker described his plan, Sammy brought the water to a level boil and turned off the heat. He put a bowl of the freshly ground coffee down on the table. Slyker pushed it toward Carson, motioning for him to pick it up.

"Go ahead, take a good whiff. See what you think."

Carson lifted the bowl and waved it awkwardly under his nose.

"Coffee. It smells like coffee," he said.

"Notice anything different from a can of Maxwell House?"

"Maybe," Carson shrugged. "I usually don't think much about it."

"OK, we'll work on that," Slyker said stiffly. "With this type of bean, some people pick up a flowery scent. Maybe some notes of citrus. Even coconut depending on the roast. Honestly, there's no right answer. Believe me, there was a time where I couldn't tell the difference between Yirgacheffe and Yoo-hoo. Sensitivity comes with exposure."

Slyker took the bowl from Carson and gave it back to Sammy, who carefully measured out the grounds into a pair of half-moon filters nested inside two thin-necked carafes. Then he slowly poured the steaming water over the grounds, keeping a steady flow dripping through the vessel. When it was done, Sammy poured out two cups and placed them on the table. Carson instinctively reached for the nondairy creamer and sugar on the next table over.

"Don't you dare!" Slyker said, glaring at the condiments. "Just take a sniff and get the aroma, then give it a good slurp. Spread it over your tongue to get a sense of the character."

Carson took a few sips and nodded approvingly. "I've got to admit, it's pretty nice. If it was always this smooth, I might lighten up on the cream and sugar."

"Damn straight you would!" Slyker said before turning back to Sammy. "This batch is good to go. Let the manager know to prepare the shipment. I'll call the buyer to finalize the deal."

"Yes, sir. Right away," Sammy said before disappearing back to the hut, leaving the men alone to their drinks.

"OK, Mr. Slyker. I'm baffled," Carson said, suddenly wide awake from a mixture of caffeine and curiosity. "Clearly, you know your coffee. So why the hell is Sammy serving crap that's not even drinkable?"

"A reasonable question," Slyker said, easing back into his chair. "Between you and me, I wouldn't touch the stuff he serves here either. However, in Sammy's defense, the problem is beyond his control. He's totally reliant on local suppliers to make margins. DRoG has maybe one or two decent producers, but the domestic industry is very undeveloped. Anything remotely drinkable is set aside for export. All that's left is the crap that Sammy scrounges up from local wholesalers and serves here at the cafe."

"But obviously you have access to better product."

"Well, of course, I do! But I don't really see anyone around here interested in cupping prime Yirgacheffe at twenty bucks a pound. I'm running a business, not a charity. Besides, I'm obligated to keep my private business interests entirely separate from my work for ESP. And even if I were so inclined, there's more to it than that. You're not seeing the big picture."

"There's a big picture to bad coffee?"

"Very big…"

"Listen, I don't need the fine print. Just tell me why coffee sucks and how can I fix it."

"Indulge me a moment and I'll give you the grade school version."

"I'm listening…"

"OK, so you've been around the Army for a while, right? Probably served in a few overseas operations?"

"Sure. Iraq, Kuwait, Haiti."

"OK, good. So, the first thing to remember is that not all missions are created equal. What we have here is a localized, limited-scope contingency involving no vital US national security interests. These things come and go at the drop of a hat; therefore, they're not especially predictable as a revenue stream. What this means for a firm like ESP is lots of uncertainty and razor-thin margins. You with me so far?"

"I'm following," Carson said, sipping his coffee, trying to maintain focus. "But what's it got to do with the problem of shitty coffee from Sujah Bean?"

"Hold on, I'm getting there. So, given these inherent risks associated with these kinds of missions, ESP offers our customers a tailored package designed to fit each unique operational profile. For example, what we have here is our basic small-footprint force sustainment package. An austere yet highly flexible arrangement providing a scalable forward presence with maximum optionality. That includes food service, facilities maintenance, uniform cleaning, telecommunications, and satellite links, among other things."

"ESP does all of that?"

"And more. The contract also contains a morale clause covering the Sujah Bean Café and the Safari Club, where soldiers can enjoy a few salty snacks and non-alcoholic beers after work. We also run the Savanna Market, where you will find an enticing selection of ESP's "exclusive reserve" non-perishable foodstuffs and sundry items, as well as Tropical Trims, the camp's full-service barbershop, styling salon, and day spa. Are you still with me? Seems like you're nodding off."

Carson suddenly realized his eyes had been closed. "Sorry, the jetlag's kicking in. Maybe we can cut to the chase."

"Gladly. Here's the bottom line. On a mission like this, the only way ESP can secure any sort of reasonable profit is by sourcing locally from non-branded, independent subcontractors. This means that we're not flying in a Seattle's Best franchise with all the bells and whistles. Beyond a pure patriotism play, there's no angle that makes the numbers work for the major players. It's low-volume business with enormous logistical nightmares and high reputational risk."

"Reputational risk?"

"Hell yeah. Do you think a major brand wants to deal with the PR nightmare after a bunch of American heroes get E. coli from a bad mocha latte? There's just no upside for them to get involved."

"OK, I get it. No Starbucks in the jungle, but there's got to be something better than Sujah Bean."

"Well, of course there is. ESP has a sliding scale of packages just like your local cable company. Believe me, I would like nothing more than to sell you the full five-hundred channel premium bundle, but there's no way in hell that Uncle Sugar is going to pony up that kind of cash for anything short of a Normandy invasion. However, ESP does offer a wide range of packages geared toward the lower end of the conflict spectrum. In fact, we have a new support line specially designed for stalemated counterinsurgency campaigns and long-term nation-building efforts. We can usually pull in some nice franchise bids on those kinds of open-ended operations. It's easy money once you get yourself established."

"Clearly you've got this down to a science."

"The business is cutthroat. It's no place for amateurs."

"So, that's the big picture. But back to Sujah Bean. How can I get it fixed?"

"Well, here's the rub. Our good friend Sammy works for me as an independent subcontractor. His operations satisfy all applicable health, safety, and nutritional guidelines. In fact, in many ways, Sammy goes well above and beyond the terms of the agreement. For example, look at this garden here," Slyker said, waving his hand in the air. "Well-maintained furnishings, mood lighting, music. These are all extras. Believe me, tasteful décor and pleasing ambiance are not easily enforceable contractual obligations. Sammy did this all on his own."

"What about drinkable coffee?"

"I can assure you, he's doing the best he can, given market constraints."

"So, what I'm hearing is that nothing much is going to change?"

"So long as Sammy is performing in accordance with the terms of the agreement, as the prime contractor, I'm not in a position to compel him otherwise. That said, I have a deep respect for his craft. Sammy is a highly trained barista with a lengthy, yet undocumented, apprenticeship in Italy. I know he's not proud to be serving a substandard product. Furthermore, at ESP, we believe that the customer is always right. We strive to offer the best possible service within bounds of reason and a legally binding contract."

"Funny, I didn't see that on your business card."

"Well, that's because I'm not in the business of selling banalities. I leave that to the State Department. However, it's clearly in everyone's best interest for us to maintain a positive working relationship. Am I safe in assuming that the purpose behind our meeting this evening is some kind of quasi-official tasking from your new boss?"

"More or less. It was all a little vague."

"Right. I'm not entirely surprised. Listen, I certainly have no interest in seeing you fail right out of the gate. But here's what I can do to help. Sammy doesn't need my help to make good coffee. He knows the business inside and out. The problem is that he can't access quality product. However, given the importance of this issue to your boss, I may have an idea for helping everybody out."

"Will this be something I'm going to regret later?" Carson asked suspiciously.

"Do you really think I'm going to compromise my professional reputation just to win you some points with your new boss? This is my backyard. My livelihood. I'll still be doing business here long after you guys are gone and have forgotten all about the Sujah Bean."

"What are you proposing?"

"For reasons I'd rather not get into, I happen to be sitting on a small truckload of Kenya AA presently stuck in a warehouse in Nairobi. I can assure you it's solid stuff. Given our mutual dilemmas, I could arrange to get it down here to Sammy.

"How much will it cost?"

"Naturally, Sammy will need to pass on the price difference at the counter, but it's not going to break the bank of anyone down here looking for their morning fix."

"What are you getting out of it?"

"Honestly, nothing. But I'd be happy to do it if it helps out Sammy and earns you a few points with the new boss. What do you think?"

"Seems like a win-win for everyone, I guess," Carson said hesitantly.

"Well, mostly for you," Slyker snorted. "However, I'm sure there will come a time when you can return the favor. Like I said, I prefer fixing problems informally whenever possible. It just makes life easier."

"How soon until you can make it happen?" Carson asked, hopeful that the meeting was nearing an end.

"I'll be on the road this week, but I can get everything set up with Sammy before I leave. I'll send you an email if we run into any snags."

"Great. I've got your contact info from the card."

"Wait! Don't use that one," Slyker said, reaching into his shirt pocket. "It's a burner card. Dummy email address and phone number. I just hand those out for show until I have a chance to check people out."

"You can't be serious?" Carson asked incredulously.

"Completely. Here's a pro tip. Never give out anything down here unless you know who you're dealing with and exactly what they want. Otherwise, you'll end up having random warlords using your name as a character reference on their visa application. Here," Slyker said, handing over a new card. "Use this one. It has my personal email and phone number."

"Thanks. Unfortunately, I don't have a card yet, but let me give you my contact info," Carson said, fruitlessly searching his pockets for a pen.

"Here. Take this one," Slyker said impatiently, handing Carson an expensive-looking Montblanc pen etched with an intricate corporate logo.

"Nice pen," Carson said. "Tantalus Holdings. Another one of your side ventures?" Carson asked, reading the engraved logo along the side.

"What?" Slyker asked, confused. "Oh, you mean the pen? I have no idea. I think I stole it from someone's desk in the billing department back at headquarters. You can keep it."

"Thanks," Carson said, jotting down his name and email for Slyker then slipping the instrument into his uniform.

"No problem. I've got suitcases full of swag back at my office. It's good for when you need to grease the skids with the locals. Not the heavy hitters, of course. Like I said, you've got to know your audience. That's the first mistake those yahoos from DC make when they get off the plane here. I can't tell you how many times I've seen some Beltway bigshot hand a twelve-dollar fountain pen to a guy who's got twenty million Swiss francs stashed in offshore accounts. They come off as if they've just given fire to a Neanderthal, then go home scratching their heads wondering why they didn't close the deal. Complete amateurs. You've got to do your homework first. Know who you're dealing with before you walk into the room. Especially down here."

"I'll keep that in mind."

"No problem. Glad to help out. The pen and advice are free. For everything else, I'll need to bill you," Slyker said, smiling as he got up to leave the table.

+++

After the meeting with Slyker, Carson went over to the mess hall looking for something to eat. By eight o'clock, he was back in his room lying in bed, struggling to keep his eyes open. The last thing he remembered was wondering if his neighbors would hear him snoring through the paper-thin walls.

Sometime later in the evening, he was roused awake by the sound of voices. With his head resting against the thin wall, he could hear a conversation in the next room almost as if he were there. One of the voices sounded distant, as if talking through the end of a long tube. Carson tried his best to ignore them, but the words burrowed into his ear like an annoying mosquito as he tried falling back asleep.

What are they saying about how much longer you'll be over there?

I have no idea, but there's a rumor going around that we could be shutting down soon. Maybe in a few months. Whether we get him or not.

Hmm. That timeline would work fine. We're still over a year away. But it would be better if we could kick things off with a bang.

Listen, I know that! But there's not much I can do. Believe me, I'm trying, but nobody gives a crap about this place.

Yeah, I get it, but that bio isn't going to write itself. We need something more to beef up it up.

Isn't that your job?

Listen, I can't just make shit up! I need something I can work with. We're not talking Profiles in Courage *here. Just ten seconds of flag-waving filler. Something to help us regain control of the narrative.*

Well, at this point that's not going to be easy. My old man made damn sure of that...

Hey, that's water under the bridge. Trust me. People have short memories. You just keep working your side and I'll take care of things back here. One way or another, we're going to get back what's rightfully ours.

OK, I'll see what I can do, but no promises. By the way, did you see the notes I sent in the last email?

Yeah. Not much there I can work with. That kind of crap might get you a few lines on the community interest page but nothing more.

Well, short of me heading into the jungle armed with a soup spoon and capturing Odoki with my bare hands, that's about all I've got right now.

But if you could possibly swing that, it sure would make my life easier.

Thanks. You're a big help. Is this really what my dad paid you for all those years?

It was a simpler time.

No doubt. Listen, just take another look at the ideas I sent and let me know. We'll talk next week.

The next thing Carson remembered was waking up to the sound of the air conditioning grinding to a halt. The room was pitch black when he opened his eyes. Carson lay there a moment trying to replay the day's events in his head. He vaguely recalled the conversation between the disembodied voices through the wall, wondering if it had been real or just something conjured from his sleep-deprived subconscious.

After a few minutes without the air conditioning, the room had become stale and humid. Carson rolled over and flipped on the bedside lamp, but to no effect. He recalled putting in a new light bulb just before falling asleep and was confused that it now wasn't working. It took a few moments before he finally deduced that the electricity must have been out for the entire building. He looked down at his watch. Two o'clock in the morning and he was wide awake.

Resigned to jetlag-induced insomnia, Carson got out of bed and pulled a flashlight from his duffel bag. He slipped on a T-shirt and gym shorts and then poked his head outside the door. The hallway was dark except for the red-tinged glow of the emergency exit sign above the doors. He tiptoed outside for a breath of fresh air. With the power off, the yard was quiet except for the distant chatter of the Gisawian soldiers on night duty. Their banter felt strangely reassuring if for no other reason than evidence that someone was awake at the front gate.

Carson sat down in a plastic chair and passed the time searching the shadows beyond the perimeter fence looking for signs of nocturnal wildlife. After several minutes without success, he decided to head back inside, but just as he stood up, he heard the sound of footsteps nearby. Carson froze in place, not wanting to be surprised, or worse, to surprise someone else. Particularly by any of the Gisawian guards, whom he feared might be somewhat careless with their weapons.

As Carson waited in the shadows, a figure moved deliberately across the yard in the direction of the headquarters building. The burly athletic build was not one of the local Gisawian soldiers. As the man cam closer, Carson noticed the man was carrying a small duffel bag strapped across his chest.

Carson decided there was no reason to announce himself and risk startling whoever it was. Instead, he watched as the figure approached the door of the operations center, punched in the security code, and entered the building. After the man disappeared inside, Carson made a mental note to ask Sid about the rotation of the nightly duty schedule.

The yard was again silent. For a moment Carson stood there pondering whether to head back into his room or go for a walk to clear his head. Then he heard the sputtering sound of a diesel generator turning over and saw a few of the exterior lights flickering back to life. With the promise of air conditioning in his room, Carson went back inside, hoping for a few hours of sleep before morning.

CHAPTER THREE

———

The next morning Major Lutalo "Louie" Bigombe arrived at the Ministry of Defense for his weekly meeting with the deputy minister. As always, he was early, believing punctuality one of the few useful habits acquired from his years at boarding school.

Louie walked through the door into a spacious, ornately decorated reception area and was greeted with a playful wink from the deputy minister's secretary, the latest of an ever-changing series of assistants. She had almond eyes and high cheekbones, her jet-black hair straightened, like the women on the roadside billboards around town. Her skirt was noticeably shorter than her predecessor's and skin a shade lighter. She motioned for him to take a seat on one of the couches against the wall.

"Mugaba is busy on a call. It will just be a few minutes. Please sit," she said in a tone suggesting that the wait could be much longer.

At the desk next to her was a tired-looking colonel, the deputy minister's overworked aide-de-camp. He looked up at Louie without expression, then went back to his paperwork.

After almost thirty minutes, waiting Louie noticed the light blinking on the intercom box at the receptionist's desk, the signal that the deputy minister was ready for his next appointment. Without a word, the secretary waved him toward the large double doors leading into the main office.

The size of the office was excessive by any standard. The sets of unmatched furniture filling the space only served to exaggerate its unnecessary extravagance. Along the wood-paneled wall was a hagiographic montage of the deputy minister posing with anyone of note who had stumbled through the country over the last twenty years. The immodest tribute was notably devoid of ideological prejudice, freely juxtaposing egregious human rights violators and tin-pot dictators alongside Peace Prize recipients and other photogenic luminaries.

Mugaba Odongo was an elephant of a man, his bulky frame fitting snuggly into the oversized executive chair behind the desk. His bald head and large, powerful hands lent themselves to the imagery. The deputy minister was still on a phone call when Louie entered the room. The man waved him to one of the large sofa chairs arranged in a semicircle to his front. Louie took a seat and waited patiently for the conversation to end. Flanking either side of the large desk was a pair of large Gisawian flags. Between them, a life-sized portrait of Gisawian President Dr. Jean Mutara Namono wearing a drab gray business suit adorned with a colorful inaugural sash draped over his shoulder.

As he waited for the call to end, Louie took out his folio and pretended to be immersed in his notes. After several more minutes, the deputy minister finally set down his cellphone alongside two other identical devices. Louie had never seen the man without all three phones by his side; however, he was only privy to a single number and not even sure which, if any, rang when he dialed it.

"Good morning, Lutalo," the deputy minister said, using Louie's given name as he always did. "How are you?"

"I am well, Uncle. And you?"

"Busy, but still alive, so I must not complain. Lutalo, you know that I visited your mother last week? Do you know what she told me?"

"No, Uncle," he said, feigning ignorance, though knowing what was coming.

"She told me that she never sees you anymore. I said to her that I was surprised by this because I see you every week. Sometimes even more. So, tell me, Lutalo, when was the last time you went home for dinner?"

Louie gazed into his lap. "I'm sorry, Uncle," he mumbled. "I will go this weekend. I promise."

"You'd better," the big man warned, waving a thick finger across his desk. "I don't want to hear her crying about this again. You know she is all alone. Your brothers and sisters are all overseas. You are the only one left. Nothing makes her happier than to cook a meal for her boy. Don't think that you are so important to this world that you cannot go see your mother. I should not be the one who must remind you of this," he said with a huff.

"Yes, Uncle. I have no excuse."

"At least you have the good sense to know that much. Your father raised you better than that. So, enough with this business. I will tell my sister that you'll see her this weekend."

"Yes, Uncle," Louie said sheepishly.

"Very good. So, I only have a short time today," Mugaba said, glancing at the messages continually buzzing into his cellphones. "Tell me what is new with our American friends?"

"Uncle, I'm sure you already heard about the mission last week. They found nothing at the two sites. The Americans said that some GLA soldiers may have been there but that they were gone by the time of the raid."

The deputy minister nodded thoughtfully, rubbing at his chin. "This is unfortunate. We had hoped that the latest information from Police Intelligence might get us closer. Perhaps we'll have better luck next time."

"But Uncle, there is more. There are rumors that the mission may end soon. Apparently, the general is under pressure from Washington for more progress."

The deputy minister's face revealed surprise mixed with skepticism. "Are you sure of this, Lutalo? Soldiers are the same in every army. Just because they talk, doesn't mean they know. Maybe this is nothing more than wishful thinking by some homesick soldiers missing their girlfriends."

"Uncle, it is not just the soldiers. The officers are talking as well."

Mugaba learned back in his chair, thinking for a moment. "It is too soon to tell the minister," he finally said. "I don't want to trouble him until we know if there is any truth to this rumor. Find out what you can and let me know."

"Yes, Uncle. I will speak to my contacts. The next mission is in three weeks. Hopefully, I'll know more by then."

"Yes, Lutalo, please tell me as soon as you hear anything. This is very important. And what about the other things I asked you to work on? Has there been any progress on getting the satellite pictures of the western region?"

"I am trying, uncle, but the request has not been approved."

"Really! Perhaps the Americans aren't concerned about defeating the GLA after all. Do they understand that without this information we cannot go forward on planning for the offensive? Lutalo, I need you to push harder. This is very important to the minister," he said, glancing impatiently at his watch. "I must go soon. Anything else?"

"Just one more thing, Uncle," Lutalo said, checking back through his notes. "The training exercise with the Americans begins next week. The arrangements have been made, just as you asked. We will be using the training area along the northern border. All of the newspapers have been notified and will send reporters to observe the training. The Americans have some other activities planned as well. A medical team will do cataract surgeries in a local village. They will also be working with our wildlife police on anti-poaching operations."

His uncle nodded indifferently, glancing at the messages on his cellphone.

"There was also something or other concerning cows," Louie continued.

"What! Did you say cows?" the deputy minister asked, suddenly putting down his phone and giving his nephew full attention.

"Yes, Uncle. I don't know the details, but I believe it's something to do with vaccinations."

"Lutalo, I must know more about this right away. By the end of the day. This is very important," he said, wagging his finger at Louie's folio, urging him to make a note.

"Yes, Uncle. I will find out as soon as possible."

"Very good. Also, let the Americans know that a few days ago the police caught several of Odoki's men trying to steal food from a village. They are being interrogated now and I expect they will provide some useful information."

"But Uncle, do you believe these low-level fighters know anything useful? We have not had much luck with anything they've given us recently."

"Lutalo, you know the old village saying: 'Hit the dog if you want to find its owner.'"

Louie gave Mugaba a wry smile. "Uncle, I've never heard anyone say this before. Are you sure this is a Gisawian saying? Sometimes I think you find these things on the Internet."

"Don't be cheeky, boy!" Mugaba snapped. "What do you even know of it? You've lived more years outside this country than inside. You don't even speak like a Gisawian anymore. My brother-in-law was a wise man, but I'll never understand why he sent you away for school. He loved this country with all his heart, but for his son, I suppose it wasn't good enough."

"I'm sorry, Uncle," Louie whispered, chastened. "I did not mean disrespect."

"Well, that's no way to speak to your elders. I only pray that you don't have fun with your mother that way. She deserves better. Now you can see what your father's plan has done to her? All her children have run off to Europe and America, believing they are better than this place. Now she is all alone. At least you, Lutalo, came back to follow in his footsteps as a soldier. I must give you some credit for that," he said, shaking his head with frustration.

Mugaba glanced down at his watch. "I must go. It's almost time for my meeting with the minister. There is just one more thing," he said, glancing at the door as if his words might somehow escape the room. "It's a sensitive matter. Concerning some troubling reports from Police Intelligence."

Louie opened his notebook, but his uncle shook his head.

"This is not for pen and paper, only your ears. Police Intelligence is worried about some outsiders who may be looking to cause trouble."

"Outsiders? Who?" Louie asked with alarm.

"We don't have all of the information yet; however, I expect the Americans will be interested. Perhaps they already know something about it," the deputy minister hinted mysteriously.

"Uncle, what people? What kind of trouble are you talking about?"

"Some of our foreign guests."

"That certainly narrows it down. There aren't very many," Louie observed. "Some Chinese. Some Indians. Maybe a few Lebanese. But why would any of them cause trouble? All they want to do is make money and keep to themselves."

"I hope that is the case. But you know what they say in the village Lutalo: 'If a donkey grows horns, people become worried.'"

This time Louie held his tongue.

"I can't say more right now, but when you speak with the Americans, perhaps ask them about the Lebanese. See what they think."

"Yes, Uncle. I will ask them at the next meeting."

Mugaba looked again at his watch and rose from his chair. "Very good. And don't forget your promise. I don't want to hear your mother crying that she hasn't seen you."

"Yes, Uncle, I promise," Louie said, rising from his chair and following the deputy minister toward the door.

+++

The following Friday, before the start of the weekly staff meeting, Carson arrived early outside the headquarters building. Sammy the barista was already waiting outside with an oversized thermos, a stack of paper cups, and a basket of fried dough balls.

"Is everything set?" Carson asked anxiously when he met him at the door.

"Yes, sir. The first shipment of beans arrived yesterday. Mr. Slyker sent enough for several months. Very good quality. You will be most pleased," he said.

"Sure, Sammy. That sounds fine. It can't be any worse than before. How much do I owe you for this?"

"Nothing, sir," Sammy insisted. "Mr. Slyker said the first tasting is on the house. A special welcome gift for you."

"OK, but here's a little something extra," Carson said, slipping Sammy a ten-dollar bill. "Thanks for the help. I'll bring the container back after the meeting."

Sammy nodded and took off back across the yard toward the café while Carson carried the refreshments inside the building. The conference room was empty except for the administrative sergeant who was sitting at the computer finishing the slides for the morning meeting.

"Good morning, sir," he said when Carson walked through the door. The mousey sergeant wore army-issue black-rimmed glasses and seemed to Carson during their few interactions as a likely candidate for an OCD diagnosis.

"Good morning, Sergeant Goodwin. I've got some special treats for the meeting," Carson said, holding up the coffee and fried dough balls. "Help yourself."

"Thank you, sir. And for your situational awareness, the colonel doesn't drink coffee. It bothers his stomach."

"Yes, Sergeant, I'm aware of that. It's for everyone to share. A sampling of the new offerings over at the Sujah Bean."

"Yes, sir. I'll add it as an agenda item," the sergeant insisted, quickly typing in a new bullet for the briefing.

"That's probably not necessary," Carson suggested.

"Colonel Kittredge doesn't like to leave out any details. My job is updating the update. I track nearly everything that goes on around this camp—from the mileage on all the trucks to the number of power outages each week."

"Really? How many did we have this week?"

The sergeant quickly scrolled to a slide showing the number of outages plotted on a dual-colored bar graph. "Nine intermittent and three triggering the backup generator."

"You're telling me that we go over all this each week at the meeting?"

"Not all of it. But if Colonel Kittredge asks a question, my job is to have the answer."

Carson read the new bullet on the agenda slide. "Presentation of new coffee and introduction of Major Carson." Then watched as Sergeant Goodwin added a clip art animation of a dancing coffee mug and donut.

"How many slides are in the briefing?" Carson asked, uncertain he wanted to know the answer.

"As of today, 387. If you are interested, I have a separate slide showing the number of slides briefed each week."

"I trust it's there if needed," Carson said, turning his attention back to the refreshments.

As Sergeant Goodwin made the final touches to the slides, the staff slowly began to trickle into the conference room. Colonel Kittredge arrived last and took his seat at the head of the table.

"Good morning, gentlemen," he said without enthusiasm. "Sergeant Goodwin, let's get this thing started."

The colonel read the first bullet on the agenda. "OK, for those of you that don't already know, this here is Major John Carson. He's our new executive officer. Please help him get settled in and learn the ropes," Kittredge said before pausing and staring at the table. "What the hell is this?" he asked, pointing a finger accusingly at the thermos and pastries.

"Sir, it's the new coffee," Carson jumped in to explain. "Sammy's signature blend. We have a complimentary sample for everyone to try."

"OK, whatever," Kittredge said, shaking his head. "Help yourself to the coffee while we push on with the meeting."

Carson passed the thermos around the table. When it came around to Sid, he hedged, adding several heaping scoops of sugar and nondairy creamer to his cup, then shrugged as Carson shot him an icy stare.

"OK. Let's start with intel," Kittredge ordered, waving away the coffee when it came around to the head of the table.

Sid laid a napkin over his plate of fried dough balls, saving them for later, while Sergeant Goodwin brought up a slide with a large map of the country. Superimposed over the terrain were several vaguely threatening red blobs adjacent to a few more benign-looking blue blobs.

"Sir, here you can see the updated enemy and friendly situation. Since our last update, there have been no new reports of GLA activity."

"Any feedback from our mission last week?" the colonel asked.

"Unfortunately, nothing of value turned up at either location. No weapons. No planning materials. Nothing. The forensics team pulled some prints and DNA samples from the camp but there were no matches against the database. If the GLA was there, it was most likely low-level fighters with no records in the system."

"What do the Gisawians make of it? They keep saying we're getting closer, but every time we come up empty-handed. I'm starting to think they don't have a clue what's going on out there."

"Yes, sir, we're still having a hard time verifying a lot of the information they're providing us. The Gisawians keep pushing this theory about the GLA bringing weapons and supplies across the western border and stockpiling the stuff in underground bunkers. They're convinced that Odoki's men are doing this to avoid detection by our overhead reconnaissance. Whenever we meet our Gisawian counterparts, it's all they want to talk about."

"Are they still bugging us about getting those satellite pictures?"

Sid nodded. "They think it will help them figure out where the GLA is burying their supplies. They're convinced it's the key to dismantling their logistical network."

"OK, for the sake of argument, let's say the Gisawians are right. Suppose the GLA is burying weapons and supplies underground and getting ready for a new offensive. How hard would it be for us to detect that kind of activity?" the colonel asked.

"Technically, it's doable. We've used overhead in other places to identify buried improvised explosives and underground storage facilities. The dense vegetation here would certainly make it a bit more challenging, but not impossible. Unfortunately, the next operation is only three weeks away. There's no chance of getting it before then. It would take weeks, maybe months to go through all the data."

"OK, let's look at the options. We're not here to fight their war for them. Our job is to get them what they need to do it for themselves. Let's try to get our hands on that information and get it to the Gisawians. It can't turn out any worse than what's already happening."

"Yes, sir. I'll check on the status of the request and try to move it along," Sid promised as Sergeant Goodwin flipped to the next slide.

"Sir, next up is Captain Burke with the Public Affairs update," Carson explained unnecessarily.

"OK, Burke, what have you got for us?" Kittredge asked.

"Good morning, sir. Per General Foster's guidance, we're revising our messaging strategy with a renewed focus on raising our mission profile. We've got a good opportunity to enhance our brand awareness with the upcoming training exercise next week. The Gisawians are sending dozens of reporters to cover the event. The general said that getting the public reengaged with our mission here is his number one priority."

"Really? I must have missed the memo," Kittredge shot back. "How are the latest M-RAT numbers looking?"

"M-RAT?" Carson whispered to Sid.

"Media Reflections Analytic Toolkit," Sid answered under his breath. "It's ESP's proprietary data analytics platform. It comes bundled along with the Sujah Bean."

"What does it do?"

"Sucks up everything from the Internet, then spits out what people are saying about us. The general is crazy about it. I heard he checks the app a couple of times a day…"

Sergeant Goodwin flipped to the next slide, an eye-straining spreadsheet listing every single US military operation around the world. Captain Burke cleared his throat as the red dot of his laser pointer traced downward toward the bottom of the matrix and the line for Operation Righteous Protector.

"Sir, as you can see from the latest M-RAT data pull, our mission's brand awareness remains suboptimal. Aggregate media reflections and mission recognition scores are still in the bottom quintile of all ongoing operations. We're continuing to lose traction among target audiences and key influencers…"

"Listen, Burke!" Colonel Kittredge interrupted. "I don't need M-RAT to tell me that no one back home gives a rat's ass about what we're doing here. We've got eighteen 'likes' on our Facebook page and at least seven of those are my kids. Clearly, we—and by we, I mean you—are doing something wrong," Kittredge fumed.

The room was silent as the colonel studied the fine print of the spreadsheet. "Burke, what's that box at the top of the slide? The one with the green arrows?" he asked.

"Sir, those are the weekly fast movers. Missions that have had the biggest jump in positive social media reflections over the last seven days. That's the gold standard back at the Pentagon."

"Hmm, OK. What's the one up there at the top of the list? OVD? I've never even heard of it."

Burke looked down into his notes for the details. "Sir, that would be Operation Vigilant Defender, US Army Corps of Engineers. They're conducting counter-infestation operations against Asian carp migration into the Upper Mississippi."

"That's a named military operation?" Kittredge asked in disbelief.

"Yes, sir. Part of the Pentagon's new branding effort. Operations are everything; therefore, everything is now an operation. OVD had a good run the past few weeks. Apparently, there have been several carp-related boating mishaps recently. It's really upped the mission profile. People seem to relate to the threat. I guess it hits close to home…"

"Damn it, Burke! We've been on a downward slide for the last six months. Now we're losing out to an undeclared war on Asian carp? The last time we made headlines was when the Dallas Cowboy cheerleaders came through here on a USO morale tour and started a riot at the airport."

"Sir, that was an unforeseen cultural misunderstanding," Burke mumbled. "Everything was fine until someone in the crowd tweeted that they were prostitutes servicing the camp. No one could have predicted that…"

Kittredge cut him off. "Listen, Burke, you get paid to show the great American public how this mission is support-ing vital national security interests while delivering peace and security to a loyal regional ally. So far, your most notable achievement has been front-page coverage of frightened cheerleaders fleeing a mob of angry natives while Gisawian soldiers fired tear gas into the baggage claim area of a major international airport..."

The room was silent as the colonel closed his eyes and massaged his temples. "OK, team. Listen up," he said after a deep breath. "Let's clear the air. You've probably all heard the rumors that this mission is on life support. I'm also guessing that some of you probably don't give a shit and will be more than happy to go home and never think about DRoG or Daniel Odoki ever again. But until that moment comes, we've still got a mission to do. That involves several things. First, no more fuck-ups," Kittredge said, glaring at Burke. "Second, sell this mission to a grateful American public. Third, go home winners. Is that clear?"

Everyone around the table nodded.

"All right then. Let's make it happen," Kittredge said, turning back to Sergeant Goodwin, who had been sitting at the computer, mostly ignoring the colonel's rant. "Goodwin, how many more slides do we have?"

"Sir, 214."

"Jesus," Kittredge muttered. "OK, no problem. We've got plenty of coffee and nowhere else to be. Let's do this..."

+++

After the meeting, Sid and Carson walked over to one of the cinder block huts tucked away in the far corner of the camp. The sign outside the door read "DRoG Army Liaison Office." Inside, a Gisawian sergeant sat at a desk typing out a report on an old-fashion manual typewriter.

"Wow," Carson said, taking a closer look at the functioning artifact. "I can't remember the last time I saw one of these."

"I know it's crazy. It seems like everyone in the country has a smartphone, but you still see people tapping away at these things. I heard they import the ribbons from North Korea," Sid explained before turning to the Gisawian sergeant who was unimpressed at their excitement over the typewriter.

"We're here to see Major Bigombe. He's expecting us," Sid announced.

The soldier got up from his desk and stuck his head through the door into the back office. "Sir, your appointment," the sergeant called into the room.

"Please, come in," Louie yelled out from his office.

"How has your first week?" Louie asked Carson once they were all seated around a small wooden coffee table.

"I'm still waking up at two in the morning. Otherwise, everything's fine."

"It's always tougher coming east," Louie said sympathetically. "It takes me at least a week or two before I adjust."

"So, you've made the trip often?" Carson asked with surprise.

"Many times. I have family in the states. My brother is a banker in New Jersey, and I lived in Washington for several years. I was an intern at our embassy while attending graduate school at Georgetown."

Sid winked at Carson. "See, I told you Louie was a worldly gentleman. He comes from a famous family here in DRoG. Kind of like royalty," Sid teased.

Louie smiled politely. "Whatever Sid may have told you is certainly an exaggeration, if not outright slander."

"Come on, Louie! Don't be modest," Sid insisted. "His father was a famous general. At least according to Wikipedia. Not to mention the fact that his uncle is the deputy minister of defense."

"I suppose you could say that my family tradition is among the warrior caste," Louie conceded. "Although, that may be coming to an end. None of my brothers or sisters heard the calling."

"Your father is out of the army now?" Carson asked.

"He died when I was younger," Louie said, without particular emotion. "It was years ago, during our border wars in the north."

"I'm very sorry," Carson said.

Louie waved away the apology. "Don't worry. Of course, there's no reason why you should know about that. It was just one of those obscure conflicts that happen down here all the time but never make headlines outside the continent."

"That must have been hard on your family," Carson observed.

"Yes, my mom, especially. I was away at boarding school in the UK when it happened. My uncle called to tell me. At the time, I doubt any of my school friends could have found our country on a map let alone appreciate the irony that my father died fighting over some arbitrary line laid down long ago by their ancestors who probably never set foot on the ground."

"My father was a soldier too," Carson said, feeling at a loss for words. "I guess it just runs in some families. I'm sure your dad would be proud to see you following in his footsteps."

Louie gave a melancholy chuckle. "Actually, I think that's why he sent me away for school. My brothers and sisters as well. He loved the army but I don't think he wanted us to follow him."

"Why was that?"

"I'm not sure. He never said so directly, but it was always my sense of things."

As Louie was speaking, the sergeant appeared at the door with a tray of tea and biscuits.

"Please, let's have something while we talk," Louie said, pouring them each a cup of tea. "I apologize for jumping straight to business; however, I must excuse myself a little early this afternoon. I'm having dinner with my mother."

"Sure," Sid said. "No problem."

"There was one issue, in particular, I was hoping to discuss," Louie began.

"What about?"

"I think you probably know. The rumors about the mission ending?"

"Wow. I guess word gets around," Sid said, shaking his head. "Listen, Louie. At this point, it's still just a rumor. And besides, that decision is way above our pay grade."

"So, there's nothing to it?" Louie pressed.

"I didn't say that either," Sid insisted, grabbing a biscuit and dunking it into his tea. "Louie, you know I always play it straight with you. It's no big secret that folks back in DC are getting impatient with the mission. It's just been going on for way too long without any signs of progress. Preferably involving Odoki's head on a platter."

"Of course, Sid. We all want this thing to come to an end. Odoki and the GLA have brought nothing but misery to my country. The sooner it's over, the better for everyone."

"No disagreement here. And I can tell you that General Foster wants to push this thing full throttle. He's looking to raise the mission profile and get us some additional resources. But that's doesn't count for anything unless we can get better intel from your side. Something actionable. Between you and me, it's now or never."

Louie nodded thoughtfully. "Sid, I can assure you that my superiors at MoD share General Foster's sense of urgency. However, you also need to appreciate our dilemma. Our army is small. We only have a few battalions who are responsible for patrolling an enormous area. Surely you realize that's not enough."

"Then maybe we need to try something different. You keep telling us that your patrols are bringing in GLA fighters. Can we talk to them? All we're getting are these secondhand reports from Police Intelligence, and that's not getting us anywhere. Maybe there's something that you're missing."

"Sid, you know this is a sensitive topic," Louie said, shaking his head. "We have a special program for reintegrating former GLA fighters. Even I don't have access to the detention facilities where they hold the detainees."

"OK, Louie, I get it. But I'm telling you that something's got to change. The status quo isn't going to last. I'd suggest you let your higher-ups at MoD know that."

"Of course, Sid. I appreciate your honesty. I'll try to help them understand the situation."

"Anything else?" Sid asked.

"Just one other thing. My superiors asked again about

the intelligence on the GLA's underground storage sites. The last time we spoke, you said that you were working on getting us access to the satellite pictures?"

"Louie, I haven't forgotten about it. But you need to realize that kind of information isn't easy to get. Even if I had it, it's all classified, and I couldn't just hand it over to you. It's going to take a little longer to get what you need."

"I appreciate that it's not a simple matter," Louie said. "But please know, we're under pressure on our side as well. I can tell you confidentially that the president's office is considering a major new offensive against the GLA. However, without information on the underground cache sites, I'm not certain the plan will be approved. It's just too risky to launch an operation without knowing the exact locations of the targets."

Sid glanced at Carson with eyebrows raised. "Louie, how certain are you about this proposed offensive?" Sid asked. "This is the first we've heard about it."

"I have no reason to doubt it. The president's office ordered MoD to develop a preliminary operations plan."

"OK, let me see what I can do. If what you say is true about a new offensive, then I may be able to expedite the request. I'll let you know as soon as I hear something."

"Thank you," Louie said, finishing his tea.

"So, I guess we should let you get over to your mother's house," Sid offered. "Nothing like home cooking."

"Very true. I always missed it when I lived overseas. You must join me sometime for some authentic Gisawian food. Not the poor excuse they serve over at that ridiculous Safari Club place across the camp. My mother always makes too much. I'll bring back some leftovers."

"Now you're talking!" Sid said as he and Carson rose to leave.

"Oh, I almost forgot. There was one other thing," Louie remembered as they turned to leave. "MoD received some new information this week from Police Intelligence."

"Something more on Odoki?" Sid asked, hopefully.

"No. A different matter entirely. It concerns some of our Lebanese guests here in the country. Unfortunately, I don't have much more information."

"Lebanese?" Carson asked with surprise. "I didn't realize there were any."

"Not a large presence, but they've been here for as long as I can remember," Louie explained. "Mostly traders and shopkeepers."

"So why is MoD worried about Lebanese bodegas?" Sid asked.

"I can't say. These people mostly keep to themselves. We haven't had problems with them in the past. However, Police Intelligence wanted to know if your side was monitoring any potential threats from that community."

"What do you mean? Like Hezbollah or something?"

"Maybe. I can't say for sure."

Sid scribbled a few lines into his notebook. "If it's something like that, then it's probably worth keeping an eye on. I'll send out a request for information to see if we're tracking anything."

"Thank you, Sid. I would appreciate it. So, we'll meet again early next week?

"Sure," Sid offered, rising from his seat and shaking hands. "And enjoy dinner with your mom."

CHAPTER FOUR

Early the next morning, Carson was startled awake by the sound of frantic pounding on his door. He stumbled across the room and opened it to find Sid outside in the hallway, still in his exercise clothes.

"Were you asleep?" Sid asked in disbelief. "It's almost seven."

"Yeah. It was the first time I've made it through the night since I got here."

"Congratulations. Listen, Sergeant Goodwin just came by. He said the colonel wants to see us in the conference room, ASAP."

"OK. Give me a few minutes. I'll be right over."

Sid was waiting outside holding two cups of coffee when Carson arrived at the headquarters building

"On me," he said, handing one over to Carson. "To make up for disturbing your beauty rest. By the way, I'm liking the new java. Whatever deal you cut with Slyker did the trick. There was actually a line outside of Sujah Bean this morning."

"I guess that's good. But I've got a funny feeling it's going to come back to haunt me," Carson confided.

"Oh yeah. I'm sure it will. But until then, let's just enjoy it. Just make sure Sammy doesn't mess with those African donuts. No need to fix what's not broken."

"Noted. So, any idea what the meeting's about?"

"No clue. Sergeant Goodwin said it was urgent. Something about us being in the shit again with the ambassador."

"Does that happen often?"

"More often than you'd think. We better get inside before the boss shows up."

The conference room was empty except for Sergeant Goodwin, who was busy setting up the video teleconference link. A moment later General Foster appeared on half the screen, dialing in from Germany. He was surrounded by his staff and clearly annoyed that the unplanned meeting had interrupted his gym time. On the other half of the screen was an empty chair, set in a nondescript conference room at the American Embassy located just across town from the camp. A young staffer suddenly appeared on the screen and flipped open the microphone.

"The ambassador will join momentarily," he said, before switching back to mute and disappearing from the room.

Sid turned to Carson. "Check it out," he whispered with a mischievous smile. "The general is about to blow his top. The ambassador always makes him wait just to fuck with his head."

"Seems to be working," Carson observed.

"Am I late? I needed to get some information before this thing started," Colonel Kittredge interrupted as he sprang into the room and slipped into his chair.

Carson shook his head just as Ambassador Claire Roberts appeared on the screen. She wore an unremarkable gray pantsuit that accentuated the silver highlights in her hair. Seeing her on the screen, Carson guessed that she was probably the same age as the General, having charted a different but equally successful career upward through the State Department bureaucracy. The ambassador had a wearied look that hinted at a late night, early morning, or possibly both. She took her seat at the table, wasting no time on formalities.

"Gentlemen, thank you all for joining on short notice," she said without emotion.

"We're always happy to oblige our colleagues at State," General Foster replied with strained congeniality. "How can I help you out?"

The ambassador offered an equally unconvincing smile, peering down her reading glasses like a teacher admonishing a misbehaving pupil. "Well, Bill," she said, pointedly using the general's first name. "It appears that I'm the one helping you out today."

"How's that, Claire? I wasn't aware we were having any problems," Foster shot back, clearly annoyed at her continued refusal to use his title.

"Late last night, I was called over to the foreign minister's residence to explain why your soldiers are planning to vaccinate cows during the training exercise this week."

The general covered the microphone and briefly conferred with his staff. From beyond view of the camera, someone pushed a piece of paper across the table. Foster quickly read it before coming back to the line.

"OK, Claire, I just got up to speed on all the details. This is a routine partnership exercise with the Gisawian military. It's been planned for months. I'm sure the military attaché at the Embassy must have briefed you on it."

"Yes, Bill," she said impatiently. "Everything except for that crucial bit of information about the cows."

"I guess I'm missing something here, Claire. We always have medical and veterinarian detachments going along on these kinds of missions. We're just building some goodwill with the locals. This is routine stuff."

"Bill, nothing down here is ever routine. Perhaps you also noticed that the Gisawians moved the exercise location to a remote training area along the northern border."

"To be honest, Claire, I didn't get a chance to look at the map."

"Well, for a little background, DRoG fought a decade-long war over that area during the 1980s, and the boundaries of the northern border remain a matter of dispute. Given our desire to maintain good relations on both sides of the line, we must officially take a neutral position. However, our good friends down here in DRoG would love nothing more than for us to weigh in on the matter, in their favor, naturally."

"Thanks for the history lesson, Claire, but I'm still not seeing the problem," the general said impatiently.

Did you happen to see the local newspaper yesterday?"

"Aw, you know us Army guys. We usually go straight for the funny pages," Foster shot back in a mocking folksy tone.

"Too bad. Because your exercise was above the fold on the front page of every newspaper in town. A big picture of American soldiers getting off a truck within spitting distance of the disputed border zone. It will almost certainly be interpreted across the region as us legitimizing DRoG's territorial claims at the expense of our friends to the north.

The general looked impatiently at his watch. "OK, Claire. Point taken. And the cows? Where do they fit into all this?"

"Ah yes, I'm glad you asked. The cows in question are not technically Gisawian."

"Just passing through on vacation?" the general interjected, eliciting a round of sycophantic chortles from his staff.

"Actually, they belong to migratory herders who spend most of the year north of the border. They only come into DRoG during the dry season when there's no surface water in their natural grazing areas. The herders have been doing this for as long as anyone can remember. They view the border as a meaningless imposition of the colonial period. In fact, they actively fought against DRoG during the 1980s when President Namono tried to close it down and stop unauthorized crossings."

"OK, Claire. Good to know about the cows. We'll watch out for them. But I still don't see why this required an urgent teleconference at 0730 in the morning."

"Because, Bill, your exercise has managed to tick off everyone on both sides of the border. Yesterday our friends to the north issued a sharply worded demarche when they saw the newspaper story about the location of the training exercise. Now they're worried that the US has changed its position on demilitarization of the border zone. Then, late last night, I got another call from DRoG's interior minister demanding that I explain why we plan to vaccinate foreign cows who don't respect the de facto international boundary."

"So, you're saying that Gisawians were trying to play us by moving the exercise to that training area up north?"

"Bill, we're the world's last remaining superpower. Everybody is trying to play us. That's just business as usual down here." The general stared blankly into the camera as the ambassador continued. "Listen, Bill, you may not believe this, but I'm not really interested in micromanaging your business."

"You're right. I don't believe it!" the general snapped back.

"Just remember. There's no such thing as coincidence down here. Things happen for a reason."

"I appreciate that reminder, but on any given day, I'm running military operations in a dozen different countries across Africa. I can't always keep up-to-date on the geopolitical implications of bovine migratory patterns. That's why we have foreign service officers. To make sure that critical national security issues like that don't turn into World War III."

The ambassador bit her lip as the microphone picked up another round of snickers from the general's staff.

"That's surprising to hear, Bill. I thought all you generals had lots of people helping you figure this stuff out. In fact, just last week, I was reading a profile of General Armstrong in the *New Yorker*. Apparently, he's created some kind of in-house think tank full of Rhodes scholars advising him on the sociopolitical implications of his military operations. He gave a great TED talk about it a few months ago. I'll send you the link. The guy seems like a real superstar. Not the type to leave things to chance…"

The general visibly stiffened at the mention of Armstrong's name.

"OK, Claire. If this is such a big deal, then tell me how to fix it because I've got another planeload of soldiers landing there in less than twenty-four hours."

"Fortunately, I think things are back under control. After a long phone call last night with Deputy Minister Odongo, we were able to reach a compromise. However, it required a few minor adjustments to the plan."

"How minor?"

"We agreed that your soldiers will have no contact with any cows during the mission, migratory or otherwise. That came with the understanding that the Gisawians will move the exercise location to a training area far away from the border zone. I know this probably seems like an overreaction to you; however, we are at a delicate juncture right now. The Gisawians have tentatively agreed to demilitarize the disputed area contingent upon an upcoming vote designating it a UNESCO World Heritage Site. In the interest of maintaining good relations on both sides of the border, we need to be viewed as an honest broker in the process. Now is not the time to be muddying the waters."

"A World Heritage Site? You mean they're going to secure the border by making it into a tourist trap?"

"Yes, I believe that's essentially their strategy. The next best thing to having soldiers patrolling a disputed border is having it recognized as an endangered ecosystem."

"How's that?"

"You'd know better than me, Bill, but I'm guessing that securing a national park from poachers also keeps out migrant herders and rebel armies. Not to mention the fact that it gives DRoG de facto recognition over their claims to the area. From their perspective, it's a win-win."

"So, from what I'm hearing, you've solved a problem that I didn't even know I had until ten minutes ago."

"I'm just trying to keep us all out of trouble, Bill. Right now, the entire region is scrutinizing every move we make. Especially while the folks back in DC are debating the location of the new counter-terrorism training center. As you can imagine, there's a lot of interest in the outcome of that decision. Until things are finalized, we can't be viewed as playing favorites. Too much is at stake."

"OK, Claire. I got it. Our exercise will steer clear of cows and the border, so everyone stays happy. And once this thing is done, we're back to focusing on getting Odoki."

"Great. The sooner that's done, the better, for everyone. We'll be in touch."

Then, without warning, the ambassador's line dropped out of the teleconference, leaving the general staring beet-faced into the camera. As it dawned on him that the meeting had ended Foster slammed his hand down on the mute button, apparently not realizing that the video link was still on. He then launched into an animated monologue, throwing his pen, sweeping papers from the table, and gesticulating wildly at his staff. As the general's outburst unfolded, Sid attempted to lip-read his ranting.

"I think I saw the B-word," Sid whispered to Carson. "Yup, there he goes again. Now the F-word, followed by the B-word..."

The colonel shot Sid a dirty look. "I'll take it from here, gentlemen. You are both excused," he ordered.

Sid and Carson got up from their chairs like scolded children and shuffled toward the door while the general's muted tantrum continued up on the screen.

+++

Late in the afternoon, Carson walked across the court-yard to Sujah Bean for an impromptu meeting with Don Slyker. He was already in the garden sitting at a table underneath the mango tree when Carson arrived.

"How's it going?"

"Well, two weeks down, and I'm still here," Carson replied with a halfhearted smile.

"Great. I heard the coffee upgrade went over well," Slyker said, winking conspiratorially. "I bet that got you some nice brownie points with the boss."

"It did. I guess I owe you one for that."

"No problem. Glad to help," Slyker said as Sammy appeared beside the table.

"Mr. Carson, will you be cupping this evening?" Sammy asked, bowing awkwardly.

"Please, join me," Slyker insisted. "We have something new. My scout just sent down some top-grade Guji beans. I'm thinking about bringing some new growers into the co-op and want to get a feel for their product."

"I guess I can't refuse."

"Very good sir," Sammy said, snapping his heels before disappearing back into the shack to prepare the tasting.

Carson settled into his seat, pulling out a small notebook and the fancy pen that Slyker had given him at their first meeting.

"So, now that you've got a few weeks under your belt, any impressions?" Slyker asked.

Carson rubbed his chin, thinking about how to respond. "Well, it's certainly not what I expected. To be honest, I still don't have a good handle on exactly what I'm supposed to be doing here."

"Defending freedom, democracy, and the American way of life?"

"Yeah, something like that," Carson chuckled.

"I'm sure it will become clear soon enough," Slyker said.

"I suppose so. Until then, I'll just take it one day at a time."

"Makes sense. So, what does the good colonel have you working on now that the coffee crisis is fixed?"

Carson doodled in the margins of his notebook, hesitating over his next words. "I almost hate to bring this up," he began." But I need to ask another favor."

"Go ahead. ESP is at your service. I can't help unless I know the problem."

"I appreciate that," Carson said before continuing. "So, there was a teleconference this morning with the ambassador. Apparently, afterward, the general told Kittredge that he wanted to bring in some kind of special advisor."

"Special advisor?"

"Yeah, someone who can answer questions."

"Well, you may actually be in luck. Our parent firm has a small boutique division called 'SME Unlimited' that offers a full range of consulting and advisory services."

"SME? Don't tell me, Subject Matter Expert."

"I know, not very imaginative. Apparently, we owned the domain name and the marketing department didn't want to let it go to waste. Anyway, the unit specializes in sourcing niche requirements like expert witnesses for class action lawsuits and cable TV talking heads. We also provide the Pentagon with a wide range of on-demand consulting services covering over eighty different areas of academic and technical research. You name the topic, and SME will find you a reasonably vetted and plausibly credentialed expert in the field."

"Wow. And I was worried this was going to be hard," Carson said.

"Rule number one, never be afraid to ask. Fortunately for you, our 'SME-On-Demand' service is bundled in with the base support contract. We have hundreds of top people on retainer at reasonable hourly rates. What sub-specialty are you looking for?"

"Hmm, the general wasn't very specific."

"Presumably someone with street cred on Africa?"

"I guess..."

"A particular academic field? International relations? Defense sector reform? Development economics?"

"Not specified."

"OK...," Slyker said, shaking his head. "Were any criteria mentioned at all?"

"Ivy League. That was all he said."

"Ah, purely ornamental then. Ordinarily, that would make things easier. We can usually dig up some disgruntled humanities Ph.D. stuck in a dead-end adjunct gig and behind on child support payments. They're a dime a dozen. Unfortunately, there's a slight catch."

"How slight?"

"Ivy League resumes are only bundled with our premium support package. That's a 'Mercle' product line."

"Mercle?"

"Sorry, I'm always slipping into billing codes. Shorthand for 'Major Regional Contingency, Land.' Unfortunately, your mission here is on an entirely different payment plan. I would really love to help you out; however, I doubt that the bean counters at the Pentagon will sign off on a premium package upgrade just for this. Especially if the rumors are true about the operation shutting down."

"The general said it was mission essential."

Slyker smiled. "Right. Of course, it is. Listen, it's not my business to get in the way of your boss's vanity project. However, in this case, my hands are tied. As much as I would love to bump you up to a premium package, I can only provide what the government is willing to pay for. And for this operation, that means no Ivy League. Sorry, no can do."

"But you came through on the coffee thing."

"Yeah, and you know what? Corporate headquarters would have my ass if they knew I was doing pro bono stuff like that. Now you come back, not even a week later, asking for another freebie?" Slyker said in exasperation.

"Didn't you just tell me that it never hurts to ask?"

"OK, OK," Slyker said, shaking his head. "What's the bottom line here? Is this something the general is just going to forget about by next week? You don't want to fire off a silver bullet unless you know it's going to be worth it."

"I don't know him well enough to guess. But Colonel Kittredge seemed pretty adamant about it after the meeting. The old man wants someone with an Ivy League resume sitting at the table the next time he dials down."

Slyker let out a full-throated laugh, slapping his hand on the table. "Man, these guys slay me. It's always a crisis, even when it's not. But of course, it's no skin off his back. Foster just made it someone else's problem to solve, so I'm sure he's not too worried about how it gets done."

"Seems that way."

"OK, let's just assume there's not going to be any extra cash thrown at this contract. In that case, the best we can do is find someone who fits the general's basic requirement but is willing to work on a reduced rate."

"How likely is that?"

"Not unheard of. People take these gigs for lots of reasons. Maybe we can find someone in a pinch. Otherwise, I'd be taking the difference out of margin and there's no way in hell I'm going to convince the home office to sign off on that. Especially if the party's almost over. They're going to be watching every nickel and dime until the curtain comes down."

"So that's what you're hearing about the mission? I guess it's not much of a secret anymore."

Slyker shrugged. "Listen, even if it's not true, it almost doesn't matter. Once rumors like that hit the street, the damage is done. I'm already getting calls from my local subs looking to jump ship for other operations. The Chinese are hiring like crazy right now, so there's plenty of work to go around. They don't pay squat, but at least they're in it for the long game. Doing business with the US government is like playing chess with a puppy. Honestly, I can't really blame my guys for wanting to work for an outfit with an attention span longer than a news cycle."

"OK, but I can't do anything about that. Right now, my problem is getting someone at that table before the next meeting. The general's only stipulation was Ivy League. Can we make it happen?"

"You're killing me, Carson," Slyker said, shaking his head. "I'll tell you what. Let me take a quick look at the on-call roster and see what I can find."

Slyker reached down into his leather attaché and pulled out an electronic tablet. His fingers tapped through a few open windows, reviewing what appeared to be personnel files. Slyker's brow furrowed as he scrolled impatiently through the data.

"Funny. I was just about to complain about the slow Internet. Then I remembered that we own the satellite link…," he said, scrolling through a few more pages. "Hmm. Interesting," he mumbled before looking back at Carson. "You may be in luck. No promises, but there's a chance I can get you an all-but-dissertation cultural anthropologist. Not that the general cares, but she has field research experience in Africa. According to our background check, she's on academic leave for a mental health exemption and currently available for worldwide assignment."

"Ivy League?" Carson asked, hopefully.

"Technically, yes. Brown. But between you and me, we can usually get lower-tier ivies at the state school billing rate."

"Great! That's good enough for me."

"OK, but don't go announcing anything until I talk with HR. I'll let you know as soon as I can."

"I can't thank you enough."

"Don't worry. I'm sure there will be ample opportunity for you to demonstrate your gratitude," Skyler said with a smile as he slid the tablet back into his briefcase. A moment later, Sammy appeared at the table carrying several bowls of roasted beans and the cupping paraphernalia.

"Now that business is done, let's move on to something more enjoyable," Slyker said, winking at the barista. "Sammy, take it away."

+++

On Friday morning, Carson walked confidently into the operations center ready to take the reins of the weekly staff meeting. He called the room to attention when Colonel Kittredge walked in the door and promptly kicked off the briefing.

"Sir, I'd like to cover a few preliminary notes before we start through our normal agenda," Carson said.

"Please proceed," Kittredge nodded, sliding down into his chair, bracing for the deluge of slides that would occupy the remainder of their morning.

"Following up on last week's business, I'm happy to report that we have received very favorable reviews on the upgraded offerings at the Sujah Bean café."

"I'll take your word on it. As long as I never hear another fucking word about the coffee I'll be happy," Kittredge said, twirling his finger in the air, signaling for Carson to move on to the next item on the agenda.

"Yes, sir. On a different topic, we may have found a candidate for the general's special advisor."

"Really?" Kittredge said, sitting up in his chair, suddenly interested. "That was quick. Good job, Carson! What are the details?"

"I'm still waiting on final confirmation from Mr. Slyker, but he's tentatively identified someone who could be here in the next two weeks."

"Ivy league?"

"Yes, sir. Brown!"

Kittredge sunk back into his seat.

"Do you want a copy of her CV so you can forward it to the general," Carson offered.

"Not necessary. I'll send him a message letting the general know that we've satisfied all stated criteria," Kittredge said before turning to his public affairs officer. "Burke. Draft up a press release announcing the arrival of the general's new special advisor. Run it through me before putting anything out."

Burke made a note to himself while Carson flipped to the next slide. "Sid will be next with the intelligence update."

"Sir, no change to the enemy situation," Sid began. "However, we did receive word that Police Intelligence is debriefing several recently captured GLA fighters. We expect a full report soon and hopefully some new information that will help us narrow the target area for our next mission."

"Yeah, that would be nice," Kittredge snapped. "Because right now we've got nothing."

Sid ignored the colonel's comment and continued on with his briefing. "Sir, if I can direct your attention to the map, I've highlighted the zones of recent GLA activity based on information from Police Intelligence. As you can see, these are mostly in the remote area along the western border, far from major roads and population centers. The GLA continues to exploit the security vacuum to recruit fighters and sustain their logistical network. MoD now believes that the only way to clear the GLA from the area is by launching a major, synchronized offensive focused on this area."

"Come on, Sid! What's the chance of that happening?" Kittredge asked skeptically.

"Sir, I recently received some confidential information suggesting that a planning effort for such an operation is already underway by direct order of President Namono. It seems like the real deal this time. The Gisawians appear to be leaning forward to make this happen."

"Really? Where did you hear that?" Kittredge challenged him.

Sid shifted in his chair, reluctant to answer. "It was from a reliable and vetted source with high-level placement inside MoD and access to…"

"You mean Louie?" Kittredge asked, cutting him off mid-sentence. "I saw you guys having coffee yesterday at the café. Is that what he told you?"

"Sir, I'd rather not discuss classified sources and methods in this venue. Not everyone in the room is cleared for that kind of information…"

"Whatever. Just tell me what Louie said," the colonel demanded impatiently.

"Yes, sir," Sid grumbled. "Apparently, MoD is drafting plans for a major offensive in the western region focused against the GLA's logistical network. But before the plan can be finalized, they need those satellite pictures to help identify suspected underground cache sites."

"Have you made any progress on getting what they need?"

"I spoke with the analysts up in Germany. They think they can use some existing satellite imagery to identify areas of recent clear-cutting and disturbed topsoil. It won't be high-resolution but should be enough to give MoD an idea of where they need to focus their operation."

Kittredge turned to Master Sergeant Jorgenson, who was sitting at the end of the table staring into his laptop, not seeming to follow the discussion. "Jorgs, what are you hearing from your guys? Are the Gisawians really prepping for something like this?"

Jorgenson looked up from his computer. "Yes, sir. They seem to be getting ready for something big. They've asked for our help developing a tactical ground plan for simultaneous raids against multiple targets, but didn't really tell us why."

"That sounds ambitious. Could they really pull something like that off?" Kittredge asked.

"It would be a stretch," Jorgs said with a shrug. "Depending on how many targets they plan to hit, the synchronization and logistics would be challenging. A major offensive like that would take up most of their army. But, if the intel is solid and they know the exact locations of the targets, there's a chance it could work."

"Sounds like a long shot to me," Kittredge said, shaking his head. "But if it did work, then that's our ticket out of here. Getting Odoki would be the icing on the cake. But maybe not even necessary if they could take down his entire network with one punch. I'll talk to General Foster later today and bring him up to speed on the developments."

"OK. What's next on the agenda?" Kittredge said, turning back to Carson.

"Public affairs, then civil affairs. Captain Burke, you're up."

"Sir, this week's public messaging campaign will focus on our joint exercise activities with the Gisawian armed forces. Per guidance from the ambassador, we've removed all references to the cattle vaccination program from our social media platforms. We also issued a revised press release noting the change to the exercise location. However, we're having some difficulty getting the local media outlets to follow suit. They're continuing to report the wrong location."

"Damn it, Burke! We need to get that fixed ASAP."

"Yes, sir. I've tried to convince them, but it seems that the local media won't budge until the Gisawian Ministry of Information issues its own press release confirming the change of venue."

"Well, how soon is that going to happen? The exercise starts on Monday, and all the newspapers are still reporting the wrong information."

"I called over to the Ministry this morning. Their spokesman said that they can't issue a formal retraction until the text has been personally approved by the minister."

"And when's he going to do that?"

"That's where it gets a little complicated. Apparently, the minister is out of the country receiving extended medical treatment at an undisclosed location outside of Geneva. His staff promised they would try to get his approval before the start of the exercise but wouldn't guarantee it."

"Jesus," Kittredge muttered. "Keep trying. The general is going to have my ass if this thing doesn't get fixed today. Anything else?"

"Yes, sir. This week we're kicking off our Sister City initiative."

"What the hell is that? This is the first I've heard about it."

"In keeping with General Foster's guidance to raise the mission profile and strengthen engagement with the local community we are looking for an American sponsor to become a Sister City with one of the nearby villages."

"I don't remember ever discussing this," Colonel Kittredge said, looking around the room for confirmation.

"No, sir. It's a new initiative," Burke stammered.

"Well, to be honest, it seems a bit out of our lane. How much work is this going to require? The last thing we need is another distraction."

"Minimal effort, sir. Once we have a sponsor city on board, then they take over most of the bureaucratic hassle. It's mostly symbolic. Maybe a few cultural exchanges and pen pals from the local schools. That kind of thing."

"OK, so how do we find a sponsor city?"

"Coincidentally, one has been identified. Centerville, Pennsylvania."

"Isn't that where you're from?"

"The next town over. But I have some contacts on city council and the local chamber. They've expressed interest in sponsoring a village."

"All right," Kittredge sighed. "Go ahead with the plan. But I don't want this thing taking up too much bandwidth. We've got enough stuff to worry about already. Anything else?"

"No, sir, that's it."

Carson nodded at Captain Dodge, the Civil Affairs officer. "OK, Dodger. We missed you last week. Bring us up to speed on your projects."

"Sir, we have a civil engineering team coming down here in a few weeks to do some work on the camp. While they're here, we're planning to have them do a few goodwill projects outside the fence. Maybe digging some irrigation wells or new pit latrines in one of the local villages."

"Sounds good, Dodge. You've got someplace in mind?"

"We're working it through Louie. MoD agreed to help us find a good location and coordinate the project with the local community. Everything should be in place once our team hits the ground."

"OK, be sure to keep Captain Burke in the loop. We'll need to get plenty happy-shots of the locals thanking Uncle Sam for their new shithouses. The general loves that crap. OK. What's next...," Kittredge said, trying his best to keep the meeting moving along.

CHAPTER FIVE

———

Carson inched the pickup truck through the chaotic traffic circle outside the airport terminal, finally making his way to the same parking spot where Sid had picked him up the month before. As soon as he turned off the engine, a woman appeared next to the truck, knocking on the window, trying to sell him a bag of boiled groundnuts. Carson bought three bags and threw them on the dashboard, hoping that evidence of his purchase would dissuade other offers.

Through the dusty window, Carson watched the steady stream of passengers flowing from the arrivals terminal. It was only a few minutes before he spotted Slyker coming out the door. Carson punched the horn several times and waved to get his attention. It took a moment for Slyker to realize that he was the intended target of the commotion. After recognizing Carson waving from the truck, Slyker crossed the plaza to where he was parked.

"Is this a coincidence or are you looking for me?" Slyker asked, sticking his head through the passenger window.

"Your assistant said you were coming in tonight and then leaving again tomorrow. I wanted to make sure I caught you. Need a ride?"

"Thanks, but I usually just grab a taxi."

"Really, it's no problem," Carson insisted. "I wasn't busy."

"This sounds like something more than a social call."

Carson shrugged without denying the charge as Slyker climbed into the truck.

"If you're going to beg me for another favor, let's at least do it over some decent food," Slyker suggested as Carson started the engine and pulled from the parking spot. "I haven't eaten all day, except for a stale croissant at the airport in Dar es Salaam."

"Business trip?"

"No. Just meeting a friend for a long weekend at the beach. Nice place if you ever get the chance. Very peaceful."

"Unlikely, but thanks for the tip."

"Yeah, I guess they keep you guys on a pretty short leash. So, have you eaten yet?"

"Nope."

"Good. Have you tried the local cuisine?"

"Not really. Just some leftovers that Louie brought back from his mom's house and it was pretty good."

"No doubt. I probably can't beat Louie's mom for authenticity; however, I do know a nice little joint on the edge of town. It's not far from camp, so I'll get you back before curfew."

"OK. Just point the way."

They drove from the airport as the sun was disappearing below the horizon. Carson flipped on the high-beam lights, trying to avoid the gigantic potholes along the badly rutted road. After fifteen minutes, they came upon what looked like a small village with a number of empty wooden tables lining the shoulder of the road. During the day, they would be piled high with thick cassavas, plantains, and burlap sacks full of dried beans and spices. Slyker motioned for Carson to turn off onto an unmarked dirt path that disappeared into the darkness.

"You're kidding, right?" Carson asked, glancing warily at Slyker.

"Trust me. We're almost there. Just follow where it goes into the trees."

Carson's mind began racing with unseen dangers. He was just about to stop the truck and refuse to go any further when the trees opened into a wide clearing. Up ahead in the moonlight he could see a dimly lit bungalow with half a dozen cars parked outside. Beside it was a small patio seating area set under a protective canopy of trees. A line of glowing luminaria marked a path from the parking lot up to the bungalow.

"Wow," Carson exclaimed, turning off the engine. "I never would have guessed this."

"It's a hidden gem. DRoG's best al fresco dining. I come here whenever I'm in town. A nice French lady owns the place. She's been here over twenty-five years."

As they walked toward the bungalow, a woman poked her head through a window and gave Slyker a friendly wave. When Carson's eyes adjusted to the light, he noticed an enormous black abyss extending far beyond the edge of the patio.

"You need to come back during daytime to see the lake," Slyker said, nodding out into the darkness. "The owner has a few cabins for rent right along the water. If you get here before lunchtime you can see the fishermen bringing their catch right up to the restaurant. The tilapia is as fresh as you're going to get. It's my go-to dish."

"In that case, I'll follow your lead."

They didn't wait long before the waitress arrived at the table with two plates of grilled fish smothered in translucent onions, red tomatoes, and peppers. She returned a moment later with big bowls of black beans and fried plantains.

"Dig in," Slyker said. "Trust me. After this, you'll never go back to the Safari Club."

"No doubt," Carson agreed as they tucked into their meals.

"So, now that we have a proper plate of food in front of us, what's the real reason you picked me up at the airport?" Slyker asked.

"I should probably start by promising that this is really the last time."

"Don't bother. It will just be more awkward the next time you need something."

"Probably right. Anyway, next on my to-do list from the Colonel is fixing up the gym. Right now, it looks like a Turkish prison. I didn't want to bother you about it, but Sid said you might have some ideas."

Slyker leaned back in his chair, taking a break from the fish. "There's a very good reason why the gym sucks."

"I'm listening."

"It wasn't in the contract. Otherwise, I could have easily built you a nice little prefab number with all the bells and whistles. Cardio, weights, yoga studio, the works."

"Don't tell me…gyms only come with a premium package upgrade."

"Bingo. It's like the HBO of base support contracts."

"So, are you saying that I'm out of luck on this one."

"Listen," Slyker interrupted. "I'm not unsympathetic to your dilemma. I know you're trying to do the right thing by taking care of the soldiers. And while I can't do anything about it in my official capacity, I still may be able to help you out."

"I'm almost afraid to ask."

"Trust me. It's nothing shady. You ever heard of the Palm Hotel?"

"That fancy place downtown where all the VIPs stay?"

"Fancy is a relative term. Five stars here in DRoG is two anywhere else in the world. And I certainly wouldn't recommend brushing your teeth with the tap water. However, they do have somewhat reliable Wi-Fi and a generator that keeps the AC running during blackouts. By local standards that gets you five stars. Anyway, I happen to know that the owner just started a big renovation. Apparently, he's trying to turn it into the country's first and only spa resort."

"That sounds nice, but I don't see how...," Carson began before Slyker cut him off.

"So, here's the deal. I'm a regular at the Palm. More importantly, every year ESP sponsors a big security conference where we fly in a bunch of talking heads and congressional staffers for a few days of chitchat, cocktails, and trinket shopping. Last year we did it at the Palm. It goes without saying that Congressional staffers focused on African affairs don't get out that much. But when they do, and when someone else is picking up the bill, they go all out. The bar tab alone was five figures. To make a long story short, I've thrown a lot of business at the Palm. The manager owes me a favor or two. Let me find out what he's planning to do with the old gym equipment after the renovation."

"Somehow you always make it look easy," Carson said, shaking his head in disbelief.

"This would be a perfect opportunity for false modesty. However, nothing is as easy as it looks. Remember, I've been at this a while. But trust me, it was a difficult learning curve."

"I can imagine. How'd you end up in this line of work anyway?" Carson said, flipping over the fish and beginning work on the back side.

"It's a long story and not really that interesting."

"I've got no place else to be," Carson said with a shrug.

"Well, like many inspirational up-by-the-bootstraps sagas, it began with me fresh out of law school, unemployed and loaded up to my ass in debt. I wasn't particularly enthusiastic about joining the rat race at a big firm but needed some quick money. Iraq was just kicking off, and I stumbled across an offer for lawyers to go downrange. The defense industry was hiring like crazy and they needed people able to write contracts under fire, literally and figuratively. At the time, I just figured it would be a quick way to pay off my school loans before getting on to something else. But I guess that's how these things always go. It's the small decisions that seem to set you down a path that lasts forever. Anyway, that's more or less how I got started in the biz."

"So, you were over there in Iraq from the beginning. You must have seen quite a bit?"

"Enough, but less than you might think. For me, it was mostly green eyeshade stuff. Sitting behind the blast walls and keeping the books straight. For the first few months, it was smooth sailing. Everyone was still doing a victory dance and feeling like heroes. At that point, it was just easy money. But of course, it didn't take long for things to change. Before I knew it, we were losing a few dozen guys each month."

"That must have been hard. I lost some friends over there too."

"Well, that's the funny thing," Slyker said, shaking his head. "They weren't my friends. Hell, I didn't even know them. Most of our employees were local hires and third country nationals. Iraqi, Pakistani, and Filipino dudes out there on the roads delivering supplies and doing the dirty work to keep the soldiers fed and the bases running. To me, they were just unpronounceable names on a personnel roster. But once they started getting blown to bits every day, my job changed to handling all the compensation payouts to the families. From a legal perspective, it was plain vanilla work. No big negotiations involved. We made those guys sign so many liability waivers that it kept things pretty cut and dry. Mostly I was just distributing next-of-kin payments to anyone willing to sign on a dotted line. Essentially, my job was making sure the C-suite guys back in DC wouldn't have to lose any sleep over it."

"That sounds like shit."

"Yeah, pretty much. Not the kind of thing that makes you excited about getting up in the morning and going into work, no matter how much they were paying me. Anyway, after a while of doing that crap, I just couldn't take it anymore. About that time, Techtron was spinning off ESP with a plan to grow the business in Africa. They were looking for someone to lead it and I was looking for a change of scenery. That's pretty much the story. I've been bouncing around here ever since."

"I guess by now, you qualify as an old Africa hand."

"Hardly. Whenever I start getting overconfident and thinking I've got it all figured out, that's when I'll get hit with something that turns everything upside down."

"But you seem comfortable over here."

"At least inside the camp, I more or less know the game. I did ROTC in college and then a brief stint in uniform before law school. Been there, done that. But of course, that was a long time ago."

"Really?" Carson said with surprise. "I wouldn't have pegged you for it. How come you didn't stick it out?"

"Let's just say that me and Army weren't a good fit."

"Should I even ask?"

"It doesn't matter. I'm over it," Slyker said with mock wistfulness. "If you really want to know, my career fell victim to a youthful indiscretion during my officer basic training."

Carson let out a chuckle. "Yeah, that happens. A general's daughter type thing?"

"Actually…his son."

Carson's gaze drifted down to the bony remains of the tilapia on his plate. After a long moment of silence, the awkwardness became unbearable.

"Damn, Carson. I feel like this has put a damper on our romantic dinner by the lake," Slyker said.

Carson shifted in his chair, unable to look Slyker in the eyes.

"You seem uncomfortable," Slyker pressed. "Listen, this

wasn't a setup. You're the one who asked me out, remember? Besides, you're not my type."

"Sorry," Carson said, shaking his head. "I'm cool. It just took me by surprise. But just to be on the safe side, I probably won't tell my wife about it."

"Sure. Makes sense. No need to make her jealous," Slyker teased.

Carson finally laughed and resumed picking at the remnants of his fish.

"So, if you don't mind me asking, what happened?"

"You know, the usual boy-meets-boy story. He was a nice kid, still in college, home visiting his folks for summer vacation. The problem was, his dad happened to be wearing a few stars on his shoulder and was still in denial about his son. No need to remind you, this was the old Army."

"But you signed up knowing that was the deal, right? Why?"

"Yeah, good question. For some strange reason, I'd convinced myself that I could make it work. I had always been careful in college. I wasn't political. Not out to rock the boat."

"Still, it must have been hard."

"I guess so. That's just the way things were back then, so I didn't really think much about it. Anyway, one night me and the kid were out in my car, parked somewhere by the side of the road, foolishly assuming it was safe. It didn't take long before some overzealous MP happened to drive by and decided to check out what was going on. I guess he saw some things that were hard for my friend to explain to his daddy the general."

"Awkward."

"To say the least. Ironically, the only thing that saved me from a dishonorable discharge was his old man. The general didn't want a big court-martial because it would have meant putting his own kid on the stand to testify. Instead, he just sent him back off to school early hoping to kill the rumors."

"Figures. And what about you?"

"Since he couldn't throw the book at me, the next best thing was to make my life so miserable that I'd eventually leave on my own. They put me in a desk job so I wouldn't be around any of the soldiers. I guess they figured I was contagious. No one would even share an office with me. They actually cleared out a utility closet and moved me in there, utterly oblivious to the irony."

"So that was it? You just waited it out in the closet until it was time to go?"

"More or less. It was about two years until my time was up. They made sure that my evaluation reports were bad enough that there was no chance for promotion. Then one day, it was all over. I was back on the street in civilian clothes. From there, I bounced around to a few jobs, trying to figure out plan B. Eventually, it became law school. That seemed like a good place to park myself while I figured out what to do with my life."

"It was a different Army back then," Carson offered optimistically.

"That's what they say…"

"You regret it?"

"What part?"

"Do you ever wish things could have worked out?"

"I guess it did, in a way. Believe it or not, I don't hold any grudges. Life's too short."

"So, what's the draw of being here now? By this point, you must have plenty of options. And I'm guessing a nice little portfolio to keep you comfortable."

"Yeah, it's not about the money anymore. I've made a pile and then some. The truth is, I met someone over here a few years back."

"Around here?" Carson asked with surprise, having completely forgotten about the tilapia.

"No, not right here for god's sake, but originally from the region. He's a lawyer too. But nothing like me. He does advocacy work for an international NGO. Good governance, human rights, democracy type stuff. We both travel a lot for work, but we've been able to make accommodations."

"OK, this story just gets crazier all the time. How does a certified merchant of death get partnered up with bleeding heart human rights activist?"

Slyker shrugged. "We don't talk much about work at home. That probably helps. But still, the travel is starting to get old. We've discussed going back to the states and settling down somewhere but he's not ready to leave quite yet. And given our respective professions, neither of us will ever suffer from a lack of work over here."

"But it must not be easy for you, given your situation...," Carson hinted.

"No, it's not. Back in the states, the worst thing I ever suffered was being humiliated by the Army. The same thing can get you killed over here. Honestly, I'd leave tomorrow if he was ready. But until then, all we can do is be careful."

"I guess that sort of puts things in perspective," Carson said as the waitress appeared to take away the plates. "Anyway, thanks for bringing me out here," he said after she disappeared back into the bungalow. "You were right. That fish was damn good."

"Glad you liked it. So anyway, I've got meetings tomorrow over at MoD, then I'm heading out for Djibouti right after that."

"Djibouti? Wow, you do get around."

"Trust me, it's not by choice. Anyway, just give me a few days on the gym thing. I'll talk to the manager at the Palm and see if I can swing a deal."

"Sure. That would be great. I guess I owe you another one."

"Don't worry," Slyker said with a smile. "I'm keeping track."

+++

The next morning Louie arrived at MoD headquarters for his weekly meeting with the deputy minister. He was surprised to walk in and find the secretary anxiously pacing the floor, waiting for his arrival. She rushed him straight inside the office without so much as a greeting. When Louie entered the room, Mugaba glanced up from his papers and waved him toward the chair in front of his desk.

"Good morning, Uncle. How are you?"

"Fine, fine. And you, Lutalo?"

"I am well, Uncle. I had a nice visit with my mother last week."

"I know," he said with a satisfied grin. "She called me the next morning. You have no idea how happy it makes her to see you. It may be a small thing to you but not to your mother. Please be a good son and don't wait so long next time. It breaks her heart to have her children so far away."

"Yes, Uncle. I promise."

"Good. I hope I don't need to remind you of this again," Mugaba added before changing the topic. "So, Lutalo, I don't have much time. Tell me the news from the camp. Are the Americans keeping you busy?"

"Yes, Uncle. There is plenty of work to do," Louie replied, unenthusiastically.

"Very good. I'm glad you are busy," Mugaba said, nodded thoughtfully. "But I can tell from your voice that something is bothering you. You don't like working with the Americans?"

"No, Uncle. It's not that. I have good friends at the camp, and they treat me like a brother."

"Then what is it, Lutalo? We don't keep secrets in our family."

"Uncle, I've been there over two years now. Almost since the Americans first arrived. Most of the soldiers have come and gone several times since then. All except for me."

"So, you think it's time for you to move on as well?" the big man asked.

"I am grateful for the opportunity you have given me, but I can't help think that there are other things I should be doing. I came back home to be in the Army, like my father. But this is not what I expected."

The deputy minister was quiet for a moment as he contemplated Louie's words.

"There was a reason why I picked you for this job. Lutalo. You may not find it exciting, but I need someone I can trust.

This is a sensitive position. Certainly, you understand why I cannot just put anyone there."

"Yes, Uncle. I understand, and I appreciate your trust in me. But two years is a long time. There must be other ways I can contribute."

"What are you thinking, Lutalo?"

"Perhaps something closer to the field. I didn't join the Army to sit in an office. I want to be a commander like my father."

Mugaba nodded but did not speak.

"The next mission against Odoki and his men is two weeks from now," Louie continued. "I would like to go with the Ranger units on the raid."

"Absolutely not!" the deputy minister said without hesitation. "It is not possible."

"But, Uncle. I am an Army officer. Why am I just sitting around an office drinking tea while the soldiers are going into the field? I remember a proverb you once told me. 'One only learns how to cut down trees by cutting them down." If that's true, then what am I learning by sitting in the camp writing memos?"

"Lutalo," the older man said with exasperation. "Let me tell you another old proverb, one that your father understood very well. 'He who refuses to obey cannot command.'"

Louie became quiet, sensing the limits of his uncle's patience.

"Don't forget Lutalo. You are helping me every day," his uncle continued. "And that is no small thing. I am the one who watched over you for many years after your father died. I am the one who made sure that you could stay in school overseas and finish your degree, just as your father always wished. I am also the one who promised your mother that I would protect you. And I have not forgotten that promise."

"But what about my father?" Louie whispered. "What would he think of me just sitting in an office doing paperwork instead of leading soldiers?"

"Lutalo, your father was a great man. A great warrior. If he had lived, I am certain he would have become president someday. He always did what was best for the country. But he also did what was best for his family. You may not agree with my decision, but he would understand why it is necessary. Lutalo, don't forget, a family is like a forest. It seems dense from the outside, but on the inside, each tree has its place. For now, your place is at the camp. I don't expect you to like it. You are too much like your father for that. But someday you will understand why it was necessary. And why I could trust no one else but you."

Louie nodded with resignation, realizing that there was no more point in the discussion.

Mugaba glanced down at his watch and then back at Louie. "I must go soon to meet with the minister. Please, tell me what is happening at the camp so I can give him the information."

"Yes, Uncle," Louie said, almost whispering. "The Americans are preparing for the next mission. They've asked for the summaries of the new interrogation reports to help them decide where to fly the drone."

The deputy minister nodded. "They will have these soon. Police Intelligence is finishing with the detainees. They will bring me the reports next week. You can pass them on to the

Americans. Have they said anything more about the satellite pictures of the western region?"

"The imagery has been requested, but they said it will take a little more time to analyze the information."

The deputy minister scratched a few notes in a small leather notebook. "Lutalo, be sure that the Americans understand that the offensive cannot go forward without this information. President Namono will not approve it unless we know exactly where the GLA are digging to hide their weapons. Without this information, the operation could fail. The minister will not take that risk."

"Yes, Uncle. I have told them. I believe it will happen. They just need more time."

"Tell me when you know more. Anything else?"

"The Americans are bringing an engineering team for projects at the camp. They've offered to do something in the local community, like drilling wells or putting in irrigation systems at one of the local villages. They've asked for our assistance in finding a suitable location."

"Really?" Mugaba said, showing more interest than Louie had expected.

"Yes, Uncle. They will bring all the equipment. They just need to know where to go."

"Very well. I will let the minister know right away. There should be no problem finding an appropriate site. I am certain the idea will be well received. Anything else?"

"No, Uncle. That is all."

"OK. Thank you, Lutalo," the deputy minister said, closing his notebook, signaling that the meeting had come to an end. "Oh, one last thing," he added as Louie rose from his chair. "Did you mention anything to the Americans about our concerns with the Lebanese?"

"Yes, Uncle."

"What did they think? Have they heard anything from their sources?"

"No, Uncle, but they said they would look into it."

"Good. Very good," Mugaba nodded. "Police Intelligence is still investigating the matter. It's probably nothing, but always good to share such concerns with our friends."

"Yes, Uncle," Louie agreed, picking up his briefcase and starting toward the door.

After leaving the office, Louie walked outside the headquarters building into the bright morning sun. He was lost in thought, replaying his uncle's words in his head when he heard someone calling his name.

"Louie. Over here," the voice yelled from the other side of the fence.

He looked up and saw a familiar face from the camp. Don Slyker was walking through the security office, coming into the compound. Louie waited as Slyker flashed his credentials to the guards and walked through the gate.

"What a surprise to see you, Mr. Slyker. I didn't know you were in town," he said, reaching out his hand.

"Just a quick trip. I got in last night, but I'm leaving again this afternoon. I probably won't make it over to the camp. How have you been?" Slyker asked.

"Fine, I guess," Louie offered, forcing a smile. "What brings you over to MoD? I don't recall ever seeing you here."

"Oh, I'm here now and then for business. Maybe you've heard about the overhaul of your armed forces training center?"

"Hmm, I recall something about it, but it's not my area of responsibility. It has been a long time since I was there for my basic officer training."

"Sure. Makes sense. Anyway, MoD put out a request for proposal on the project. ESP happens to have a specialized unit that does that sort of thing. In fact, we've built half a dozen armies from scratch over the last few years."

"Interesting," Louie replied, feigning curiosity.

"It's a niche market but tons of opportunity."

"Really?"

"Sure, we're talking double-digit growth. Initially, we focused the business model on professionalizing irregular militias in post-revolutionary conflict zones but ran into some complications with invoicing."

"To be expected, I suppose."

"Yeah, apparently failed states don't leave forwarding addresses. Anyway, now we're focusing more on capacity building with established partners like DRoG. I'm pitching the new product line to the minister today."

"Well, good luck, Mr. Slyker. Let me know how it goes. I'll see you around camp."

"Absolutely. Let's get together for coffee. And please give my regards to the deputy minister. He was a guest speaker at our last regional conference. He brought down the house. The guy has a catchy proverb for every occasion."

Louie nodded and smiled politely before continuing out the gate and back to the camp.

+++

On Friday morning, the staff gathered in the conference room for the weekly meeting.

"OK, Carson, let's get this thing started," Colonel Kittredge said, sliding into his seat.

"Yes, sir. I have a few issues to cover before we go around to each section," Carson began.

"First off, I'm pleased to announce that our new special advisor will arrive next week." The colonel appeared buoyed by the news. "That's great, Carson. What's his name?"

"*Her* name," he corrected. "She's a woman. Anna."

The colonel seemed momentarily confused, then shrugged. "Whatever. She meets the general's requirements, right?"

"Yes, sir. And she'll be here before the next mission."

"That's good enough for me. Captain Burke let me see that draft press release before the end of the day."

"Yes, sir. Right away," Burke piped in.

"Major Sidwell is up next with the intelligence update," Carson continued.

"Good morning, sir," Sid began. "No major changes to the enemy situation. I've received word that Police Intelligence is nearly done questioning the new detainees. I expect to have the summary reports sometime next week. We're hoping that information will generate some actionable targets for the next mission."

"Good. We really need a win. The folks in DC are looking at every mission with a microscope. Speaking of which, Captain Burke, how'd we do with last week's M-RAT ratings? Are we breaking out of the basement yet?"

Burke looked up from his briefing notes. "Sir, the latest data shows continuing declines in our brand recognition score."

Sergeant Goodwin brought the slide up on the screen. The room was silent as Colonel Kittredge studied the information. "It looks to me like we slipped down another notch."

"Yes, sir."

"What about all that press coverage from the exercise? Didn't we expect some kind of bump from that?"

"Unfortunately, the bump was less robust than anticipated. After the exercise was moved from the northern training area, the local media lost interest. Since then, I've been digging through the numbers trying to figure out why we're still stuck at the bottom. I ran a regression analysis of the latest M-RAT data hoping to tease out a snapshot of our core audience."

"How the hell do you do that?" Kittredge asked.

"M-RAT allows us to track the online behavior of our social media followers, then generate an inferred demographic profile."

"I think I'm already starting to see the problem...," Kittredge said, glaring at Burke. "Just explain it to me in plain English."

"Yes, sir. Basically, M-RAT tells us, in general terms, what kind of person is following us."

"And..."

"Unfortunately, the data was somewhat ambiguous. The best I can figure, most of our digital traffic is likely a result of user error."

"What do you mean user error?"

"Apparently, our brand has several digital doppelgangers."

"Burke, you've lost me again. What are you saying?"

"When you analyze the online traffic, most of our hits come from people looking for something else. For example,

Operation Righteous Protector, or ORP, is frequently confused with the Organization for Responsible use of Pesticides, also known as ORP. Then there's a thing called Oxidation Reduction Potential, also ORP, having something to do with technical measurements used in water treatment. There's also an Eastern European porn site that comes up as a related hit; however, for obvious reasons, I didn't explore the details of that connection."

"So, you're telling me that the few hits we're getting are from people lost on the Internet?"

"Yes, sir. That seems to be the case."

The colonel lowered his forehead to the table while everyone waited for the meeting to proceed. After an awkwardly long pause, Kittredge looked up and turned back to Captain Burke.

"OK, Burke. I'm going to look at the bright side. Maybe this is a blessing in disguise. Until we have something positive to report, it's probably best that we stay under the radar. All we're doing now is drawing attention to failure," the colonel said, before turning back to Carson. "OK, let's keep this thing moving along. I don't want to be stuck here until lunch."

Sergeant Goodwin had just flipped to the next slide when suddenly the entire building felt like it was jolted sideways off its foundation, followed by an ear-splitting blast. Coffee cups spilled over the table, bulletin boards tumbled from the wall, and the room turned pitch black as the power failed. For a few seconds, everyone was frozen in darkness before the backup generator kicked on, filling the room with the amber glow of the emergency lighting system.

"Is everyone all right?" the colonel shouted, looking around for injuries. "What the hell was that?"

Everyone leaped to their feet and charged for the door. Outside in the courtyard, they could see a large plume of smoke rising above the tree line at the edge of the camp. They sprinted toward the front gate as the debris and dust settled to the ground. As they rounded the corner they saw that the wooden guard shack where the Gisawian soldiers checked identifications was gone. There was nothing but a gaping hole in the spot where the camp's front gate had been. Several nearby palm trees had been sheared off and flung like twigs across the road.

"Medics!" Colonel Kittredge screamed at the top of his voice as he sprinted toward the gate and began sifting through the rubble, searching for survivors.

As the rest of the staff joined in and began digging through what was left of the front gate, a second blast suddenly reverberated in the distance. All eyes turned to the horizon as another plume of dust rose into the air several miles away, closer to the center of town.

Colonel Kittredge stood frozen in the pile of splintered timbers and shredded palm fronds, staring up at the sky. It took his mind a moment to process what was happening. Finally, he awoke from the trance and seized Sid by the arm.

"We've got this!" he yelled at Sid through the pandemonium. "I need you to get on the phone with the Embassy ASAP! Find out what the hell is going on!"

Sid nodded, turned, and sprinted back toward the headquarters building.

+++

Late that night, Carson finally got back to his room and collapsed into bed without bothering to take off his uniform. His mind was reeling from the lingering effects of adrenalin, too much coffee, and too little food. He closed his eyes and soon fell into a fitful sleep, only to be disturbed a few hours later by the sound of Captain Burke's voice on the other side of the wall.

What the hell happened there? It's all over the news.

Really? We've been scrambling like crazy here. I haven't even had time to check my messages. It was some kind of bomb at the front gate. Then another explosion about a minute later downtown at Police Intelligence headquarters.

Holy shit! Are you OK?

Yeah, I'm fine. We were in a meeting when it happened. Totally leveled the front gate. All the Americans are OK, but a few Gisawian guards got hurt pretty bad.

Well, I don't need to tell you what this means.

Hmm…maybe you do. It's been a long day. My brain is fried.

Your mission is going to be on the front page of every newspaper in the country tomorrow morning. We've got one, maybe two news cycles before they move on to something else. It's now or never.

What are you saying?

I'm saying that we need to get you some face time. If we miss this opportunity, we may not get another chance.

I don't see how…I'm just too tired to think about this right now.

Listen. Are you guys set up for remote broadcast?

Yeah, I think so. We have all the equipment. My assistant can run the camera and patch us into a satellite link.

OK, here's what we're going to do. I'll call the local affiliate in Centerville. We'll offer them a live exclusive direct from DRoG. I guarantee they'll eat this shit up. Especially if there's a local angle.

You really think it will work? It could be risky putting me on. What if they just want to rehash old news?

Don't worry. I'll grease the skids. I know the general manager. He's an old friend of your dad's. I'll make sure they don't try to muddy the waters. All you need to do is be ready to talk. Get some sleep and make sure things are set on your end tomorrow morning. I'll text you the details once I have them.

OK, if you're sure about this.

Trust me. This is the best thing that could have happened.

+++

"Testing, one, two, three…" Burke said into a mini microphone pinned to the lapel of his uniform. Behind him were the charred remains of the guard shack, next to an improvised gate that had been built during the night with oil drums, industrial piping, and concertina wire. A pair of armored military jeeps were parked on either side of the road with Gisawian soldiers perched high in the turrets, AK-47s at the ready.

"Operations Righteous Protector, this is Centerville affiliate KCTV," said a voice through the earpiece. "We're live in thirty seconds."

"Ready on this end," Burke replied, waiting for his cue.

"And five, four, three, two, one…This is Leslie Jenkins from KCTV Centerville with a breaking news exclusive live from the Democratic Republic of Gisawi where just yesterday an American forward operating camp came under attack by unknown assailants. We are live with Captain Stephen J. Burke III, spokesman for Operation Righteous Protector. Captain, can you hear me?"

"Yes, Leslie, I hear you. Please, go ahead."

"Super. Let me start by asking you to explain exactly what happened yesterday."

"Leslie, we're still gathering information, so I can't go into details concerning an ongoing investigation. However, I can tell you that yesterday morning at approximately 0930 local time there was a large explosion outside the security perimeter of the American camp. Two minutes later there was a secondary explosion several miles away outside the Gisawian Police Intelligence headquarters building."

"You have reason to believe these two incidents are related?"

"Leslie, at this point I don't want to speculate. However, initial indications suggest a coordinated and deliberate attack. We are working closely with our Gisawian counterparts to gather information and identify those responsible."

"Can you give us an update on casualties?"

"Thankfully, the explosion happened outside our perimeter. No American personnel were injured. The Gisawian guards were conducting a shift change at the time and miraculously no one was killed. Unfortunately, we received word that several Gisawian police officers were badly hurt as a result of the second attack downtown; however, none of those injuries appear life-threatening."

"Captain Burke, is the US government treating this as an act of terrorism? Are there any suspects?"

"Leslie, there have been no claims of responsibility. We are in the process of conducting a forensic analysis of the blast sites and working closely with our Gisawian partners to review all available intelligence. Until that process is complete, I don't want to jump to any conclusions."

"Captain Burke, until this morning, when the world awoke to news of the bombing, I'm guessing many of our viewers had never even heard of the Democratic Republic of Gisawi or Operation Righteous Protector. Can you explain to our audience why American soldiers are there and what you're doing?"

"Of course, Leslie, I'd be happy to. Your viewers may recall the name Daniel Odoki. He is the leader of a rebel group known as the Gisawi Liberation Army, or GLA, who several years ago ruthlessly attacked a village in the far western region of the country. They burned an entire settlement to the ground, kidnapping dozens of children and conscripting them as fighters. Since then Odoki and the GLA have operated with impunity across remote parts of the country, terrorizing innocent civilians and challenging government control. Following that attack, Gisawian President Namono asked the United States for assistance in bringing Odoki to justice and neutralizing the threat from the GLA."

"Captain Burke, that certainly seems a noble cause, but can you explain to our viewers why it takes several hundred American soldiers to capture one man who poses no obvious threat to our homeland?"

"Leslie, I realize that for most Americans this may not

seem like a pressing national security concern; however, this is about much more than one evil man. For the last thirty-two years, President Namono has been a close ally of the United States. During the Cold War, DRoG was a loyal partner helping to contain the spread of Soviet-backed communism in Africa. More recently, they have aided us in countering the threat of global terrorism. Your viewers certainly understand that in a time of need, America does not turn its back on old friends. DRoG has been, and remains, an anchor point of peace and stability in the region. Daniel Odoki and the GLA represent a direct threat to the Gisawian people, as well as to American interests and credibility across the region."

"Well, that seems good enough for me! Captain Burke, we only have a few minutes left, so I want to ask you something on a personal note. I understand that you have a local connection to the tri-county region."

"Indeed, Leslie, I do. I was born and raised not too far from Centerville. I graduated from Jefferson High before attending Harvard and then joining the Army."

"And I expect that many of our viewers recognize your name as well. I believe you are the son of Stephen J. Burke Sr., who represented the tri-county area and Forth District for over twenty-five years in Washington until his sudden death last year."

"That is true. Our family roots go back many generations there. My mother still resides just outside of Centerville. I hope to return someday once my military service ends."

"Well, Captain Burke, until then, please stay safe and thank you for your service to our country."

"Of course, Leslie. It's been my pleasure."

"For KCTV Centerville, I am Leslie Jenkins. This has been an exclusive live report from the Democratic Republic of Gisawi, where yesterday a US forward operating base came under attack. I have been speaking with one of our hometown heroes, Captain Stephen J. Burke, currently serving with the American special advisory mission in that country. For more information on Captain Burke and Operation Righteous Protector, please see expanded coverage at our website."

CHAPTER SIX

———

Two weeks later, everyone again gathered around the conference table. Colonel Kittredge glanced up at the time-zone clock and then scanned the room one last time, making sure everyone was ready. On the screen, General Foster trooped into view, followed ducks-in-a-row by his staff.

"Foster here! How do you read me?" he barked into the microphone.

"Loud and clear sir," Kittredge replied from the other end of the line. "We have an ETA of approximately twenty-three minutes over our first target area."

"Roger. We're tracking the same thing on our end," the general said. "Colonel Kittredge, before we get started I want to give a big thumbs-up to your team down there. You all did a magnificent job handling the attack a few weeks ago. It's a testimony to your determination that you kept the camp fully operational and the mission on schedule. Good work."

"Thank you, sir. We appreciate the kind words. We have a few things to cover before turning to tonight's mission. Major Sidwell will provide an update on the status of the bombing investigation."

"Good evening, sir," Sid said. "As you are aware, we still have no claims of responsibility for the recent attacks."

"What do you make of that, Major?" the general interrupted.

"Right now, we have two working hypotheses. The first focuses on the GLA. They have the capability to conduct such an operation; however, their intent is less clear. Up to this point, it has not been their modus operandi to conduct direct attacks against hard targets outside their area of operation. If it was them, then these attacks represent a major escalation of the group's tactics and methods."

"And the other theory?"

"We haven't ruled out the Hezbollah link; however, we still view this scenario as highly unlikely. To the best of our knowledge, the group doesn't have a significant presence in DRoG. While they likely maintain low-level sleeper cells around the region, they haven't used these to conduct major operations. Nevertheless, MoD and Police Intelligence continue pushing this hypothesis. Last week they initiated a major crackdown targeting Lebanese merchants around the country. They've also been tightening security screenings at ports of entry and scrutinizing all the cargo traffic coming into and out of the country. Despite this, we're still not finding much evidence to support their suspicions. If it was Hezbollah, the question remains, why here and why now?"

"So, it sounds like you're leaning toward the first scenario?" the general asked.

"Possibly sir, but until we have all the information I don't want to jump to conclusions. The forensic evidence we gathered from the bombing sites was sent back to the States for analysis. Once we get the results back, we should have a better idea about who made the bombs and where they learned their technique. That will be a big help in narrowing down a list of possible suspects."

"Good work, Major. What's next?"

"Now I'd like to give you a quick overview of tonight's operation," Sid said, turning to the animated map up on the screen. "As you can see, the drone is approximately nineteen minutes from the first target area. We'll be observing two additional sites after that. The locations were derived from recent interrogations of GLA fighters who were picked up by DRoG Army patrols. According to the detainees, some of the camps in these areas may still be active. If we see anything interesting, we have the assault teams up in the air and ready to move on the targets."

"Very good, Major. When I woke up this morning, I had a good feeling about this one," the general said. "Let's hope I'm right."

Colonel Kittredge took back the mic. "Sir, we have a few minutes before the mission gets underway. If you don't mind, we have a few other items of business to cover. First off, I wanted to let you know that your new special advisor arrives tonight."

The general looked blankly at his staff until someone discreetly slid a note across the table. Foster read the paper and then exchanged a few words with the unseen officer before looking back into the camera.

"Good work. Have we sent out a press release yet?"

"Yes, sir. We sent it out today."

"OK. Send me a copy when you get a chance. What else you got?" the general asked while keeping an eye fixed on the animated map showing the drone inching toward the first target area.

"Just one other item of note. Captain Burke has some exciting news on the latest M-RAT data."

The general's interest suddenly piqued. "Let's hear it. But make it quick. We're getting close to game time."

Captain Burke leaned toward the microphone. "Good evening, sir. Since the bombing attack, Operation Righteous Protector has become the top trending mission in the department's portfolio. Brand awareness has been steadily rising, moving us firmly into the top quintile of all named operations. The latest perception response index shows an overall positivity rating of sixty-one percent. The highest since the president announced the deployment over two years ago."

"Outstanding!" the general enthused. "We're finally getting this thing back on the map."

"Yes, sir, literally and figuratively," Burke added. "Audience knowledgeability feedback shows that nearly three percent of respondents were able to correctly identify DRoG on a world map. That's nearly double the pre-bombing numbers!"

"Excellent! It's good to see the American public finally becoming engaged in global affairs. Any negative indicators we should be worried about?"

"A few minor things, but only when you really start digging down into the data. For example, we're detecting a strong correlation between low-knowledgeability respondents and higher levels of support for our mission."

"Just give it to me in plain English, son. What's the bottom line?" the general said.

"Yes, sir. It appears that respondents who are least able to place DRoG on the map seem to be the strongest advocates for escalation in response to the bombing."

"Hmm, interesting. Is there a way we use that to our advantage?"

"Possibly, sir. The public affairs playbook has some advanced strategic messaging techniques for targeted ambiguation. Basically, we attempt to localize the threat perception to better resonate with our core…"

The general suddenly became distracted by something on the screen.

"What the fuck…," Foster murmured into the open mic. Everyone watched the dotted blue line of the drone's flight path making a 180-degree turn back in the direction from where it came.

"Oh shit…," Colonel Kittredge said as he flipped open the intercom. "Sir, we have a secure chat room open with special operations headquarters. We'll ping them and find out what the hell is going on with the bird."

"I'm on it," Master Sergeant Jorgenson said without looking up from his laptop.

Kittredge fixated on the time zone clock, counting the passing seconds. He glanced periodically back to the map, watching in disbelief as the drone continued its retreat from the target area. The room was silent except for Jorgenson's fingers tapping furiously on the keyboard, shooting off rapid-fire notes to an unseen interlocutor. Finally, Jorgenson stopped typing and looked up from his computer.

"Sir, the mission was scrubbed."

"Equipment malfunction?" the general asked, having heard Jorgenson's words through the speaker.

"No, sir. The aircraft was diverted," Jorgenson clarified.

"Diverted? What the hell do you mean by *diverted*? That platform was allocated to us for the mission," the general said incredulously. "It's been on the books for weeks!"

"Apparently a higher priority target popped up. A national level, tier-one objective. Those missions come with blanket authorization for the designated commander to pull all available assets without pre-notification."

"According to who?"

Jorgenson, in a rare moment of uncertainty, glanced across the table at Colonel Kittredge before answering the general's question.

"Sir, the diversion was ordered by General Armstrong. He's the only one authorized to make that call."

"Like hell he is! Get fucking Armstrong on the line right now, god damn it!" the general screamed into the mic.

Everyone froze except for Jorgenson, who was tapping furiously at the keyboard. Meanwhile, the staff watched helplessly as the drone continued its path toward the edge of the screen. After what seemed like an eternity, Jorgenson suddenly grimaced as if poked in the ribs with a sharp stick.

"Sir, General Armstrong is unavailable," he said.

"What do you mean unavailable? If he just ordered that thing to turn around, then he must be someplace I can talk to him. Did you tell his staff that I need to speak with him directly?"

"Yes, sir. He's aware. But he's on a secure line with POTUS right now and can't break away. They said the general's schedule is tight for the next few days, but he might be able to squeeze you in sometime early next week. He's speaking at Davos and will be in your time zone. His staff said that they'd call to set something up."

The general's lips tightened. His eyes narrowing to snaky slits as patchy blotches crept up over his collar.

"Foster out!" he said as his hand slammed down on the mic like a hammer and the screen went blank.

+++

Early the next morning Carson walked over to the camp's VIP quarters, a modest brick bungalow surrounded by a grove of withered palm trees. Anna Devore was already waiting outside the building when he arrived.

"Wow, I figured you'd still be asleep," Carson said, reaching out to shake her hand.

"I'm fine. I slept on the plane," she said with a smile.

She looked younger to Carson than he guessed from reading her resume. In her late twenties or early thirties, with shoulder-length hair still wet from the shower and hastily arranged into a simple ponytail. She wore lightweight nylon pants, a long-sleeved travel shirt, and sturdy hiking boots that signaled a pragmatic indifference to fashion. Yet she projected a wholesome, mid-western attractiveness that reminded Carson of the sporty, overachieving girls he knew in high school.

"Need a cup of coffee before we head over to meet the colonel?" Carson asked.

"Maybe later. I'm anxious to get started."

Carson nodded and led her across the yard toward the headquarters building. Inside, Sergeant Goodwin was already at his desk and glanced up from his computer when they walked through the door.

"Goodwin, this is Ms. Devore, the general's new special advisor," Carson explained unnecessarily. "She's here for her meeting with the colonel."

Goodwin nodded and unceremoniously handed her a stack of papers as thick as an epic novel. "Ma'am, this is your in-processing paperwork. Please fill it out and get it back to me as soon as possible. I'll let the boss know you're here."

He disappeared into the back office and returned a moment later, motioning for her to go inside.

"I'll be back here to pick you up after you're done," Carson said before she disappeared into the colonel's office.

Kittredge rose from his desk when she entered the room. "Welcome to the DRoG. Have a seat. I'm Colonel Kittredge, the commander here."

"Ann Devore. Good to meet you," she said over the sound of rapid-fire pings announcing the arrival of several new emails into the colonel's computer.

"Sorry about that," Kittredge said, gesturing at the computer. "It never stops. So, is this your first time here?"

"Not in Africa. But yes, my first time in DRoG."

"In that case, hopefully there won't be too many surprises. We've put you up in the VIP quarters. They probably don't deserve the name, but it's the best we've got. If the general happens to come down for a visit, then we'll need to move you. Otherwise, it's yours."

"Don't worry. Anything is fine. I've stayed in far worse."

"Good. What do you know about our mission here?"

"I have a basic idea. The HR manager from ESP filled me in a bit. I had a week or two to do some background reading so I wouldn't show up unprepared."

"Well, that's more than I can say for most of the people around camp. I usually start my welcome talk by asking new arrivals if they can locate themselves on a map. I probably don't need to tell you how that goes. Anyway, let me be the first to tell you that General Foster is really excited to have you on board. His intention is that you be fully integrated into our operations. When you have ideas, I want to hear them."

"Perfect. So, when do I get to meet with General Foster to discuss my role here? I have several things I'd like to go over with him."

"Right," Kittredge replied, hesitating. "Actually, he has delegated that responsibility down to me. The general's schedule is extremely tight, so it may be difficult for you to get on his calendar right away."

"I see...," Anna replied. "If I recall correctly, the job listing stated that I would serve as the special advisor to a senior US defense official responsible for crafting American political-military strategy across Africa."

"Yes, that is absolutely the case. However, in that capacity, you will be reporting through me to General Foster. It's simply a matter of protocol. When you speak with me, it's the same as talking with him. Practically speaking."

"Hmm. OK. Since I'll be reporting through you then perhaps now is the time to discuss the exact nature of my duties."

"Right now?"

"Preferably."

The colonel sighed and glanced at his watch. Then he began searching his desk for something misplaced. After looking through the piles of paper, he looked up in frustration and yelled through the door into the front office. "Sergeant Goodwin. Are you out there?"

"Yes, sir."

"Can you please bring me the press release that Captain Burke put out yesterday? The one announcing the arrival of the new special advisor?"

The colonel smiled uncomfortably as he waited for Sergeant Goodwin to arrive with the information. Goodwin handed Kittredge the paper. He briefly reviewed the text, nodding with interest as if seeing it for the very first time.

"Here's a copy for your reference," he said, sliding the page across the desk to Anna. "I think this pretty much lays out all the expectations. The general approved it, so you should consider it as coming directly from him."

Anna carefully read through the words on the page.

UNCLASSIFIED. FOR IMMEDIATE RELEASE. Major General William G. Foster, commander of Operation Righteous Protector (ORP), is pleased to announce the arrival of Dr. Anna Devore as senior special advisor to the US mission in the Democratic Republic of Gisawi (DRoG), assisting that country's effort to neutralize the notorious warlord Daniel Odoki and his Gisawian Liberation Army (GLA). Dr. Devore comes to the mission with an impressive Ivy League pedigree, deep experience in conflict resolution, and an extensive record of scholarship on African security issues.

In her capacity as senior special advisor, Dr. Devore will provide ORP with tailored, actionable analysis relating to the complex social-cultural dynamics of the multi-dimensional operating environment. She will lead a highly specialized cell focused on planning post-conflict stabilization and assisting DRoG civil authorities in the Disarmament, Demobilization, and Reintegration (DDR) of former GLA fighters.

As an "outside the box" thinker, General Foster has been a strong advocate for leveraging multi-disciplinary experts from academia as a "force multiplier" in support of his military operations. Foster has received widespread praise as a paradigm-breaking leader and unconventional problem-solver who welcomes disruptive thinking and process innovation into his decision cycle. As a "world-class expert" in her field, Dr. Devore will add another "arrow in the quiver" of the ORP mission, helping to defeat a highly adaptive and menacing adversary.

"You're kidding, right?" Anna asked, looking up from the page after reading it.

"What do you mean?"

"Just that I don't understand a single word of what I just read. It's complete nonsense."

"What do you mean? It's a press release. There's nothing to understand," Kittredge insisted, nodding at the paper. "The general approved it. We already sent it out. Is there something wrong?"

"Where do I start?"

"OK. I've got five minutes," Kittredge said, glancing again at his watch.

"Well, for starters, I haven't finished my dissertation, so I'm not sure where you guys got the idea of adding the honorific in front of my name."

"OK, we may have been misinformed about that detail. But you're Ivy League, right?"

"I am enrolled as a Ph.D. candidate at Brown. So yes, that part is technically correct."

"Good enough. Anything else?"

"How about everything else! 'Deep experience in conflict resolution and scholarship on African security?'" Anna continued, reading directly from the page.

"Well, that's what ESP told us we were getting."

"At the very least, I would describe it as a willful misrepresentation of my academic research and experience."

"I'm sure you're just being modest. What exactly do you study?"

"Cultural anthropology."

"It doesn't really matter. The point is, we were very specific with ESP about the required qualifications for this position. They assured us that you fully satisfied the criteria."

"Those criteria. It's plural."

"Right. Anything else? I've got three minutes left."

"It says here that I will provide tailored, actionable analysis relating to the complex social-cultural dynamics of the multi-dimensional operating environment."

"Yes. That's true."

"I don't have the slightest idea what that means. It's just a bunch of random words put together into a sentence."

"It means you answer questions when we have them."

"What kind of questions?"

"Ones pertaining to complex social-cultural dynamics of the multi-dimensional operating environment. I think the press release lays that out pretty clearly."

"It also says here that I'll be leading a highly specialized cell focused on planning post-conflict stabilization and assisting DRoG civil authorities in Disarmament, Demobilization, and Reintegration of former GLA fighters."

"Yes. That's correct."

"Let's overlook the fact that I'm completely unqualified for any of those tasks. That issue aside, can you tell me more about this highly specialized cell that I'm supposed to be leading?"

"For the time being, it's just you."

"Presumably that's what makes it so highly specialized."

"In effect, yes."

"Can you at least provide some guidance on where my focus should be?"

"OK. In a nutshell, you need to help us understand Odoki and how to get him."

"The first part I can try. The second part is not my problem. If you're OK with those terms, then I'll stay. Otherwise, I'm on the next flight out of here."

As she spoke, Kittredge became distracted by another rapid-fire series of pings emanating from his inbox. "OK," he muttered impatiently. "I'll let the general know. I don't anticipate any problems."

"And as head of this so-called planning cell," Anna said, using air quotes with her fingers. "I report directly to you?"

"Actually, it would probably be best if you just went through Sid. He's our intel guy. You should run things through him first. He'll keep me in the loop," Kittredge added as he glanced back at his computer screen. "So, I apologize, but I'm just about out of time…"

"Just one last thing," Anna interrupted. "Then I'll be out of your hair."

"OK, shoot."

"If I'm going to do this, then I want to start at the beginning."

"Sure, that makes sense to me. Go right ahead."

"I mean, all the way back to the beginning. I want to see the site of the attack. The village where Odoki launched his movement."

"I don't think that's advisable. Perhaps you're aware that we just had a bombing outside the front gate a week or so ago?"

"Yes, I think I saw something about it on the news. But I don't see why that should interfere…"

"Listen," Kittredge interrupted. "The massacre site is very remote. It would probably take you three or four days just to drive there. Not to mention the fact that the area isn't even under government control."

"You've never been out there?"

"Of course not. There's nothing left to see. The village was completely burned to the ground. According to the government, there were no survivors."

"I'm aware of that. I read all the newspaper accounts. In any case, I'd still like to get out there."

"I can't justify the…"

"Fine," she interrupted. "I'll inform ESP of my departure." She rose from the chair and prepared to leave the office.

"OK, OK," Kittredge said with exasperation. "If you really want to go, then I'm not going to stop you. But the Gisawians get the final word. It's their country. If they say no, then there's nothing I can do about it. Talk to Carson and Sid. They'll put you in touch with the liaison officer, Major Bigombe. The guys call him Louie. He'll take the request over to MoD and we'll see what happens."

"Thank you." Anna nodded and handed the press release back to Colonel Kittredge.

"Don't you want to keep it for reference?" he asked.

"Not really."

"Welcome to the team. Let me know if you need anything. Better yet, ask Carson or Sid. They can get you whatever you need."

"Got it," she added quickly, sensing that Kittredge would be more than happy never to see her again.

After leaving the meeting, Anna spent the next hour filling out forty pages of administrative paperwork before Sergeant Goodwin would let her leave. Afterward, she stepped outside the building, slipped on her sunglasses, and took her first good look at the camp. She was trying to decide what to do next when Carson suddenly appeared from a grove of trees across the yard.

"I was just waiting at the café until you got out. How'd it go?"

"Great. No problems."

"Really?" Carson said with surprise. "Colonel Kittredge can sometimes be hard to read."

"He seems pretty transparent to me," Anna said, her eyes hidden behind her sunglasses.

"Good. Did he say what he wanted you to work on?"

"In basic terms. He told me to start at the beginning."

"And where would that be?"

"The village where Odoki first attacked."

"Do you really think you'll find anything there that can help?"

"Only one way to find out," she said, giving Carson a smile. "The colonel said that you and somebody named Louie would help make all the arrangements."

"OK, if that's what he wants. Louie should be here later today. We'll plan to meet him over at the café."

"That would be perfect. The colonel told me you would figure everything out."

+++

Later in the afternoon, Carson took Anna over to the Sujah Bean for a coffee.

"Wow. This is clearly the place to see and be seen," Anna said sarcastically as they walked into the garden.

"Alcohol is off limits on camp. This is the closest thing we have to a neighborhood bar. It also doubles as our office. Sid and Louie said they'd meet us here," Carson said, motioning Anna over to their regular table beneath the shade of the mango tree.

"Coffee any good?"

"Better than it was," Carson said, spotting Sid and Louie walking across the yard in their direction.

After exchanging pleasantries, the four sat down and waited for Sammy to take their order.

"So, did you have an interesting first meeting with the colonel?" Sid asked Anna

"You could say that. It didn't exactly inspire confidence in my decision to take the job," she replied with a shrug of resignation.

"Hmm. Since you mentioned it, I was kind of wondering about that. Why exactly did you take the job?" Sid asked. "I mean, me and Carson didn't have much of a choice about being here. The Army decided that for us. And as for Louie, well, it's his country after all, so I guess he's got to be here too."

"At least as far as my uncle is concerned," Louie chimed in.

"So that explains us. But why on earth did you take this gig?"

"You want the truth, or should I just make up a good story?"

"Your choice. We're among friends, so either one is fine," Sid assured her.

"OK then, let's just call it self-medication for dissertation-induced anxiety."

"The press release had a 'Dr.' before your name" Carson noted. "You're not finished yet?"

"Don't look at me! I didn't know anything about that thing until your boss showed it to me this morning. I'm already stressed out enough about the situation. Believe me, I'm not going to add to my problems by misrepresenting the source of my anxiety."

"OK, so you wanted a change of scenery to get over a bad case of writer's block?" Sid speculated.

"I wish. Writer's block is the least of my worries. The dissertation is already eight hundred pages long and nowhere close to ending. That's the problem. My advisor told me to take a break until I could figure out how to get it under three hundred. To make a long story short, I'm on academic leave to clear my head."

"And DRoG is where you decided to do that?" Sid asked incredulously.

"Not exactly. Originally, I was just planning on finding a temp job. Maybe pick up some work as a paralegal just to cover the bills until I was ready to tackle it again. Then I happened to see a notice on a grad school job board saying that some company called SME was hiring academics for short-term contracts in Africa. The money was good, and I didn't really have anything else on the burner. I sent in my resume. A few weeks later, I received this call from an HR manager asking me if I wanted to come over. That, in a nutshell, is the story."

"And now you're stuck with us," Sid said, smiling. "A new immigrant to the land of misfit toys."

"Speak for yourselves," Louie countered. "I warmly welcome anyone able to rescue us from the banality of our normal lunchtime conversations."

"No promises, but I'll do my best." Anna winked across the table.

"What is your academic field?" Louie asked.

"Cultural anthropology."

"And how does that relate to the mission here?" Louie asked.

"No idea. Presumably, ESP pulled my resume out of a hat. It must have checked some block off their list."

"And your dissertation topic?"

Anna shook her head defiantly. "No way! I'm not falling into that trap. The whole reason I'm here is to get it off my mind for a while."

"Amen to that," Sid interrupted. "I'm hungry. Let's order. Sammy just added a new Panini press to his menu. I haven't been able to identify the source of the meat and cheese, but as long as you don't think about it, the sandwich isn't half bad. In honor of our new team member, Paninis are on me today."

"Thank you, Sid," Louie chuckled. "However, my mother sent me some leftovers. I'll stick with home cooking if you don't mind."

"Suit yourself," Sid said with a shrug as he read over the menu.

After ordering, Carson pulled out his notebook and started going through the lines of chicken scratch on the page. "Louie, I've got a few things I need to discuss with you."

"At your service," Louie replied, opening up his backpack and pulling out a Tupperware container of rice and vegetables.

"Anna and Colonel Kittredge discussed her going out to the village where Odoki and the GLA did that first big attack."

"I'd just like to take a look," Anna interrupted. "Maybe talk to some people in the area."

Louie looked surprised. "I don't think there's anyone left to talk to. I've never been out there myself; however, I understand it was completely burned to the ground. I'm not sure that going out there would be much help."

"Maybe, maybe not. I guess I just can't escape my old fieldwork habits. I'd feel more grounded in the problem if I could see it for myself."

"Transportation is not a problem," Carson said. "ESP's pilots can fly her out to the closest airport. They don't have much else to do between missions. The colonel said to give Anna our full cooperation."

"But it's simply a matter of security," Louie insisted, looking at Anna with genuine concern. "Our forces don't fully control that region. As far as we know, the GLA is still operating in the area."

"Come on, Louie!" Sid interrupted. "Someone just tried to blow up the front gate of the camp last week. Clearly, it's not very safe here either. Can't MoD arrange to send Anna out with a security detachment? No one from the camp has ever been there. At this point, we need any help we can get. If the colonel is OK with it, then I don't see any problem with Anna going out there."

Louie nodded, though he still seemed unconvinced. "I'll ask my uncle and see what he says. But no promises."

"Good enough. Thanks, Louie. You always come through for us," Sid said as Sammy appeared at the table, delivering the tray of Panini sandwiches before scurrying off to another table.

"Business is really picking up here," Sid said, nodding at Carson. "Thanks in no small part to you."

"Sammy's doing all the hard work. All I had to do was sell my soul to Slyker. But I still have a funny feeling that's going to come back to haunt me. There's no such thing as a free lunch," Carson said.

"At least today there is," Sid said, taking an enormous bite of his sandwich. "Just enjoy the Panini and don't worry about it."

As the others began eating, Louie opened the plastic container of his mother's leftovers. Suddenly, Sid's eyes widened as Louie took an olive drab plastic utensil from his pocket and stuck it into the food.

"Wait a second! Is that a first-generation NDS-H2P multi-tool? Where'd you get that? Those were phased out years ago."

"NDS-H2P multi-tool?" Louie replied, staring at Sid in bafflement.

"Yeah, Nutritional Delivery System, Hand-Held, Plastic. That thing was a classic during the war. The Army pushed them out to Iraq by the millions until there was a recall because of some big investigation."

Louie pulled the utensil from the food and held it up for everyone to see. One end was a fork-spoon combo and the other a dull, serrated knife edge.

"Everyone complained about them, but once they were recalled, it became an instant collector's item. I haven't seen one in years," Sid explained excitedly.

"Really? I can give you two shipping containers full of them if you like," Louie said.

"You've got to be kidding me?"

"I wish I was. Your government sent us an entire planeload a few years back as part of a counter-terrorism assistance program."

"No shit?" Sid exclaimed in stunned disbelief, admiring the utensil. "It sure looks like the real deal, but there's only one way to know for sure. Let me see if I've got something for a quick function test."

Sid rummaged through his camouflage backpack, eventually finding a half-eaten breakfast roll wrapped in oily paper. "Not perfect, but this will do," he said, setting the stale pastry down on the table. "Just try to cut it gently with the knife and see what happens. Careful...not too much pressure. Just a nice, gentle stroke."

Louie slowly worked the serrated edge back and forth across the flaky bun. The surface compressed slightly but not enough to penetrate the bread.

Sid smiled knowingly. "OK. So far, so good. Now just put a little bit of torque on it. Not too much! Just enough to get the tip of the knife inside the roll."

As soon as Louie applied the slightest bit of torsional pressure the knife end broke away from the fork-spoon combo, leaving two unusable remnants in his hand.

"Yep, it's the real deal!" Sid cried with glee. "Back during the war, some congressman's son won a low-cost bid to replace all the Army's plastic forks, knives, and spoons with a single device, promising to cut back on two-thirds the production cost. Apparently, no one bothered to realize that you can't cut with the knife end at the same time you're eating with the spork end. Once they hit the field, everyone started carrying around three or four with them at the same time just to get through a meal. The fiasco lasted about three months before there was so much bad press that the Pentagon ordered a complete recall. This must be where all the surplus inventory ended up. Amazing..."

"You know about this?" Louie asked Anna, who was sitting across the table and clearly enjoying the demonstration.

"I vaguely recall the story doing a few rounds on the Internet before disappearing into digital obscurity. It even got some play in anthropology circles. Someone cited it in an academic paper as evidence of human cultural devolution."

"Check this out," Sid interrupted, pulling out his smartphone. "It's an old website called 'Broken GI Spork.' Before the recall, soldiers all over the world were uploading pictures of their broken NDS-H2P multi-tools. Then somebody got the bright idea to use the photo metadata and geo-locate all the pictures in real-time. The next thing you know, the counter-intelligence guys at the Pentagon were freaking out when they realized that broken sporks were popping up in places where there weren't supposed to be any US troops deployed. It was such a big security breach that it went all the way to the White House. They threatened to throw the book at anyone caught posting pictures of broken sporks on the web," Sid explained.

"Yeah, now it's coming back to me," Anna said. "I remember some commentator describing the 'Broken GI Spork' map as the apogee of American empire. The Romans gave us roads and aqueducts; we leave a trail of broken plastic cutlery. All hail Caesar salad!" Anna said, winking at Louie.

"Nice," Sid chuckled. "I can tell you're going to have no problem fitting in here. Anyway, I can't wait to tell my buds back home that all the sporks ended up here in DRoG. Louie, is there any way you can get me a few dozen of these to send out in the mail?"

"Given that it was such a generous gift from your government, I feel obliged to return the favor. Do you want two dozen or two million? Either can be easily arranged."

"Hot damn! Now we're talking," Sid squealed, unable to conceal his elation. "A blast from the past. I'm getting my spork on tonight," he said, breaking into a goofy little dance move in his seat.

"Happy to be of service," Louie replied before pulling another spork from his bag and starting in on his lunch.

+++

The next day Louie arrived at MoD for his meeting with the deputy minister. As soon as he walked into the office, he sensed his uncle's impatience.

"You're late," the big man said, tapping at his watch.

"I am sorry, Uncle. I had to go to the MoD warehouse to find a few things for the Americans."

"What! Now we're giving supplies to them?" the deputy minister said in a huff.

"No, Uncle, it is nothing," Louie assured him.

Mugaba Odongo sniffed indignantly. "Tell me. What is happening at the camp."

"It has been very busy, Uncle, but unfortunately, this week's mission was canceled at the last minute."

"Yes, I heard. Do you know why?"

"Not exactly. Something to do with the drone not being available."

"At least they can't blame us this time," Mugaba said. "What else?"

"There is still a lot of talk about the bombing."

"Yes, so what are they saying?"

"Very little. At least to me. However, I sense they are skeptical of the Hezbollah connection. They think that the analysis of the bomb residue will lead in a different direction."

"The Americans put too much faith in their technology," the deputy minister said, shaking his head. "What will the bomb tell them that we have not already said? You know the old saying, Lutalo. 'No one buys a cow by looking at its hoof marks.' Police intelligence has been watching these Lebanese merchants for months now. Something is not right there. That's why we told the Americans to be careful. But they ignored us and look what happened!"

"Yes, Uncle," Louie said, unwilling to argue with him.

"Just keep me informed if they say anything else. Until then, we'll continue our investigation in our own way. What else do you have?"

Louie looked down into his notes. "The engineering team arrives tomorrow to begin work on the camp. They will repair the front gate that was damaged in the bombing. After that, they plan to begin the well drilling project in the local village, just as we discussed."

"Good. And you gave them the proposed location?"

"Yes, Uncle, they have all the information you provided."

Mugaba nodded thoughtfully. "Please keep me informed when work begins. Is that all for today?"

Louie glanced down once more into his notebook. "Oh, I almost forgot. The Americans have a new advisor. She is helping them to understand the GLA."

"Yes, yes," the deputy minister said, nodding distractedly.

"She has asked to visit the site of Odoki's massacre in the western region," Louie added.

"What for?" his uncle asked, suddenly becoming interested. "There is nothing there anymore. No reason for her to go out there."

"I told her that, Uncle. But she insists it's necessary for her work. She's not a soldier. Just an advisor. An academic."

The deputy minister shook his head. "It is not advisable. The area is too dangerous. We cannot guarantee her safety."

"That's what I told her, but she seems very determined. The commander asked that we cooperate with her request, if possible."

Mugaba was quiet for a moment, thinking to himself. "If the Americans think this is important, then we will accommodate her request. But for her own safety, she must stay with an escort, although I am certain she will find nothing there of value. You know the old saying, Lutalo. 'War has no eyes.' In any case, go ahead and make the necessary arrangements for her travel."

"Yes, Uncle. I will."

CHAPTER SEVEN

Two weeks later, Carson stepped outside the officer's quarters as the sun cracked above the horizon. Sid was already out in the yard jogging in place, vigorously pumping his fists and holding what appeared to be two neon-colored bocce balls.

"What the hell are those?" Carson asked, observing Sid's frenzied routine.

"It's a new thing," he said breathlessly. "If you carry them around all day it increases your resting caloric burn rate by fifteen percent. Nothing extra required," Sid said, wheezing as he dropped the balls to the ground and bent over his knees.

"Where'd you find them?"

"Hack-my-diet-dot-com. It's totally legit."

Carson kicked one of the balls, testing its mass. "You know, I read somewhere that not eating two dozen fried dough balls each day can reduce caloric burn rate by fifteen percent."

"Don't be a hater," Sid said, snatching the balls from under Carson's toe and resuming his jerky boxer shuffle. "So, are we going jogging or did you just come out here to talk shit?" he taunted Carson.

"Yeah, we're going. Just give me a minute to stretch."

As they warmed up, Carson heard what sounded like chanting coming from the direction of the front gate. "That's weird. You hear that?"

"Yeah. Strange. Maybe we should check it out."

Sid dropped the bocce balls and followed Carson toward the front gate. When they arrived, they found the Gisawian guards standing shoulder to shoulder outside the fence, weapons slung defensively across their chests, fingers dancing on the triggers. They were watching nervously as a crowd of locals marched in a circle at the entrance to the camp. Sid counted about fifty people, with more trickling in. They were chanting in the local dialect that he couldn't understand, so he waved over one of the Gisawian guards, hoping to find out what was going on.

"Sergeant, what's this all about?" Sid asked the head of the security detail.

"Protest, sir."

"I see that, Sergeant. But what exactly are they protesting?"

"America."

"And why may I ask…"

"They say you poisoned their village."

"Thank you, Sergeant. Please, carry on," Sid said calmly, before turning to Carson with a look of panic. "Not good. We better wake up the colonel. Now!"

Half an hour later, the entire staff had assembled in the conference room while Sergeant Goodwin frantically set up an emergency teleconference.

"OK, what do we know about what's going on out there?" Colonel Kittredge asked, looking around the table.

"Right now, not much," Sid explained. "The guards weren't very helpful, so we called Louie at home and asked him to get over here right away. Hopefully, he'll be able to go out there and talk to them."

"Sir, General Foster is coming on the line now," Sergeant Goodwin interrupted.

A moment later Foster appeared on the screen clad in gym clothes, his shirt damp with perspiration, and a towel wrapped around his neck like a boxer in his corner between rounds.

"Kittredge, what the hell is going on down there? They just pulled me off the treadmill and said there was some kind of problem."

"Yes, sir, we're still trying to gather information…"

As Kittredge spoke, Ambassador Roberts suddenly appeared on the other half of the screen, dialing in from the Embassy across town.

"Good morning, Bill," she said coldly.

"Hello, Claire. I understand that we have a little excitement there at the front gate."

"Excitement? Yes, Bill, I suppose that's a word for it."

"Well, how can we help? Do you need me to call in the cavalry?"

"I don't believe it's a matter of you helping me. Particularly since your folks seem to be the cause of this little crisis."

"Crisis? That sounds like a bit of an overstatement, Claire. It's probably just some local kids blowing off steam at the expense of old Uncle Sam. Nothing to get worked up over. If I had a dime for every time…"

"Bill," the ambassador interrupted. "Turn on your TV."

Colonel Kittredge nodded at Sergeant Goodwin, who grabbed the remote control and flipped on the multi-channel TV panel mounted to the wall. All six international networks were broadcasting live images from outside the front gate. Since Sid and Carson had left the scene, several hundred more people had gathered. Meanwhile, a smaller group of young men had broken off from the crowd and overturned several cars, setting one of them on fire.

"Bill, I'm not sure your definition of a crisis, but in my book, this is about to qualify," the ambassador said.

"OK. You've got my attention," Foster replied, throwing his sweaty towel to an unseen assistant standing somewhere off-camera. "Bring me up to speed on what's going on."

"We're still trying to piece that together," the ambassador replied. "I was told that you had an engineering team down here doing some work a few weeks ago. Is that correct."

"Yes, ma'am, that's correct," Colonel Kittredge interrupted. "They repaired the front gate after the bombing. Then did a few goodwill projects in the local community. They dropped a wellhead and put in some irrigation pipes at a local village just on the other side of the airfield."

"Right," the ambassador nodded. "So, here's the rest of the story, as best we understand. Apparently, a few days after that well went in, the village chief showed up at the Ministry of Health claiming that all their crops had died. He reported a bad smell coming from the well and said some of the children had been taken to a local clinic complaining of upset stomachs."

"Bad water?" The general asked.

"Seems that way."

"Listen, Claire. I realize this doesn't look so good, but that project was fully vetted through MoD. They told us where to drop the damn wellhead. If anything, those people should be burning cars in front of MoD headquarters," the general said in frustration.

"I'm guessing that the Gisawians are not very eager to step up and take the blame," the ambassador said. "Yesterday afternoon the Ministry of Health ordered the entire village evacuated due to suspected water contamination. The government's announcement specifically mentioned the fact that the US military had recently put in a new well there. That's probably what set off the protests this morning."

As the ambassador spoke, Sid and Carson kept their eyes fixed on the television, watching as a small group of young men tore a canvas tarp from a flatbed truck parked on the side of the road. The vehicle contained what appeared to be a load of plum-sized paving stones being used to build a new sidewalk. A few seconds later they heard a metallic pinging sound above their heads. Colonel Kittredge glanced up at the ceiling, trying to identify the source of the noise, as a few more strikes came in rapid succession. Kittredge turned to Sid, mouthing an obscenity in place of a question. Sid discreetly pointed at the television screen, now showing a gaggle of young men swarming into the bed of the truck and launching volleys of paving stones over the fence into the camp.

"Psss," Kittredge hissed at Sid as he finally comprehended what was happening. "Get Louie. Now! Have him call MoD. Tell them to get some backup over here ASAP. I think they're about to overrun the gate."

Sid nodded and leaped from his chair, heading outside to find his cell phone.

"OK, Claire," the general continued. "What's our game plan to calm this thing down?"

"Right now, the government has us in a corner. Even if we're on the right side of this thing, it's not going to play well if we start making counter-accusations. It will come off heavy-handed and probably just backfire on the street."

"So, you're telling me that we're just going to roll over and take it up the ass? Is that what you consider a winning course of action over at State?" the general fumed.

"Listen, Bill, I realize you may not like it, but we don't have many options here. You have my word, we're not going to concede blame. However, our immediate concern is de-escalating the situation before it gets out of hand. First, we need to convey our concerns for the people in the village. Then we express a firm desire to support the government in a full and thorough investigation."

On the TV, they watched the group of young rock-throwers fleeing down the street as the Gisawian soldiers began lobbing tear gas canisters into the crowd.

"An investigation!" the general scoffed. "Into what? How they just screwed us over for trying to help?"

"Bill, we need to be patient. Once the protestors understand that we're not going to openly challenge their claims, it will lower the stakes. The offer of a joint investigation is just a red herring. Whatever happened, I can assure you that the government doesn't want us poking around in their business. They'll make a big show of pretending to work with us, then almost certainly try to brush it under the rug at the first opportunity. By then, the only ones who'll remember what happened will be the poor people who lost their village."

"I still don't like it," Foster said in a huff. "Seems like no good deed goes unpunished."

"Unfortunately, in our case, that's probably true. There's an old saying here in DRoG. 'The flea troubles the lion more than the lion troubles the flea.'"

"By the looks of it, the fleas are pretty busy right now," the general said, shaking his head at the scene unfolding on the television.

"Listen, Bill, let me make a few phone calls to some trusted contacts in the government. I'll get a read on what's happening behind the scenes and do my best to calm things down. For now, I think it's best if we keep a low profile around town. Now is not the time to be out there waving the flag. I'll send someone from my team over to the Ministry of Health to find out what really happened at that village. Maybe you could do the same with your contacts over at MoD."

"Right," the general agreed. "I'll have Colonel Kittredge get right on it. Foster, out," he said before dropping from the line.

After the teleconference ended, Colonel Kittredge and the staff sat there watching the television, fixated on the drama unfolding outside. Suddenly the colonel grimaced, then yelled to the outer office.

"Sergeant Goodwin! For god's sakes, turn off the fucking air conditioning. It's sucking all the tear gas in from outside!"

+++

Early the next morning, Carson stood at the front gate watching a group of local laborers clear away remnants from the riot. During the night, a bulldozer removed the charred wreckage of several cars, clearing the road into the camp. As an added precaution the Gisawian soldiers had placed a row of enormous concrete barriers extending a hundred meters down the road, creating a vast no-go zone between the camp and adjacent village. The hasty renovations gave the camp an appearance of a medieval fortress under siege.

Out beyond the concrete barriers, Carson noticed a large truck driving slowly toward the Gisawian guards. There was a large plastic tarp draped over the back, concealing whatever was being carried on the flatbed. Carson saw the guards anxiously fingering their weapons as the truck rumbled closer toward the barriers. Before it could advance any further, the officer in charge raised his hand and ordered the driver to stop. Several soldiers cautiously approached the vehicle, weapons raised at the ready, preparing for the worst. The truck stopped about fifty meters away and revved its engine.

Carson felt his heart racing. He watched helplessly as the officer-in-charge slowly approached the truck. Then he turned back and said a few words to the soldiers in the local dialect. They lowered their weapons and smiled with relief when Don Slyker stuck his head out of the passenger window of the truck. Then the guards waved the driver through the zigzag maze of concrete barriers into the camp.

"Hey, stranger!" Slyker yelled over the rumbling engine when the truck pulled to a stop inside the compound. "What the hell happened here?"

"I guess you haven't been watching TV," Carson said.

"Nope. I try to avoid it," Slyker said with a smile. "But I love what you've done with the place. It brings back fond memories of Baghdad."

"It wasn't my idea," Carson said lamely. "The general insisted that we beef up security outside the perimeter."

"A bold maneuver in the battle for hearts and minds," Slyker said sarcastically.

Carson shook his head.

"I got something that may brighten your day," Slyker said, thumbing back at the flatbed. "It's your new gym. Courtesy of the Palm Hotel. Where do you want me to drop it?"

The truck pulled up to camp's open-air exercise area. A concrete pad covered by a ramshackle wooden pavilion with walls made of tattered mosquito netting. Slyker got down from the truck and gave some instructions to his work crew. A few minutes later, half a dozen men began unloading a small mountain of lightly used, high-end gym equipment.

"What do you want me to do with the old stuff?" Slyker asked. "If you want, I could have my guys throw it into a giant pile outside the gate. It might help scare away the locals. Unless of course, they're looking to do a little toning before overrunning the camp."

"Very funny," Carson said, admiring the new equipment.

"So, this should be the last item on your to-do list from the colonel, right?" Slyker asked. "Not too bad for only two months here. Hopefully, that will get you a good evaluation."

"Has it really only been that long?" Carson said with an exaggerated moan. "Seems like a lot longer."

"Ah, come on. It can't be that bad," Slyker reassured him.

"I guess not. But I can't shake the feeling that I don't really have any idea what's going on here."

"Welcome to DRoG. The place is like an onion. Layers upon layers to peel away."

"And the tears?"

"I didn't want to pummel the simile. Besides, it's not really that bad, is it? You're getting paid. You've got plenty to eat. There's a roof over your head. Best of all, no one's shooting at you. What's not to like about it?"

"Maybe the locals chanting anti-American slogans and throwing rocks over the fence all before eight o'clock in the morning?"

"Come on. That could happen anywhere," Slyker said encouragingly. "At least the people you work with are OK."

"Hmm," Carson murmured. "I'm still trying to figure them out."

"Like who? Sid needs no explanation. He's a good guy. What you see is what you get. Who else is there?"

"Dodge."

"Who's that?"

"The civil affairs guy."

"I doubt I could pick him out of a lineup," Skyler said, scratching his head.

"Big help you are. What about Burke? That guy seems a little off."

"OK. You're right on that one. You know the backstory, right?" Slyker asked.

"I guess not," Carson shrugged.

"His dad was some bigwig politico. A congressman from somewhere in flyover country. Apparently, Junior was on track to inherit Daddy's seat. Checking off all the boxes: Harvard, military service, then probably some hedge fund time to fatten up the bank account before dedicating his life to selfless public service. Unfortunately, Daddy suffered an untimely heart attack in the company of a young lady friend who was not his wife. The acquaintance in question also happened to be unofficially on the congressman's payroll when not pursuing her primary career interest as an exotic dancer."

"Nice," Carson said, shaking his head. "I can't believe we give these guys here a hard time about corruption. We wrote the damn book on it."

"Anyway, that tells you pretty much everything you need to know about Burke. But, just some advice, stay on his good side. He'll probably be running the Pentagon someday."

"I'll keep that in mind. What about Kittredge?"

"No mystery there. He's standard Army issue. A full-on company man. Does what he's told. Probably harmless, so long as his boss doesn't order him to do something crazy. Who else is there?"

"Louie?"

"Ah, Louie Bigombe. What can I say? I think the kid's in a tough spot."

"How so?" Carson asked, genuinely interested.

"From what I gather, his father was something of a legend back in the day, before suffering an untimely but heroic death. That kind of thing sets a high bar for a son to live up to."

"I guess so," Carson agreed. "Louie seems pretty well connected."

"Yeah. Have you noticed how the DRoG soldiers treat him when he walks through the gate? He's like minor royalty. I'm sure it doesn't hurt that his uncle is the deputy minister of defense. Barring an unforeseen coup, I'd bet that Mugaba gets the top job someday. He has the minister's ear and, according to the rumors, he's really the one pulling the strings behind the scenes at MoD. That said, it's all pretty opaque. Probably by design. I've met him a few times, but it's hard to read his game."

"So, all of that must bode well for Louie's future," Carson speculated.

"Maybe," Slyker said, shaking his head. "But my hunch is that Louie is a bit out of his league. And probably stuck in the middle of some things he doesn't quite see."

"How so?"

"Don't get me wrong. Louie's a sharp guy and has a heart of gold. I just don't think he has the instincts to operate down here. After his father died, he spent most of his time overseas in boarding schools and university. That's his world. He'd have no problem making it in London or New York, but down here, he's a fish out of water. I know it seems weird to say that, but I'm guessing he's never really learned the rules of the game. I hope I'm wrong about that because I really like him. I'd hate to see anything bad happen."

"Interesting," Carson said, scratching his head. "I guess that's pretty much everyone."

"Almost everyone," Slyker added. "Except for…The Specimen."

"Who the hell is that?"

Slyker nodded across the yard at Master Sergeant Jorgenson, who was walking a beeline in their direction. He had already changed out of uniform into his jungle fever workout ensemble, weathered cargo pants, a skin-tight olive drab T-shirt, and combat boots. As he crossed the yard, he came to a sudden stop, his brow furrowed over his aviator sunglasses as he noticed the gym equipment being unloaded from the truck.

"What the fuck is this?" he said, dispensing with formalities and skipping straight to business.

"New gym equipment," Carson explained. "Colonel Kittredge asked me to get rid of the old stuff."

"Well, nobody asked me about it," he said with unconcealed disdain. "I spend more time here than anyone on camp. The old stuff was just fine."

"It was all rusted out from the humidity," Carson countered. "Someone was going to get tetanus. It was a safety hazard."

Sergeant Jorgenson spit on the ground. "Where'd the old equipment go?"

"You're looking at it," Slyker said, pointing to the pile of junk underneath the truck's tarp.

"Where's it going?"

"Probably to the local dump," Carson said.

"Well, I'm sure as hell not working out on that chick-gym shit," he said, nodding at the fitness equipment from The Palm. "I'll be taking some of that stuff off that truck before it leaves."

"Your call, boss," Slyker said, glancing nervously at Carson for support.

"Whatever," Carson replied, unwilling to make an issue of it. "Just find someplace else for it. There's not enough room on the pad for everything."

Without a word, Jorgenson turned and began walking away.

"By the way, man. I love your work," Slyker called out at Jorgenson's back.

Jorgenson stopped in his tracks, turned, and glared at Slyker through his sunglasses. "What the fuck does that mean? You trying to be funny?"

"Of course not," Slyker said. "Just expressing my respect for a fellow entrepreneur."

Without warning, Jorgenson suddenly lunged forward like a predator seizing helpless prey. Slyker flinched but somehow held his ground without breaking his smile. Jorgenson planted himself inches from Slyker's face and jabbed a meaty finger into his sternum.

"You're about to make a big mistake," Jorgenson snarled through his teeth. "Maybe your last mistake." Then, as if nothing had happened, he turned, walked back toward the truck and began digging through the old equipment.

"What the hell was that about?" Carson stammered.

"Nothing," Slyker said, quickly regaining composure and adjusting his tie. "Just having a little fun."

"Didn't seem like fun to Jorgenson. He was about to rip your head off."

"Forget about it. At least now you know everything you need to know about Jorgenson. He's a hothead. My recommendation: stay clear."

"Yeah, thanks. I'll take that advice," Carson said, watching as Jorgenson began tossing pieces of the rusty gym equipment to the ground.

"Anyway. Thanks again for getting all this stuff," Carson said, admiring the new equipment. "Jorgenson may not like it, but everyone else will. I don't know how to thank you."

"My pleasure," Slyker said, slipping on his sunglasses. "But since you mentioned it. There is one thing I could use some help with."

"Sure, just let me know," Carson said.

"I need a meeting with General Foster."

Carson turned and stared at him. "You're kidding, right?"

"Nope. Just a few minutes of face time. That's it."

"Come on, Slyker! You know I can't do that. First off, I don't even know him. Colonel Kittredge has all the contact. He's the only one who ever talks to him. Besides, it's probably not even legal. What the hell are you're trying to do?"

"Calm down, Carson. I'm not trying to get you into trouble. In fact, I'm actually trying to help you out."

"How's that?" Carson snapped. "It seems to me like this has all been some kind of setup. Is that what the gym equipment was all about?"

"Listen, Carson, don't be such a baby. I've gone out of my way to help you out with your little to-do list from the colonel. I've made you look like a rock star. I hope you haven't already forgotten about the coffee and special advisor… what's her name again?"

"Anna."

"Right. Anyway, remember what I told you at the beginning? Things go best when we work together. All I'm asking is for you to grease the skids a bit. It's not like I want to play a round of golf with the guy. I just need ten minutes of face time, privately."

"Then tell me what it's about!" Carson demanded. "I want to know what I'm getting myself into before I get my ass chewed by Colonel Kittredge."

"Sorry. Can't do that. It's proprietary information. ESP channels only. Certainly, you understand."

"What the fuck, Slyker? I've got top secret security clearance and you can't even tell me what it's about?"

"Nope. Sorry. I really wish I could."

"Are you kidding me? You really expect me to walk into the colonel's office and give him that line of bullshit?"

"Listen, I sense you're a little upset. You probably think I've been playing you all along; however, I can assure you that's not the case. In fact, I like you. And I just wanted to help you succeed. But now, I'm the one who needs a favor. All I'm asking is for ten minutes with the guy. Not even any slides! A secure video teleconference will be fine."

"No way," Carson said, shaking his head. "I've got a wife and three kids at home. I need this job. I'm not getting court-martialed just so you can make a few extra bucks to finance renovations on your god damn coffee plantation."

"Hey, there's no need to make this personal. Business is business. All I ask is that you trust me a little. While I'm not at liberty to go into details, I can say that it concerns a potential solution to a lingering, unresolved problem for this command."

"You mean getting Odoki?" Carson sniffed in disbelief. "Give me a break! What are you going to do? Poison him with Sammy's old coffee?"

"I'm sorry. I wish I could tell you more. All I can say is that it's a serious proposal. I just need ten minutes with the general to lay it all out. I guarantee you won't be sorry."

Carson kicked at the dirt, angry with himself for trusting Slyker. "You're a jackass," Carson mumbled under his breath.

"I know that," Slyker replied with the hint of a smile. "It goes with the territory. So, are you going to help me out?"

"If I get fired, my wife is going to hunt you down and have your ass. You think Jorgenson is scary? Just wait until you get her pissed off. I guarantee it will be the last thing you ever do."

"Great. I knew you'd come around," Slyker said, taking off his sunglasses and tucking them into the breast pocket of his blazer. "I'm available whenever the general has time. Just let me know."

+++

The next morning Sid and Carson made plans to meet Anna at Sujah Bean to catch up over coffee. She was already waiting at a table when they arrived.

"Welcome back," Sid said, offering her a weary smile. "Your trip was perfectly timed to miss all the excitement."

"So I gather. I leave you guys alone less than forty-eight hours and all hell breaks loose. When I got back into cell phone range, I had a dozen emails from friends asking if I was OK. Of course, I had no idea what they were talking about until I saw a local paper. What on earth did you guys do to start a riot?"

"You mean what did we get framed for," Carson corrected.

"I didn't have time to read past the headlines, but the gist seemed to suggest that you poisoned a local village?"

"Allegedly poisoned," Carson corrected again. "But the media here doesn't seem big on nuance like that."

"Apparently not. So, what's the rest of the story?"

"We're still trying to piece it together," Carson continued. "All we know for sure is that a few weeks ago we sent an engineering team out to drop a wellhead and irrigation lines at a village just on the other side of the airfield. Everything seemed to go fine. The team did the work and brought back pictures of the happy farmers watering their crops and kids frolicking around the new tap."

"So far, so good," Anna said.

"Yeah, but then a few days later some of the villagers started complaining about a bad smell coming from the water. Then all their crops died, and some of the kids ended up in the hospital feeling sick."

"Good lord. Not so good," Anna said, shaking her head in disbelief.

"Yeah, that's an understatement. So, then the government sends someone out to test the water. They come back and tell the locals that it's all contaminated and they can't use it."

"And that's what kicked off the riot?"

"No, it gets even better," Carson added sarcastically. "Then the health minister announces that the entire village will need to be relocated because of the bad water. Lo and behold, the next morning, they all show up outside our front gate demanding an apology and reparations."

"Wow," Anna said. "But didn't the government tell you where to drop the wells in the first place? They must have done some kind of groundwater assessment first."

"Apparently not. But naturally, that information never made it into the news. The Health Ministry was quick to pin the blame on us. The next thing we know there's an angry mob outside the front gate and a local TV news crew beaming live footage of the protest out to the entire world. Things went downhill quickly from there once the trigger-happy Gisawian guards started throwing tear gas into the crowd. So, that was our wonderful week. How was your little sojourn out to the jungle?"

"Clearly, much better than being here," Anna said sympathetically as Sammy appeared at the table to take their orders. "Just tea for me, Sammy," Anna said. "And whatever these guys want. It's on me. They seem like they've had a rough few days."

Sammy took the order, then disappeared back into the hut to prepare the drinks. Meanwhile, Anna opened her journal and began running through her notes.

"The trip was interesting, to say the least," she began. "Louie wasn't kidding about the place being remote. It's in the middle of nowhere. It took us the better part of two days just to get there. On the first day, we flew to the closest government airfield and stayed there overnight. The next morning we drove almost three hours over rutted dirt roads to get to the village. Or at least what's left of it."

"I hope you asked about a forwarding address for Odoki. Maybe he left a business card after burning down the village," Sid joked.

"No such luck. Whatever was there is now gone. The jungle has already started taking it back over."

"Then I guess it really wasn't worth the trouble after all," Sid said.

"I wouldn't say that," Anna corrected. "After walking around a while, we drove to the next village over. The soldiers escorting me wanted to see if they could find something to eat before starting the drive back to the airfield. I got the feeling they were under strict orders not to let me out of their sight. MoD sent along an interpreter that I was supposed to use whenever I wanted to talk to the locals, but he really seemed like more of a minder. Not to mention the fact that he was doing a bit of selective translation."

"What do you mean?" Sid asked.

"You know, paraphrasing a lot. Maybe not giving me the full answers to the questions I was asking. Especially when I brought up anything about the attack. It's hard to describe, but when I asked some of the local women about Odoki, their expressions weren't what you would expect when someone brings up the name of a guy who massacred the neighboring village."

"That does seem a little weird," Sid conceded. "But maybe they misunderstood the questions. They probably don't get too many young white women showing up in town asking about their run-ins with sociopathic warlords suffering from a messiah complex."

"Believe me, I considered that explanation. I've done enough field research to know that you don't just drop in unannounced and start asking random questions. At least not if you want good results. Unfortunately, in this case, I didn't have much choice. Anyway, I wanted to sniff around a little on my own, so while the soldiers and the interpreter went off to find some food I wandered down to a stream where a few local women were washing clothes. On a whim, I said hello to one of them in French. She seemed to know a bit, so I started asking her some questions about the attack."

"Anything interesting?"

"Hard to say. My French is a little rusty, and hers was even worse. But she seemed to understand the gist of my questions. The woman said a few things that were interesting.

"Such as?"

"She kept talking about soldiers, or at least men in uniform."

"What was interesting about that?" Carson asked.

"Just that the chronology was a little odd. According to the official government reports, DRoG army troops didn't arrive at the massacre site until a full three days after the attack. That was long after the GLA had allegedly left the area. But this woman insisted that there were men in uniform around the area *before* the attack."

"Maybe just a case of misidentification," Sid speculated. "The GLA has been known to wear surplus military gear stolen during raids on army checkpoints. The people in those remote areas probably don't see DRoG soldiers very often. Maybe she was just confusing the GLA fighters for government soldiers."

"Sure, that's possible, but she kept nodding at the soldiers who were escorting me. Sort of like she was saying that they were the same kind of men who were there before the attack. She seemed pretty adamant about it."

"Hmm, it's certainly interesting," Sid said. "Anything else?"

"Just one other thing. She didn't take the bait when I asked about Odoki. She just shook her head and kept babbling on about *creuseurs*."

"What the hell does that mean?" Carson asked.

"It's French. Literally, a person who digs. Diggers."

"Well, it does seem strange that she didn't respond when you brought up Odoki. But I guess the comment about the diggers could make sense. MoD keeps insisting that the GLA is out there in the jungle burying weapons and supplies. Maybe that's what the woman was getting at."

"Perhaps," Anna said skeptically. "Unfortunately, I didn't get a chance to press her on it. The conversation was slow-going, and by the time I finally started getting somewhere when the translator suddenly realized what was going on and rushed over to intervene. He seemed really alarmed that I was talking to someone without his supervision. Once he got involved, the woman just clammed up. She wouldn't say another word."

"You think he was trying to keep something from you?" Carson asked.

"I'm not sure, but after that, I never got another chance to wander off on my own. The translator stayed right by my side until we got back on the plane."

"Strange," Sid said. "So now that you've been there, what's next?"

"Well, since it seems like I probably won't get another chance to go out to the village, I guess I'll start digging a little deeper into the movement. How Odoki got started. What makes him tick. Why people follow him."

Sammy arrived at the table with the drinks and Sid pulled out his wallet to pay the bill, but Anna waved him down. "Really, this one's on me," she insisted. "Sammy, can you please put it on my tab?" she asked, searching fruitlessly for something to sign the ticket.

"Here," Carson offered, handing her a pen from one of the many pockets on his uniform.

"Wow," she said, admiring the instrument. "The Army's gone from plastic sporks to Mont Blanc pens? I think I need to write my congressman about this," she joked, signing the ticket and adding a generous tip for Sammy.

"Don't worry. The pen's not Army issue. Slyker gave it to me," Carson said, suddenly reminded of the promise he had made outside the gym.

"Who's Slyker?"

"What? You haven't met him yet?" Carson said with surprise. "He's the camp's absentee landlord. And technically, your boss."

Anna had a confused look on her face.

"He runs all of ESP's operation here," Sid clarified. "Which pretty much includes everything you see around you."

"Right. I knew the name rang a bell," Anna said. "I think he was cc'd on the email for my liability waiver. I guess now that I'm here I should make an appointment to meet him."

"Just watch yourself," Carson warned. "He's an operator. I just learned that the hard way."

"Thanks for the warning," Anna said as she read the logo etched along the side of the pen. "Tantalus Holdings," she said. "One of Slyker's business interests, I presume?"

"No idea," Carson said with a shrug. "Probably just some defense contractor."

"That's kind of a funny name for a defense contractor," Anna said.

"Why is that?" Sid asked.

"Just that Tantalus was a villain from Greek mythological," she explained. "If I recall correctly, he was condemned to eternal deprivation in the afterlife. Forced to stand forever in knee-deep water from which he could never drink, just beyond the reach of a fruit tree that he could never touch. His name is the origin of the word 'tantalize,' describing something desired yet unattainable."

The table fell silent as Sid and Carson stared at Anna, grinning in disbelief.

"What?" she finally exclaimed. "For god's sake, I was a Classics major as an undergrad! Do you realize how infrequently that comes in handy? You couldn't really expect me to pass up on the rare opportunity to flaunt my accumulation of useless knowledge?"

"OK," Sid laughed. "I'll give you a pass this time, but only because I feel sorry for you. At least now we know who to pick for our team on trivia night at the Sujah Bean."

"Game on!" Anna said, smiling.

"Since you're lording over us with your superior intellect, at least tell us why Tantalus was damned to eternal longing," Sid insisted.

"There are a few variations of the story. The one I remember says that after tasting ambrosia, the sustenance of the gods, Tantalus tried to steal it from Olympus and give it to the mortals. I suppose he was punished for hubris. Believing that he was smart enough to fool the gods."

"Interesting," Carson said, looking more closely at the pen before passing it back to Anna. "Here, you can keep it," Carson said. "I've had my fill of Slyker for one week. I don't need to be reminded of him every time I jot something down in my notebook."

"I don't want it either," she insisted. "Too fancy for my taste. It would blow my image as a suffering grad school ascetic."

"Whatever," Carson sniffed. "Leave it for Sammy. He deserves it for having to put up with Slyker as his boss."

+++

On Friday morning the staff shuffled unenthusiastically into the conference room for their weekly meeting. Colonel Kittredge looked ragged as he slumped in his chair at the head of the table. Dark bags under his eyes hinted at late nights in the office. Sergeant Goodwin flipped to the first slide, showing a long, bulletized cascade of agenda items. Kittredge closed his eyes as if summoning a hidden reserve of strength to go on.

"OK. Let's do this thing," he said, more pleading than demanding. "Carson, what's the latest on the fallout from the protest?"

"Sir, we've completed all the security enhancements around the camp. The mobility barriers have been extended out a hundred meters beyond the gate. We've reinforced all the perimeter fencing and added triple strand razor wire on top. The undergrowth along the fence has been cut back and treated with defoliant. No one will be able to get near the wire without being spotted by the guards in the watchtower."

"What about the manpower?"

"It's been doubled. We told the MoD that we needed enough guards to inspect all the vehicles entering the compound. They also sent over some heavy weapons and enough soldiers to man a quick reaction force. MoD wasn't happy about it, but after the bombing, followed by the riot, there wasn't much they could say."

"Good. The general made it clear that we're not taking any more risks," Kittredge said. "Until further notice, there will be no more off-camp movements except for official duties. No exceptions. We are now operating in a zero-risk tolerance environment. Force protection is our number one priority."

The staff nodded solemnly, realizing that their universe had just been condensed down to a five-acre island of boredom surrounded by razor wire and concrete blast barriers.

"OK. What's next?" Kittredge asked, trying to sound upbeat.

"Captain Burke with the public affairs update," Carson said.

"Burke, what have you got?" the colonel said.

"Sir, I'm happy to report that we are seeing some very positive trend lines in the latest M-RAT data."

"You mean our numbers are still up? Even after the riots last week?" Kittredge asked with surprise.

"Yes, sir. In fact, we're at all-time highs for mission recognition across the entire target demographic. ORP is now firmly in the top fifteenth percentile among all active operations worldwide. Over eighty percent of domestic respondents now hold a positive view of the mission."

"That's amazing!" Kittredge said, his mood suddenly brightening. "Does the general know about this?"

"Not yet, sir. The latest data dump just came in last night. We're still doing our preliminary analysis of the numbers."

"Write up a quick summary and get it off right away."

"Yes, sir..." Burke said, hesitating.

"Is there something wrong, Burke?" Kittredge asked, sensing his reluctance.

"It's probably nothing. Just some noise in the data."

"Please elaborate," the colonel said, sipping at a cup of coffee and wincing. "I'm not in the mood for any more surprises."

"Yes, sir. It appears that most of the increase in our

mission recognition score is being driven by low-information respondents."

"You mean those people who didn't know that we're operating in Africa?"

"Yes, sir. However, that was the case before the riots. With all the recent media coverage, that demographic now seems fully informed of our location."

"That's good news, right?

"One might think so. However, it gets a little more complicated. The data suggest that our highest level of support is now coming from those under the impression that we're actually at war *against* the Democratic Republic of Gisawi."

"How is that even possible?" the colonel asked, burying his head in his hands.

"It seemed odd to me as well. All I can think is that the surge of news coverage in recent days has been misinterpreted by some viewers. Particularly those watching the TV on mute."

"What do you mean? Why would that make a difference?"

"Respondents who reported seeing the images of young black men attacking the front gate of the camp also expressed the highest levels of support for a major expansion of US military operations in DRoG."

"Jesus," Kittredge muttered. "Anything else of interest?"

"The data did show one small sub-group of respondents adamantly opposed to our operations here."

"What's their deal? Do they have some kind of an ax to grind?"

"Hard to say. However, M-RAT regression analysis shows an almost perfect correlation between this anti-ORP sub-group and those able to correctly identify DRoG on a world map."

"Could that be coincidental?"

"Certainly. There's always a margin of error in the data."

"OK, until you get to the bottom of this I don't think we need to bog down the general with all the details. Just give him the bottom line. Focus on the all-time highs for mission recognition. Lord knows we need a little bit of good news. Anything else?"

"Just one last item, sir. We're charging ahead on the Sister City initiative. A VIP delegation from one of the local villages is on their way to Centerville now."

"Not the one we poisoned, I hope?"

"No, sir. We wanted to spread the goodwill, so we picked a different village a few miles in the other direction."

"Good. Keep me updated on the progress. What's next?"

"Intel update is next," Carson said, as Sergeant Goodwin flipped to the next slide." Cut "showing a satellite image of the camp and surrounding area.

"Good morning, sir," Sid began. "No new updates on the GLA or Odoki. However, I did find some interesting stuff relating to the contamination of the well."

"I wasn't aware we were treating that as an intelligence issue," the colonel said without enthusiasm.

"Technically, it's not. But I came across some satellite photos of the area around the village in question. I found a few things that I thought you should see."

The colonel twirled his finger in the air, signaling for Sid to speed things up. Sid brought up the image showing an overhead view of the camp and adjacent area. With a laser pointer, he made several circles showing the area around the village.

"Sir, here you see the village. And you will also notice that it sits in an area of sparse vegetation adjacent to the international airport. This bare patch of earth surrounding the village is almost perfectly symmetrical. Clearly a man-made phenomenon," Sid explained.

"It's shaped like an airstrip," Kittredge observed.

"That's what I thought too. And it turns out that there was a small airfield there built before the current international airport."

"Before? Who built that one?" Carson asked.

"We did. Or more specifically, the allies during World War II. It was one of the nodes in the trans-African resupply network stretching all the way from Ghana to Egypt. They used the airfields to ferry supplies and troops around the continent during the war."

"Nice detective work, Nancy Drew, but so what?" the colonel asked impatiently.

"Well, the satellite imagery clearly shows that the village was sitting right on top of the old runway. But that didn't make any sense to me, so I asked Louie to pull the old cadastral maps from the colonial administration archives. It confirmed my suspicion. There was no village there before the airfield was built in the early 1940s."

"So, you're saying that the village was built on top of the old airfield?"

"Yes, sir. I'm guessing that the locals simply occupied the space once it fell into disuse at the end of the war."

"I guess that makes sense, but I still don't see why it matters. What's the point?"

"If it was that easy for me to figure out that the village was sitting on top of an old airstrip, then certainly MoD must have known as well. And it should have been no surprise to anyone that there would be toxic residue buried in the ground. Under an old airfield is the first place you'd expect to find groundwater contamination."

"Sid, are you suggesting that MoD told us to dig a poisonous well there on purpose?"

"I'm not sure I'd go that far, but it does seem a little suspicious."

"But why?" Kittredge asked. "It doesn't make any sense that they would tell us to drop a well there if they suspected it might be contaminated."

"It didn't make any sense to me either until I saw a headline in yesterday's paper. The government just announced a major expansion of the adjacent airport with a plan to add a second runway and lots of new ramp space."

"An interesting coincidence, Sid, but not actionable. It's a little too late for that now. In the future, please keep your conspiracy theories to personal time rather than staff meetings. Carson, what's next on the agenda? We haven't got all day…"

When the meeting was over, Colonel Kittredge asked Sid and Carson to stay after. Once the others left the room, Kittredge pulled out a red folder and slid it across the table.

"Gentlemen, the shit's about to hit the fan over this bombing thing. The Pentagon just ordered a full investigation. This is coming down from the highest levels," Kittredge explained.

"I don't understand. Aren't we already investigating it?" Sid said. "The forensic report should be back any day now."

"Not that kind of investigation. The kind where they look for someone to blame."

"Blame for what?" Carson said indignantly.

"Poor risk assessment…insufficient force protection… basically, anything they can find to show that we were unprepared for the attack."

"You've got to be kidding me!" Carson said, shaking his head. "How could we have been prepared for something that was completely out of the blue."

"Well, gentlemen, that's the rub," Kittredge replied. "Apparently some folks in DC got wind that the MoD gave us advanced warning of a possible threat. Now they're wondering why we ignored it."

"That's crazy!" Sid exclaimed. "There was no advanced warning! Louie told us that Police Intelligence was looking at some suspicious Lebanese businessmen. That was it! For god sakes, he was asking us if *we* had any information to give to *them*. There was nothing more to it."

"OK, but after you spoke with Louie you sent up a request for information that mentioned possible Hezbollah presence in DRoG, right?"

"Of course, I did. It was a routine request for information. But not because I thought there was anything to it. Just the opposite. It was completely out in left field. In fact, the query was completely ignored. Meaning that there was no information in the system suggesting an imminent attack."

"That may be the case, but they're still going to ask why we didn't implement additional security measure around the camp if we had suspicions about threat actors operating in the area."

"Sir, you've got to be kidding me," Sid blurted. "There were no suspicions. No threat actors. There was nothing at all. Besides, what the hell would we have done anyway? So, is that the real reason General Foster ordered us to turn the camp into Fort Knox? To cover his ass in case something else happens?"

"I agree with Sid," Carson chimed in. "They must be looking for a fall guy. These things always roll downhill until they can find somebody at the bottom to crucify."

Kittredge nodded sympathetically. "Usually, I'd agree with you. But this time I think you've got it backward. They want to push this thing uphill. To the very top..."

"General Foster?" Sid asked.

"Hell no! They don't give a crap about Foster. This thing is coming from the Hill. It's a classic fishing expedition. They're looking for anything that will embarrass the president. It's less than a year until the election. They're going to throw whatever they can find against a wall and see what sticks. It's the old who-knew-what-and-when-did-they-know-it game."

"But that's ridiculous. No one paid any attention to that query when I sent it up. Certainly, not anyone at the White House," Sid insisted.

"That's probably true," Kittredge agreed. "But also, completely irrelevant. The important thing is that you created a paper trail. That's all they need. The wheels are already in motion. The bombing and the riot put this mission back on the front page. Now people are going to use that for leverage. Unfortunately, we're getting caught in the middle. I just wanted to warn you guys. We should be expecting some visitors soon. They'll probably want to ask you two some questions."

Sid sighed and shook his head.

"Listen, no one's out to get you, Sid," Colonel Kittredge reassured him. "When the time comes, just tell them the truth. But until then we need to keep this thing quiet. There's no need to worry the others. We've got enough problems as it is."

"What about Louie? Should we let him know?" Carson asked.

The colonel tapped his pencil on the table, thinking about the question. "No, not yet. Right now, it still doesn't involve them. Besides, I'm guessing that word will get out soon enough. The people pushing this thing back in DC don't have any incentive to keep it a secret for very long. That's not the point of their game."

CHAPTER EIGHT

Slyker glanced impatiently at his phone for the third time in a minute as he waited for Sergeant Goodwin to finish reviewing the thick stack of forms. Goodwin squinted at the page through his army-issue glasses, going meticulously through every single line.

"Just a few more pages and we're done sir," Goodwin assured him.

"Sure, no problem," Slyker replied with forced geniality.

"Mother's maiden name and place of birth?" Goodwin asked, deeply absorbed in the minutia of the boxes.

"Didn't I already give you that on forms three, five, and eight?" Slyker snapped, no longer able to conceal his frustration.

"Sir, it would be easier if you just told me again rather than have me go back through all the pages to find it."

"Simon. SIERRA, INDIA, MIKE, OSCAR, NOVEMBER. Middletown, Connecticut. Do you need me to spell that out too?"

"No, thank you. Next question. Have you ever been married to a foreign national or naturalized US citizen?"

"For the third time, no!"

"Have you recently traveled to any countries designated as State Sponsors of Terrorism?"

"Define recently," Slyker asked, then immediately regretted his flippancy as Goodwin began searching through the form's detailed explanatory notes.

"The last ten years," Goodwin clarified after finally locating the appropriate reference.

"No. Not that I'm aware of. Wait! Are Seychelles on that list?"

Goodwin looked up, unamused. "Do you have an ownership interest in any foreign corporations, partnerships, or other commercial entities?"

Slyker glanced at his watch. "Listen, Sergeant. I realize you're just doing your job, and I respect that, but is this absolutely necessary? I'm just going to walk into that room, have a ten-minute conversation with General Foster, then leave. I can assure you that I'm not an evil mastermind plotting the demise of constitutional order. I would appreciate it if you could just cut me some slack. I'm about to be late for the meeting."

"Sir, the forms are required by regulation before you can enter the room."

"I have no doubt about that, Sergeant. However, do you appreciate the irony that I'm being asked to fill out dozens of forms in order to access a facility that I built? Then talk on a teleconference system that I lease to the government? Over a secure satellite data link that is provided by my company as part of the base support contract?"

Goodwin stared blankly at Slyker, flummoxed by multiple breaches of protocol and uncertain of his next move.

Settling for tactical retreat Goodwin pushed the stack of papers across the desk at Slyker. "Please, sir, have them done before you leave the building."

"Thanks, Goodwin. You're a great American. Please take one of these complimentary ESP keychains for your trouble," Slyker said, tossing Goodwin the trinket before following him into the operations center.

Once inside the conference room, Slyker sat in the large leather chair at the head of the table, usually occupied by Colonel Kittredge. Goodwin turned on the teleconference system then gave Slyker a thumbs-up before leaving the room. A few minutes later, General Foster appeared on the screen absent his usual entourage. He flipped the mic and wasted no time getting down to business.

"You've got ten minutes. No, wait. Make that five. What's the pitch?" the general said.

"Yes, sir. I'll dispense with the formalities. I trust you're familiar with ESP and our parent company, Techtron Industries."

"Damn straight about that. I've been eating in your crappy chow halls and sleeping in your shoddy prefab barracks all over the world for the better part of the last decade."

"Indeed. Just like the Army, we do our best under sometimes challenging conditions. But at the end of the day, of course, we're all on the same team. My number one priority is helping you achieve your mission while offering high-quality performance and competitive-value solutions in the best interest of the American taxpayer."

"Cut the bullshit. Your job is to make money so let's dispense with the chitchat. I was told you had something to discuss that's close-hold."

"Yes, sir. Our legislative liaison team in Washington has become aware that this command is functioning under some unique operational constraints. And that this situation has led to several missed opportunities. We are also aware that the budget authorization for ORP is about to get the ax, with or without achieving your primary objective."

"Listen, Mr. Slacker."

"Slyker, sir, with a Y."

"You know damn well that I'm not authorized to discuss operational matters with you. If that's where this conversation is going, then let me just save you the time by cutting it off right here."

"Yes, sir, I fully understand. At ESP, we believe that protection of national security always comes first. In fact, that's the reason why I asked to see you. To make you aware of a new capability that could help bring your mission to a desirable end-state."

General Foster leaned back in his chair, smirking into the camera. "Really! No kidding, Slacker. So, what's your great plan? We've been hunting that pissant Odoki for almost three years without any luck. Now you're just waltzing in here with some bright idea that we haven't thought of yet? Give me a fucking break!"

"General, we both know why you haven't got him. You've been given an impossible job, without the tools to get it done. That's like sending a fireman into a burning building without a water hose. If you ask me, that's no way to do business."

The general stiffened in his chair. "What are you going to do, Slacker, sell me an armed drone?" he asked incredulously.

"No, sir, actually, I'm going to rent you one. Well, not exactly you. President Namono's name will be on the lease."

"Yeah right," Foster scoffed. "What is this, some kind of Uber for UAVs?"

"Our lawyers have advised us against making that comparison. Think of it more like a fractional ownership plan for airborne precision targeting."

"Like a vacation time-share?"

"Exactly! Except with high explosives and no holiday blackout dates."

Foster leaned into the table like a gambler joining a hand of poker.

"OK, Slacker. I'll bite. But why DRoG? In case you haven't noticed, no one gives a crap about what's happening down there."

"On the contrary, it's the ideal testbed for the proof of concept. According to our market analysis, places like DRoG are going to be the sweet spot of the sector."

"I don't see it. Why would they want something like this?"

"Put yourself in their shoes, General. Players like DRoG are priced out of the market for cutting-edge military technology. Sure, they can always pick up second-hand junk from a former-Soviet Bloc yard sale, or maybe some knock-off gear from North Korea. But think about the message that sends to potential adversaries and rivals?"

"Kind of like shopping at Target?"

"Precisely! Instead, we aim to market ourselves as an aspirational brand. Appealing to up-and-coming regional military powers who want to show they're ready to play in the big leagues."

"OK, I get that. But it still seems a tough sell. I just don't see them going to all the trouble."

"Well, there's also a matter of reputational interest. Countries like DRoG have long resorted to…how shall I put this? Exercising more blunt instruments of state authority. Of course, this has caused them nothing but headaches with the international community. But let's face it, a targeted airborne precision strike is not going to get you indicted by the ICC. It's a gentleman's game. Like pistols at dawn. We think there's a real untapped demand for that kind capability in this neighborhood."

"Interesting…," Foster said, rubbing his chin. "But how does it work on the ground?"

"Good question. Our flexible fractional ownership plan including full technical and logistical support across a wide range of customer-directed missions. We retain full ownership and end-use control over the hardware, thereby avoiding complications with sensitive technology transfer and proliferation. We offer turn-key deployment with on-site customer support for operations, maintenance, and piloting. However, final targeting authority is left entirely with the client. But for an additional fee, we can offer non-binding legal consultation services to advise our customers on applicable law-of-war conventions and pertinent human rights considerations."

"OK, so you're telling me that we provide the targeting information, ESP brings the drone, and DRoG pulls the trigger?"

"Yes, sir. In a nutshell, that's the concept."

The general nodded thoughtfully. "Slacker. As much as I like the idea, I'd say you're crazy if you think the White House is going to sign off on this."

"On the contrary, sir, we're confident it will go through. ESP enjoys regular, informal consultations with senior administration officials and staffers of the relevant oversight subcommittees. This helps us anticipate potential pitfalls and adjust our business strategy accordingly. Naturally, in our line of work, we prefer to shape policy determinations rather than be shaped by them."

"I'm still not buying it, Slacker. Why would DC go for this? I don't see the angle."

"General, you and I both know that Washington is sick and tired of hearing the name Daniel Odoki. Everyone wants the hell out of this thing at the first opportunity for a dignified retreat. This proposal offers the perfect exit strategy. They can take the credit if it works, or shift blame elsewhere if something goes wrong. It's a perfect win-win strategy for risk-averse policy planners."

"I'll believe it when I see it. Besides, once word gets out on the street about this, you're going to have every bleeding-heart NGO in the world accusing you of arming dictators."

"Our marketing team is already way out ahead of that. We're promoting this as a responsible-use model offering highly controlled access to a legitimate military technology. In our view, the private sector is much better positioned to establish and maintain norms for acceptable use. After all, we have brand value to consider. Not to mention liability. Unlike Uncle Sam, we can't just write off reckless behavior under the guise of sovereign self-defense. We have shareholders to consider. They're going to hold us accountable for any fuck-ups."

"Well, Slacker, I got to admit it's an interesting concept. What kind of firepower are we talking about?"

"We are prepared to offer customers a wide range of lethal and non-lethal strike options as a part of the entry-level package. The standard payload is what we call a 'Low Objective Radius Small Kinetic Munition,' or LORSK-M. The warhead is not much bigger than a magnum of Dom Perignon, with a very tight blast radius. If one of these babies detonated inside your living room, it probably wouldn't even crack the dishes in the kitchen. Our design engineers worked closely with the legal team specifically to mitigate potential liability concerns with unintended collateral damage."

"Nice. And the non-lethal version?"

"Even cooler. Our research lab has developed a fast-acting adhesive that is highly effective against large crowds as well as point targets when deployed from a hovering quad-copter. The payload is derived from sugarcane extract and one hundred percent certified organic. Basically, we're talking aerosolized molasses. Targets are stuck to the first thing they touch and completely immobilized until authorities arrive with a patented dissolving solution."

"There's a market for that?"

"Are you kidding? We've already received at least a dozen private inquiries from European governments wanting to have it on hand before the next World Cup. We expect it to totally revolutionize precision airborne crowd control."

"So, you really think DRoG is going to pony up the cash for this?"

"Given that this is an untested scenario we've elected to waive all fees and commission for the initial demonstration. We're offering the entire package to DRoG at cost."

"Slacker, it seems like you've done your homework. But at the end of the day, I'm still a soldier, and this is still my mission. I'm not exactly comfortable with the idea of handing the entire thing over to ESP. Even if it means finally getting Odoki. I'm kind of old school that way. It just feels like the guys in uniform should be on the front lines pulling the trigger."

"General, please don't get the wrong idea. I couldn't agree with you more. Of course, the soldiers will still be in charge. You'll be the ones telling us where to fly and what to do. And if we get Odoki in our crosshairs, it will be someone from DRoG who pulls the trigger. Just think of it as just another tool in your rucksack. Like a can opener. Just because you didn't build it doesn't mean that someone is going to tell you how to open the can."

"Well, when you put it that way, it makes a lot more sense. So how long would it take to get this capability operational here on the ground? We're running out of time."

"Six to eight weeks, as long as we don't run into any snags back in DC."

"So, what do you need from me? I could make a few calls back to the Pentagon to grease the skids."

"I appreciate the support; however, I think we've got that part well in hand. But there is one last issue I'd like to discuss. Hypothetically, as the first commander overseeing this new targeting protocol, naturally, we would hope to leverage your unique perspective and experience. Perhaps somewhere down the road in a consulting capacity..."

"Go on..."

"Well, we're not selling used cars after all. The business is all about relationships, the people behind the technology. Before signing on the dotted line, any prospective client would expect to have personalized, professional consultations with a senior-level subject matter expert. Particularly with such a new technology."

"Hmm, very true," Foster said, rubbing at his chin. "So, hypothetically, how would someone like me help to facilitate such relationship building?"

"Hypothetically, someone of your experience and seniority would be critical for concept socialization among key influencers. After the initial product demonstration, we anticipate some strong reactions. There will inevitably be a lot of uninformed speculation about where this program goes in the future. The chattering class always goes straight for the slippery slope. For that reason, we find it essential to preemptively shape the narrative. Inevitably the skeptics will simmer down once confronted with a seasoned personality who really gets the new technology. Someone able to lend credibility and put a human face on something that might otherwise seem frightening."

"And you think someone like me is the right fit for that role?"

"Absolutely! A respected officer, with substantial wartime bona fides, backed up by actual experience using the technology in the field. That kind of influence is hard to come by. And naturally, the scarcity of such expertise would be reflected in the compensation package."

"Slacker, you do realize that you're talking to a general officer still in uniform?"

"Of course, sir. That's why we're only speaking about hypotheticals."

"Right. I just wanted to make sure that we both understand the situation. So, hypothetically speaking, what does something like this involve?"

"We have a standard package for senior-level product representation. The agreement provides maximum optionality for the relationship to evolve over time if the business grows as expected. We'd probably start with a few speaking engagements around the Beltway think tank circuit. Maybe some TV talk shows and radio appearances if the media engages with the story and wants a talking head."

"That sounds a bit hands-on…"

"Not at all. We'll have a robust product launch support team that handles all the heavy lifting. They'll be writing the press releases, prepping talking points, ghostwriting articles for trade publications and professional journals. Trust me. These guys are real pros. Their job is to make your job look effortless."

"Very interesting," Foster said, taking notes for the first time. "Since we can't talk about compensation, I won't ask about compensation."

"Naturally. However, if we were to discuss it, I'm confident that you would be pleased with the nature of that conversation. More importantly, what we're offering here is a chance to be on the ground floor of an entirely new business model. The drone is just the tip of the iceberg."

"How so?"

"We've recently identified significant unrealized potential on the margins of our core defense-related business. Specifically, in the areas of cultural production, family entertainment, and merchandising. Our goal is to move up the value chain and capture some of this higher-margin production."

"What? Is that even possible?"

"The numbers will blow you away. The Global War on Terrorism spun off hundreds of books, movies, themed apparel lines, and children's toys. While our industry played a vital role in defining how this conflict was waged, we essentially ceded the commodification of these activities to the so-called creative class. And believe me, they've done very well for themselves by exploiting the value of our contributions. Since the end of the Cold War, we've basically given up the entire market without a fight."

"So, what's the angle?"

"We're going to horizontally integrate our traditional defense and security business with a newly formed media and entertainment unit. Our analysts see an enormous opportunity for post-conflict revenue streams flowing from things like personal memoirs, movie adaptations, merchandising, and other spinoffs. The fact is, war sells, especially after it's over. Ultimately, we're aiming to reduce volatility for our shareholders by moving into these niche areas as a hedge against countercyclical fluctuations."

"Countercyclical fluctuations?"

"Sorry. B-school jargon. Peace and stability. That's what I'm getting at. We find it a very challenging business environment."

"Makes complete sense to me. I trust we can follow up on all the details somewhere down the road. Once we're both in a better position to talk specifics?"

"Indeed, sir. I look forward to that opportunity."

"But back to our immediate concern. When are we getting the rent-a-drone?"

"I've recently pitched the concept to our friends over at MoD. Obviously, we need to get their buy-in before we bring the platform in-country. As you're probably aware, dealing with Gisawians can be somewhat unpredictable. However, I think they see this as a win-win proposition. I expect we'll have them on board soon. I'm guessing they'll want to show DC that they're willing to play ball. Facilitating a near-term resolution to the Odoki problem is certainly one way to do that."

"And if the Gisawians sign on the dotted line, we're getting the real deal, right? The one with a dick on it?"

"Sir?"

"I don't want some damn molasses-spraying helicopter. I want the one that's going to finish the job."

"Yes, sir, that's the plan."

"OK, then. It was good meeting with you, Slacker. We'll be in touch. I really like your can-do style. I only wish we had more guys like you in the service."

"Thank you, sir. I've always had a soft spot in my heart for our men in uniform."

"And the girls!" Foster reminded him. "Don't forget. We've got them now too."

"That's right, sir. Can't forget about the girls," Slyker said with a theatrical snap of his fingers.

"Foster, out," he said as the screen went black.

Slyker gathered up his things and stepped outside the conference room. The outer office was empty and the lights off. Slyker passed by Sergeant Goodwin's desk and tossed the stack of unfinished security forms into the trashcan. He was just about to leave when he realized that he wasn't alone.

"How'd the meeting with the general go?" Kittredge called out from his darkened office. The colonel was sitting at his desk, bathed in the pale glow of his computer screen.

"Good meeting," Slyker answered cautiously. "Sorry I couldn't fill you in on all the details. It's all still pretty close-hold."

"Yeah, right," the colonel replied. "For some reason, I was operating under the impression that I was in charge down here. But I guess that's not the case anymore."

"Hey, no hard feelings. Once things move forward, I'll be sure to bring you into the loop."

Kittredge didn't reply, so Slyker moved toward the door, but just as he reached for the handle, he heard the colonel's voice call out from the darkened room.

"I remember you," he said. "Back from officer training. What's it been? At least twenty-five years now?"

For a moment Slyker froze at the door, trying to decide what to do. "Yup, must be about that," he finally replied.

"The first time I saw you here I couldn't believe it. After what happened back then, I figured you'd never have the balls to show your face around the Army again."

"Small world, I guess."

"Yup. I suppose so. I guess you probably think you got the last laugh on all of us, don't you? You got booted out of the Army for sucking dick, and now you're probably making two or three times what I pull in each month."

"At least," Slyker replied with a chuckle.

"So. What's the moral of that story? I guess it doesn't pay to play by the rules and keep your nose clean, does it?"

"What the fuck does that mean, Kittredge? Did you even know me then? Other than the rumors and jokes you heard around camp?"

"I knew all I needed to know, Slyker. There were rules and you broke them."

"Yeah, well, I'm sure it was pretty easy for you to follow the rules. Because they were made by guys like you. You really think it was all just a bunch of fun and games for me? Getting to spend two years of my life as the big joke on camp?"

"Seemed like you were having fun until you got caught."

"At least you're right about that. I was having fun. He was a nice kid, and we were minding our own business, not hurting anybody."

"Well, Slyker, maybe you didn't like the rules, but they were there for a reason."

"Yeah, thanks for reminding me," he shot back.

"But then, I guess now it doesn't really matter anymore," Kittredge added. "The Army's happy to welcome in guys like you now. We're just one big happy family."

"Yeah, I'm sure it's just peachy. But you know what, as nice as that sounds, I'm fine with my current gig," Slyker said, turning the handle and pushing open the door. As he stepped outside, he heard Kittredge call after him.

"Watch yourself, Slyker. You may be able to fool the general, but I know what you're all about…"

+++

The next morning Sid, Carson, and Anna met at the café for their mid-morning fix. Sammy arrived at the table with their usual order: two coffees, one tea, and a small plate of sweet biscuits.

"So, Anna, how are things going on cracking the Odoki case?" Sid asked while popping a biscuit into his mouth. "You've been here over a month now and still haven't revealed his hidden location."

Anna rolled her eyes. "Well, Sid, you've been here almost a year and haven't done much better."

"Touché," he replied, throwing up his hands. "Speaking of which, I'm getting a little worried about how my annual evaluation is going to read. So far, I've failed to catch Odoki, entertained wild conspiracy theories during staff meetings, and possibly become the first person in Army history ever to gain weight on a deployment to Africa."

"Those bullets will get you promoted for sure," Carson said, smiling mischievously.

"Well, at least Carson has some real concrete achievements to show for his time here," Anna said.

"Yeah, involving actual concrete," Sid piled on.

"Mock if you will," Carson said. "But how many times have we been attacked since I surrounded the camp with those giant barriers and razor wire? In case you haven't been counting, the number is zero. I'd say that's a pretty solid performance statistic," he added with a wink.

"Hard to argue with success," Sid said. "But I still give Anna high marks for effort. Since she arrived, I'm guessing she's probably read everything ever written about Odoki. By now, you qualify as a genuine authority. At least compared to anyone else in the camp."

"Admittedly, a low bar. Unfortunately, I still don't feel any closer to figuring things out," she lamented. "It seems like most of what's been written about him is complete nonsense. Based on little more than rumors, speculation, and wild exaggeration."

"Par for the course. Rumor, speculation, and wild exaggeration are currency down here," Sid noted.

"OK, Sid, so you've been here a lot longer than the rest of us. You must at least have a few theories by now. Who do you think Odoki is?" Anna challenged.

"That depends on who you're asking. Like you said, people can hardly even agree on the basic facts. I guess the standard version puts him somewhere between fifty and sixty years old, born in a remote part of western DRoG, of normal stature and unremarkable in appearance. His personality profile is what you'd expect from your typical warlord. He's deeply narcissistic and suffers from messiah complex, prone to irrational outbursts of extreme violence, and probably has mother issues. Yet despite this charming personality, somehow the guy has managed to build a cult-like devotion among his followers."

"What about those stock pictures of him that the newspapers always use? Are those legit?" Anna asked.

"We think so, but honestly, no one knows for sure. Only a few Westerners have ever seen him face-to-face. And that was a long time ago. The first time he seems to pop up in the public record was during the border wars of the late '80s. He made a minor name for himself as a mid-level rebel fighter, credited with leading a few raids against government forces. At the time, there were rumors he was on the payroll of a neighboring government, fighting for treasure more than ideology. At least that's the story you get from MoD. But we've never been able to confirm most of those details. So, it goes without saying that anything you hear about Odoki should be taken with a grain of salt."

"What happened to him after the border wars?" Carson asked.

"Good question. He fell off the radar for a while. At least until the late '90s when he suddenly reappeared for a second act as a religious leader. He had a reputation as a magnetic proselytizer and gradually built up a base of support in the rural western parts of the country. However, according to some accounts, the sudden profession of faith was more entrepreneurial than heartfelt."

"But from what I read he attracted a real following in areas where the central government didn't carry much influence," Anna added.

"True, but that's where the story starts getting a bit fuzzy," Sid explained. "As he gained notoriety, the government took notice. Particularly when his sermons became more political. According to MoD, he began calling on his followers to challenge the regime. The government will tell you that the religious furor was nothing but a ruse and that Odoki was really acting as a proxy for outside forces. By then, folks here in the capitol were starting to get nervous about a return of the border wars."

"Is that version of the story plausible?" Carson asked.

"Maybe. It's a fairly safe bet that any of DRoG's neighbors would have jumped at the chance to stick it to President Namono. After thirty years in power he hasn't exactly endeared himself to his fellow regional despots," Sid surmised.

"Either way, I can imagine that Odoki was tilling fertile ground out west," Anna added. "When I traveled there last month it was obvious that the place is a complete backwater. You'd be hard-pressed to find much evidence of any development money trickling down into the area. Even by Africa standards, the place seems pretty marginalized."

"In a way that makes sense," Sid agreed. "Apparently, part of Odoki's appeal was his call for the transfer of land rights from the central government to local communities. That strategy certainly wasn't going to win him any friends in the presidential palace. But that's the point where I start losing track of the storyline. Once it gets down into the details of all the different tribes and their histories, I can't keep any of it straight. If you really want the nitty-gritty, you need to ask Louie. He can explain it all."

"But at some point, Odoki's followers decided to give up praying and start fighting," Carson asked. "How come?"

"I don't think we really know what triggered it. One day he just pops back up on the radar with that big attack on the village. Suddenly, he was on the front page of every newspaper in the world. At least for a few days."

"And that's when we got pulled into this mess...," Carson said, sipping at his coffee.

"True, but only because of a few more odd twists in the story," Sid continued. "Probably the only reason that the massacre even made the newspapers back at home was because of that church he burned down along with the village."

"You mean the one sponsored by the American evangelical group?" Anna asked.

"Yup. I can't remember all the details, but some ministry down in Texas had been supporting missionaries working here in DRoG. The church happened to be associated with them. Coincidentally, a few of those Texas evangelical fundraisers had connections with the administration. The next thing you know, an obscure tragedy halfway around the world becomes an agenda item during a National Security Council meeting. The rest, as they say, is history."

"But there was a little more," Anna continued. "Apparently, all the news coverage also attracted the attention of the IRS. It turned out that there was some shady accounting behind the church's good deeds here in DRoG. Eventually, the feds discovered that most of the donations never made it over to Africa."

"Why am I not surprised?" Sid said, shaking his head.

"They linked some of the diverted funds back to a vacation property developer somewhere on the Gulf Coast. Six months later the church's charity office in DRoG was quietly shut down. But of course, by that time President Namono had already asked for our help in tracking down Odoki."

"And here we are today," Carson chuckled in disbelief.

"Well, it's an interesting plot twist, but it doesn't get us any closer to finding Odoki or getting the hell out of here," Sid sighed.

"Sid, while we're on the subject. Didn't you say that most of the intel you're getting on Odoki is coming from detainee interrogation reports?" Anna asked.

"Yeah, what little there is. From time to time DRoG army patrols bring in GLA fighters. Usually, these guys are caught sneaking around villages, trying to steal food or supplies. Other times they just give themselves up for one reason or another. After that, they get turned over to Police Intelligence and run through a standard line of questioning. We never get to see the detainees face to face, but MoD provides summary reports of all the interrogations. That's mostly what we've been using to develop our target sets for the raids. It's not much to go on, but for now, it's the only game in town."

"Interesting," Anna said, absently tapping her pencil against a teacup, lost in thought. "Any chance I can look at those interrogation reports?" she finally asked.

"Nope. Sorry," Sid said. "As soon as they touch my hands, they become classified information. If I give them to you, I'll be finishing my career in Leavenworth making small rocks out of big ones."

"Oh, come on, Sid, they don't really do that anymore, do they?" Anna asked.

"I have no idea, but I don't want to find out."

"But why are they only classified once they get in your hands. What are they before then?"

"Nothing as far as I'm concerned. Property of the Gisawian Ministry of Defense."

"Where do you get them?"

"Louie brings them over every few weeks. If you really want to see them, nothing is stopping you from asking him. If he's willing to show you, that's his business, not mine."

"Nice ethical flexibility," Anna winked. "You've got a bright future in government service. I'll talk to Louie and see what he says."

"Yeah, better that you ask him," Sid suggested.

"What the hell is that supposed to mean?"

"Come on, Anna. Don't think I haven't noticed a little chemistry between you guys."

"Please, Sid! Don't be such a child," she scolded, stifling a laugh.

"Don't feel bad," Sid assured her. "It's his funny little accent. He's irresistible."

"Fuck off," Anna said under her breath, sipping at her tea and concealing a smile.

+++

On Friday, the weekly staff meeting lasted 242 slides with attendant discussion. In the early afternoon, when the session finally adjourned, Colonel Kittredge kept Sid and Carson behind while the rest of the staff rushed off to the Sujah Bean for a late lunch.

"Gentlemen, sorry to keep you here, but I had a few things I didn't want to discuss in front of the group," Kittredge began. "The bombing investigation seems to be moving ahead at full steam. I heard through the grapevine that we should expect visitors next week."

"Visitors?" Carson asked.

"Investigators," Kittredge clarified. "They'll be poking around here for a few days and interviewing everyone in the camp."

"Everyone!" Sid exclaimed, already on the defensive. "The three of us were the only ones who knew anything about that nonsense coming out of MoD. Why in the hell do they want to talk with everyone else?"

"Sid, you can probably guess the answer to that," the colonel said. "They're looking to make a case."

"And what case is that?" Carson interrupted. "I still don't get why they are wasting their time here. Unless they're just looking to screw us over."

"Listen, guys!" the colonel said, slamming his fist on the table. "Just calm down. Trust me, they don't give a shit about us. This is all inside-the-Beltway theater. The only thing they want is some fodder for cable TV news."

"But it doesn't make sense," Carson said. "Why put us under the microscope just to score points back in DC?"

"Think about it. The headlines write themselves. President deploys troops without congressional authorization for combat activities. President withholds vital resources needed to get the job done. President puts soldiers in harm's way without proper gear and protection. President's national security staff ignored advance warnings of attacks. Don't you see how this plays out? We're just pawns in the game. All you need to do is answer their questions, briefly and truthfully. If you can manage to pull that off without screwing up, then you've got nothing to worry about."

"If you say so, boss," Sid sighed. "It just gets me worked up. This may be business as usual in DC, but it's still our careers. I don't like being made a toady for somebody else's political agenda."

"Well, Sid, like it or not, you better get ready for it. I guarantee the investigators will be using a shotgun blast approach. They're going to want to see everything. The notes on the threat warning from MoD. Slides from all our weekly staff meetings. Email traffic. Social media posts. Probably even an audit of our computer network activity. They're not going to miss a chance to find out something that will embarrass the administration."

"Super. I can't wait," Sid said sarcastically. "If they really wanted to see something interesting, they might start with the forensic report from the bombing. It came back last night."

"Really? What'd they find?" Kittredge asked.

"I just started looking at it before the meeting, but so far it doesn't make a damn bit of sense."

"What do you mean?"

"For starters, the bomb design was really unusual. It wasn't like any IED I've ever seen before. From what was left of the device, it didn't seem designed to fragment or create any shrapnel."

"Why would someone build a bomb like that?"

"I was wondering the same thing. Either we're dealing with complete amateurs, who had no idea what they were doing, or whoever built the thing did it that way on purpose, not intending to kill anyone."

"You mean the bombs were just for show?" Kittredge asked.

"I don't know, sir. I suppose it's possible. Both devices had a similar design; therefore, they likely were built by the same individual. If the plan was just to grab attention, then it worked as intended. The explosions caused a hell of a lot of noise and threw up a nice plume of dust, but that was about it. The design is what explains the so-called 'miracle' that no one was killed," Sid said, making air quotes with his fingers. "Non-lethality was a feature, not a bug."

"Wow. Strange," Carson said. "Anything else?"

"Maybe. The triggers were nothing fancy. Standard technology for improvised explosives. Remote detonation using a radio frequency trigger. Probably a cheap Nokia phone or something similar. We didn't recover the phone, so there's no way of tracking down the supply chain or tracing the SIM cards back to an owner. But there was one other thing that was a bit curious. The choice of explosives."

"How so?" Kittredge asked.

"Well, if it had been a professional. Say someone trained by al-Qaeda or Hezbollah, we would have expected to see a home-cooked brew. Probably some type of peroxide-based explosive. You can find recipes all over the Internet, and it doesn't take much technical knowledge to whip up a batch in your kitchen."

"But that wasn't these bombs?" Carson asked.

"No. Not according to forensic analysis. The chemical residue matched what is commonly found with industrial-grade explosives. Stuff you might use for construction or mining applications."

"What does that mean to you?" Kittredge asked.

"I suppose it's possible that the bomb builder just happened to have some of it lying around; however, it also could mean that we're not dealing with an experienced terrorist cell. To me, the combination of clues points more toward a local connection. But what I can't figure out is the motive. If the bombs were just intended to send a message, then what the hell was it? It just seems too ambiguous."

"Interesting," the colonel said, jotting down a few notes. "Presumably, the investigators will have seen the forensic report before they arrive. Although, it might not matter if the facts don't support the talking points they're looking for. Here's my advice, just tell them what you know. Nothing more. Nothing less. We'll get through this the best we can," the colonel said before getting up and leaving the room.

+++

At the end of the day, Louie rushed over to MoD for his weekly appointment. As soon as he entered the room, he could see that Mugaba was in a foul mood.

"Good morning, Uncle. I'm sorry I couldn't be here

sooner. The Americans didn't finish their meeting until late. I had to stay until I was able to speak with them."

Mugaba looked down at his watch, then back at Lutalo. "Whatever information you have, it's too late," he grumbled. "I already met with the minister and won't see him again until next week."

Louie looked down into his notebook, uncertain of what to say.

"Go on, Lutalo," his uncle relented. "Stop feeling sorry for yourself. Just tell me what you have. Are the Americans any closer to getting us the satellite pictures of the western region?"

"I think so, Uncle. Maybe a few more weeks."

"Hmm," Mugaba said, tapping at his desk. "Keep reminding them. Be sure they know that planning for the offensive will not move forward until we have this information. If things are delayed, it will be their responsibility."

"I will keep asking."

"What else?"

"They've completed the new defensive measures around the camp. The commander asked me to convey his thanks to the minister. They were very happy to receive the extra platoon of guards outside the perimeter."

"It sounds as if they are finally taking our warnings seriously," the deputy minister observed.

"Yes, Uncle, it appears so. But they still have questions. They asked to see our final investigative report on the bombing."

"This is not possible," his uncle said. "Police Intelligence is still working on it. They must not be rushed. And what about their report? Should we expect the Americans to share this with us?"

"I asked about it, but they cannot give all the details."

"Really? So, what exactly did our friends tell you, Lutalo?"

"They're still skeptical about Hezbollah. They believe it is more likely something local. Maybe something not even related to terrorism."

"What do they know!" Mugaba blustered. "I suppose they can tell this from their satellites when they fly overhead? The Americans never leave their camp, but they still think they can see everything that goes on outside the fence! Police Intelligence knows the Lebanese are up to no good. We told this to the Americans, and they ignored it. I tell you, Lutalo, they think we know nothing. They treat us like little children!"

"No, Uncle. It is not like that. They just see things from a different perspective. They listened to me when I told them of our suspicions, but there wasn't enough information to act."

"Of course, that is what they say after the fact. Somehow the Americans are always the victims," he sniffed indignantly. "Next time, when we tell them something, perhaps they ought to listen more closely. You know what they say in the village, Lutalo, 'The one who has the stick always finds the trouble.' They hide inside their camp and behind the fences, but still, the Americans always seem to find trouble..."

"Uncle, is there anything else I should tell them?" Louie said, hoping that the meeting was coming to an end.

"Just one thing. Work has begun on the new airport project. It is progressing quickly, ahead of schedule. The president wants a dedication ceremony as soon as the runway is complete. Maybe less than two months from now."

Louie looked surprised. "That is amazing, Uncle. The project was just announced a few weeks ago."

"You tell our American friends to pay attention to this. When we have an aim in mind, we can achieve it! Even without their help…"

"Yes, Uncle. I will be sure to let them know."

"Good. I don't have anything else for you now," he said.

Mugaba seemed on the verge of ending the meeting before remembering something else. "Are you going to see your mother this weekend?"

Louie nodded. "Yes, Uncle, I will."

"I had dinner with her a few days ago. She told me that she was worried about you."

Louie shrugged.

"She said that you don't seem happy. She is frightened that you will leave her and go back overseas, just like your brothers and sisters. Lutalo, you know this would break her heart. You are the only thing she has left."

"I don't want to hurt her," Louie whispered.

"Then what is it? Why does she think you want to leave?"

Louie hesitated, unable to look his uncle in the eyes. "I am fine, Uncle. It's just what we spoke of before. I want to be doing something else. I am not making any difference at the camp."

His uncle surprised him with a sympathetic nod. "You are just like your father. You cannot stand to be still, even for one moment. But remember, Lutalo, the patient man eats the ripest fruit."

"Please, Uncle, stop with the village sayings! I know that you mean well, but a few words cannot fix what is wrong. It won't make me feel any differently."

The moment the words left his mouth Louie regretted speaking them. But to his surprise, his uncle showed no anger. Mugaba sat calmly at his desk, waiting for Louie to regain his composure.

"Lutalo, I know you are frustrated," he finally said. "I just ask that you wait a little longer. Often, we cannot realize the importance of something until it is done and have the opportunity to look back on it. When you asked me for another position, I told you that I needed someone at the camp I could trust. That is truer now than ever."

"Why does it matter so much? I am nothing more than a messenger boy. Running back and forth between your office and the camp."

"That's not true, Lutalo. You are my eyes and ears. I trust no one but you."

Louie said nothing, feeling like a child sitting in the giant overstuffed chair, unable to meet his uncle's gaze.

"Lutalo. I wanted to wait to tell you, although perhaps now is the time. Something big is coming soon. I cannot give you all the details just yet, but you must know that you will play an important role. This is the reason I have kept you there. I just ask that you wait a little longer. Please, have patience."

Louie looked to the wall, realizing there was no decision to be made.

"As you wish, Uncle," he whispered.

"Thank you, Lutalo. Soon enough, you will understand why."

CHAPTER NINE

Sid and Carson sat in their cramped office staring blankly at their computer screens. The room was just big enough for two desks pushed together, one faux-leather chair and a four-drawer metal security cabinet that was missing its padlock. Mounted on the wall between their desks was a single air conditioning unit circulating room-temperature air that smelled faintly of rotten eggs. The only other adornment was a government-issued clock hanging above the door. Sid and Carson looked up from their computers as the hands inched toward ten o'clock.

"Coffee break?" Sid asked.

The suggestion prompted a quick nod from Carson, eager for any excuse to escape the office. As they rose to leave, there was a knock at the door followed by Sergeant Goodwin poking his head into the office.

"Glad I found you. The ambassador just requested an urgent teleconference with General Foster. The colonel said you two should listen in."

"Any idea what it's about?" Sid asked.

"Nobody tells me anything, sir. The colonel just said to get you two right away."

Sid and Carson grabbed their notebooks and chased Goodwin across the yard. Colonel Kittredge was already in the conference room waiting for the meeting to begin. He snapped his fingers at Sid and Carson, pointing at the empty seats. A moment later Ambassador Roberts and General Foster appeared on the screen.

"Good morning, Bill," the ambassador said unenthusiastically.

"Claire, to what do I owe the pleasure? It seems like it's been a few months since any major crisis down there. Hopefully this time it's just a social call."

"You know how it is, Bill, there's always something interesting going on down here," she said, forcing a smile.

"Seems that way," the general agreed. "You know, Claire, I've been meaning to come down there for a visit to see you in person."

"Well, now might actually be a good time for that," the ambassador continued. "We've had a bit of tension in the relationship lately."

"Between you and me, or us and them?" the general said, eliciting a round of muffled guffaws from his staff.

Ambassador Roberts finally cracked a genuine smile. "Touché, Bill. But rest assured, I'm referring to the bilateral relationship with our friends here in DRoG. Right now, a bit of high-level engagement from you might help calm the waters a bit."

"Anything I should be worried about?"

"Hopefully not. However, I wanted to let you know that yesterday I received an invitation from the President's office to attend the dedication ceremony for the new airport expansion."

"Didn't they just start that project a month or two ago?"

"Correct. In fact, they broke ground just a few days after ordering the relocation of the village with the contaminated well."

"You mean the one they pinned on us?"

"Yes, that one," the ambassador confirmed.

"Wow, with friends like these…"

"Indeed. And believe it or not, they even had the gall to ask me to make some remarks at the dedication ceremony."

"Do you have a choice?"

"I'll be expected to make an appearance unless I can find a convenient excuse to send the chargé. In any case, I'm putting my foot down about making a speech. Even diplomacy has its limits," she sighed.

"I don't get it, Claire. Why the hell do they want us there for their little party after the stunt they pulled with the bad well?"

"That's probably all the more reason to invite us. It gives them some top cover. Not to mention a little reminder for the public about who was, quote-unquote, responsible for the village being moved. That way President Namono can bask in the glory of his new, utterly unnecessary runway without having to deal with any awkward questions about how it got done."

"Do we know what his plan is for the new airstrip?" Foster asked.

"Actually, I was hoping that you might tell me. The current airport isn't running anywhere near capacity. Even if tourist and business traffic doubled overnight, there's still no logical reason why DRoG needs a second runway. Not to mention all the extra ramp space they put in across from the passenger terminal. I was just wondering if you had any theories about that?" she asked.

"One second, Claire," the general said, flipping the mic to mute and conferring with his staff around the table. After a few minutes of discussion, Foster came back on the line.

"The regional counter-terrorism center."

"Bingo!" the ambassador said wryly. "That was my guess as well."

"But Claire, from what we're hearing out of the Pentagon, DRoG isn't even on the short list of finalists," the general countered.

"Right. We're hearing the same from Foggy Bottom. But then again, maybe President Namono thinks his odds are better than we do. No doubt he's aware that the infrastructure assessment is one of the key criteria in the final decision. Perhaps the runway expansion is a Hail Mary pass to get DRoG back into contention."

"Maybe," the general pondered. "But the announcement is just a month away. I'm not sure how much he can really influence the decision at this point. The Pentagon planners have been studying the basing options for the last eighteen months. Of course, the final decision will be up to the White House, so who knows what will happen, but if I were a betting man, I think DRoG is still a long shot."

"I'd tend to agree, but MoD may have different ideas. Sometimes it's hard to see what game they're playing. Sort of like this Hezbollah thing they keep pushing."

"We're still not seeing any evidence in that direction," the general confirmed.

"Neither are we. It could just be a red herring. But it certainly hasn't stopped them from putting a squeeze on some of the ex-pats around town. I am afraid that some of this activity is crossing the line."

"What do you mean?"

"Well, from down here, it looks more like a witch hunt than a counter-terrorism operation. However, given the climate in DC right now, no one has the stomach to call them on it. At least as long as the bombing investigation is still ongoing. The administration won't risk looking soft on terrorism or undercutting the Gisawians while we're still working with them to get Odoki. Too much is at stake."

The general nodded, thinking for a moment. "OK, Claire. My team will let you know if we hear anything more about new threats."

"Thanks, Bill. I appreciate the support. But before you go, there's one other thing that came up this week that I wanted to ask you about."

"Go ahead."

"Two days ago, we received an unusual cable from DC concerning the delivery of some new military equipment into DRoG."

Foster stared blankly into the screen, waiting for the ambassador to continue.

"The cable said that MoD is receiving temporary access to a reconnaissance platform and payload delivery system via an approved commercial vendor. We were asked to submit a customs clearance request on behalf of the contractor. Do you know anything about this?"

"Nope. First that I've heard about it," the general said.

"Interesting...," the ambassador said. "Apparently, the contractor providing the equipment is ESP. Aren't they the same guys running your camp down here?"

"Yup. And almost every other forward operating base in the world. But they also have some business with the Gisawians. I wouldn't be surprised if they've got some new contract deal with MoD. If I hear anything more about it, I'll be sure to let you know."

"Please do, Bill. Something about it smells a little fishy."

"Sure. Anything else, Claire? I'm about to run up against another meeting."

"No. That's it for now. And if you feel like coming down for a visit next week, I can save you a seat at the grand opening of the new runway."

"Hmm, my schedule may be a little tight, but thanks anyway," the general said, seeming eager to end the conversation.

When both parties dropped off the line, Colonel Kittredge turned to Sid and Carson. "What do you make of it?"

"Which part?" Sid asked.

"First, the runway," Kittredge clarified.

"The ambassador is probably right to be suspicious," Sid said. "DRoG has plenty of things to be spending money on. An airport vanity project should probably be pretty low down on that list. But then again, last year they borrowed fifty million from the Chinese for a new national soccer stadium. I'm guessing that also wasn't an urgent need for the welfare of the Gisawian people."

"What about the crackdown on the Lebanese shopkeepers? That doesn't seem a logical response to a bombing attack," the colonel asked.

"I agree. It doesn't add up. I asked Louie about it, but he didn't have much to say. He told me that the investigation falls under Police Intelligence, not MoD, so he's totally in the dark."

"Can you ask him again next time you see him?" Kittredge asked. "The general will want to be in the loop on this. He played it cool today with the ambassador, but I could tell that he didn't like being caught off guard."

"And what about that thing with ESP?" Sid added.

"Whatever it is, I'm guessing Slyker's fingers are all over it," Carson chimed in.

"Probably the case," Kittredge agreed, gathering up his things and preparing to leave.

"Sir, I don't want to overstep my bounds here," Carson interrupted as the colonel got up from the table. "But did you get the sense that General Foster knew a little more than he was letting on?"

Kittredge shrugged. "Gentlemen, that's above my paygrade. Unless we're given specific instructions to get involved, it's best to leave it alone. Let's keep focused on our own business. Any questions?"

Sid and Carson shook their heads as the colonel closed his notebook, signaling that the meeting had come to an end.

"OK. See you tomorrow at the staff meeting. Let's try to keep this one short for a change."

+++

The next morning Sid began the staff meeting with a slide showing a large map of DRoG marked with clusters of yellow stars.

"Sir, if I can direct your attention to the map, you can see here where I've highlighted several areas along the western border region. We received some new information from MoD suggesting the possibility of a high-level GLA leadership meeting taking place around this area in the near term."

The colonel took a moment to study the map. "Sid, that's a long way from where we've been conducting our recent raids. Why the major shift in the target area? Has something changed MoD's thinking about where Odoki may be operating?"

"It seems that way. Based on some recent detainee interrogations, Police Intelligence now suspects that Odoki may be hiding in a sanctuary location just across the border from this area. That's why they think our raids have been coming up empty for the last few months."

"So, what's so special about that location?"

"MoD believes that Odoki may be planning to cross the border around there sometime in the next few weeks for a rendezvous with his lieutenants. They asked us to focus all available collection assets on that zone."

"OK, but that's still a lot of terrain. What the hell are we supposed to be looking for?" Kittredge asked.

"If a meeting takes place, they expect that his men will likely move into position ahead of time to secure the area. Then wait there for him until he's ready. If that's the case, then we may be able to identify some activity around the meeting site in advance of the link up. It's a sparsely populated area. If anyone is out there wandering around, there's a good chance we could pick up some signs. Maybe this time we'll get lucky."

"I'll let the general know. He'll be happy to see some kind of progress. Anything else?" the colonel asked.

"Just one other thing. I finally received the imagery data on the suspected GLA cache sites in the western region. The ones that MoD has been bugging us about for months."

"It's about time," the colonel said. "Anything useful?"

"Maybe. It's hard to tell exactly what we're looking at. It's all low-resolution data from commercial satellites. The multispectral imagery doesn't give much detail, except to highlight areas where vegetation has been cut back or the soil recently overturned. But that's not necessarily a smoking gun for GLA activity. It could be any number of things, like subsistence farming or even wild animals digging up burrows."

"Well, we're giving them what they asked for. So, what's next? Are we authorized to hand it over?"

"Yes, sir. I'll give it to Louie later today. I expect that this may kick-start MoD's planning for the offensive."

"Excellent," Kittredge nodded. "We'll need to let General Foster know as soon as we hear anything about their timeline. You got anything else?"

"No, sir. That's it," Sid replied, handing the clicker over to Captain Burke and taking a seat.

"OK, Burke, what have you got?" the colonel said, his mood momentarily buoyed after hearing Sid's news.

Burke quickstepped to the podium and flipped to his first slide. A complicated scatter plot with a dozen different colored dots displayed across an unmarked x-y axis.

"Sir, as you can see here, we continue to see all-time highs for our mission recognition score."

"I can't see that at all, Burke!" the colonel said. "What the hell am I looking at?"

"My apologies, sir. This graph highlights the most recent public awareness tracking data. As of this week, Operation Righteous Protector is the number one trending operation across the department's entire portfolio. We're approaching the eightieth percentile on the mission recognition index. In the public affairs community that's considered the gold standard for sub-regional, limited-scope contingency operations."

"Eighty percent is the gold standard?"

"Yes, sir. The last twenty percent is virtually untouchable. They're considered a highly information-resistant audience."

"What does that mean?"

"Active avoiders of news or simply lacking a reality-based cognitive framework for processing our messaging."

"So, we're talking tin foil hat guys?"

"I'm not a clinician, so I don't want to draw any conclusions, but penetrating that last twenty percent is considered the Holy Grail of the business. In fact, it's the central pillar of the department's growth strategy. We're spending a huge chunk of the R&D budget trying to lower that threshold down to fifteen percent."

"There's an R&D budget for Public Affairs?"

Burke nodded with excitement. "The SCARPA program—Strategic Communications Advanced Research Projects Agency."

"Hmm, interesting," Kittredge said, still puzzling over the slide. "Why do you think we saw such a huge surge last week? We haven't had any major news on the operational side."

"I haven't finished crunching all the numbers yet, but I'm guessing its related to the media chatter over the investigation.

Probably rumors about the congressional committee preparing a memo accusing the White House of a cover-up."

"Covering up what?" Sid interrupted.

"That's not entirely clear; however, the administration is hitting back hard, doubling down on the fight against the GLA. Last week was the first time the president mentioned Odoki by name in over two years. I'm guessing that's what caused the spike."

"So, what's our strategy going forward?" Kittredge asked.

"Stay on message. Right now, any news is good news. We're fielding dozens of media requests every day. Print and television, local and national. Our social network platforms are getting more hits per hour than ever before. We're steering clear of the controversy over the investigation and deferring all those questions back to DC. Our core audience is not looking for a nuanced discussion of substantive policy issues, so there's no point in heading down that rabbit hole. We need to stay focused on top-line messaging."

"Good. That's exactly what the general wants. Don't overwhelm them with details," Kittredge said, nodding appreciatively. "Anything else?"

"One last thing. The sister city delegation just returned from Centerville following a three-week visit. The event generated a lot of good press. I'll be meeting with them soon to go over the final details before making a formal announcement and scheduling the signing ceremony."

"Icing on the cake!" Kittredge gushed. "Burke, I'm glad to see you finally hitting your stride. You've come a long way since the cheerleader incident. Let's keep up the good work."

"Thank you, sir," Burke beamed as he handed the clicker over to Sergeant Goodwin.

After the meeting, Colonel Kittredge asked Sid and Carson to stay. Once the room was empty, he slid a red file across the table.

"Take a look," he instructed. "It's a copy of the preliminary report from the investigators."

"That was quick. They just left last week," Carson said while he and Sid scanned through the pages. "Anything worth noting?"

"I guess they found what they were looking for. But during the investigation, a few other things came to light that were a bit unusual."

"Such as?" Sid asked.

"Either of you ever heard of an underground blog called Black Ops?"

Sid and Carson shook their heads.

"Turn to Annex C of the report. Apparently, it's a members-only website that's popular among military fanboys. The investigators stumbled across it after receiving an anonymous tip. Whoever made this blog is claiming to be an American soldier embedded with the Gisawian Rangers."

Sid flipped quickly through the pages to a series of screenshots with photos of Gisawian soldiers on patrol in the jungle accompanied by an unidentified white man.

"This is *really* weird shit," Carson mumbled.

"Not to mention a bit racist," Sid added. "It's like *Call of Duty* meets *Heart of Darkness*. But why are the investigators digging into this? It's more ridiculous than anything else. The guy doing this is clearly a dumbass but probably harmless."

"Turn to the last few pages," the colonel said.

The final series of photos depicted a mock interrogation, showing what appeared to be a captured GLA fighter, blindfolded and bound to a tree with a rope wrapped around his neck. The man was surrounded by angry-looking Gisawian soldiers brandishing weapons. Meanwhile, the anonymous white soldier, with his back turned toward the camera, appeared to be leading the interrogation."

"Oh shit…," Sid whispered, quickly flipping through the last few pages. "This will blow sky high if it goes public."

"Could it be one of Jorgenson's men?" Carson asked. "They're the ones on the ground with the Rangers."

"That was the obvious assumption," Kittredge explained. "The investigators went there first. But whoever was taking the pictures did a good job of concealing the identities. The guy's face is obscured in every photo. But after multiple interviews with Jorgenson's men, including a polygraph, they decided it wasn't any of them. The investigators are redirecting focus to personnel here on the camp."

"That makes no sense," Sid said. "Why would someone go to all that trouble?"

"I don't know, but they asked for our help to narrow down the search. They want this handled quietly. Nobody outside this room needs to know. I want you to go through the evidence in the package and let me know if you have any ideas."

"Got it, boss," Carson said. "Anything else?"

"Just one other thing. When the investigators were sniffing around, they did an audit of our network traffic. They noticed some unusual patterns of data flowing from our IP address."

"What was unusual about it?" Sid asked.

"It wasn't going out over the secure network and was happening at odd times of the day, and usually during the middle of the night."

"Probably just someone using a work computer for an erotic video chat with home," Carson guessed.

"That's what I thought too, but it was originating from here inside the conference room. You don't need to use a high-end, classified video-teleconference suite just to say hi to the kids. The connection was routed through an overseas VPN, as if the person doing it didn't want anyone tracing it back to the source."

"Strange," Sid said, suddenly more interested.

"The investigators want some answers, but it's not a high priority. For right now, they've got bigger fish to fry. But eventually, I'll need to give them some answers so we can close this thing out and move on."

"Sure, Colonel. We'll let you know," Carson promised as Kittredge got up and left the room. Once he was gone Sid put the report back in the envelope and looked across the table at Carson.

"What do you think?" he asked.

"About which one?"

"First, the blog," Sid clarified.

"It's Burke, no doubt," Carson said without hesitation. "I even recognized some of the so-called Rangers in the pictures. It's some of the DRoG soldiers who guard the front gate."

"Yeah, that was my guess too," Sid agreed. "Lord knows what Burke thought he was doing out there running around in the woods taking fantasy photos. He hides it well, but that kid is a freak."

"Seems to run in the family," Carson chuckled.

"So, what do we do about it?"

Carson rubbed his chin, thinking for a moment. "Nothing for now. It's clearly a stupid hoax. Not to mention a strange fetish. But having this thing blow open right now is not exactly what we need. Especially if this offensive is about to kick off. We've got to keep our eyes on the prize."

"Whatever that may be…," Sid sighed. "This thing is just getting crazier by the day. The sooner we're out of here, the better."

"Agreed, but now's not the time to blow the whistle. Especially since we're not one hundred percent sure it's him."

"Are you kidding?" Sid insisted.

"OK, OK. It's him," Carson conceded. "But for now, let's keep this between you and me."

"And what about the other thing?" Sid asked. "The stuff being beamed out of the conference room late at night."

"I have a theory, but it's too soon to say for sure," Carson said. "Give me a little time to dig around. I'll let you know."

+++

Later in the afternoon, Sid, Carson, Anna, and Louie all met at the Sujah Bean for coffee. After their drinks arrived, Sid reached into his backpack and pulled out an overstuffed manila envelope held together with heavy-duty wrapping tape. Sid put it on the table and pushed it toward Louie.

"It's what you've been waiting for," Sid said, nodding at the package. "The imagery showing the locations of the suspected GLA cache sites. Best not to open it here."

"Of course!" Louie said. "Thank you, Sid. I know it wasn't the easiest request to fulfill, but I can assure you it is greatly appreciated by my government."

"I hope it helps," Sid said.

"I'm certainly no expert, but isn't it kind of a longshot to premise a major military operation on a bunch of holes in the ground," Anna pointed out as Louie slipped the package into his backpack.

"Perhaps, but we don't have much else to go on," Louie explained. "The GLA are like ghosts. They disappear into the jungle whenever we get close. The minister has convinced the president that the only way to defeat them is by going after their logistics network. It may not be a perfect strategy, but it's the best we can do."

"And the interrogation reports…," Anna hinted.

"Don't worry, I didn't forget!" Louie said defensively. "But getting my hands on the original reports was a little more complicated than I'd expected. Fortunately, I have an old friend who works in the records department at Police Intelligence. He promised me that he would try to get copies."

"Don't worry, Louie. I know you're doing your best," Anna reassured him.

As she spoke, Sid winked and smiled mischievously across the table. Anna glared back, letting him know she was unamused by the insinuation.

"But please, can we just keep this between us at the table?" Louie asked, sipping his tea. "The reports are sensitive. It would be complicated to explain."

"No problem. Your secret is safe with us," Sid reassured. "Nobody rats out a member of the coffee club."

"So, Louie, now that you have the pictures, how long do you think until MoD moves ahead on the offensive?"

Carson asked. "Is President Namono really ready to make this happen?"

Louie shrugged his shoulders. "It's difficult to say. I've heard that the minister wants something soon. Between us, the rumors about your government pulling out of the mission has created pressure to accelerate the planning."

"I agree, the clock is ticking," Carson said. "If you don't mind, please let us know if you hear anything about the timeline. General Foster wants to know ASAP."

"I'm meeting with my uncle today and plan to give him the photos," Louie said, patting his backpack. "I should know more after that."

Just then Sammy appeared at the table with a plate of warm scones and the check.

"Wow, Sammy!" Sid exclaimed. "A new item on the menu?"

Sammy smiled, nodding excitedly. "Yes, sir. A free sample for my best customers."

"Oh, Sammy, you know me too well," Sid laughed. "I have a feeling these may become my new bad habit."

Sammy laid the scones on the table and tucked the bill underneath the plate. Carson and Louie both reached for it at the same time, Louie beating him by an instant.

"Please put it on my tab," Louie said, signing the slip and handing the paper back to the barista. As Sammy retreated to the hut, Louie noticed Anna staring at something on the table.

"What is it?" he asked.

"Your pen. It looks familiar. Isn't that the same fancy pen you left on the table for Sammy a few weeks ago?" she asked Carson.

Carson picked it up and looked at the logo etched along the side. "Tantalus Holdings," he read. "Yup. Same one. Did Sammy re-gift this to you?" he asked Louie.

"Of course not," Louie insisted with mock offense.

"Is Slyker trying to butter you up too?" Carson speculated.

"No, not Slyker," Louie insisted, taking the closer look at the pen and trying to jog his memory. "I'm pretty sure my uncle gave it to me. A few weeks ago, when I was in his office for a meeting."

"Any idea where he got it?" Anna asked, suddenly intrigued by the coincidence.

Louie shrugged. "I have no idea. The Ministry's acquisition and supply programs fall under my uncle's portfolio as deputy minister. He's always meeting with foreign businessmen and defense contractors. I suppose he got it as a gift during one of those meetings. His desk drawers are overflowing with that kind of stuff."

"Have you ever heard of Tantalus Holdings?" Anna pressed.

"No. Never."

"Sid, out of curiosity, do you have any way of checking them out? Maybe finding what kind of business they're involved in?" she asked.

"Nope. Not my line of work," Sid said, shaking his head. "I do military intelligence, not corporate spying. After being interrogated a few weeks ago by those investigators from DC, I've learned my lesson about sticking my nose into things that aren't my business. Sorry."

"Don't worry about it," Anna said. "I guess I can't blame you. Anyway, my Odoki research is a bit stalled right now. I have some time to look into it. Let me sniff around and see what I find."

"Great. I'll be waiting on the edge of my seat," Sid teased as he bit into a scone.

+++

After finishing at the café, Louie raced over to the MoD headquarters with the package from Sid. His uncle's secretary and the tired-looking colonel were surprised to see him when he appeared in the office without an appointment. Louie breathlessly explained that he had an important message for the deputy minister and needed to see him right away.

After a few minutes of waiting, Louie saw the red light blinking on the secretary's phone, signaling that the deputy minister was ready to see him. Without a word, she waved Louie toward the door and into his uncle's office.

"Uncle, I am sorry to come unannounced," Louie blurted as he rushed into the room. "But I have something very important."

His uncle waved him over to the chair in front of his desk.

"It is fine, Lutalo," his uncle reassured him. "I've finished my meetings for the day. What do you have that couldn't wait until next week?"

"The satellite pictures from the Americans. They finally arrived," he announced, pulling the thick folder from his backpack.

"Good. Very good." His uncle nodded, clearly happy at the news. "The minister will be pleased. We must take these to the planners right away so they can begin analyzing the information."

Louie handed the package to his uncle who opened it with a penknife. He browsed through the pages, grunting approvingly as he examined the images.

"They show all the areas with recent activity that has disturbed the ground," Louie explained unnecessarily. "Perhaps not enough detail to know exactly what is going on, but good enough to know where things are happening."

"It will be sufficient for our purposes," his uncle replied, still studying the pictures. "There are some things about the GLA that we understand but the Americans do not see. With these pictures, we should have more than enough information to deliver them a blow. I am confident the offensive will be successful."

"Yes, Uncle. I hope so," Louie said. "How soon do you think until it begins?"

Mugaba shook his head. "There are many factors to consider. Once the information is analyzed, then the minister will present a final plan to the president for approval. If he is satisfied, then we can begin our preparations. The challenge will be striking so many locations at once. We can only do this if we can retain the element of surprise. This will not be easy, Lutalo."

"No, Uncle, of course not," Louie agreed.

"However, it will not be enough just cutting them off at the feet. We must take the head of the snake at the same time."

"Odoki?" Louie asked, surprised to discover uncle was considering such an ambitious plan.

"We cannot miss another opportunity. If we attack the network without taking him down first, we may never get another chance. The strike against Odoki must start the offensive. From there, the rest will follow."

Louie was quiet, lost in thought as his uncle continued paging through the satellite images. Finally, he mustered the courage to speak.

"Uncle, may I ask a question?"

Mugaba nodded without looking up from the photos.

"I want to request reassignment to the field. If the army is preparing for the offensive, I want to be out there with the soldiers. Please, Uncle, give me a chance," he pleaded.

His uncle finally looked up from the pages, staring at Louie over his reading glasses.

"No. It is out of the question."

"But Uncle, I have done everything that you've asked!" Louie insisted, his voice quivering with emotion. "You cannot deny this. My place is with the soldiers, not sitting at a desk on the camp with the Americans."

"Lutalo, I am sorry, but there are things you don't understand. You will play an important role as these events unfold, even if you cannot see this now."

"How can you say this?" Louie stammered. "I am nothing more than an errand boy. My father would be ashamed if he could see me."

"No, he would not!" Mugaba snapped. "Do not forget what they say in the village. 'A good family eats from the same plate.' You are where you are for a reason. I cannot trust anyone else but you.

"But Uncle, what is this reason? You keep telling me this, but why can't I see it?"

Mugaba sighed deeply. "There are many things that you don't yet see, Lutalo. It is not your fault. You are a good man.

A good soldier. If your father were here, he would be proud of you. I have no doubt of that. But the world is not as simple as you wish to make it. Each of us has a role to play. Perhaps you do not care for your part. Or feel that it is unimportant. But I tell you, it is. Please, trust me."

"But can you just explain it, so I can understand?"

"Not yet. I am sorry. The reasons will become clear soon enough. All I can tell you is that you will play a critical part. Perhaps the most important one of all."

"How? By sitting at the camp with the Americans drinking coffee?" Louie said with exasperation.

"Don't be so sure," his uncle said with a smile. "Interesting things are happening, Lutalo. Just be patient a little longer."

Louie had lost the spirit to argue any longer, realizing that his uncle would never compromise. Without another word, he rose from the chair and turned toward the door.

"Lutalo. One more thing," Mugaba called after him.

"Yes, Uncle," he replied, resigned to whatever the request.

"The ceremony for the opening of the new runway. It is three weeks from now. Do you plan to be there?"

"I suppose. I hadn't really thought about it."

"You should go. The president and the minister will be there. I will keep a seat for you in the VIP section. It will be a grand show. You will not want to miss it."

Louie nodded obediently, then turned and walked toward the door.

CHAPTER TEN

Sid wobbled unsteadily on his feet, feeling lightheaded from the fumes of freshly laid asphalt. Rivulets of perspiration trickled down his neck, soaking through the collar of his uniform. Without the hint of a breeze, it felt twenty degrees hotter than when they left camp earlier that morning.

"For god sakes. How much longer until this thing starts?" Sid pleaded to no one in particular, dabbing his brow with his perspiration-soaked bandanna.

Carson looked down at his watch. "Forty-five minutes ago. Don't forget, we're on DRoG time."

"I can't take it anymore! We've been standing out here in the sun for almost two hours!"

Carson looked over at the rows of VIPs seated atop an elevated reviewing stand under the shade of a linen canopy. Directly to their front was an empty dais, awaiting the arrival of the guest of honor.

"Still no sign of President Namono," Carson reported, gazing off into the horizon.

Next to the seating area, a military band played half-heartedly, the musicians suffering under the weight of woolen uniforms and bulky instruments. Adjacent to the band, a large fest tent had been erected for a reception. White cloth-covered tables overflowed with bottles of sparkling wine, plates of finger sandwiches, hors d'oeuvres, and decorative pastries. A squad of waiters stood at the ready in starched, single-breasted serving coats and white gloves. Several unsmiling Gisawian soldiers were posted around the tent's perimeter, presumably to deter the curiosity of any non-VIP interlopers.

"Slyker looks all nice and comfy sitting there in the shade," Sid said, almost spitting out his name.

Carson pulled out a set of mini-binoculars from his pocket and scanned the faces in the crowd. It was mostly an assortment of Gisawian bigwigs. Politicians, businessmen, local celebrities, and generals all decked out in full regalia. At the far end of the first row, he spotted Ambassador Roberts, sitting by herself, concealing her face under the brim of an oversized silk sunhat.

In the middle of the second row, Carson saw Louie's uncle, the deputy minister. Next to him was Don Slyker, wearing a khaki linen suit, white shirt, baby blue tie, and expensive-looking Italian sunglasses. He was having a friendly chitchat with the deputy minister, occasionally checking his watch and looking out toward the end of the airfield.

"No one in the VIP section is sweating," Carson observed through the binoculars. "I think they must have blocks of dry ice hidden underneath the platform."

"What a load of shit!" Sid whimpered. "If this thing doesn't start in the next five minutes I'm leaving."

"Nice try," Carson taunted. "Colonel Kittredge said our attendance was mandatory."

"That's funny," Sid snapped. "Because I don't see him out here getting heatstroke."

"It's protocol, man. Someone had to represent the mission. That meant us."

"If our presence was so vital you'd think we might have at least rated a chair or an umbrella," Sid said.

Carson glanced over his shoulder back at the gaggle of other non-VIPs mingling around the edge of the runway. There was a platoon of bored-looking Gisawian soldiers who had spent the morning setting up the VIP seats and party tent. Some members of the local media chatted amongst themselves, apparently untroubled by the heat. A few bored-looking, low-level European diplomats were talking on their cellphones, carelessly tossing smoldering cigarettes butts around the aircraft refueling zone.

Suddenly, Carson saw a few of the Gisawian soldiers pointing off in the distance to where a dust cloud was rising beyond the perimeter fence. Carson lifted his binoculars and scanned the horizon, trying to identify the cause of the commotion.

"Looks like the wait is over," he reassured Sid.

By then the VIPs in the bleachers had spotted the approaching storm and rose to their feet in anticipation. A moment later a convoy of military vehicles raced into view, followed closely behind by several armored sedans. Two technical trucks with machine guns mounted on top skidded to a halt on either side of the reviewing stand. A squad of soldiers from the presidential guard leaped from the vehicles and formed a tight perimeter around the dais.

Right on cue, the military band struck up the Gisawian national anthem with renewed vigor while four S-Class

Mercedes sedans with blacked-out windows rolled to a stop in front of the reviewing stand. The front passenger doors opened and several thick-necked men in tight-fitting suits and reflective sunglasses emerged from inside. The lead man from the first sedan quickly assessed the situation and then gave an "all clear" sign to the others. Then one of them opened the rear passenger door of the middle sedan. The tip of a wooden walking cane appeared first, followed by the unsteady hand of President Namono struggling to pull himself from the bucket leather seat. The steady hands of two burly bodyguards lifted the octogenarian to his feet and ushered him toward the stage.

"Looks like he could drop dead at any moment," Carson whispered to Sid.

"Yeah, we've been saying that for two decades, but somehow he's outlasted six US administrations. I wouldn't bet against him making it seven," Sid replied.

As the band finished playing, the guards set President Namono on the podium like a celebrity wax figurine, staying close enough for quick intervention just in case a stiff breeze threatened to topple their charge. The president smiled and waved at the adoring VIPs, finally begging them to take their seats. As the crowd settled in, the president searched his suit jacket for the prepared remarks. He carefully flattened the pages on the podium, donned his glasses, and began reading the words in a raspy, barely audible voice.

"Friends, compatriots, distinguished guests. I welcome you to this celebration as we dedicate the opening of this magnificent new facility. Like our nation itself, this runway was built upon the ruins of good intentions…"

Carson glanced at Ambassador Roberts, her nose buried deep into the pages of the official program, immersed in some minutia of the ceremonial agenda. She tugged nonchalantly at the brim of her hat, deftly evading notice of the press pool photographers.

"But today, my friends, we are here to look forward, not backward," the president continued. "For the spirit of the Gisawian people is to make lemonade from lemons," he said, pausing patiently for laughter and polite applause.

"What we dedicate here today is more than just concrete and asphalt. It is the realization of a vision. A vision of our destiny. For the Democratic Republic of Gisawi to take its natural place as a leader of nations. Setting an example for all to follow by our spirit and ingenuity. What we have here before us is not only the region's longest improved runway surface, with state-of-the-air instrument landing systems, optimized for continuous all-weather operations of civil and military aircraft. It is also a symbol of peace and security."

"This runway demonstrates our openness to the world, as well as our solemn obligation to support the security needs of the entire region. And sadly, my friends, these needs are many. Even in this moment of celebration, we cannot forget the many dangers we face. In fact, we saw this with our own eyes just a few months ago, right here in our very own capital city. Of course, I am speaking of the cowardly bombings directed against our American friends and Police Intelligence headquarters. Those attacks were a dark reminder that even upon our peaceful streets, we can never be truly safe until those who wish us harm are defeated."

As the president bathed in a healthy round of applause, Carson noticed a small black dot appear in the sky, gradually expanding on the horizon with a dirty contrail in its wake.

"What the hell is that?" Carson asked as Sid looked up and noticed the object.

"Give me those!" Sid demanded, nearly ripping the binoculars from Carson's hands. "Holy crap…," he whispered as he locked the binoculars onto the target.

"What is it?" Carson demanded.

"That, my friend, is the An-225. The largest cargo aircraft ever built. There's only one in operation. Russians made it during the Cold War but never put them into full production."

"Damn," Carson said, marveling at the giant aircraft lumbered into the pattern. "Is it really as big as it looks?"

"Bigger. It can carry twice as much as a fully loaded 747. I think some Ukrainian transport firm rents it out for moving oversized loads," Sid said, handing the binoculars back to Carson. "It's the first time I've ever seen one except in photos."

"Why the hell is it here?"

As Carson asked the question, Sid glanced over at the VIP reviewing stand. Don Slyker was tapping his watch, grinning ear to ear as he whispered something to the deputy minister.

"I've got a pretty good idea…," Sid said, nodding over at the stands.

"Of course," Carson said, shaking his head. "I should have guessed."

The audience tittered with excitement as the massive aircraft settled onto final approach toward the new runway.

President Namono nodded with approval at the deputy minister before continuing his remarks.

"Today, we inaugurate the most capable multi-use airfield in the entire region. We will use this resource to access the most sophisticated technologies to assist us in our fight for peace and stability across the region. And we will offer these resources to any friend who is with us in this struggle. I will conclude by saying that very soon our government will announce details of a new military offensive. An operation that will eliminate, once and for all, the last remnants of the Gisawian Liberation Army and the scourge of Daniel Odoki. We have been burdened by this terror for too long, and soon it will end. I make this promise to you, the proud people of Gisawi."

The audience erupted in frenzied applause at the conclusion of the president's speech. Meanwhile, Ambassador Roberts slipped unnoticed from the platform into an awaiting staff car while everyone's attention was focused on the plane's arrival. The cheers of the crowds were drowned out by the earsplitting roar of six enormous turbo-fan engines as the jet touched down and taxied toward the podium.

"I think I'm getting a hard-on," Sid yelled at Carson as they stared in awe at the massive machine.

As the crowd pressed toward the edge of the runway, Carson saw the motorcade speeding away in a cloud of dust. The audience hardly noticed the president's departure as they scrambled for position, snapping selfies with the giant metal albatross as the backdrop.

Once the jet came to rest in front of the reviewing stand, Don Slyker walked confidently out onto the tarmac and greeted the pilots with a familiar handshake. A few minutes later, the airplane's hydraulic nosecone lifted toward the sky, revealing the cavernous cargo space inside. Once the wheel rails were lowered to the ground, a full-size tractor-trailer and several smaller trucks rolled from its belly out onto the tarmac. The vehicles were painted in metallic gray with the circular ESP corporate logo stenciled on the side. Once the convoy cleared the ramp Slyker exchanged a few words with the pilot, who then proceeded to lead the VIPs and local media on an impromptu tour of the plane.

"I don't know whether to love the guy or hate him," Sid said to Carson as they watched the scene unfold.

"I know," Carson sighed. "He's a jackass. But at the same time, it's hard not to admire the professionalism."

"So, you want to check it out?" Sid asked sheepishly.

"Are you kidding? No way in hell I'm missing this," Carson replied as they jogged out on the runway and joined the crowd scrambling into the belly of the aircraft.

+++

The next morning the staff shuffled into the conference room for the weekly meeting.

"Sorry to keep you all waiting," Colonel Kittredge announced, arriving late and taking his seat at the head of the table. "The general had some things to discuss. It seems that people are finally starting to pay attention to what we're doing down here. I want you all to keep that in mind going forward. We need to be on our 'A' game. No more fuck-ups. Everybody got that?"

The colonel waited patiently until satisfied with the round of nods and compliant murmurs.

"OK then, now that we've got that straight, let's get on with this. Sid. Carson," the colonel said, looking at them across the table. "Sounds like you guys had some excitement out at the airfield yesterday. Did everyone have a good time playing on the big, big airplane?" he said in mocking baby talk.

"Yes, sir. As requested, we represented the mission at the dedication ceremony," Carson said, playing it straight.

"Well, it also would have been nice if you two had bothered calling back here to give me some heads-up before Slyker's convoy showed up at the front gate."

"Sir, we knew as much as you did!" Sid insisted. "It was all hush-hush until those trucks rolled off the plane. Even Louie didn't know about it!"

Colonel Kittredge shook his head in disgust. "You know what, guys? Every now and then, I would just like to pretend that I'm still in charge here instead of being the last guy to know about everything. So I don't end up looking like an idiot, maybe you could indulge my little fantasy by providing just a little bit of useful information. Is that too much to ask? What do you think, guys?" he begged sarcastically.

"Sir, we were in the dark on this one too," Carson said in Sid's defense. "But now that the cat is out of the bag, we should able to stay on top of things."

"Well, I sure hope so. I imagine it should be a wee bit easier now that ESP has set up their entire command center just on the other side of this wall. Keep up the great detective work, guys."

"Yes, sir. We'll do our best to keep you in the loop," Carson promised. "I can give you a quick rundown of what we know now."

"By all means, please do…," Kittredge begged.

"Yes, sir. Yesterday after the ceremony, ESP downloaded all their equipment next to the new runway and started flight line activities. They set up an integrated air operations center with the flight control and targeting cells at the camp. This morning they began initial equipment checks of the satellite links and control systems. Once those checks are complete, next week they plan to begin the initial flight tests over at the airport."

"What's the timeline to full operational capability?"

"That depends. The critical factor is the training piece."

"How much training can there be? ESP is running the entire show. In fact, I'm not even sure why we're here anymore!" Kittredge fumed.

"ESP does almost everything, except pull the trigger. They won't go operational until the LTA has been fully trained on the equipment and launch sequence protocols."

"LTA? What the hell is that?" the colonel asked impatiently.

"Sorry, sir. It's a proprietary acronym. Local Targeting Authority."

"Right, of course. How silly of me not to know that. And who might this person be?"

"Uhhh, Slyker didn't tell you?" Carson muttered.

"No! Since when did Slyker become my source for situational awareness? Isn't that why you guys are here sitting around this table?"

"Yes, sir. Louie is the TLA. He just found out last night."

"For the love of god…," the colonel moaned, burying his face into his hands. "So, you're telling me that Louie

Bigombe, our liaison officer, is now in charge of the entire operation?"

"No, sir. Not strictly in charge," Carson clarified. "However, legally speaking, he is the designated local authority empowered to make the final decision on pulling the trigger. According to ESP's targeting protocol, the physical act of launching the warhead must reside with an authorized LTA. Louie was designated as that last night by order of the DRoG minister of defense."

"So, you're telling me that Louie is sitting next door right now in that geodesic dome, learning how to launch a missile from a drone?"

"Yes, sir. That's what one of the ESP technicians told me while we were standing in line for coffee at Sujah Bean. They've already started running him through the ropes. He'll spend the next few days on equipment familiarization followed by some digital simulations. Once he's comfortable with the protocols, then they'll get an actual bird up in the air and take him through a week of basic flight operations. They'll gradually increase the complexity of the mission profile to include running multiple strike scenarios. His final check ride involves a full-blown attack simulation against a mock-up target somewhere out in the jungle. Once Louie passes that final training gate, then it's just a waiting game until we get some actionable intel pointing us to Odoki."

"Jesus H. Christ…," the colonel muttered. "I can't believe what I'm hearing. So, what's my role in all this?"

The table was quiet as the colonel looked around to each officer in turn. After what felt like an eternity, Carson finally spoke up.

"Sir, technically speaking, there is no change to your authorities as commander of Operation Righteous Protector. Our mission here remains the same."

"Well, if you ask me, it sounds like Slyker just took over this mission!" Kittredge said, staring across the conference room table littered with half-empty cups of coffee and crumbs of freshly baked scones. The colonel closed his eyes, taking a deep breath before turning back to Carson.

"OK. What's next on the agenda?"

"Public Affairs update."

"Right. OK, Captain Burke, maybe you can provide us with some good news," the colonel said with forced serenity.

"Good morning, sir. It's been a busy week on the data front, and we're seeing some increased volatility inside the latest M-RAT numbers."

"Volatility?"

"Yes, sir. While our overall mission recognition score remains off the charts, we've been detecting some divergence within the public perception feedback data."

"English, Burke! Please...," the colonel begged. "Just tell me what the hell is going on."

"Well, sir, like I said, more people than ever are aware of our mission."

"That's good news, right?"

"One would think so. However, at the same time, we're also seeing a polarization of public opinion. Apparently, we've become something of a lightning rod at home. That's where we're getting the statistical variance in the favorability response scores."

"You mean people are turning against us? I thought our

ratings were sky-high after the bombings and the president's statement about Odoki. What happened?"

"Unfortunately, it's hard to attribute these short-term sentiment shifts to any single variable. Popular opinion can be fickle. And it's not necessarily correlated with anything happening here on the ground."

"OK, Burke, I get that. But can you at least tell me who's supporting the mission and who's not?"

"Yes, sir. We've got a good read on the profile of our core supporters. In a nutshell, the pro-ORP demographic is strongly correlated with high-volume viewing of certain cable TV news programs."

"What? Why on earth does the Army track what TV channels people are watching?"

"Mostly as a proxy for patriotism. The data is used for precision recruiting."

"OK, then what demographic is not supporting our mission?"

"At the risk of oversimplifying, it could be described as 'urban,'" Burke said, making air quotes with his fingers.

"Urban? What does that mean?"

"Young, male, non-Caucasian."

"They don't like the mission? What the hell do they have against it?"

"That's what we're trying to figure out. The best we understand, Odoki seems to have attracted something of a following among this particular demographic."

"Warlord fanboys?" Kittredge said in disbelief.

"Yes, sir. I suppose you could call them that. It came to light last week when our SMART unit detected a pro-Odoki video going viral on the Internet."

"SMART unit? Should I even ask?"

"Social Media Analysis and Response Team. They're the Navy SEALs of the Public Affairs community."

"Right. So anyway, you're saying that this video is somehow causing people to turn against our mission?"

"Yes, sir. A rap video, to be specific. The SMART unit tagged it for heightened surveillance, given the potential risk to our strategic communications campaign."

"So, you're telling me that rap videos are now considered legitimate military threats?"

"Yes, sir. Information is a weapon. We can't ignore direct assaults against our narrative any more than we would overlook an IED outside our gate. It would be a dereliction of duty. The video in question was intentionally provocative and a willful misrepresentation of US policy objectives vis-à-vis DRoG."

"So, this rap video, or whatever it is, has been under surveillance? What does that even mean?" the colonel asked.

"The SMART unit does dynamic meme monitoring and real-time assessment of trending informational threats against our narrative. We use this information to isolate adversarial content and conduct counter-proliferation."

"Then you've seen this video?"

"Yes, sir. And personally, I would not recommend it. I was unfamiliar with the so-called artist. A gentleman by the name of de chisel."

"Let me see it," Kittredge demanded.

Burke hesitated. "Sir, this individual is clearly attempting to exploit a complex national security crisis for the purposes of self-aggrandizement and personal gain. Viewing this shameless propaganda only serves to legitimize his message and undermine US policy in the region."

"Cut the shit, Burke. Bring it up. Now!" the colonel ordered.

At the computer terminal, Sergeant Goodwin typed the name "de chisel" into the search engine. Within a few seconds, he found multiple links to the video. After navigating to the site, the video opened with an image of a man dressed in combat boots, cargo pants, and a T-shirt emblazoned with a black-power fist superimposed over an outline of Africa. He was flanked by half a dozen women of ambiguous ethnicity, standing in a darkened alleyway, similarly attired except for the undersized leather bikini tops in place of the T-shirt. When Goodwin started the video, the women broke formation into a synchronized gyration as de chisel began rapping to the beat of a thunderous bass.

Keeping my profile low key
Playing it cool like Odoki
A ghost in the jungle who can't be caught
Renegade motherfucker that won't be bought
Out conjuring witches, gathering bitches
A chocolate messiah turned into pariah
An outlaw with an AK
Turning it into a payday
Out representing like a black Jesse James
Confusing and confounding the white man's games
Living like a king in an African dream
Evading, retrograding, never abdicating
So I'm calling my brothers in America
It's time to get whitey out of Africa...

"That's enough! Goodwin, shut it down!" the colonel demanded.

"It just goes on and on from there," Burke interjected as the sergeant cut the video. "There's no redeeming artistic value whatsoever. Nevertheless, it's generated quite a buzz in the alternative media. As well as sparking numerous street protests against our involvement here in DRoG."

"Is the Pentagon treating this as a high-priority threat?" the colonel asked.

"Yes, sir. In fact, we're running aggressive counter-messaging intended to retake the informational high ground."

"A competing rap video?"

"No, sir. Infomercial. It is a more familiar format with our target demographic."

Kittredge nodded. "Good. Keep me informed on how this plays out. Anything else?"

"No, sir. Not really...," Burke said, hesitating. "Just a minor snag with the Sister City campaign."

"Nothing significant, I hope. I already told the general all about it. He is looking forward to the big announcement."

"Yes, sir. I'm confident we can resolve the issues and move forward ASAP. The local delegation here just requested some additional time to study the proposal."

"What's there to study? You just put up a sign up in front of the village and take a few pictures of happy Gisawians waving to their new friends in America. That's all there is to it," the colonel said, suddenly regretting asking the question.

"Well, it should be that simple!" Burke said defensively. "The Centerville Chamber of Commerce spent ten thousand dollars bringing the village delegation over for the visit. Believe me, they are not exactly thrilled with the delay."

"What information are the Gisawians asking for?"

"It's a bit academic. Not worth taking everyone's time," Burke insisted.

"Where else have we got to be?" the colonel sighed.

"The villagers had some concerns with the optics. The chief wanted to explore other partnership opportunities before committing to Centerville."

"You mean they're looking for a better deal?" Sid blurted out, barely suppressing a smile.

"Not a better deal!" Burke snapped. "They simply wanted additional information regarding Centerville's development statistics. It's just a matter of context. The delegation had some unrealistic expectations about life in the US. It's not uncommon among native peoples whose understanding of America is derived largely from pop culture."

"They were expecting Baywatch, PA?" Sid snickered.

"No, they were just surprised by a few things they saw during their visit. They've asked for some statistics on how Centerville ranks against several UN development benchmarks. It's just a formality. We're gathering the information now and expect to close the deal once the village elders are able to review the data."

"OK, thanks, Burke," the colonel said, eager to end the discussion. "I'll let the general know that everything's still on track. Keep me informed…"

The meeting concluded, the colonel signaled for Sid and Carson to stay while the others left the room.

"OK, gentlemen, the investigators haven't forgotten about that blog thing or our mysterious midnight web surfer. Did you two dig anything up yet?"

Sid and Carson exchanged glances, waiting for the other to reply.

"Nothing yet, sir," Carson finally blurted out. "We went through all the blog posts. Whoever made it was really careful not to leave any clues."

"Come on!" the colonel insisted. "How many people could it be? Don't you have any ideas?"

"Sir, given the nature of the subject matter, this could be a pretty serious offense. We don't want to jump to any conclusions," Sid chimed in, feeling guilty for putting Carson on the spot.

"OK, OK," Kittredge relented. "What about the data traffic coming from the command center."

"That one should be a bit easier," Carson explained. "Only a few people have access to the headquarters building. We'll check the access control system and cross-reference the entries with the dates of the transmissions. I'll talk to Slyker and see if his technical guys can give us a printout of the logs then we should be able to narrow down the list. We'll let you know as soon as we have an idea."

"OK, thanks," the colonel said. "Speaking of Slyker. I want you to keep an eye on him. He's been playing fast and loose around here. Whether he likes it or not, I'm still the one in charge. Let me know if you see anything out of the ordinary."

"Will do, sir," Carson promised as the colonel got up and left the room.

Sid waited for the door to close before turning to Carson. "So, was there a particular reason why you didn't say something about Burke being behind that blog?"

"Louie still needs to talk to the gate guards in the photos and see if they fess up. If they pin it on Burke, then there's nothing more to discuss. I'll take it straight to the colonel."

"OK then," Sid said, looking down at his watch. "Coffee?"

"Sure. We were supposed to meet Anna there a half-hour ago," Carson said, getting up from the table.

At the café, they found Anna waiting at their usual table, flipping through a local newspaper and sipping a cup of tea.

"Long meeting?" she asked, looking up from the paper.

"Not the worst," Sid said, trying to look on the bright side.

"Sorry I didn't wait," she said.

"No problem," Carson said, waving for Sammy's attention.

"So, I see there was some excitement out at the airfield yesterday," Anna said, holding up the local newspaper and the front-page picture of the giant cargo plane landing on the new runway.

"Yeah, it was quite a show," Carson chuckled. "All courtesy of Don Slyker. It was a bit over the top, but the locals were eating it up."

"I'll say," Anna agreed. "It was on the cover of almost every newspaper in Africa this morning. I guess it's not too often that the world's largest airplane inaugurates a new runway. I also spotted an unfortunate picture of Ambassador Roberts on page two, along with an exhaustive exposé of how you guys poisoned the village before the government bulldozed it for the new runway."

"Wonderful," Sid said, shaking his head.

"So, it seems like Slyker brought quite an entourage with him," Anna said, nodding at the caravan of pods, tents, generators, and satellite dishes filling the courtyard next to the Sujah Bean. "Are you guys planning a party or something?" she asked sarcastically.

"Anna, you know we can't discuss operational details. All that stuff is top secret," Sid said, suddenly turning serious.

"Oh, don't worry, Sid. Louie already told me everything," she said between sips of tea.

"What the fuck?" Sid exploded. "You're not cleared for that information."

"Come on, Sid! It's not like you guys are any good at keeping secrets," she insisted, waving her hand at the high-tech encampment next to the café. "Besides, President Namono already let the cat out of the bag yesterday at the airfield. He basically announced the offensive to the entire world. What's the big secret that you're still trying to keep?"

"Whatever," Sid fumed. "Your boyfriend should still keep his mouth shut."

"What, are we back in grade school now, Sid? Grow up. Louie's not my boyfriend. And besides, you should be more appreciative of his help. This morning he gave me copies of all the original interrogation reports."

Sid sat up in his chair, suddenly forgetting about the breach of security. "No kidding? That's great. What's in them?"

"Calm down," Anna insisted. "It's almost three hundreds of pages of handwritten notes by someone with extremely poor penmanship. I haven't even had time to look at them yet. It's going to take me at least a week or two just to figure out what's what."

"Well, we're running out of time," Carson hinted. "We

need anything we can get that might tell us where Odoki is meeting his lieutenants. That is if that story's even true."

"I can't promise I'll figure it out just by looking through a bunch of old interrogation reports, but I'll do what I can."

"What about your other mystery?" Sid asked.

"Hmm, remind me again what we're talking about?"

"The mythology guy. What's his name? Tantalus?" Sid reminded her.

"Oh yeah. Unfortunately, I didn't find out very much. As far as I can tell, Tantalus Holdings is just some off-shore holding company registered in Mauritius. I asked a lawyer friend back in the states to do a database search, but nothing much turned up."

"So much for your conspiracy theory," Carson consoled.

"Almost nothing," Anna clarified. "He did come across one interesting tidbit. Tantalus Holdings was listed on a public document filed by the Chinese engineering firm that just did the runway expansion project."

"That's interesting," Sid said. "So, maybe there's a local connection after all. I'll ask Louie if any of his contacts over at MoD have ever heard of it."

"I guess it couldn't hurt," Anna agreed. "Speaking of Louie. Have you guys spoken with him recently?"

Sid and Carson both shook their heads.

"I think his uncle has been keeping him busy over at the Ministry," Sid guessed. "Why do you ask?"

"No reason, really. I know he's been busy. But the few times I've seen him, he just hasn't seemed like himself."

"What do you mean?" Sid pressed.

"I don't know," she said, shaking her head. "He just seems...preoccupied."

"I can't really blame him, given everything that's going on," Carson said. "He had this whole thing dumped in his lap last night with no warning."

"But it's more than that," Anna said. "His mood has been off for a few weeks. I think he had an argument with his uncle. He won't say much about it, but I could tell something happened."

"Hmm," Sid murmured. "Now that you mention it…"

"Anyway, just keep an eye on him, will you? Make sure he's all right."

"Sure. You bet," Sid agreed.

"Thanks," Anna said, getting up to leave the table. "Sorry for cutting out early but I've got a pile of interrogation reports to start working through. I'll let you guys know if I find anything interesting," she promised, grabbing her backpack and heading off toward her quarters.

+++

Later that the day Carson wandered through the maze of prefab tents and shipping containers that served as ESP's mobile command center. He was looking for Slyker and eventually found him standing outside one of the gray geodesic domes checking messages on his cell phone. Slyker looked up and smiled when Carson walked up.

"Long time, no see," Slyker said, offering out a hand.

"I was at the airport a few days ago for the ceremony. You probably just didn't notice me standing out there in the cheap seats."

"Oh, sorry about that. I was a little busy escorting the VIPs around."

Carson shrugged. "You put on quite a show. President Namono seemed pretty happy before he zoomed off in his motorcade."

"It went pretty well," Slyker said modestly. "The owners of the plane owed me a favor. I've thrown them some business over the years, so they gave me a nice discount on the hourly rate."

"Seemed like a bit of an overkill given the cargo," Carson observed, nodding at the modular camp.

"Yeah, between you and me, the plane was totally unnecessary," Slyker conceded. "We could have easily fit two or three of these expeditionary packages into that thing, but the president wanted to generate some buzz for the runway expansion."

"I didn't realize it was such a high priority."

"Listen, Carson, here's a little bit of friendly advice. Don't take these guys for fools. They've got a plan for this country. The runway is only a small part of it. That was just a little bit of free marketing."

"To who?"

Slyker shrugged. "Anyone who's listening. Capacity creates its own opportunity."

"But a runway expansion? That seems like an expensive way to attract foreign investors."

"Hey, if you want to mingle with the players you've got to look the part. An underutilized ten-thousand-foot runway with extra ramp space is like putting on an Armani suit. It shows people that you're there to do business."

"You make it seem like some kind of big conspiracy."

"'Conspiracy' is a strong word. I'd probably just chalk it up to misaligned incentives."

"How do you mean?"

"Put it this way, weren't you a little surprised when those Chinese bulldozers showed up just two days after the Gisawian government relocated that village with the poisoned well?"

"Yeah, now that you mention it…"

"Exactly. So, I'd say that was a curiously well-executed operation. In my experience, things like that don't happen by mistake at this latitude. Now, I don't claim to know anything more about the runway project than you do. However, I do know this much. The Chinese don't break ground on a major infrastructure project unless they've got buy-in behind the scenes."

"So, you think it was all planned out ahead of time?"

"Well, let's not give them too much credit. But I will say that our friends here are quick to seize upon an opportunity when they stumble across it. I'm guessing that the village was going to be moved one way or another to make way for that runway. They just went for the path of least resistance. Blame it on Uncle Sam, then hire the Chinese to do the dirty work."

"It all seems a bit Machiavellian."

"Confucius once said, 'When your goal is blocked, do not adjust the goal, adjust your route to get there.'"

"Did he really say that?"

"I have no idea, but it sounds good. All I'm saying is that the runway project is particularly well-timed to impress potential suitors."

"I suppose you mean the new counter-terrorism support base?"

"It's no small beans, my friend. Any kleptocrat worth his salt would love to have that little prize land in his backyard.

Believe me, that's one game I do know. Those bases are the gift that keeps on giving. The local cronies get a nice cut of the sub-contracting, plus plenty of opportunities for skimming some cream off the top. With a deal like that, you can buy plenty of friends when you really need them. You probably won't even need to bother rigging the next election. It'll already be in the bag long before international monitors show up to babysit ballot boxes."

"Wow, what a little slice of paradise we have here."

"Fair enough. But before you start acting all high and mighty, just remember who brought the keg to the party. Besides, it could always be a lot worse."

"How's that? Everything you're describing already seems bad enough."

"Listen, Carson, this place isn't perfect by any stretch of the imagination. But on the other hand, look around here," Slyker said, waving his hand at nothing in particular. "Nobody's dying in the streets. Most of the kids are going to school and have enough to eat. Sure, not everybody's getting a fair shake. But that's a sad fact of life no matter where you go. Hell, I'm living proof of how the gods can fuck with you for no apparent reason."

"So, you're just saying that we should go along to get along? Look the other way while we get played by the locals?"

"I'm not saying that exactly. But you've got to ask your-self, what price are you willing to pay to fix it? Is it really worth toppling the whole apple cart just to dig out a few pieces of rotten fruit at the bottom? If you recall, we've tried that a few times, and it hasn't worked out so well."

Carson shrugged but said nothing.

"Don't worry, it's a rhetorical question. There's no right answer. I guess when you've been working down here as long as I have, you start getting comfortable with ambiguity."

"Then maybe that's a sign it's time to go."

"Could be…," Slyker pondered. "Anyway, I hope there are no hard feelings about that thing with the general. I just needed to get my foot in the door. And at that moment, you were my best option."

"I'm over it," Carson grumbled. "If it wasn't me then I guess you would have figured out some other way to get it done."

"Hey, business is business," Slyker said with a shrug.

"No doubt. But since we're on the topic of favors, maybe you could do one last one for me," Carson hinted.

"Such as…"

"Remember that run-in you had with Jorgenson outside the gym?"

"Oh, you mean when he threatened to detach my limbs from my body? Yeah, I sort of recall that interaction," Slyker said.

"Right. Anyway, he seemed a little defensive about something you said."

"Listen, I'm not getting involved," Slyker said, shaking his head.

"I'm not asking you to go mano a mano with the guy. Just tell me what he's up to."

"Why do you need to know?"

"I can't go into that. Just like how you couldn't tell me about the reason you needed to see the general," Carson said, waving at the prefab village behind Slyker.

"OK, OK, simmer down," Slyker begged. "But I'm telling you, it's not what you think."

"How do you know what I think?"

"Trust me. This thing has never entered your mind," Slyker assured him.

"Try me," Carson said, beginning to lose patience.

"Swedish meatball. That's all I'm going to say."

"Are you fucking kidding me?" Carson fumed. "Is that some kind of joke?"

Slyker shook his head. "That's all you're getting. And it didn't come from me. That guy is a maniac. I'm not taking any chances."

"Jesus," Carson sighed. "This is ridiculous."

"Sorry," Slyker shrugged. "Anything else I can help you with? Besides that."

Carson turned and started walking away when he remembered the conversation at the café with Anna.

"Tantalus Holdings. What do you know about it?" he called back to Slyker.

"Never heard of it."

"What do you mean you never heard of it? You gave me a goddamn Mont Blanc pen with their logo on it!"

"Oh, that? I don't have any idea where I got it. Honestly, I've got piles of that shit in my office."

"Louie has the same exact pen. Does that ring a bell?"

"Hmm, maybe. It's possible that I picked it up from his uncle during a meeting over at MoD. Really, I'm not trying to bullshit you, Carson. I just don't remember."

"OK. One last question. Any idea who signed that contract for the runway expansion?"

"Nope. The Gisawians like to keep those things pretty opaque. It makes accounting easier."

"Do you mind asking around a bit? I'd be curious to know more."

"Sure. But between you and me, I'm not pushing this too hard. ESP does a lot of business down here. If you go poking your nose too much into their business, it kind of hurts the relationship, if you know what I mean. Due diligence can be considered impolite among friends."

"Yeah, I get it. But if you come across something, let me know. I don't consider us even yet."

"Sure. You got it, boss."

Just as Carson was about to leave, he remembered one last thing.

"Slyker. You know Louie pretty well, don't you?"

"Sure. I wouldn't call us best pals, but I've known him for a while."

"How's he doing?"

"Great. He's diving right into the training. He should be ready to go in no time. But between you and me, it doesn't really matter," Slyker confided.

"What do you mean? Isn't he the one pulling the trigger if we find Odoki."

"Yeah, sure. But I could teach a goldfish to do that in about five minutes. The training program is mostly about keeping the lawyers happy. The client needs to demonstrate functional awareness of the platform's capabilities before we hand them the keys. Think of it as a liability waiver."

"Man, you guys really make sure to cover your asses, don't you?"

"Hey, this is war. Or something sort of like it. It's no place for amateurs."

"Yeah, I'll be sure to keep that in mind," Carson said over his shoulder as he turned and walked away.

CHAPTER ELEVEN

Two weeks later, the entire staff was packed into the conference room. The mood was a mixture of anxious anticipation and subdued revelry—like a college football kick-off party in a Midwestern suburban basement. But instead of a pregame marching band, the big screen at the front of the room showed a live feed from an airborne video camera cruising at ten thousand feet over the patchy, subtropical forest.

The staff mingled around the table, chatting and sipping complimentary cups of Sammy's special roast. They nibbled on banana fritters, vegetable samosas, and fried plantains, while an untouched fruit sculpture sat in the middle of the table. When Colonel Kittredge walked through the door, he froze in disbelief, waiting for someone to acknowledge his presence.

"Goddammit!" he finally exploded after a moment of standing in the doorway unnoticed. His finger quivered at the trays of food and cups covering the conference room table. "This is a military operation, not a fucking dorm room movie night! Get that shit off the table. Now!"

Like scolded teenagers, the staff scrambled to clear away the snack trays while Colonel Kittredge threw his notebook on the table and took his seat.

"Bring me up to speed on the situation," he said.

Sid, recognizing his cue, moved to the front of the room, discreetly placing a large chai mocha latte under the podium and grabbing the laser pointer.

"Good evening, sir. I'd like to direct your attention to the image on the monitor."

"Just tell me what I'm looking at. It's too damn dark to see anything."

"Roger, sir. Let me switch to the thermal infrared camera. That might be a little easier to make things out."

Sid nodded to Sergeant Goodwin, who was sitting at the computer terminal controlling the presentation. A moment later, the frame toggled to a grainy, false-color image, only slightly better than the first.

"I'm still not seeing anything," the colonel said.

"It's mostly forested terrain. Not a whole lot to see," Sid explained. "The platform is about five minutes away from the mock-up village that will be the target for tonight's exercise. If all goes well, this should be the final certification check ride for the Local Targeting Authority."

"So, Louie is behind the controls right now?" Kittredge asked.

"Yes, sir, so to speak. He's next door in the targeting cell. Once the platform enters the engagement area, I'll have Sergeant Goodwin patch us into the audio channel. We can follow along with the cross-talk between mission control and the targeting cell."

"He's actually going to launch a missile?"

"Yes, sir, it's the real deal. Everything tonight is meant to be an exact simulation for when we get Odoki in the crosshairs."

"You mean *if* we get Odoki," Kittredge corrected.

"Yes, sir, of course."

"Speaking of that, what's the latest from MoD?"

"Based on the most recent reports, MoD still believes that he's planning to cross the border sometime soon. But until that happens, there's not much we can do. None of DRoG's neighbors are willing to grant authorization for the drone to across the border. Even if we knew where he was hiding, we couldn't touch him on the other side. At least not without causing an international incident."

"Good call to hold off on that. Instigating an African border war is not what I need on my resume when I start looking for work after the Army," Kittredge said. "How long until they think Odoki will make his move?"

"It's anyone's guess. He certainly won't be advertising his movements. But MoD has reason to believe that it could be soon. A few patrols have detected some unusual activity over the last few weeks in an area about fifty kilometers east of the border."

"What kind of activity?"

"Small groups of armed men moving around an area where there aren't many villages. The region is known as a hotbed of support for the GLA, although it's been relatively quiet lately. Based on the satellite imagery we gave MoD, there appears to be a high concentration of suspected digging sites around the area. The Gisawians think that GLA fighters may be using them to stockpile weapons and supplies in preparation for new attacks."

"So, that's why they think Odoki is coming across now? To launch a new offensive?"

"Yes, sir. At least, that's their theory. The government has a minimal presence in the area; however, Police Intelligence still has a few sources in some of the nearby villages. They're probably going to be our best chance of getting a tip when Odoki makes his move across the border."

"OK. So, assuming Louie gets certified tonight, then it's just a waiting game?"

"Yes, sir. Basically, that's it. ESP's ground crew over at the airport can load the warheads and launch the platform in less than thirty minutes from notification. Unfortunately, it is a damn slow flyer. Depending on the target location, it could take us a few hours to get over an engagement area along the western border. On the bright side, the platform has almost thirty hours of flight time on a full tank of gas. If we suspect that Odoki has moved into an area, we should have plenty of time to fly around looking for him."

As Sid finished his explanation, everyone's attention turned to the screen. The drone's camera showed a break in the ocean of vegetation. A few small buildings and several parked cars came into view.

"OK. That's the mock-up village," Sid said. "They should be getting ready to start the targeting protocol. Sergeant Goodwin, please patch into the audio so we can monitor the operation."

A second later the speakers crackled with voices on the radio.

"This is Flight Ops. Trigger Man, how do you read us?"

"Flight Ops, this is Trigger Man. I read you loud and clear," came Louie's voice through the speaker.

"Trigger Man, please be advised that the platform has entered the engagement area. We are moving into a holding pattern at an elevation of nine thousand feet. Skies are clear with thirty percent illumination. Winds are west-southwest at four knots. Barometric pressure steady with favorable conditions expected for the next three to four hours. Vegetation in the engagement area is sparse with few line-of-sight obstructions. At this time, there is no observable civilian activity inside the engagement area. We assess minimal risk for collateral damage. I repeat, minimal risk for collateral damage."

"Roger, Flight Ops. This is Trigger Man. I read you loud and clear. Request permission to arm the warhead."

"Roger, Trigger Man. Permission granted."

"This is Trigger Man. The arming sequence has been initiated," Louie said in an emotionless monotone.

Seconds later, a voice from the operations center came back to the line.

"Trigger Man, this is Flight Ops. We confirm that the warhead is armed. We will maintain a holding pattern at this elevation. We are now turning mission lead over to the targeting cell."

A new voice cracked on the line. "All stations, this is the targeting cell. Initial analysis suggests a meeting of high-level GLA operatives. We detect three vehicles. Two cold, one hot. We estimate five to seven military-aged males occupying the main structure. Possibly two additional MAMs in the smaller structure approximately fifty meters to the northeast of the main building."

The colonel turned and looked at Sid, clearly surprised to see several active heat signatures moving around in the target area.

"Goats...," Sid said, reading his mind. "They're using them to calibrate the thermal sensors," he added as targeting protocol continued.

"Trigger Man, this is the targeting cell. Visual analysis indicates both structures are likely made of unreinforced wood siding and thin-gauge metal roofing panels. We do not anticipate any problems for warhead penetration or munition effectiveness. All other signatures indicate a good target. Trigger Man, you are cleared to engage when ready."

"Roger, targeting cell. This is Trigger Man. I read, clear to engage when ready. Please confirm."

"Trigger Man, this is the targeting cell. That is affirmative. You are cleared to fire."

Everyone in the conference room waited breathlessly. A moment later a blinding flash blotted out the screen as the missile's rocket engine flared and the projectile released from the mounting bracket beneath the wing. An instant later it was followed by another flash from the opposite wing as a second missile fired.

"This is Trigger Man. The target has been engaged. I repeat, target engaged," echoed Louie's voice through the speakers.

All eyes were fixed on the screen as the two warheads spiraled downwards toward their targets. There was a small burst of light when the first projectile plunged through the roof of the building. The second missile struck moments later, hitting a smaller structure visible on the edge of the screen.

"Targets engaged," came the voice through the speaker. "Munitions impacted within the acceptable error radius. The targeting cell is conducting an initial battle damage assessment. Please stand by..."

In the darkness, thousands of feet down below, they could see a fire burning in the larger of the two structures. The drone's infrared camera picked up a few of the surviving goats stumbling around the edge of the clearing. The remainder of the herd was nowhere to be seen, presumably incinerated inside the buildings, simulating the surgical demise of a hardened GLA fighter. A few moments later, the voice from the targeting cell came back on the line.

"Initial battle damage assessment indicates that all targets have been neutralized. I repeat, all targets neutralized. This concludes the final training exercise and LTA certification. Exercise is complete. We are now turning mission control over to Flight Ops. Targeting cell, out."

The burning shack faded from view as the drone turned from the clearing and began the long flight back to the airport.

"That's it," Sid announced to the room. "Louie is officially ready to go. Now, all we need to do is find Odoki..."

+++

The next day Sid and Carson met Anna at the café for their usual morning rendezvous. The mood around the table was subdued as they waited for Sammy to bring around the drinks.

"You guys seem exhausted," Anna said. "Late night?"

"What do you mean?" Sid asked, defensively.

"Well, it just seemed like the entire camp was abuzz until the wee hours," Anna said. "I got up to go to the bathroom around two in the morning and noticed all the lights on over at the command center."

"So, now you're spying on us?" Carson said, half-joking. "We may need to look at what's in that little notebook of yours."

"I can assure you, nothing very useful," Anna insisted.

Sid and Carson were especially grateful when Sammy arrived with the coffees. After the barista disappeared back into the shack, Anna pressed harder for information.

"So, the chitchat in the breakfast line this morning made it sound like Louie passed his test with flying colors. I guess that means the operation is a go?"

"Jesus," Sid said, shaking his head. "Can't we at least pretend that this stuff is classified? You're not cleared for any of this. We shouldn't even be talking about it. Especially not over coffee at Sujah Bean."

"OK, Sid. Just lighten up a bit. I'll keep your little secret safe," Anna whispered mockingly. "And just so you feel better. Nobody told me anything at breakfast. I just guessed. After a week of not hearing anything from Louie, he finally texted me early this morning and invited me over to his mom's house for dinner. I just figured that if he had time for dinner, then his training must finally be over."

"I cannot confirm or deny anything," Sid said, still sulking over the breach of security. "Wait a second!" he blurted out as an afterthought. "Dinner at his mom's house? Seems like things are getting a little serious."

"Stop it, Sid. We're just friends. I seem to recall that he has invited you two jerks over to his house on several occasions, but you've never taken him up on it. I'm sure he wouldn't mind if you came along tonight. I'd be happy to ask."

"No can do," Carson said. "You know we've been restricted to camp ever since the bombing. No one is allowed off-base, except for official duties."

"Your loss. But I'll try to bring back some leftovers," Anna promised. "Anyway, while we're on the topic of things that I'm not supposed to know about. I finally finished going through all of the interrogation reports."

Sid perked up with interest. "What did you find?"

"Unfortunately, no smoking gun if that's what you were hoping for. All in all, I'd say they left me with more questions than answers."

"How so?" Carson asked.

"Well, you said that these reports have been the primary source of intelligence on Odoki and the GLA for the last few years, right?"

"Basically, yes," Sid said.

"And during that time, all the raids have more or less had the same outcome. No sign of Odoki. No major defeat of the GLA. And no capture of any senior leaders," Anna clarified.

"True. But the Gisawians have rounded up plenty of lower-level fighters. Not to mention uncovering plenty of weapons and supplies."

"OK, but would you agree that the results have been rather modest given a three-year military campaign that is supposedly the number one priority for the Gisawian army?"

"Fair enough," Sid agreed.

"So, why do you think that is?"

Sid took a sip at his coffee as he considered the question. "Probably a combination of factors. Obviously, the biggest issue is that we have very few resources trying to collect intelligence over a huge piece of terrain. Plus, DRoG's army is just stretched too thin. There's no way they can cover such a large area. And I'm guessing that they're not getting much help from the locals either. People in the area are probably more scared of the army than the GLA."

"But with our help, shouldn't they be doing better?" Anna asked.

"Come on, Anna!" Sid said. "Look around here. This mission has never been more than a PR stunt for the United States. Sure, we put a few hundred boots on the ground to make a show of it, but that's about it. No one was even paying any attention to this operation until a few months ago."

"I get that, but it still doesn't explain why the Gisawians haven't at least made more progress in tracking down Odoki's men. They haven't captured a single high-level leader in years."

"Well, it just comes back to a lack of intel. Those summaries of the interrogation reports are usually weeks old by the time we get our hands on them. And who the hell knows if any of it is even true? You've been reading them for the last two weeks. What do you think?"

"You want my honest opinion?"

"Sure," Sid nodded. "Although, you'll get your paycheck either way."

"I think something fishy is going on. The stuff in the reports doesn't add up."

"What's so strange about them?" Carson asked.

"Well, for starters, you told me that MoD only sends you the sanitized summaries, not the original reports, right?"

"Yup," Sid confirmed. "A few times per month. Unfortunately, they're usually pretty vague. Sometimes it's hardly anything more than some grid coordinates where they think the GLA might be operating. But, when that's all we get, we don't have much choice but to rely on it. At the end of the day, it's still just a cat and mouse game. And our cat is blind."

"I won't argue with you there. But after reading through the original reports, I'm not surprised that the information you're getting isn't useful."

"You mean they're not giving us a complete picture?" Carson asked.

"It's kind of obvious when you see the full reports. You get a sense of what the interrogators are really after. Not to mention what the detainees actually know."

"So, you suspect that the Gisawians are giving us a cherry-picked version of the truth in the summaries? Gee, what a surprise," Sid said sarcastically.

"Well, you're certainly getting the version of the story that they want you to have. It seems like those detainees are either highly trained masters of evasion or else completely clueless. My guess is the latter."

"Why do you think so?"

"Well, for starters, a lot of them are just kids. But of course, you wouldn't know that since MoD strips out all the biographical data from the summaries. However, it's all there in the full reports. Most of these so-called rebel fighters should be on playgrounds, not battlefields."

"But Anna, that shouldn't come as a surprise," Sid insisted. "We've known all along that the GLA uses child soldiers.

We have plenty of reports about them kidnapping kids from villages and turning them into fighters. It's horrific, but apparently not uncommon."

"Right. But in the reports, there's almost no mention of Odoki or the GLA. Most of the questions are about the camps. The locations. How many people live there. How long they've been there. Things like that. Even more interesting is the fact that the interrogators didn't seem to ask any questions at all about Odoki."

"I agree, that is a little strange," Sid said. "But you need to realize, these guys over at Police Intelligence probably aren't highly trained interrogators. From their perspective, finding the locations of the training camps is probably a legitimate concern. That seems to be the focus of their entire strategy. Take down the network, camp by camp, hoping it will lead them to the big fish."

"Then why do all the raids keep coming up empty?" Anna countered. "Shouldn't they have found at least some of the GLA senior leadership hanging out in these camps? Doesn't it strike you as a bit odd that all these places keep turning up empty by the time you arrive there?"

"Maybe, or maybe not," Sid said, still unconvinced. "The GLA fighters are highly mobile. They survive by moving around. They know we're out there looking for them, so they never stay too long in one place. Based on what we've found at the camps, most of the locations are occupied only for a few days at a time, maybe a week at the most."

"So, your explanation for all the near misses is that MoD just isn't getting timely information?" Carson asked.

"I guess so," Sid said with a shrug.

"Any alternate hypothesis?"

"Anna, I don't see what you're getting at," Carson said, frustrated that the conversation seemed to be going in circles.

"Well, is it possible that someone inside MoD is tipping off the GLA before the raids?"

"That doesn't make any sense," Sid challenged. "What's the motive? Besides, I seriously doubt that the GLA could place a source inside MoD. They may be an irritant to the government, but they're still just a ragtag rebel group operating in a remote part of the country. It's not like they're going to overthrow President Namono anytime soon."

"I'd have to go with Sid on this one, Anna," Carson added. "I love a good conspiracy, but that one seems a bit far-fetched."

"OK," Anna relented. "I admit, it doesn't seem particularly plausible, but we need to consider other possibilities. Let me throw one more idea at you. What if it's not really the GLA using those camps?"

"You mean another rebel group that we haven't heard of?" Sid said skeptically.

"Maybe. Or even a rogue element within the Gisawian army. Who knows? I'm just trying to brainstorm possible explanations."

"Any evidence for that theory?" Carson asked.

Anna tapped her pencil on the table, scanning through the pages of her notebook as she considered the question.

"I don't know yet," she murmured, lost in thought. "I just keep thinking back to what those women in the village told me. They kept insisting that soldiers were in the area before the attack. But all the media reports, and the government's official account, all stated that DRoG army troops didn't arrive at the scene until three days after the massacre. I'm still kind of stuck on that discrepancy in the timeline."

"OK, let me play devil's advocate," Sid countered. "It easily could have been anyone out there dressed up as government soldiers. The GLA is known to wear military-style uniforms. I still think it's possible that the women were just confused about who they saw out there."

"I'm not necessarily saying it was the DRoG army. What if there is another force operating out there besides the GLA?" Anna asked.

"You mean another group using those camps? Who? And for what purpose?" Sid questioned.

"I don't know yet. I'm still trying to get all this straight inside my head. It's just a bunch of unconnected dots that don't really form a picture," Anna said, staring into her notebook.

"Is this something we should run by Louie?" Carson asked.

"No," Sid said, shaking his head. "So far, this is nothing more than speculation. No sense dragging Louie into this unless we have something firm. We can't just go ask him if he thinks MoD is playing both sides."

"You're probably right," Carson agreed. "That would put him in a tough situation, particularly given the fact that his uncle runs the show over there."

"But you guys trust Louie, don't you?" Anna asked.

"Of course, one hundred percent," Sid insisted. "But I also wouldn't be surprised if there's some stuff going on over at MoD that he doesn't know about."

"Any evidence for that theory?" Anna said.

"Not really," Sid conceded. "Just a gut feeling."

Anna let the thought sink in as she finished her tea. Then she suddenly got up from the table. "OK, guys, I'm sorry to cut this short, but I've got some research to do."

"What now?" Carson asked.

"I'm putting together a database to organize all the information from the interrogation reports. It may not help, but I want to check out a hunch."

"Good luck," Sid said, raising his coffee cup in a mock toast. "Let us know when you track down Odoki's mailing address."

"Will do," Anna said, smiling. "Same time tomorrow?"

Sid and Carson nodded as she turned and walked away.

"So, what do you think?" Carson said, once Anna was out of earshot. "Is she on to anything?"

"Who the hell knows? At this point, I don't know what to believe. Things just keep getting crazier by the day. We have Louie over there in a geodesic dome getting ready to fire a missile at a rebel leader who no one has seen in almost three years. At the same time, the Gisawian army is preparing to kick off a major ground offensive based on nothing more than low-resolution satellite photos of holes in the ground. Meanwhile, President Namono seems to be hatching a secret plan to turn the international airport into a regional counter-terrorism center. Oh yeah, and don't forget that MoD is still trying to convince us that our camp was attacked by Hezbollah. While Police Intelligence has been shaking down every rinky-dink Lebanese grocery store in the country, trying to dismantle an imaginary terror network. So, you tell me, what part of any of this makes sense?"

"My head hurts just thinking about it," Carson said.

"Me too," Sid agreed, sipping his coffee. "So, what about our other issues? The mystery blogger and midnight data transmissions coming from the conference room? Made any progress cracking the case?"

"Well, it seems like the mystery blogger is solved. I had Louie talk to the soldiers at the gate," Carson explained. "At first, they denied everything. But when he showed them the pictures, one of the guys finally fessed up. He said that Burke put them up to it and gave them some extra pocket money for their trouble."

"What a fucking little freak," Sid said, shaking his head. "Are you confident enough about the confession to tell Kittredge?"

"I guess so. Particularly if it gets him off our back," Carson added.

"What about the other thing?" asked Sid.

Carson stared down into his coffee cup, shaking his head and smiling to himself. "You're not going to believe this one."

"Try me. Nothing you tell me can be any crazier than what's already going on around here."

"We'll see about that. Remember I told you that I confronted Slyker about that run-in we had with Jorgenson?"

"You mean when he threatened to kill Slyker with his bare hands?" Sid laughed.

"Right. At first, Slyker wouldn't tell me anything. When I finally convinced him to talk, all he gave me was that stupid phrase."

"Swedish meatball?"

"Yeah, exactly. I was so pissed off that I didn't even bother thinking about it for a few days. Then last night, I finally gave in to curiosity and started doing a little research online."

"And you discovered that Jorgenson moonlights at Ikea?" Sid joked.

"Very funny, but not too far off."

"OK, I'm on the edge of my seat," Sid said.

"So, when not serving in his official capacity as a disgruntled, sociopathic Green Beret, Jorgenson is a face man for a global, multi-level marketing enterprise aimed at lonely, sex-starved housewives."

"You're fucking kidding me!" Sid gasped in disbelief.

"I am not."

"So that's what he was doing sneaking into the conference room late at night?"

"As far as I can tell, he's been using it as a studio for his side gig," Carson explained. "The buyers' club is hosted on a restricted-access web domain. It's impossible to see anything unless you're a member. Unfortunately, to become one, I would have needed to sign up five new members within thirty days to recoup my initial fee. Naturally, I declined the opportunity."

"You're smarter than you look," Sid said, smiling. "So, what on earth is Jorgenson selling?"

"More like, what isn't he selling. The club pushes everything from dietary supplements to knock-off Tupperware and pre-paid legal services. You name it, and he's probably hawking it."

"Wait a second, if you weren't able to access the members-only domain, how'd you figure out it was him?"

"That's the kicker," Carson said. "You can find bootleg copies of his routine posted to other online forums."

"How'd you ever find them?" Sid asked, now fully enthralled in the story.

"Guess," Carson demanded, trying to suppress a smile.

"Swedish meatball?"

"Bingo! Slyker was actually trying to help me out after all."

"But how on earth did he know about it?"

"Apparently, Jorgenson has something of a cult following among Slyker's circles."

"You mean soulless merchants of death?"

"No, not those circles. His *other* circles."

"Ohhh, *those* circles…"

"Yeah," Carson confirmed with a serious nod.

"But I don't get it. What's the draw?"

"You've got to see it to believe it. Jorgenson's infomercials are way over the top. It's like some weird combination of Dale Carnegie, the Village People, and CrossFit."

"Jesus. No wonder he threatened to kill Slyker to keep his secret safe. So, you think he's been taping episodes during those nighttime trips to the conference room?"

"Yup. That's my best guess. He's only on-air for an hour a day, but his show is the top-ranked segment on the entire marketing network. The guy is probably making a mint on the side when he's not busy killing terrorists with his bare hands."

"OK, I got to admit. You did surprise me with that one," Sid said, sinking into his chair. "I don't even know what we do with it."

"At some point, we'll need to tell Kittredge," Carson suggested.

"I suppose so. But I'm not even sure that it's technically illegal to run a global online pyramid scheme from inside a top-secret government facility. It just seems like one of those things that must happen all the time," Sid pondered.

"Probably right. The worst they'll do is slap him on the wrist for misuse of government property," Carson said.

"Maybe it's best just to tell the colonel now," Sid said. "But for god sakes, make sure he keeps it quiet. If word ever gets back to Jorgenson that we ratted him out, we'll both end up in a shallow, sand-covered grave somewhere outside the fence."

"Agreed," Carson said. "Behind those chiseled pecks beats the heart of a ruthless killer. We need to be careful."

"Don't worry," Sid reassured him. "My business is all about keeping secrets."

+++

The next afternoon Louie made his way over to MoD to meet with the deputy minister. When he arrived, his uncle was already at the door, waiting for him.

"Lutalo, I'm very happy to see you," he said, squeezing in behind his oversized desk and motioning Louie toward one of the plush leather chairs. "We have much to discuss."

"Thank you, Uncle. It is good to see you as well," Louie said, somewhat taken aback by the unexpected warmth of the greeting.

"So, I understand that you have completed your training. We are now ready to begin the operation."

"Yes, Uncle. The program was very thorough."

"Good, good," Mugaba enthused. "But Lutalo, you don't seem excited. What is the matter?"

Louie turned and stared at the wall as he searched for the right words. "I'm sorry. It's just that I don't understand what is happening," he finally answered.

"What do you mean?" Mugaba said.

"Why didn't you tell me about any of this beforehand? You must have known about it for some time. But I never heard a word until Mr. Slyker showed up at the camp with all the equipment. He told me that you were the one who decided that I would fire the missile."

"Not just me, Lutalo! The minister himself approved the plan. He knew that you could be trusted. That is no small thing. I should think you would be honored by this!" his uncle insisted.

"Uncle, please do not misunderstand. I respect you and the minister. However, I dislike being treated as a child. You're keeping secrets from me. It's as if you think that I'm not able to understand things. You tell me just enough to do your bidding, but never anything more."

Mugaba leaned back in his chair, thinking for a moment before looking back across his desk at Louie.

"Perhaps you are right, Lutalo. Sometimes I do treat you as a boy, not a man. But this is only because I wish to protect you. You are my sister's son. You are the only thing she has left here. After your father died, I promised her that I would always protect you. I will not break this promise, no matter what."

"But protecting me doesn't mean that you must keep treating me like a child?" Louie said.

"No, Lutalo. That is a fair criticism. I know that you are a man. A very good man. One that your father would be proud of. I am certain of this."

"Then tell me what's going on? Why did the minister invite Slyker here? Why did he pick me to fire the missile?"

"Lutalo, I know this doesn't make sense to you. All I can say is that someday you will understand the big picture. But for now, the most important thing to know is that we are depending on you. I trust you because we are family. And, when the time comes, I know that you will do your duty."

"But how can you be sure, Uncle? I don't even know what the right thing is anymore! None of this makes any sense."

"You will know, Lutalo. I am certain."

Louie said nothing. He stared down into his hands until his uncle finally spoke.

"Lutalo, you remember the old saying from the village. 'He who earns calamity eats it with his family.'"

Louie nodded indifferently, having lost all patience for his uncle's endless stream of proverbs.

"The same is true when a family finds great success. These fruits are shared. Do you understand what I mean?" his uncle asked.

"I suppose so," Louie said with a shrug.

"It means that we will succeed or fail together as a family. Many people will be watching what happens in the coming weeks. A great deal rests upon our success. And not just for us, but for the entire country. I know that you have not been happy with the arrangement, but I am certain you will be rewarded for your loyalty. The minister thinks very highly of you. He knew your father well and respected him. That is partly why he entrusted you with this important task. When the time comes, you must not let him down."

Louie simply nodded, still unable to meet his uncle's eyes.

CHAPTER TWELVE

———

Colonel Kittredge glanced at his watch, drumming his fingers against his chair while they waited for the meeting to begin. Ambassador Roberts came on the line first, dressed in her signature gray business suit, sitting alone at the end of a table with a notebook and pen at hand. A few seconds later General Foster appeared on the other side of the split screen. He was still in his gym clothes and flush with exertion, flanked by half a dozen of his staff all identically attired.

"Hey there, Claire. I almost didn't recognize you without your hat," Foster said, inviting muffled chortles from his staff around the table. "The press got a few good shots of it at the airfield dedication ceremony."

"Thanks, Bill. Maybe you can give me some tips on ceremonial camouflage next time you're in town," she replied with an annoyed smirk. "Obviously, I would have preferred to skip that charade all together; however, I was overruled by Washington. In any case, I did my best to avoid lending too much credibility to President's Namono's little circus show out there."

"I heard he brought down the house when that An-225 came flying in out of nowhere," Foster chuckled. "You've got to give him credit, the guy knows how to play a crowd."

"Indeed. He's been holding center stage for almost thirty years now with no end in sight," the ambassador observed dryly. "I guess I didn't realize that you were such an admirer of his Excellency. You military guys are always accusing us of going native. Now it seems the shoe is on the other foot."

"Come on, Claire! I don't trust that little bastard any more than you do. But that's just the way it is with allies. Can't live with them. Can't kill them. Anyway, we've got bigger things to worry about right now. Kittredge, are you there?"

"Yes, sir," the colonel said, breaking into the conversation.

"Good. Bring us up to speed on what's happening with the operation. And make it snappy."

"Yes, sir. This morning I got an update from the ESP technicians. The platform is now on full-alert status over at the airport. It can be fueled, armed, and airborne within thirty minutes of notification. The flight crews are on ten-minute recall in the event we receive actionable intelligence on Odoki. On the Gisawian side, it appears that MoD is nearly ready to kick off the offensive, code name Operation Brushfire. They're just waiting for the order from President Namono to move troops into place."

The ambassador leaned forward and flipped on her mic. "Colonel Kittredge. It should go without saying that this is a potentially sensitive, not to mention utterly unorthodox application of military force. At this point, there's no use getting into a lengthy philosophical debate over the inadvisability of this course of action. The fact that we are sitting here right now is evidence that my concerns have been roundly dismissed by the powers that be in Washington. Nevertheless, can you at least offer me some kind of assurance that we've done due diligence regarding DRoG's legal authority to conduct such an operation?"

"Yes, ma'am," Kittredge said, glancing down into his notes. "The Local Targeting Authority, or LTA, has completed an intensive two-week familiarization program covering all aspects of the platform's operational characteristics and capabilities. This training included a culminating live-fire exercise where the LTA demonstrated a full and complete understanding of all targeting protocols and risk mitigation best practices. Ultimate and final decision-making authority concerning the lawful application of deadly force resides solely with the designated LTA, acting on behalf of, and responsible to, the sovereign power of the Democratic Republic of Gisawi."

"Did ESP give you those talking points?" the ambassador asked flatly.

"Yes, ma'am. It's all right here in the liability waiver," Kittredge said, waving a thick stack of papers in front of the camera.

"How reassuring," she sighed. "Bill, do you have any concerns about what's happening here?"

Hearing his name, the general broke away from a separate conversation with his staff and flipped on the mic.

"At the moment, Claire, my major concern is getting some good intel on Odoki so we can finally get that little son-of-a-bitch. Kittredge, any progress on that front?"

"Yes, sir," the colonel popped back on, ignoring the ambassador's question. "According to the latest information from MoD, Odoki's move back across the border may be imminent. Police Intelligence believes that he has called a leadership council to discuss plans for a new offensive."

"Do we have any idea where this meeting is going down?" the general asked.

"No, sir. Nothing specific just yet. There's a good chance we won't know the location until just before it happens. We expect that his men will assemble at a rendezvous point just before the meeting, then wait for the boss to show up. But they don't think that Odoki will make a move across the border unless he feels secure. For that reason, MoD doesn't want to flood the zone with ground patrols and risk scaring him away. For the time being, they're going to maintain a low profile. No preemptive moves until they get something definitive from their sources on the ground."

"Then what's the plan?" the general pressed.

"If they get a tip that Odoki is on the move, then we get the bird up in the air ASAP. From there we'll just start looking and keeping our fingers crossed that we can catch him out in the open."

"And exactly how is this operation linked to the plan for the ground offensive," the ambassador interrupted.

"Ma'am, it's all interconnected," Kittredge explained. "MoD wants to deliver a one-two punch. First, take down Odoki and his key lieutenants with the drone strike. Then launch Operation Brushfire to break the GLA's logistical network in the western region. That part will focus on seizing and holding the underground cache sites where they believe the GLA has been storing the weapons and supplies. But above all, President Namono wants to maintain the element of surprise. He's not going to kick off the ground offensive without taking down Odoki first."

"It's a good plan, Claire," the general interrupted. "Namono's instincts are right on this one. You've got to go for the whole enchilada. If we piecemeal this thing, then we'll just end up pissing away our advantage."

"OK, Bill, I get it. I'm not going to second-guess your professional military judgment on the relative merits of the strategy. However, we still need to consider the broader implications of what we're about to do. The stated US policy goal has always been neutralization of Daniel Odoki. But now we've expanded that narrow objective into support for a broader plan to pacify the entire western region. I don't need to tell you, that's not what we signed up for. By linking these two operations together, even symbolically, we've made ourselves silent partners in whatever President Namono has planned for the offensive. Do we even know what the end game looks like?"

"Claire, with all due respect, you're over-complicating this thing," the general said impatiently. "There are bad guys out there. Namono is going in to clean them out. That's all there is to it. Isn't that the whole reason we're here, for god's sake?"

"To be quite honest, Bill, I'm not even sure anymore. And I say that as the senior US official in this country. And frankly, I don't think anyone in Washington knows either. As far as I can tell, the folks in DC are hedging all bets, just waiting to see how this thing turns out before deciding whether to walk away or double down. Yesterday we even heard that the White House is delaying the decision on the new counter-terrorism training center until after Operation Brushfire."

"Well, Claire, if you ask me, I'm just happy that someone is finally taking charge down there. I don't really care if that's ESP, President Namono, or goddamn Mickey Mouse. We've been screwing around with this thing for almost three years with nothing to show for it. It's time to close the book on this. And the only way to do that is by finishing off Odoki."

Ambassador Roberts took a deep breath and forced a smile. "Obviously, gentlemen, this train has left the station. And we're probably not going to get anywhere useful by arguing over the price of the ticket. At this point, I suppose we'll just hope for the best."

"Agreed," the general said. "Colonel Kittredge. Do you have anything else for us?"

"No, sir. We are leaning forward on our public affairs posture. Once the operation kicks off, we expect significant media interest. We've prepared draft press releases and talking points covering multiple scenarios. When the time comes, we'll be ready."

"Excellent. We need to be aggressive on perception management. I want to own the narrative from start to finish."

"Roger, sir. We'll keep you and the ambassador up-to-date as everything unfolds. If we get a read on Odoki's location and transition into a launch sequence, we'll dial you both into the operations center to monitor the situation."

"No need for that," the general said.

"Sir? It would probably be best for you to take part in…," Kittredge began.

"Damn straight it would!" the general said, cutting him off. "But I'm sure as hell not going to be watching the action from up here. I'm gonna be down there with you. I've got a

G5 fueled up, and we can be at your location in ten hours. Don't you dare launch that thing without me there. Any questions?"

"No, sir."

"Anything else?"

"No, sir."

"OK, then. Good luck with the hunting. Let me know when things get hot. Foster, out," he said as the video screen abruptly went dark.

The ambassador was alone on the screen, waiting for a sign that the meeting had come to an end. After a moment of awkward silence, she rolled her eyes, reached out and cut the video link without another word.

"I guess that's a wrap," Kittredge announced. "You all heard the general. It's game time. Let's stay sharp!"

Everyone around the table nodded solemnly, sensing that their moment of collective destiny was near at hand.

"OK, back to work," Kittredge ordered. "Everyone out of the room except for Carson and Sid."

The three of them waited for the room to empty before the colonel spoke.

"Gentlemen. This is it. From this point forward, everything needs to be perfectly coordinated. I want this organization running like a finely oiled machine. We are now operating in a zero-defect environment. Mistakes are unacceptable and will not be tolerated. Am I making myself understood?"

Carson and Sid nodded.

"Good. It goes without saying that there's a lot riding on this operation. But before things get hot, we need to finish up a bit of house cleaning. There were two things you guys were working on," he said, glancing down into his notes. "That underground blog and the midnight shenanigans in the conference room."

"Yes, sir," Carson jumped. "I think we've almost gotten to the bottom..."

"Let me finish," the colonel snapped. "From this point on, mission success is our number one priority. And like the general said, controlling the narrative will be the key to that success. Therefore, anything that threatens the narrative also jeopardizes our success. Does that make sense?"

"Yes, sir. I think so," Carson said. "But regarding the two issues, I think we have sufficient information..."

"No longer necessary," the colonel interrupted, cutting off Carson before he could finish. "I was informed last night by General Foster's staff that those two issues are no longer under review. The investigators already have everything they need. The incidents were determined to be tangential to the primary focus of the investigation."

"But sir," Sid cut in. "That doesn't erase what happened. Those were serious issues. Maybe not to the outcome of this mission, but to good order and discipline."

"Control the narrative...," the colonel interrupted, calmly raising his finger in the air like some wizened Ninja master. "We must ask ourselves, does the pursuit of these concerns enable our mastery over the narrative? Or does it lessen our ability to control the message? I think we probably all know the answer to that question."

"Sir, so you're telling us just to drop the entire thing and forget about it?" Sid asked incredulously.

"There is no 'thing' to be dropped," the colonel countered,

emphasizing his point with air quotes. "The blog has been deleted. It's no longer accessible online. Furthermore, the investigators felt that any formal inquiry would require the testimony of several foreign nationals against a US person. They didn't like the optics. As of today, that case is officially closed."

"And the other 'thing'?" Carson asked, mimicking the colonel's air quotes, inching precariously close to insubordination.

"Unauthorized use of government communications equipment. That's what it was. The matter has been dealt with administratively and the individual in question appropriately reprimanded. While I do appreciate the time that you both spent on figuring this out, it's no longer a matter of our concern."

Sid and Carson sat in stunned silence.

"Any questions?" the colonel asked, without waiting for an answer. "Good. Then we need to move on. Our plates are already full. We don't need any more distractions," he added as he rose from the table and headed out the door.

"What the fuck was that?" Sid blurted out, once they were alone.

"Beats me," Carson said, shaking his head. "But with all the other crazy shit going on, I guess I'm not that surprised."

"Just out of curiosity," Sid said after a moment's contemplation. "The colonel said that the 'Black Ops' blog had been deleted from the web. But you still have that archived copy of the screenshots on your computer, right?"

"Hmm, yeah, I guess so…," Carson said. "Why do you ask?"

"No reason. Just make sure you keep it somewhere safe. We may need a little insurance policy in case this thing comes back to haunt us."

"Consider it done," Carson agreed.

+++

Later that day Sid and Carson met Anna over at Sujah Bean for a midafternoon break. When they arrived, Anna was already at the table tapping away at her laptop.

"New office?" Sid asked as they sat down.

"The air conditioning in my office conked out this morning. It's like a sauna in there. I'm staying here until I can find someone to fix it."

"Try talking to your boss," Carson suggested.

"What?"

"ESP. They'll do all the maintenance work on the camp."

"I should have guessed…," Anna said, shaking her head.

"Don't worry," Carson said. "I'll call the supervisor after coffee. He'll have it fixed before dinner."

"Thanks," Anna said, sipping her tea. "So, the excitement seems to be building," she observed, nodding at the buzz of activity around ESP's encampment. "Prepping for the alien invasion?"

"Very funny. But even if we were, you know we can't talk about it," Sid reminded her. "It's probably best just to change the subject so we can all stay out of trouble. So…what else can we talk about?" Sid said, playfully scratching his head. "Oh yeah, how about your date last week with Louie and his mom? How was the big dinner?"

"You missed out. The food was amazing. Much better

than anything you'll find around here. And Louie's mother is charming," she added. "I had a really nice time."

"Sorry we missed it," Carson said. "Maybe we'll go next time if things ever quiet down around here."

"Hopefully," Anna urged. "It would mean a lot to Louie if you guys took him up on the offer. For reasons I can't fully grasp, he seems to like you two. Plus, he wants you to have a few memories of his country that don't involve sitting inside this wretched little camp."

"Me too!" Sid agreed. "And we're probably running out of time to make that happen," he said, nodding at the workers shuttling back and forth between the geodesic domes.

"It sure seems that way," Anna agreed.

"So, what are you working on so diligently?" Carson asked, sneaking a glance at her laptop.

"That spreadsheet with all of the information from the interrogation reports. The records Louie gave me were a complete mess. I was hoping to find some way to analyze the content, although I'm not sure this really helps that much."

"Any major discoveries so far?" Sid asked, genuinely interested.

"Nope. Nothing yet. I'm still doing data entry. It may be hard to make heads or tails of it until everything is loaded."

Sid peeked at the screen. "Hmm, interesting," he mumbled, examining the columns of data. "I think you went into the wrong profession. Ever consider doing intelligence work?"

"Come on, Sid!" she laughed. "You know how good I am at keeping secrets. It's my nature to blab about everything. I can assure you, I'm much better suited to life in academia than espionage."

"Good point," Sid nodded thoughtfully.

"Speaking of secrets and intrigue," Anna said, turning back to Carson. "Did you find out anything more from Slyker about Tantalus Holdings?"

"Sorry, no luck," Carson said. "Slyker seems to have his fingers in everybody's business but claimed not to know anything about it."

"And you actually believe him?" she asked incredulously.

"Strangely, this time, I do. Slyker usually gets me what I ask for, even when it's wrapped up in the process of him getting what he needs first. But I got the feeling that if he knew something about it he would have at least given me a hint. Were you able to find out anything on your end?"

"Not really. My lawyer friend back in the states is still sniffing around but warned me not to get my hopes up. Apparently, it's not so easy tracking down the paper trail for offshore shell companies."

"I guess that's the whole point of having a shell company, isn't it?" Carson added.

"True. I suppose we may end up like poor Tantalus," Anna chuckled. "The answers forever dangling just beyond the reach of our fingertips."

As she spoke, Sid was scrolling through images on his smartphone, finally stopping on one and turning the screen to show Sid and Anna.

"Don't do the crime if you can't do the time," Sid joked, showing them an image of Tantalus suffering his fate. The mythological figure was mired knee-deep in a pool of water, just beyond the reach of a fruit-laden branch.

"That looks like a pretty grim way to spend eternity," Carson observed. "Why did he ever think it was a good idea to steal ambrosia from Olympus? It seems like kind of a bold play to screw with the gods like that."

"I think the same reason that anyone does anything," Anna said with a shrug. "He wanted to impress his friends."

"Well, at least you were right about one thing," Carson added. "It's the perfect name for a shadowy shell company."

"By the way, miss smarty pants," Sid interrupted, still reading from his smartphone. "Here's some trivia I bet you didn't know. Our friend Tantalus also lends his name to the mineral Tantalum, a rare, highly corrosion-resistant metal used in electronic equipment such as mobile phones, computers, and videos game systems."

"Touché, Sid. You got me there. But don't forget, I studied classics, not chemistry," Anna reminded him.

"Hmm, this is interesting...," Sid said, continuing to scroll down through the information. "It says Tantalum is extracted from Coltan, a so-called conflict mineral. There are believed to be major untapped deposits all over this part of Africa."

Anna suddenly sat up in her seat. "What did you say?"

"Apparently, mobile phones have created an enormous demand for the stuff over the last decade," Sid explained, holding up his phone in the air, marveling its inner workings.

"I see wheels turning in your head," Carson said to Anna, who was now lost in thought.

"It's probably nothing...," she said, snapping from her hypnosis. "I need to keep working on this," she said before abruptly closing her laptop and getting up from the chair, leaving her unfinished cup of tea on the table.

"I'm going back to my office where I can concentrate."

"What about the broken air conditioning?" Carson called after her.

"Please be a sweetie and call Slyker to get it fixed," she called over her shoulder as she trotted off in the direction of her office.

+++

Forty-eight hours later, General Foster's jet touched down at the international airport. With the turbofan engines still spinning, the passenger door swung open, and General Foster stepped onto the tarmac like MacArthur wading ashore on the Philippines. Colonel Kittredge rushed out on the runway and greeted him with a crisp salute.

"Good to see you, Ed," the general said, taking his hand in a bone-crushing grip.

"Likewise, sir. I hesitated to call you down so soon, but we've had some developments since yesterday morning. The Gisawians received what they consider to be highly reliable information from one of their sources in the western region."

"What are they saying?"

"Several reports concerning small groups of armed men converging into an area near the border. This could be the sign we've been waiting for."

"That's good news, Ed. No problem calling me down. If this turns out to be the real deal, I don't want to take a chance of missing the action. Is ESP ready to launch the platform?"

"No, sir, not quite yet. We're just waiting on a few more indicators. We can't risk putting the bird in the air until we're certain that Odoki is on the move. Once it's up, there's no turning back. The clock starts ticking, and we've only got a narrow window of opportunity."

"OK. So, what's on the agenda?"

"That's up to you, sir. If you're amenable, Mr. Slyker offered to give you a tour of ESP's operations center so you can see the capabilities firsthand. Of course, there's no obligation. I'm happy telling Slyker to pound sand."

"No need for that. I'd be very interested to see the operation. Let Slyker know that I'm available whenever he has time."

"Yes, sir. Will do," Kittredge said unenthusiastically.

When they arrived at camp Colonel Kittredge had the driver stop in front of the headquarters building, intending to take General Foster over to the VIP quarters to get settled in. As they crossed the yard, Kittredge suddenly spotted Anna struggling in their direction, dragging two large duffel bags and her laptop case. Kittredge abruptly pulled Foster aside and steered him in the opposite direction.

"Sir, unfortunately, your room is not quite ready yet. We just need a little bit of last-minute housecleaning. My apologies."

"No problem," the general insisted. "I could use a little walkabout after being on the jet all day."

Just then Don Slyker appeared outside the door of ESP's operations center. Spotting Kittredge and Foster standing in the yard, Slyker made a beeline in their direction.

"General Foster," Slyker smiled, reaching out to take his hand. "Great to see you. It's a real honor to have you here."

"Likewise, Slyker. From the looks of it, you've got quite an operation going on here," the general said, nodding approvingly at the high-tech equipment scattered around the yard.

"Our engineers have really outdone themselves," Slyker said, waving his hand at the sprawling encampment. "What you see here is state-of-the-art modular design, scalable to meet any customer need. The package is fully transportable on any mid-sized cargo aircraft. From this command module, we can control up to five additional aircraft, even running concurrent missions against multiple target sets."

"This is great stuff, Slyker!" the general said. "How about a little tour inside?"

"Sure thing, General," Slyker said, leading Foster through encampment with Colonel Kittredge sulking silently behind.

When they entered the first geodesic dome, they were suddenly hit with a blast of frigid air.

"Jesus, Slyker. This place is an icebox," the general said, shivering as his eyes adjusted to the dim light.

"There are insulated parkas over on the rack if you need one," Slyker pointed out. "As you can tell from the temperature, our units are one hundred percent environmentally self-contained and able to operate in any climate zone from arid desert to subarctic. We generate our own power using a combination of conventional and renewable sources, making us fully independent of the local grid. As you can imagine, that's a big advantage down here. Our goal is to provide customers with turn-key service requiring minimal reliance on local infrastructure and logistics. All we need is a patch of ground for the command pods and eight thousand feet of improved runway. Then we're in business."

"Slyker, I like what I'm seeing," the general nodded approvingly. "Tell me more about this," he said, pointing to a control panel embedded into the desk.

"Yes, sir. From these work stations, we manage all flight operations. Basically, everything that happens once the bird is in the air. It probably looks similar to your military version; however, we've added some executive upgrades to make it more appealing to our private clientele."

"Such as?"

"Well, for starters, note the comfort-oriented design and customized features. An ergonomically correct profile, heated leather seats, inlaid mahogany and brushed aluminum trim around the command center. We hired a top-notch Scandinavian design firm to consult on the prototype."

As Slyker described the equipment, an attractive ESP technician clad in a formfitting cherry-red jumpsuit suddenly appeared beside them with a tray of refreshments.

"Warm hand towel or sparkling water, General?" she asked.

Foster blushed, self-consciously waving away the hand towel but helping himself to a bottle of water.

"Slyker, you've done quite a job here. I need to get your guys over to my house to fix up the basement," he joked, prodding Slyker with his elbow.

"Yes, sir. But don't let the bells and whistles fool you. What really matters is under the hood. Let me take you over to the targeting cell and show you the nerve center of the operation."

The general followed Slyker into an adjacent module with computer terminals lining the walls and several high-resolution video monitors dangling from the ceiling.

"General, this is where the magic happens, the targeting cell," Slyker continued. "Things are slow right now, but once we ramp up operations this room will be buzzing. Here you see the terminals for the analysts. They're responsible for providing the client with real-time situational awareness based on a set of predefined targeting parameters and live data feeds transmitted from the platform."

"Fascinating...," the general murmured. "How do you develop the targeting parameters?"

"Excellent question, sir! Prior to an operation, we conduct a detailed customer needs assessment so we can fully understand the nature of our client's geopolitical objectives and desired military end-state. Believe me when I say that there's much more to our business model than just putting warheads to foreheads. We're aiming higher up the value chain by offering our clients an agile, customer-led design process."

"That's where you see the growth potential?"

"Absolutely," Slyker said, lowering his voice and leaning closer toward the general. "Despite what you see here, we're not looking to be in the hardware business. Quite frankly, if you just want to put steel on target, there are plenty of firms out there that can handle that kind of basic tactical work. Between you and me, we're more than happy to let the Russians and Chinese fight over that low-end segment of the market. Believe me, the margins are crap and clients more trouble than their worth."

"Hmm, makes sense," the general said, nodding thoughtfully.

"As the technology proliferates, we're betting on a highly differentiated marketplace for on-demand precision targeting. We intend to position ourselves as a value-added provider catering to a more discriminating clientele. That business is more about relationship-building and trust. It's about understanding our clients' long-term security goals, as well as helping them to identify emerging threats and unrealized vulnerabilities. That means offering a horizontally integrated process linking strategic decision-making to tactical execution, all in a competitively priced package."

"What's that over there?" Foster asked, pointing at the front of the room and what appeared to be the cockpit seat of an advanced jet fighter.

"General, that is where the rubber meets the road, the trigger seat. You'll notice the head-up display surrounding the cockpit. It has an integrated augmented reality feature providing the Local Targeting Authority with immersed visualization of the engagement area. We also have a patented friend-or-foe identification tool that visually disaggregates the kill zone, thereby greatly reducing the chance of unintended civilian casualties."

"So, once we reach that point, the LTA is making all the decisions alone?" the general asked.

"For legal reasons, the final act of employing the munition rests entirely with the client. That part of the contract is non-negotiable. However, we are with the customer every step of the way. Our basic subscriber package includes a pre-mission risk estimate, full analytical support, target characterization, as well as a complimentary post-strike effectiveness assessment. All of that comes with a one hundred percent customer satisfaction guarantee. We're the only ones in the industry offering that!"

"Sounds complicated…"

"That's an understatement. We're talking two hundred pages of fine print in the contact. All I can say is, thank god for sovereign immunity."

"Well, Slyker, I can clearly see that you've got your shit together."

"Thank you, sir. At the end of the day, that means everything."

Colonel Kittredge, who had been sulking along behind them, tapped at his watch and edged himself into the conversation.

"Sir, I'm sorry to interrupt, but I need to check and see if the VIP quarters are ready. I'm sure you'll want to freshen up after the trip. I'll get your bags and then send someone to pick you up."

"Great. Thanks, Ed. I'm just going to stay a few more minutes here to finish up with Slyker. Just come get me when the room's ready."

"Will do, sir," Kittredge said, turning and leaving them alone. Once Kittredge was out the door, Slyker resumed their conversation.

"General Foster, I want to thank you again for coming down. It's a real honor to have you here."

"Well, Slyker, our discussion last month really piqued my interest. But I got to admit, at first, I figured you for just another defense industry bullshitter trying to steal taxpayer money. When you made that pitch, I didn't give you a snowball's chance in hell of getting it through the wickets back in DC."

"I wish I could take credit for that, sir. But really it was all the hard work of our congressional team liaison team back in Washington. They're top-notch operators," Slyker assured him. "Best in the industry."

"I guess so. And what I'm seeing right now is damn impressive as well. You guys are running a real professional outfit," Foster said, gazing admiringly at the spotless, high-tech interior.

"So, General, did you put any more thought to the other part of our discussion?" Slyker hinted.

Foster cleared his throat as if dislodging an errant peanut. "Let's just say that contingent upon our success here, I remain very interested in exploring future, mutually beneficial opportunities."

"That's good to hear, General. I believe we understand one another," Slyker confided. "I think we both also appreciate that a lot is riding on the outcome of this endeavor."

"Perhaps more than you realize...," Foster hinted.

Slyker said nothing, trying to read the general's expression.

"You know this thing has become a real hot potato in DC?" Foster continued.

"So I gather."

"Between you and me, the president is scared shitless that something's going to go wrong. After that investigation over the bombing, he didn't want to hear anything more about DRoG or Odoki. It only got worse after that damn rap song kicked off the street riots back home. With the election coming up, he doesn't want to touch this thing with a ten-foot pole. I'm guessing that's why your little scheme got the green light. If it succeeds, the White House will be first in line to take credit. But if it fails..."

"We're hung out to dry," Slyker said, finishing the thought.

"Yup," Foster nodded. "So, perhaps you can appreciate why I'm somewhat hesitant to dive into a relationship prematurely."

"I can't say that I blame you, sir. However, in my experience, when a prospective partner shows a willingness to put some skin in the game, one becomes more favorably inclined toward future generosity."

The general was quiet for a moment, carefully considering Slyker's words before replying. "You remember that I said a lot was riding on our success here?" he finally said.

"Yes, sir."

"Well, I'm sure you're aware of the pending decision on the regional counter-terrorism base?"

"Yes, sir."

"You are also probably aware that the decision has been temporarily put on hold."

"I am aware of that as well."

"I have reason to believe that success here. And by that, I mean a decisive and conclusive end to the problem of Odoki. The kind of success we can all feel good about. That kind of outcome will weigh heavily on the decision-making concerning the final location of the base."

"Very interesting," Slyker said, stroking his chin.

"In any case, once the announcement is made, the Pentagon will want to move fast on getting things set up. I would think there would be a decided advantage for any outfit that came to the table prepared with a plan. Especially one who already knows the game down here and has an established track record on the ground."

"Indeed," Slyker said. "A detailed specification for such a requirement would certainly be helpful if one desired to pursue such an opportunity."

"I imagine that would be extremely helpful," the general agreed. "Well, anyway, Slyker, it was great talking with you," the general said, reaching out his hand. "I'm sure we'll be seeing plenty of one another as this thing unfolds. Let's hope for the best," he said, putting on his hat and turning for the door.

CHAPTER THIRTEEN

Carson was startled from a deep sleep by the sound of frantic pounding on his door. He shot up in bed with heart racing. As he gathered his wits, there was another round of drubbing, this time accompanied by Sid's voice yelling through the door.

"For god's sakes, wake up!" Carson heard Sid yelling from outside in the hallway.

"What is it?" Carson yelled back, stumbling out of bed in his underwear.

"Man, you are one deep sleeper," Sid said when Carson finally opened the door. "Get on some clothes. We need to be over at the headquarters building ASAP."

"Why? What's going on?" Carson demanded.

"Louie just called about an hour ago. MoD got a tip on the meeting location. There's a chance Odoki is already on his way across the border. Kittredge just ordered ESP to prepare for launch. He wants everyone over in the conference room right now. This could finally be it…"

Carson nodded, suddenly wide awake. "Give me two minutes and I'll be there."

"OK. I'm going over now to get ready," Sid said, already in full stride toward the door.

A few minutes later, Carson was walking across the yard toward the command center. The camp was already buzzing with activity. Inside the headquarters building, he found Sergeant Goodwin putting on a fresh pot of coffee. Colonel Kittredge and most of the staff were already in the conference room when Carson sat down at the table. Sid was at the podium studying his briefing notes.

"The general will be here any minute. You about ready?" the colonel asked him.

"Yes, sir. I don't have much to go on, but I'll do my best."

Kittredge nodded and left him alone to concentrate. A moment later Sergeant Goodwin appeared with coffee and a handful of tannin-stained mugs all chipped around the rim. No one dared take a mug while the general's seat was still empty. Suddenly, the door flung open and Foster burst into the room.

"Good morning, team!" he bellowed as the group leaped to attention. Foster moved straight for the last empty chair at the head of the table, seized the coffeepot, and poured himself a large, steaming mug.

"Let's get to it," he demanded, wasting no time on formalities.

Kittredge nodded to Sid at the podium.

"Good morning, sir. My name is Major Sidwell, the intelligence officer for Operational Righteous Protector. I'd like to bring you up to speed on what we know about the current situation. At 0045 this morning I received a phone call from our MoD liaison officer, Major Lutalo Bigombe. He notified me that last night a Police Intelligence source reported that Daniel Odoki was preparing to cross the border within the next twenty-four to forty-eight hours. After receiving that call, I immediately woke up Colonel Kittredge and briefed him on the situation. Colonel Kittredge then issued a warning order to the ESP operations center instructing them to begin pre-flight procedures in preparation for launching the platform. That is the situation as we know it now. The time is now 0210. Sir, what are your questions?"

"Hot damn, Sidwell, good briefing!" the general said, spilling coffee from his mug as he slammed his fist down on the table.

"Ed, what do you make of this?" the general asked, turning to Colonel Kittredge.

"Hard to say, sir. We've been here a few times before and thought we were getting close. But from what Sid says, MoD seems convinced this time. Of course, this could easily turn into a wild goose chase just like the last few times."

"Major Sidwell, what's your take?" the general pressed.

"Sir, I'd agree with the colonel. It's all still a bit murky. Without our own collectors on the ground, we can't confirm or deny any information we're getting from MoD. The only way to know for sure is to get eyes on the target and make the assessment ourselves."

"That sounds to me like a vote to launch," Foster insisted.

"Yes, sir. I think that's the only way we're going to know for sure," Sid said, glancing over at Kittredge, trying to read his thoughts. "However, there's also a risk in moving too soon."

"Go on," Foster said.

"Yes, sir. As you are aware, the platform has about twenty-eight hours of endurance time, depending on weather conditions and payload. It will probably take a quarter of that time just to get us over the target area. Then about the same amount of time to get back to the airfield. Not to mention the fact that we don't know exactly where this meeting is taking place. MoD has a general idea, but there's still a lot of terrain to cover. We'll need time to search. But if we launch too soon, before we know whether Odoki is making his move, then we could miss our chance. The entire meeting could go down while the platform is back at the airport refueling for another sortie. Either way, this may just come down to dumb luck."

"Ed, does that sound right to you?" the general said, turning back to the colonel.

"Sid's basically right, sir. Our flexibility is limited by having only one aircraft. Our best chance may be to launch now and then hope for more information once the mission is underway. If Odoki and his men are really on the move, there's a chance we'll get another tip while we're up in the air. But, one thing is for sure. As long as that bird is sitting on the runway, we have zero chance of getting him."

"What's the status of the Gisawians? Are they ready to move forward on the offensive?" the general asked.

"Yes, sir. We believe they're fully postured," Kittredge continued. "MoD has allocated nearly four full brigades to Operation Brushfire. That's almost their entire army. They've spent the last several weeks preparing their assault forces for the mission. But they'll need at least twenty-four hours to mobilize once President Namono gives the order to launch."

"When do you think that order will come?"

"We've been told that nothing will happen until we've taken our shot at Odoki. They won't risk moving large formations into the area and possibly scaring off the big fish."

Foster closed his eyes and nodded, appearing lost in thought. The staff held their breath, anxiously awaiting his next move. Finally, General Foster opened his eyes and stared decisively off at the far end of the room, as if gazing into an unseen horizon.

"Gentlemen. We all know this is a long shot. But the cards have been stacked against us from the get-go. We were given an impossible mission. Without the tools to get it done. And that's no damn way to run a war," he said, shaking his head in disgust. "It's no secret that the shot clock has run out on this operation. The damn politicians back in DC have failed us once again. But this evening, by the grace of God, we have been given one last opportunity to set things right. And there is no way in hell we're going to pass up on that chance. Men, the time is now. We must seize this opportunity and go home winners. Are you with me!" he demanded.

As he awaited their answer, Foster leveled a beady-eye gaze around the room. His eyes seemed to interrogate their very souls, weighing the substance of their manhood. In return, he received a few hesitant nods and uneasy murmurs of acquiescence around the table. Then, Foster exploded like a hair-trigger bomb.

"I - SAID - ARE - YOU - WITH - ME!" he bellowed, pounding his fists on the table, punctuating each and every word. The staff leaped from their seats, hearts racing, uncertain what would happen next. Then someone, somewhere, began methodically slapping their hand on the table. Then another joined in, then another, and another. Soon the entire room was rocking in a frenzied chorus of rhythmic percussion. Fists pounding on the table. Coffee mugs tumbling to the floor. Chanting in manic unison, "USA, USA, USA…"

Amid the pandemonium, General Foster leaned back in his chair and unsheathed a massive cigar from a secret pocket sewn into his uniform. Foster broke into a smile as he erotically caressed the fat Cubano between his fingers while utter chaos erupted around him. The feverish chanting built to an ear-splitting crescendo before gradually fading. Then Foster's expression turned deadly serious, squinting under the bright, fluorescent lights.

"Gentlemen, it's game time," he growled. Then he rose from the chair, slipped the stogie between his lips, and dramatically exited the room.

+++

Louie arrived at the camp a few hours later. As he approached the headquarters building, he spotted Sid and Carson standing outside, silhouetted in the pre-dawn twilight.

"Good morning, sunshine," Sid said as Louie joined them.

"Is the entire place awake?" he asked, nodding at the ESP technicians scurrying around the compound.

"More or less," Carson said. "You're just in time. They launched the drone about two hours ago."

"Armed?" Louie asked, uncertain if he wanted to know the answer.

Sid and Carson both nodded. "Seems like it's the real deal," Carson added.

The three of them stood there for a moment without speaking, watching as dawn broke over the horizon.

"I just came from MoD headquarters," Louie finally said. "It's busy there too. They woke the president and told him about the new intelligence report. He spoke with the minister, then gave the order for mobilization. The entire ground force should be ready to move by tomorrow morning if he decides to go forward with the operation."

"Anything new on Odoki?" Sid asked.

Louie shook his head. "Nothing yet. Police Intelligence alerted all their sources in the area. If they see anything unusual hopefully we'll hear something soon."

"OK," Carson said. "Let us know. The general wants an update every hour."

"What do you think about our chances?" Sid pressed.

Louie shrugged. "I guess when you know what you're looking for, it's always easier to find it."

Sid gave Louie a quizzical look. "Is that one of those wise African proverbs that I'll need to think about for a few days before it makes sense?"

"I doubt it," Louie chuckled. "I don't remember my uncle ever saying it."

"In any case, I hope you're right. The general was pretty fired up this morning. He wants this thing to happen. You'll probably see him wandering around the pod farm today giving impromptu Patton-like pep talks."

"Thanks for the warning," Louie said, sighing without enthusiasm. "I guess I better get inside and see what's going on."

"You've still got a little while. It will be at least an hour until the platform gets over the first engagement area. But we should all probably get ready for a long day."

"Sujah Bean opens in about an hour," Carson said, stifling a yawn as he looked at his watch. "You want us to bring you over a coffee?"

"Not my usual habit, but today probably calls for an exception. Thanks," Louie said, before turning and disappearing into the encampment.

+++

Just before noontime, the general called the staff back to the operations center for an update. The exhilaration of the pre-dawn pep rally had since deflated into sedate anticipation. The conference room table was littered with half-empty coffee cups, plates of uneaten fried dough, discarded briefing slides, and dog-eared maps. Colonel Kittredge glared at the clutter as he walked into the room a step behind the general.

"Attention!" Kittredge shouted, sending everyone scrambling to their feet.

"Take your seats," Foster said as he took his place at the head of the table. "OK, what's the situation?"

Sid was already at the podium ready to brief. Behind him the video screen showed a live feed from the drone's onboard camera, cruising high above a vast expanse of patchy jungle.

"Good afternoon, sir. As you can see on the display behind me, the mission is well underway. Right now, we have favorable weather conditions and good visibility. Barring any deterioration of conditions, we expect to have somewhere between fourteen and fifteen hours of flight time before we'll need to turn back to the airfield for refueling."

"Got it," the general said impatiently. "Let's hear about what you've found so far."

"Yes, sir," Sid said. "We have three engagement zones based on the recent information provided by MoD. Earlier this morning we completed the flyover of the first zone but found nothing of interest. No signs of unusual activity or obvious indicators of GLA presence."

"So, we've written that area off?"

"Yes, sir, at least for today's mission. We could take another look during the next flight tomorrow; however, if we stayed any longer, it would have jeopardized our chances of getting to the other two areas. The flight operations center gave us very specific windows of overflight based on estimated fuel consumption rates. The bird is currently en route to the second location. We anticipate two or three hours of surveillance time once we get there."

"Anything more from MoD?"

"Nothing, sir. Our liaison officer was just on the phone with them. He said there's been no new reporting since yesterday."

"Well damn it, have him call again! We can't just be flying around all day hoping that we stumble across something. I need actionable information!" the general demanded. "Failure is not an option!"

"Yes, sir," Sid said. "We'll call right away to see if they have anything new."

"Good. And don't be scared to push these people. We aren't going to let their lack of urgency drive the pace of our operations."

"Yes, sir."

"When do we expect to be over the next engagement area?"

"Around fifteen hundred hours sir."

"OK, let's reassemble then for another update."

The group shot to attention as the general rose from his seat and stormed out of the room. Kittredge followed a step behind, pausing for an instant at the door and glancing back over his shoulder.

"Clean this shit up before the next meeting!" he yelled, before slamming the door shut behind him.

+++

After Carson and Sid finished cleaning up the conference room, they walked over to the Sujah Bean for lunch. They sat in their usual table under the mango tree while Sammy prepared two Panini sandwiches. As they waited for their food, Sid spotted Anna coming across the yard with a determined look on her face.

"Where's Louie?" she demanded, forgoing pleasantries. "I've been texting him all morning, and I haven't heard back."

"If you hadn't noticed, there's a military operation going on here," Sid said, sipping at his double mocha latte. "He's probably a little busy."

Anna cocked her head with annoyance. "Is he over there in one of those pod thingies? Just tell me which one. I'll go over and knock on the door myself."

"Come on, Anna, you know I can't discuss details of where Louie is, or what he's doing," Sid said with a shrug.

"For god's sakes, Sid! Enough with the secret squirrel bullshit. Everybody knows what's going on here! The entire camp has been awake since two in the morning. There was someone in the breakfast line taking bets on whether you guys get him. Sammy just put a sign up next to the cash register announcing that he's extending the café hours until the drone lands! Exactly what secrets are you still trying to keep?"

"OK, OK," Sid said, head shaking in frustration. "Louie's over in the targeting cell, but he's probably too busy to be checking his messages. As long as that thing is up in the air, he needs to be ready to go at any moment."

"Well that's fine, but I still need to speak with him. Doesn't he get a pee break or something?"

"The modules are completely self-contained, including accommodations for all bodily functions. He doesn't need to leave the pod as long as the mission is going on. Anyway, what's so important that you need to see him right now? I'm guessing he's probably got other things on his mind."

Anna threw her notebook onto the table and collapsed into one of the chairs. "I need to ask him some questions. I was up all last night, going through everything in my files, but it still doesn't add up."

"What doesn't add up?" Carson asked.

"Any of it," Anna sighed, flipping distractedly through the pages of her notebook. "Last night I went through every single interrogation report again. Over two hundred pages of indecipherable chicken scratch."

"Did you think you were going to find something new?" Sid asked.

"No. That's just it. There's nothing there. Now I'm even more convinced that the interrogators were looking for something other than Odoki and the GLA."

"How can you know that for sure?" Sid challenged. "You said yourself the notes were a mess. The guys asking the questions probably had no idea what they were doing."

"That's where you're wrong, Sid. I think they knew exactly what they were looking for. Almost all of the questions were about locations of those mysterious camps."

"But why do you think that's a smoking gun for some kind of conspiracy?" Sid countered. "Those are perfectly reasonable questions to ask if you're trying to dismantle an insurgent network. That's exactly what they should be asking."

"Listen, Sid, I just want to see what Louie thinks. Doesn't it strike you as a bit odd that he's sitting over there at the controls of an armed drone, trying to kill a mysterious warlord whose name is almost never mentioned in three hundred pages of interrogation reports?"

"Yes. I admit. It's a little strange. Next issue?" Sid said.

"OK, you remember that information you stumbled across about that mineral Tantalum?"

"The stuff inside cell phones?"

"Yes, among other things. So, I did a little more research and discovered that DRoG is probably sitting atop one of the world's largest unexploited deposits of the stuff."

"Is it valuable?" Carson asked.

"Not when it's in the ground," Anna said.

"So, the stuff is just sitting out there?" Sid asked. "If it's worth something, then why isn't anyone out there digging it up?" he said, suddenly more interested.

"Well, maybe someone is," Anna said. "Most of the assessed deposits are scattered around the western region where the government doesn't have control."

"The same areas where the GLA has been operating?" Carson asked.

"Yup, as far as I can tell. You know that database I made from the interrogation reporting?"

"Overachiever," Sid teased her.

Anna ignored him and pulled out a sheet of paper from her notebook. "Look at this," she said, pushing the page across the table at Sid and Carson.

"What is it?" Carson asked.

"A map of western DRoG. I marked all the locations that were mentioned in the interrogation reports. Unfortunately, most of the descriptions were not specific enough to be identified. Things like, 'the tree at the big rock past the second turn in the road.' But every now and then one of the detainees would mention a village by name or some landmark that I could locate. When I came across something like that, I marked it down on the map."

"Interesting…," Sid said, studying the pattern. "You can really see the areas where they seem to be operating. But you know what's strange?" Sid observed. "Most of this location data wasn't in the interrogation summary reports. Our missions have been focused on an entirely different area."

"Maybe that's intentional. Check this out," Anna said, pulling a sheet of vellum paper from her notebook. The translucent film was covered with yellow blobs drawn with a highlighter. Anna placed the film on top of the map, carefully aligning the grid markings so that the corners matched up.

"OK, so what have we got here?" Sid asked. "It looks like a map with lemonade spilled all over it."

"There's a little more to it than that," Anna snapped. "What do you notice about the areas underneath the lemonade stains?"

"It seems like all the location markers from the interrogation reporting fall underneath them," Carson observed before Sid had a chance to answer.

"Exactly," Anna confirmed.

"OK, now my curiosity is getting the best of me," Sid said, studying the map more closely. "What do the lemonade stains represent?"

"A rough outline of the locations containing likely deposits of Tantalum. I pulled them out of some old geologic survey data I found online. When you superimpose those areas onto the map, you can clearly see a correlation between areas of suspected mineral deposits and places mentioned in the interrogation reporting."

"So, you think that's what this is all about? Odoki and the GLA are trying to hold onto mineral deposits?" Carson asked.

"Right now, that's more than I can prove. But it's hard to dismiss the hypothesis," Anna hinted. "That's why I needed to speak with Louie. He may have some ideas that could explain the connection. Also, I wanted to ask him a few more questions about Tantalus Holdings."

"Did you find anything new?" Sid asked.

"Maybe. Last night I got an email from my lawyer friend back in the states. The one who helped me track down the location of the firm's registration."

"Where was that again?"

"Mauritius. Anyway, my friend was doing some follow-up work trying to locate some of the company's transaction records."

"Any luck?"

"Nope. Nothing at all. But that's still kind of interesting. As far as he could tell, the company has no public record of any revenues or expenditures. In fact, there's almost no paper trail whatsoever."

"But that's the whole point, isn't it? Trying to keep that kind of information away from people poking their noses into your business," Carson said.

"True. Certainly, whoever set up the holding company was trying to avoid attention. However, my friend did come across a few instances where the company's name popped up in public filings by other firms. Including several major infrastructure projects here in DRoG where Tantalus Holdings was listed as the local partner with some Chinese engineering firms doing business here."

"So, you're convinced that Tantalus Holdings has a local connection?" Sid asked.

Anna leaned back in her chair, shaking her head. "I'm not sure of anything right now. All I know is that all of this seems to be connected somehow. I'm just not sure where the pieces fit together."

"But you think Louie knows something that could help?" Carson asked.

"Maybe. I just wanted to run it by him," Anna said, looking around the garden, making sure that no one was within earshot of their table. "There is one other thing," she said in a low voice. "I need to ask you guys a favor…"

Sid glanced hesitantly over at Carson before turning back to Anna. "OK, what do you need?"

"The plans for the government's offensive. I need to know all the targets for Operation Brushfire."

Sid closed his eyes and took a deep breath. "Hell no. I can't do it."

"Come on, Sid!" she begged. "It's not like I'm going to send it to the *New York Times*. This thing could kick off in a few hours. I just need a quick look. Nothing more. I promise!"

"Have you gone completely insane?" Sid hissed at her. "We could all go to jail if I gave that to you. You already know too much as it is. You're not cleared for any of this information!"

"Why do you want to see it?" Carson interrupted, more curious than upset.

"The reason doesn't matter!" Sid interrupted before Anna could answer. "There's no way in hell you're getting that. Trust me, Anna, I'm protecting you from yourself. It's not worth it. Not for any of us. I know you want to solve your little mystery, but I've got a wife and kids at home. I'm not much good to them if I'm doing ten to twenty in Leavenworth."

"Just calm down, Sid," Anna said, patting his arm maternally. "Take deep breaths and think happy thoughts."

"Fuck you, Anna," he murmured, yanking his arm away. "You think this is some big joke, don't you? Listen to me. This isn't some grad school research project. It's a military operation. People could get killed."

"I know that, Sid!" she said. "And that's exactly why I'm asking for your help. Believe me, I don't think it's a joke at all. In fact, I haven't slept for the last two days because this is all I've been thinking about. Whether you like it or not, we're part of this now. Or at least unwitting accomplices. Don't you at least want to know the reason why it's all happening?"

Sid sunk into his chair, sulking as he sipped his coffee. "Tell me why you want to know?" he finally said.

"I need to understand what President Namono is planning. I need to see the locations of the targets."

"It's not going to happen," Sid said, shaking his head defiantly. "It's completely out of the question. Anyway, even if I wanted to give you that information, I don't have it."

"What do you mean you don't have it?" Anna said in disbelief. "I thought we were partners with the Gisawians. Didn't they show you their plans for the offensive? How can you possibly not know that?"

"It's not our mission," Carson explained. "We're here to help them get Odoki. Nothing more. Nothing less."

"So, you're really telling me that you have no idea about the targets for the offensive?"

"Pretty much," Sid admitted. "Operation Brushfire is entirely separate from what's going on here with Odoki. President Namono is using the strike to kick it off, but once that happens, we're just spectators in whatever comes next. That isn't our war, Anna."

"You may want to believe that, Sid, but it's not really true," she insisted. "Our fingerprints will be all over this thing, no matter what happens."

Sid shook his head. "Maybe you're right. But at this point, it doesn't matter. DRoG is mobilizing the army. President Namono issued the order last night. And if you want my honest opinion, MoD is going to do this thing whether we get Odoki or not. The wheels are in motion. It's a done deal."

"But what about the targets? Just tell me what they're going after?"

"Anna, I wasn't kidding about that part," Sid insisted. "I really don't know. We have a general idea of the engagement areas, but they didn't give us specifics about the individual targets. None of our advisors are embedded with the units leading the offensive. It's not our ball game."

"Can you at least give me a general idea of what's going to happen?"

"Jesus, Anna, you're killing me!" Sid griped. "You must really want my kids to be visiting Daddy in jail on Father's Day?"

"OK, OK," she finally relented.

For a moment, the three of them sat together in silence until Sid put down his coffee and turned back to Anna.

"Here's what I'll do," he said with a pained expression. "Come by my office later. I'll show you a copy of the satellite pictures we gave to the Gisawians. By now, everybody and their brother has probably seen them."

"Why show me those?" Anna asked.

"Because I'm pretty sure that will tell you exactly what they're going after. We gave them a detailed laydown of all the areas with recent digging in the western region. My bet is that's where they're going to focus the assaults."

"You're the best, Sid," Anna said, smiling at him across the table. "Just one more tiny…little…thing," she begged, playfully rubbing her fingers together in front of her nose.

"For god's sake, Anna, does it ever end?" Sid exclaimed.

"Don't worry. This one's easy. Just go inside that dome thingy over there and tell Louie I need to see him. I know he's busy, but let him know it's important," she pleaded.

"OK, but this is really it. I'm not kidding this time. No more favors. And don't forget, you owe me big time," Sid said, jabbing his index finger at her across the table.

"Thanks a million, guys," Anna replied, bounding out of her seat and taking off across the yard toward her office.

+++

Later in the afternoon, the staff gathered once again to update the general. Foster wasted no time getting down to business as he sauntered into the room.

"OK, Sidwell, let's have it," he demanded as soon as his butt hit the seat.

Sid accidentally fumbled his laser pointer, nervously dropping it on the ground. He disappeared behind the podium to retrieve it before reappearing above the lectern like a prairie dog popping up from its burrow. He took a deep breath, trying to regain his composure, then began the briefing.

"Sir, as you can see on the screen, we're continuing the high-level sweep over the second engagement area. It's a big chunk of terrain, so we've plotted a wide-area surveillance pattern covering the maximum amount of ground in the minimum amount of time."

"Got it," the general said, cutting him off. "Let's get to the meat and potatoes. Have we found anything yet?"

"No, sir. Nothing yet," Sid answered.

"Goddammit!" the general said, pounding his fists on the table. "This thing is turning into a fiasco. How much longer have we got over this area before we need to move on to the next location?"

Sid looked down into his notes. Everyone waited as he made a few calculations in his head and then jotted some figures on a yellow sticky pad.

"Sir, about one hour more in this area before we'll need to divert to the third site. If we spend any longer here, we won't have enough fuel for a complete run over the final area of interest. Unfortunately, the bulk of that reconnaissance will take place after the sun goes down. That will reduce the effectiveness of the camera, making it harder to identify potential targets."

"This thing is a goat screw!" the general fumed. "What happens if we don't find anything there?"

Before he could reply, Colonel Kittredge cut into the conversation, trying to take the heat off Sid.

"Sir, once the platform gets back to base, ESP's crew can do a quick maintenance check, refuel the aircraft, then launch again in less than ninety minutes. After that, it will take another two or three hours to get back over the engagement area. Best-case scenario, we could resume operations over the area sometime late morning or early afternoon tomorrow."

"For all we know, Odoki could be long gone by then. Maybe back across the border," the general said.

As Foster ranted, Sid noticed Sergeant Goodwin poking his head through the door, waving frantically for his attention. Sid pointed to his chest, trying to confirm that he was the intended audience.

"Sir, please excuse me," Sid pleaded, sliding from the podium once he realized it was urgent. He scurried from the room, leaving General Foster and the staff staring mindlessly at the video feed from the drone's camera, searching for signs of Odoki hiding somewhere down below.

A few minutes later, Sid slipped back into the room, out of breath and sweating profusely after sprinting across the compound. At the podium, he pulled a crumpled sheet of paper from his pocket with some notes scribbled on it.

"Sir, I apologize for the interruption," Sid said, panting. "I just received some new information and needed to confer with flight operations on a revised fuel consumption estimate."

"What have you got?" the general demanded.

"A new report just in from Police Intelligence. Late this morning one of their informants reported some unusual activity approximately forty-five kilometers northeast of the border."

"What kind of activity?" the general asked, momentarily forgetting the image on the screen.

"We don't have many details, but the source reported seeing a patrol of men moving toward what was described as an abandoned military camp."

"Is this an area we've patrolled before?"

"No, sir. At least not recently. We had a mission around there late last year but didn't find anything unusual. It's sparsely populated. Just a few small villages and not much else around. The source said that it was unusual for people to be passing through the area, especially armed men. MoD seems to be taking this seriously."

"How seriously?"

"Seriously enough that they want us to divert from the original flight plan. They've asked to reroute the platform over the new area."

"All based on one source? Are you kidding me?" the general scoffed.

"Sir, I'm skeptical as well. But they claim it's from a well-vetted informant. Someone who has provided valuable information in the past. Police Intelligence has confidence in his story. Also, there's hasn't been any recent reporting from the area scheduled for tonight's reconnaissance. MoD feels we'll be wasting our time by sticking with the original plan."

"Do you agree with that assessment?"

"Sir, I have no way of evaluating the information. MoD doesn't share background on their sources and methods. We only receive sanitized versions of everything. However, at this point, we don't have much else to go on. These engagement areas were planned several days ago. Probably based on information at least a week or two old. The reporting we got today is the first tip we've had since then. It seems risky to ignore it."

"OK, Sidwell. Now, play devil's advocate. Tell me why we shouldn't do this. What's the downside of changing the plan at the last minute?"

Sid looked down into his notes, checking his figures one more time before answering the question. "Sir, it all comes down to a time-space problem."

"Explain."

"The new engagement zone is farther out than the one initially planned for in the fuel burn-rate estimate. It will probably take us another hour and a half to get the platform over the new target area. About the same amount of time for the return trip. Based on my rough calculation, that will give us a maximum of thirty or forty minutes over the new engagement area. That's not much time to check things out."

"Thirty minutes? Fuck. That's no room for error," the general grimaced, as if physically in pain. "How much do we know about the target?"

"We have a grid coordinate but not much else. Police Intelligence describes it as an abandoned military camp, but that's all we know. We won't have a good idea until we get overhead and can take a closer look."

The general was lost in thought, staring vacantly at the video on the screen. After a moment, Colonel Kittredge leaned over and whispered into his ear.

"Sir, every minute we wait is one minute less over the target area. We need to decide now. One way or another. It's your call, sir."

The general rubbed the stubble on his chin, pursing his lips as he weighed the options. Suddenly, he looked up at Sid, still standing behind the podium.

"Divert. Divert the mission now! Get us over that new target!" Foster yelled out. "Those bastards at Police Intelligence better be right on this one. You go back and tell them, I'm not going home without a scalp. Are we clear on that!"

"Yes, sir," Sid said, frozen behind the podium, uncertain what he was supposed to do.

"Make it happen!" the general bellowed.

Sid leaped back from the podium and bounded for the door, racing across the compound toward the flight operations center to deliver the general's message.

CHAPTER FOURTEEN

———

Anna was sitting by herself at the café, lost in concentration as daylight faded. Papers, notebooks, maps, and empty cups of coffee were scattered around the table. She was squinting into her laptop when Sammy appeared beside her carrying an old-fashioned oil lamp.

"It is too dark for reading, Ms. Anna. Please, take this," he said, setting the lamp down on the table.

"Thank you, Sammy. You're very kind," she smiled, rubbing her eyes and suddenly aware of the time.

"Not working in your office tonight?" he asked.

Anna shook her head. "The air conditioning broke again. Besides, I have a better view of the excitement from here," she explained, nodding across the yard at ESP's encampment.

"Yes, it's very busy," Sammy agreed. "The café is open late tonight, so please stay as long as you wish. Can I bring you another coffee?"

"No, thank you, Sammy. I've had too many already. Maybe a decaf later."

Sammy smiled and retreated back to the hut to start on another round of Paninis and fresh lemonade for delivery to the ESP compound.

An hour passed with the sun now completely below the horizon. The decorative Chinese lanterns woven through the branches of the mango tree cast the garden in a pale light. Anna continued working on her computer while keeping a close eye on the comings and goings across the yard. The geodesic domes glowed brightly under cones of industrial lighting, giving the camp the surreal appearance of a science fiction movie set or high-security prison.

Anna yawned deeply and was almost ready to give up her vigil when she spotted Sid leaving the headquarters building and walking across the yard. Before he could escape, she whistled and waved him over to the table.

"Didn't I see you here four hours ago? Have you been sitting at this table all day?" he asked in disbelief.

"More or less. The AC is still out in my office."

"What about your room? That's got to be better than sitting out here in the dark."

"What room?" Anna snorted. "I got booted out when the general arrived. They put me in some windowless shoebox with walls made of whitewashed plywood. It's like a prison cell, only less homey."

"Welcome to my world. Where do you think I've been sleeping for the last eleven months?"

"Oh, sorry," she said. "I guess I shouldn't complain. Anyway, how are things going with mission impossible?" she asked, nodding in the direction of the command center.

"You know I can't talk about it," Sid reminded her.

"Right. I keep forgetting. It's all a big secret," she said sarcastically. "Don't worry, Sammy gave me an update a few minutes ago. He said you guys diverted the drone to an unplanned target based on some new information from MoD."

"Fuck!" Sid yelled at no one in particular. "This is ridiculous! Now you're telling me that the damn Gisawian barista is chit-chatting about sensitive operational information? Why do I even bother? Maybe we should just do a pay-per-view over here at the café so everyone can sit down in the garden with some popcorn and watch it all on the big screen. I'm sure it would be great for Sammy's business!"

"Calm down, calm down," Anna said, barely suppressing a smile. "Sammy didn't do anything wrong. He's been running trays of Paninis and coffee back and forth between the café and the operations center all day long. It would be hard for him not to pick up on a few details when he's over there delivering food every twenty minutes. Besides, it's all in the family, right?"

"What the hell does that mean?" Sid snapped.

"ESP," she reminded him. "It's the common denominator. Me. Sammy. The people flying the drone. How could you forget? We all work for Slyker."

"Whatever," Sid sniffed. "As far as I'm concerned, this is still a military operation. Until someone tells me otherwise, I'm going to treat it that way."

"OK, Sid. If that makes you feel better," Anna said with a shrug. "Anyway, before you go, I need to ask a favor."

Sid was silent, kicking at the dirt, still angry over the breach of security.

"Pretty please…," she begged.

"What do you want?" he said, already annoyed for letting himself be manipulated.

"I still haven't seen Louie. He hasn't been out of the pod all day."

"Listen, Anna. I'm telling you, he's busy in there. It's not like he's just hanging out at the café all day, drinking lattes and scribbling in his notebook," Sid said, waving a hand dismissively at the clutter on the table.

"Just tell him I need to see him. It's important. I'm not leaving this table until he comes out here."

"OK, fine. I'll tell him. But you may be waiting all night. At least until this thing is over."

"Thanks. I knew I could count on you," she said as he turned and began walking away. "Sid," she called after him. "You look tired."

"It's been a long day. And probably will be a long night."

"Please take care of yourself. OK?"

"Yeah. I will," he mumbled before setting off back toward headquarters building, having completely forgotten the coffee he came outside to get.

+++

For the first time since arriving in the country, Anna felt herself shivering. The nighttime air was dry. A light breeze blew across the yard, and the mango leaves shimmered in the moonlight, casting strange shadows across the garden. Anna glanced down at her watch, surprised at how long she'd been sitting there. Sammy's deliveries across the yard gradually tapered off when the operation seemed to enter a lull. Inside the hut, she saw him slumped over the counter, fighting to stay awake as he counted the day's receipts.

With the moon high above the horizon, she felt her resolve finally ebbing. Closing her laptop, she began gathering up the notebooks and maps from the table. She took one last sip from a cup of cold tea, then started off toward her room. Halfway across the yard, she felt her cellphone buzzing in her pocket. She pulled out the primitive Nokia and glanced down at the screen, seeing Louie's number flash up on the incoming text.

"Five minutes" was all it said.

Anna immediately changed direction and walked over to the darkest part of the yard across from the cluster of pods where Louie was working. She found a concealed spot inside a small grove of palm trees where she could watch from the shadows without being seen.

After a few minutes, one of the pod doors opened. She spotted Louie stepping outside. For a moment he stood in the yard stretching his arms over his head, then began jogging in place as if he'd just come outside to clear his head. Once she was certain that he was alone, Anna whistled for his attention. Louie heard her call and scanned the yard trying to find her. She stepped out from the shadows just long enough for Louie to see her. Glancing over his shoulder, he checked to see if anyone was watching, then jogged over to join her in the palm grove.

"I've been trying to reach you all day!" Anna whispered, reflexively reaching out and touching his hand.

"I know. I'm sorry," he said. "Please understand…"

Anna shook her head, letting him know that she didn't blame him.

"How are you?"

"OK. I guess. It's been a long day," he said, nervously checking his watch. "I only have a few minutes. Sid told me you needed to talk. Is everything OK?"

"I'm fine. It's not really that important. You know my little obsessions," she said, kicking at the bag of notebooks and maps on the ground. "Also, I just wanted to see you," she whispered, feeling emboldened by the darkness.

"Me too," Louie said, realizing they were still holding hands before self-consciously letting his slip down to his side.

"Sid told me you found something from the interrogation reports," Louie said, trying to change the subject. "Anything interesting?"

"I'm not sure how interesting. Just strange, I guess. How closely did you read through the reports?" she asked.

"Not very," he admitted. "I glanced over them before I gave them to you, but honestly, I really didn't give them much time."

"Don't worry. They're not great reading. But there are a few things I still haven't been able to figure out."

"Such as?" Louie asked, glancing back at the compound.

"Such as, why did the interrogators never ask the detainees anything about Odoki? His name never comes up in the questioning? He's this big notorious warlord supposedly leading a rebel army, yet the interrogators never even talk about him. I can't figure that out."

"I don't know," Louie said, shaking his head. "I agree, it doesn't make much sense."

"Or maybe it does make sense. Especially if he's not really what they're looking for."

"What do you mean?" Louie said, confused. "That's what this entire thing is about! Look around here. Have you noticed what's going on?" he said, jabbing his thumb back at the silvery domes glowing under the lights.

"Listen, Louie, I know it sounds crazy, but what if this offensive is really going after something else?"

"Anna, my uncle is the deputy minister of defense," he said impatiently. "If that was the case, don't you think I'd know about it? We've been trying to get Odoki and shut down the GLA for years. Even before the Americans arrived. Now you're suggesting that it's all some elaborate ruse? That just doesn't make any sense."

"When was the last time anyone saw him?" Anna challenged.

"Come on, Anna," Louie sighed. "You know the answer to that."

"Do I really? All I know is what I've read in the papers. That three years ago, Daniel Odoki and his men supposedly mascaraed that village. Since then he's been in hiding across the border, and no one has seen him."

"Right. But just because he's in hiding doesn't mean that he's any less dangerous. He's still in command of the GLA. His fighters are still operating all over the western region."

"Then why isn't any of that mentioned in the interrogation reporting? There's nothing there about Odoki or the GLA attacks. It's all about the locations of these camps and logistical routes. It's like they're trying to take down a postal system, not a rebel army."

"Listen, Anna, we've been over this before. I know you think it's suspicious, but there are plenty of explanations. Unfortunately, I don't work for Police Intelligence, so I can't tell you why they asked the questions they did," Louie said, glancing down at his cell phone, checking for messages. "Anna, I'm sorry, but I really need to get back inside," he said distractedly.

"What do you know about Tantalum?" Anna blurted out, ignoring his attempt to leave.

"What? You mean that mythology guy you told us about? Are you still obsessing about that pen?"

"No. I'm talking about the mineral, not mythology. It's a rare metal used in electronic equipment."

"Never heard of it."

"Would you be surprised to learn that there are significant unexploited deposits in the western part of your country. More or less the same areas occupied by the GLA."

Louie became quiet, forgetting for a moment his urgency to return to the pod. "What are you saying?" he asked.

"I'm not exactly sure. That's why I wanted to talk. The target zone for the offensive. Does it look like this?" she asked, showing him the map with the yellow highlighted overlay. Louie stepped into the moonlight to study the details.

"Where'd you get this?" he asked.

She could see the worry in his eyes. "I made it. It's from some old geologic survey data showing areas likely containing large deposits of Tantalum. The pin markers underneath the yellow shading are the places I was able to identify from the interrogation reporting. Notice the correlation?"

Louie handed back the map and glanced over his shoulder before turning back to Anna. "It's the same area as the targets for the offensive," he finally said. "Anna. What do you think is going on?"

"I don't know, Louie. I really don't," she said, shaking her head. "Is there a chance that the army is going after miners, not rebel fighters?"

"Children?" Louie asked incredulously.

"No, M-I-N-E-R-S, not M-I-N-O-R-S," she clarified.

"Oh right," Louie said, embarrassed. "Clearly, I need some sleep. Anyway, it doesn't seem possible, but right now, I just don't know what to believe."

Louie's cell phone began buzzing in his hand. "I need to go," he said after glancing down at the message.

"Wait!" Anna begged, impulsively grabbing his hand before he had a chance to leave.

"Anna, I'm sorry. I can't talk anymore. I've got to be back inside. They can't do this without me."

"Louie, one last question. Then I promise I'll let you go."

He nodded anxiously, hoping to end the conversation.

"Does your uncle ever travel to Mauritius?"

"What? Anna, I don't have time for this now! How can my uncle's holiday plans possibly be relevant?"

"So, he's been there?"

"Yes. I'm sure he's been there!" Louie said with exasperation as his cell phone buzzed again. "My uncle is a senior government official. He goes to meetings all over the world. But why does it matter?"

"More than once?" she pressed. "Please, Louie. I just need to know."

Louie nodded, still not understanding but realizing that she would not relent. "Yes, I'm sure he's been there several times. He goes to some big defense conference there each year. But I still don't see the point? What does this have to do with Odoki and the GLA?"

"Maybe nothing. I just needed to ask," Anna said, as Louie's phone buzzed yet again.

"I'm sorry. I've got to go," he said. As he turned to leave, he realized she had grabbed his hand again. "We'll talk more after all this is over," he promised her.

Anna wouldn't let him go when he tried to pull away. "Is this the right thing to do?" she whispered.

Louie dropped her hand and shook his head. "I'm not sure of anything anymore," he said, glancing anxiously back at the command center. "Please, try to get some rest. We'll talk tomorrow. I promise."

Then he turned and broke into a jog back toward the glowing dome. Anna waited until he disappeared inside, then picked up her bag of notebooks and maps. She walked slowly back to her temporary room, hoping to forget about it all, at least long enough to get some sleep.

+++

During the short time Louie had been away, the mood in the targeting center had transformed. Everyone wide awake, sitting at the workstations, sipping steaming cups of Sammy's special blend.

"Where the hell have you been?" Slyker snapped the instant he saw Louie walking through the door. "I've been texting you for the last ten minutes!"

"I just stepped out for some fresh air. I've been stuck in here all day. I needed to clear my head before things got busy," Louie said.

"OK. I was worried that you might be getting cold feet or something," Slyker said, in lieu of an apology. "We're almost over the engagement area. The targeting cell is waiting to start pre-mission checks. They need you in the seat and ready to go."

Louie nodded. "How much time?"

Slyker glanced at his watch. "Ten minutes until we're over the grid coordinates that we got from Police Intelligence. I just spoke with the flight engineers. Apparently, we hit some headwinds during the last leg of the flight. It took longer than expected. If we're lucky, we'll probably get about twenty minutes over the engagement area before we need to turn back around."

"What's plan B if we don't make that?" Louie asked.

"What do you mean plan B? There is no fucking plan B! If we don't turn that thing around on time, we run out of gas and crash into the goddamn jungle. That's plan B!"

"Don't you have some kind of contingency for that?"

"You're kidding, right?" Slyker asked in disbelief. "The only contingent thing about that scenario is my job! Corporate headquarters will have my ass if that thing goes down on the proof of concept mission. There's too much riding on this."

"You mean getting Odoki?"

"What? Oh yeah, sure. That too," Slyker said as an afterthought.

"So, will you be here when this goes down?" Louie asked.

"Nope. My boys have all the technical stuff covered. Just listen to them, and everything will be fine. It's no different than the rehearsal last week. Focus on your job, and we'll take care of the rest. Once they get you over the engagement area, the analysts will let you know if they see anything that looks remotely like a target."

"Then it's all on me?"

Slyker nodded. "Yup. We'll help you assess what you're seeing on the camera, but at the end of the day, you've got to decide if what you see is actionable. That's the only part of this that we can't do for you. At least according to the lawyers..."

"Where are you going to be?"

"Over in the conference room babysitting General Foster. At least for today, my main job is keeping him happy," Slyker said, walking toward the door. Before stepping outside, he stopped, turned and looked back at Louie. "Everything's cool, right? No second thoughts?"

Louie shook his head.

"OK. Good. Just remember. If we find something, we're not going to have much time. Happy hunting," Slyker added, giving Louie a thumbs-up before disappearing out the door.

A few minutes later Slyker arrived into the headquarters building. The operations center was packed wall-to-wall, and every single seat around the table was occupied. General Foster and the staff were all staring at the large monitor on the wall, watching the grainy images from the drone's infrared camera. When Foster noticed Slyker standing against the wall without a place to sit, he motioned for one of the junior officers to relinquish his seat. Slyker wedged the chair up to the table between Colonel Kittredge and the general. Kittredge shot him a dirty look as he scooted over to make room.

"It's go-time," Foster said giddily.

"Yes, sir. But we're looking at a very tight window."

"How tight?" Foster asked with a furrowed brow.

Slyker looked down at his watch. "About twenty-five minutes until we'll need to pull the platform back to base."

"Damn…," Foster said under his breath.

Slyker looked over to where Sergeant Goodwin was manning the computer. "Sergeant. It's time," he called out. "Please patch us into the audio channel so we can listen in."

Goodwin tapped a few commands into the keyboard, and a moment later, they heard the sounds of disembodied voices crackle through the speakers. During a break in the chatter, Slyker flipped on the intercom.

"Flight Ops, this is Slyker over in the conference room. I have General Foster here with me. We are patched into your communications channel and observing the video feed from the platform. Please provide us with an update of the situation, over."

"Roger, sir. At this time, we are moving over the engagement zone and preparing to enter a surveillance pattern at ten thousand feet. Skies are clear with sixty percent illumination. We have light winds from the east at two knots. Barometric pressure is steady."

"Thank you, Flight Ops," Slyker continued. "Please provide an estimate of our available time-on-target based on the current fuel-burn rate."

The line went quiet for a moment as flight operations performed the calculations.

"Mr. Skyler, this is Flight Ops. Based on anticipated weather conditions and burn rate, we have approximately twenty-one minutes remaining over the target area before end-of-mission."

Slyker flipped the mic back to mute and then called over to Sergeant Goodwin at the computer terminal. "Sergeant, please put the time up the board so we can monitor."

Goodwin reprogrammed the digital clock display, showing the time remaining on-station. As the numbers flipped to under twenty minutes, the voice from flight operations came back on the line.

"This is Flight Ops. We are over the engagement area and beginning the surveillance pattern. Targeting cell, please give us your status."

A new voice came on the line.

"This is the targeting cell. All onboard sensors operating normally. The payload is in weapons hold status."

"This is Flight Ops. We copy, all sensors operating normally." Then, after a brief pause: "This is Flight Ops. Trigger man, please give us your status."

Slyker, General Foster, and everyone else in the room stared at the countdown clock as it ticked under nineteen minutes.

"This is Flight Ops. I say again, Trigger man, please provide your status."

Slyker's finger danced over the intercom button as the entire room awaited a response. When the clock was halfway to eighteen minutes, Slyker stood up from his chair in frustration and slapped the mic.

"Louie, where the hell are you!" he yelled into the microphone, abandoning all concern for radio protocol.

"Trigger man here," Louie finally replied. "I read you loud and clear. All systems are Go."

Slyker shook his head and sat back down in his chair. The next voice was flight operations, seemingly unruffled by Slyker's panicked intervention.

"Trigger man. We read you loud and clear. All systems are Go. Please stand by for updates from the target assessment section."

The radio was silent for several minutes as the drone zigzagged over the engagement area. The staff in the conference room appeared hypnotized by the images on the screen. Far down below the dense layer of treetops looked like a moonscape through the drone's thermal camera. Occasionally the sensors picked up what appeared to be animals bounding through clearings or huddled in shallow burrows. Each false positive sent everyone's pulse racing in the operations center, keeping alive the faint hope that something more sinister would be found.

As twelve minutes, General Foster leaned over to Slyker. "This is turning into a goddamn clusterfuck. There's nothing down there but jackrabbits and hyenas."

Slyker ignored Foster and calmly flipped the switch on the mic. "This is Slyker. How much of the engagement area have we covered so far?"

The clock ticked under ten minutes as they awaited the answer.

"This is Flight Ops. We estimate approximately forty percent of the engagement area has been covered."

"Targeting cell. Have you detected any indicators yet?" Slyker replied.

"This is the targeting cell. Negative, Mr. Slyker. Nothing yet. We're also monitoring the shortwave radio frequencies. Nothing there either. If anyone is down there, they're not moving around or talking on the radio."

The sputtering air conditioning had long since become ineffective, and the temperature in the conference room was unbearable. Slyker was sweating through his tailored dress shirt, dabbing his forehead with a handkerchief as the clock hit nine minutes. He leaned over to General Foster, who was stewing in his seat and gnawing on the stub of an old cigar.

"Sir, may I speak with you privately?" Slyker whispered, nodding over to an unoccupied corner of the room beyond earshot of the others.

The general pushed away from the table in disgust and barged across the room like an agitated bull, sending the staff scurrying from his path like frightened animals.

"Sir, we've got five minutes left," Slyker explained unnecessarily. "Tonight may not be our night. We need to make the call to abort the mission. We can't afford to cut things too close."

"Not yet," the general growled, his lips clenched around the stub of his cigar. "We're not quitting until we have to."

Slyker glanced nervously back at the clock. "Sir, it's not about quitting. This is about getting a very expensive prototype design back to the airfield in one piece," he said, gesturing frantically at the screen. "Look, General. There's nothing out there. It's not worth running our baby into the ground just to confirm what we already know. We got to keep our eye on the prize. Think about the big picture. It's time to turn it around," Slyker pleaded.

The general stared despondently at the screen as the seconds ticked by. Finally, Slyker could wait no longer.

"Sir, as the senior on-site representative for ESP International, I am making a command decision to turn the platform around. We'll get it safely back to the airfield, refuel, then be back out here again by tomorrow afternoon."

"You wouldn't dare...," the general threatened, jabbing his finger in Slyker's chest.

"General, with all due respect, the contract clearly stipulates that ESP is empowered to assume operational decision-making at any point when a company-owned asset is jeopardized by client negligence or willful deviation from established flight protocols. In my professional judgment, we've reached that point. Therefore, I'm ordering the platform back to base."

Slyker made a move for the nearest microphone but not quickly enough to escape Foster's reach. The general seized his arms in a vice grip as Slyker squealed in surprise. The general proceeded to lift him off his feet and slam him hard against the wall.

"Listen, you little faggot!" Foster hissed, so close that Slyker could feel the spittle hitting his face. "Don't think I don't know your deal. You're turning that thing around over my dead body."

As Slyker struggled to free himself from the general's grasp, Colonel Kittredge suddenly realized what was happening and leaped from his chair to intervene, less out of concern for Slyker than to protect Foster from the unintended consequences of his rage. With Slyker yelping in pain and Kittredge pushing his way across the room, Sid suddenly called out from the podium.

"Something's down there!"

In an instant, everyone's attention shifted back to the screen and the live feed from the drone's infrared camera. The grainy image revealed a large clearing down below and several humanoid-like blobs moving around on the ground.

General Foster, now distracted by the images on the screen, unconsciously released his captive. Slyker dropped to the floor, then went scrambling for the nearest microphone, throwing himself on the table and frantically slapping at the button.

"Flight Ops. This is Slyker. What the hell are we seeing down there?"

A moment later, a voice replied through the speakers.

"All stations, this is Flight Ops. We are entering a holding pattern above a possible target and awaiting an assessment for multiple unidentified objects. Please stand by…"

The general joined Slyker at the table, having already forgotten about the attempted assault just seconds before. "What do you think?" Foster asked.

"I don't know, but we better find out soon," Slyker said, nodding up at the clock.

After what felt like an eternity, the voice came back on the line. "This is the targeting cell. Initial assessment indicates one structure and two vehicles. We observe between eight to ten military-aged males moving around the perimeter. All personnel appear armed with light automatic weapons. Two additional individuals, also armed, are positioned outside the structure, possibly guarding an entrance. Thermal signatures suggest the possibility of an unknown number of additional personnel inside the structure."

Before Slyker could respond, General Foster pushed him aside and yelled into the microphone. "Is it Odoki or not?"

The radio was silent as the clock ticked under five minutes. Foster tapped impatiently on the button, leaning over the microphone. He was just about ready to speak when the voice came back on the line.

"Target location and observable signatures are consistent with reporting provided by Gisawian Police Intelligence. We assess with medium to high confidence that patterns of life match known GLA profiles. Remote location, presence of armed security, and nighttime activities are all consistent with known GLA operational templates."

"You didn't answer my question!" the general yelled back. Slyker cautiously reached down to the table and covered the microphone with his hand.

"General Foster, sir, it's not your call. We can't take this any further. That's how it's designed to work."

Foster blinked with confusion, staring blankly back at Skyler. Without a word, he stepped back and ceded control of the intercom. With visible relief, Slyker felt the situation returning under his control. He looked up at the clock, took a deep breath, then leaned over the microphone.

"Louie. This is Slyker. You've heard everything we know. You've got about two minutes and forty seconds left to assess the situation and make your decision. After that, I'm ordering the platform back to base. The ball's in your court."

On the screen, two more figures suddenly appeared at the edge of the frame, walking in the direction of the building. They joined the two others standing outside. The four men appeared to exchange a few words before disappearing inside the structure. Meanwhile, the shot clock on the wall ticked under two minutes.

"That little fucker is going to let them get away," the general muttered in disbelief.

Slyker ignored him as he pressed the intercom button. "Louie, two minutes left. What do you want to do?"

Suddenly Louie's voice came over the speaker.

"Flight Ops, this is Trigger Man. Request permission to arm the warhead."

"Roger, Trigger Man. Permission granted."

"This is Trigger Man. Initiating the arming sequence and locking on target," Louie said, his voice devoid of emotion.

"This is Flight Ops. We confirm that the warhead is armed. I say again, the warhead is armed and locked on target. You may engage when ready."

The room waited as the clock passed under sixty seconds. Slyker held his finger over the intercom button. At fifty seconds Slyker flipped the mic off mute, preparing to give the order turning the drone around. Suddenly a flash of light filled the screen, followed a second later by another. Then came the sound of Louie's voice confirming what they had just witnessed.

"This is Trigger Man. Payload released. I say again, the payload has been released."

On the screen, they watched the fiery plums of the missiles' engines marking their path toward the target. A few seconds later they saw two small flashes, milliseconds apart, as the warheads penetrated the building.

Slyker exhaled with relief. Turning to Foster, he saw the general's eyes tearing with pride. Then, without warning, an intense flash of light momentarily blinded the drone's optical sensors.

"What the fuck was that?" Foster said, dumbstruck, cigar drooping from his lips.

"That wasn't the warhead," Slyker stammered, trying to understand what had just happened. "The LORSK-M doesn't pack that kind of punch. Something else must have been inside that building."

As the drone's sensors recalibrated, the image gradually sharpened and revealed the aftermath of the blast. Everything in the clearing had been consumed in the fireball. Trees and vegetation vaporized. A crater was left where the shack had stood. The vehicles at the edge of the clearing were burning, and nothing was left standing anywhere. Slyker took a moment to regain his composure and then flipped open the mic.

"Targeting cell, this is Slyker. Please provide a post-strike assessment."

As they waited for the response, Foster leaned toward Slyker, so close that he could smell the stench of stale cigar on the general's breath.

"If this goes bad," Foster whispered, "it's your queer little ass on the line. Not mine."

Slyker looked straight ahead and said nothing, watching the fires burning across the remnants of the encampment.

A moment later, they heard the voice from the targeting cell back on the line.

"Initial post-strike analysis suggests that the LORSK-M likely triggered a secondary explosion of materials stored inside the structure."

"What kind of materials. How much?" Slyker asked into the mic.

"The amount and type of explosive materials cannot be determined from remote sensing. However, judging from the blast radius and area of collateral damage, we assess at least several thousand pounds of explosive materials."

"Is anything still moving down there?"

"Negative, Mr. Slyker. No signs of movement. There's nothing still alive down there."

Without warning, the general pushed toward the microphone. "This is General Foster. I want some fucking answers right now! Who was down there and how many of them did we get!"

"Sir, the time is up," Slyker said calmly, nodding to the clock on the wall, now showing a string of zeros. "I'm ordering the platform back to the airfield."

Slyker reached for the mic, half expecting Foster to break his arm before he could press the button.

"Flight Ops, this is Slyker. Mission complete. Return to base. I say again, return to base immediately."

"This is Flight Ops. Acknowledge. Platform returning to base. ETA, two hours and forty-seven minutes."

Everyone in the room watched as the drone turned away from the target. The residual light from the burning car fires gradually disappeared, replaced by the monotone moonscape of scrub brush and trees.

"Colonel Kittredge, I want someone out there ASAP," the general demanded. "I need to know what the hell just happened."

At the sound of his name, Kittredge was startled back from a trance. He looked around the room in a state of befuddlement. The rush of adrenalin already giving way to exhaustion.

"Sir?"

"I said, I want someone standing on the pile of rubble. Now!" Foster ordered.

The colonel turned to Master Sergeant Jorgenson.

"Jorgs, how soon until we can get one of your teams out there for site exploitation?" the colonel asked.

Jorgenson shook his head. "Sir, that's going to be tough. DRoG is kicking off Operation Brushfire in a few hours.

They don't have any units to spare. It's too dangerous for our guys to be out there on the roads while the Gisawians are conducting combat ops."

"What about ESP's helicopters?" Kittredge asked, turning to Slyker. "We can use those to get a forensics team out to the blast site."

"Or alternatively, I can get the platform refueled and be over it by late tomorrow morning," Slyker suggested as a counter-offer. "In daylight that should get us a good view of whatever's left out there."

"That's not enough," Sid interjected. "We won't know anything unless we get boots on the ground. We need to collect residue from the secondary explosion. We need DNA samples. There could be major intelligence value in whatever's left out there. We're not going to get that by flying overhead at ten thousand feet."

All eyes fell on Slyker, awaiting his answer. Sensing that the moment for negotiation had passed, Slyker relented and pressed the button on the mic.

"Flight Ops, this is Slyker. Call the airfield. Tell them to get the choppers ready. They'll be taking a team out to the blast site first thing in the morning."

+++

The next afternoon, after a few hours of much-needed sleep, the staff reassembled in the conference room. Sergeant Goodwin was at the computer trying to link up the large video screen to a satellite television feed. After a minute of fiddling with the settings, the monitor finally flickered to life.

Captain Burke suddenly appeared on the television screen standing just outside the front gate of the camp. Visible over his shoulder was a large sign emblazoned with the crest of Operation Righteous Protector, which had been hastily fabricated during the night by the camp's maintenance crew. The logo featured a pair of crossed American and Gisawian flags superimposed over the outline of an eagle's claw extending down from a cloud. Trapped in the predator's talons was what looked like a plague-infested rodent. Beneath the dramatic imagery was a scroll with the phrase "*Acta non Verba.* Actions not Words."

"Let the circus begin," Sid whispered over to Carson as they watched Burke fiddling with his earpiece.

"Testing, one, two, three," his voice blasted through the speakers.

"For God's sake, Goodwin, turn down the volume!" the colonel pleaded, rubbing his temples and sinking into his chair.

"This is KCTV Centerville. How do you read us?"

"Loud and clear," Burke said, flashing a thumbs-up into the camera.

"Perfect," said the unseen speaker on the other side transmission. "Two minutes to air. Once we start, Leslie will do a brief intro and then cut to your location for the interview. Any questions?"

Captain Burke shook his head and checked his uniform one last time. A moment later the shot switched from Burke to a live view of a bustling newsroom somewhere in Pennsylvania. A blond woman of indeterminate age was sitting behind the anchor desk smiling into the camera. The frame tightened around her as the dramatic set-piece music faded.

"Good morning, Centerville and the greater tri-county

region. This is Leslie Jenkins from KCTV with a breaking news exclusive. In a moment we are going live to a sensitive US military operating base in the Democratic Republic of Gisawi where for the past three years American forces have been waging a campaign aimed at capturing the notorious warlord Daniel Odoki. I'm on the line now with Captain Stephen J. Burke the Third, spokesman for Operation Righteous Protector. Captain Burke, are you there?"

"Yes, Leslie. I hear you loud and clear," Burke said, as the image went to a split-screen.

"Captain Burke, I hope you don't mind is we start off with a little quiz. Can you tell our viewers how far you are from Centerville?"

"Well, Leslie, as the crow flies, about 7,300 miles. However, I might be off by a few miles, so don't hold me to that."

"A long way for sure, but certainly not far from our thoughts and prayers."

"Thank you, Leslie. That means a great deal to us."

"So, Captain Burke, let's move on to the big news of the day. I understand from our producer that we are the first affiliate in the country to report on a major development in the hunt for Daniel Odoki."

"That's right, Leslie. Late last night this command led a precision strike operation against a suspected GLA compound believed to be hosting a high-level GLA leadership meeting.

"Captain Burke, can you tell our viewers how this went down?"

"Unfortunately, many of those details remain classified; however, I can tell you that we employed an innovative new targeting methodology while working in close collaboration with our Gisawian partners."

"So, can we assume this was some kind of drone strike?"

"Leslie, I can't go into the specifics of the particular platform. However, I will say that through a unique public-private partnership, we were able to leverage a sophisticated military technology previously unavailable to regional allies such as DRoG."

"OK, Captain Burke, let's get to the question on everyone's minds. Did you get Odoki?"

"At this time, we're still in the process of conducting a post-strike assessment. It would be premature for me to speculate on who or what may have been in that compound."

"But you did say the strike was against a GLA leadership meeting. Can we assume that Odoki was the intended target?"

"All l can say is that preliminary analysis suggests a successful engagement of a high-level meeting of rebel fighters."

"Odoki among them?"

"I can't comment on that specifically, except to say that the absence of evidence is not evidence of absence."

"Well, that sound to me like confirmation!"

"We don't want to jump to conclusions, Leslie. While we cannot confirm that the operation took out Odoki, we have no compelling reason to believe that he was not in the compound at the time of the strike. Our forces are currently conducting site exploitation, and we expect to have additional information soon."

"Well, that sounds like a big win for team America! So, Captain Burke, with the successful conclusion of this operation, what's next? Is the mission there over? Will our troops be coming home soon?"

"That's a decision for our political leadership in Washington. However, from our perspective here on the ground, significant security challenges still remain. Early this morning Gisawian President Namono announced the start of a major offensive aimed at taking back parts of the country still under GLA influence."

"Is the US assisting in this effort?"

"No, Leslie, not directly. While the US strongly supports Gisawian efforts to bring peace and stability to this unstable region, we have no direct role in these operations. It is their fight, and we can't do it for them. While we will continue to provide advice and assistance to local forces, I want to emphasize that there is no military solution to these complex security challenges. That is why this morning President Namono announced a major economic development program aimed at filling the security vacuum in the western region. He has solicited the help of several foreign partners to unlock the country's vast natural resources, bringing jobs, education, and prosperity to a volatile region. We are very optimistic about the prospects for success of this multi-dimensional, whole-of-government approach."

"That is fabulous. I'm sure our audience is thrilled to hear about how our military is making a difference in the lives of people so far away. Captain Burke, thank you for enlightening us on this important national security development."

"It's been my pleasure, Leslie."

"Captain Burke. I know you are busy, but I have one last question before I let you go."

"Please, go ahead."

"My producer just slipped me a note saying that you may be here in Centerville sometime soon. What does the future hold for you?"

"Leslie, I must say that your question has taken me a bit by surprise. I don't want to get myself into trouble by going off script," he said chuckling.

"Don't worry. I promise, we won't tell," she said, beaming at the camera.

"Leslie, as you know, my family roots go deep in the tri-county region. It was always my dream to serve our nation as a member of the most powerful military in the history of mankind. But I also knew that one day, I would lay down arms and return home to continue my public service. Once Operation Righteous Protector ends, I intend to complete my military duty and then realize that dream."

"So, should we be expecting to see your name on the ballot for the second district race next year?"

"Leslie, it would be inappropriate for me to focus on such things while we are still in the middle of a challenging fight over here. Let's just say that I'm looking forward to returning home and will certainly keep all options on the table."

"That's fabulous, Captain Burke. I know a lot of folks in this community will be planning a hero's welcome when that day comes. We look forward to seeing you home safely."

"Thank you, Leslie."

"I'm Leslie Jenkins. This has been an exclusive KCTV report with Captain Stephen J. Burke the Third, live from an undisclosed location in the Democratic Republic of Gisawi. We return now to our regularly scheduled programming."

CHAPTER FIFTEEN

———

Two weeks later, Sid and Carson stood together out in the yard watching the sun rising over the mango tree.

"The place feels like a ghost town," Carson said, searching for signs of activity.

"Yup. It's like we're the only ones left," Sid agreed.

"You ready for this?" Carson asked.

"I guess so. Hard to believe this is the last one."

"Your wife must be happy. How long has it been?" Carson asked.

Sid looked down at his watch for no particular reason. "Next week will be one month shy of a year. When I told her that I was coming home early, the first thing she asked about was my diet."

"Oh yeah," Carson chuckled. "I completely forgot about that."

"Me too," Sid sighed, shaking his head. "I figure I can drop at least ten pounds if I don't eat anything between now and when I get off the plane."

"Seems like a reasonable strategy," Carson replied, straight-faced. "Just remember to hydrate so you don't collapse when she sees you."

They walked together across the dusty yard in the direction of the headquarters building. Outside the door, they hesitated for a moment, not yet ready to go inside.

"So, when are you flying out?" Sid asked, stalling the inevitable.

"Right after the meeting. This is my last official duty, then I'm heading straight to the airport. How about you?"

"Not until later tonight. I've got a few things to finish up before I go. On the bright side, it gives me a little extra time for the crash diet," Sid said.

Carson smiled, then nodded at the door. "I guess there's no putting this off any longer. After you," he said, waving Sid ahead.

Inside the conference room, they made their way to the usual seats. Only a handful of the staff was sitting around the table, the rest having trickled away over the past week. Colonel Kittredge entered into the room appearing more relaxed than usual but still wasted no time getting down to business.

"OK, team, I know a few of you have flights to catch so let's get this done with," he instructed. "Who's up first?"

Captain Burke raised his hand. "Sir, I'll be leading off with our final public affairs update."

"Go ahead," Kittredge sighed, seeming relieved to be hearing the last of Burke's nonsense.

"Sir, at 0800 this morning, Eastern Standard Time, the Pentagon will formally announce the de-activation of Operation Righteous Protector. I'm pleased to report that we're ending the mission with the highest M-RAT numbers of any recent operation. Our stats have been through the roof since the president made the announcement last week about the strike. Our public perception index score briefly edged into the low nineties when the news came out about Odoki. Once it was confirmed that we got him, the media quickly forgot about the bombing investigation and controversy over the rap video. We're still seeing sky-high public approval marks across almost every demographic."

"Great news, Burke," Kittredge said, nodding approvingly as he studied the numbers on the slide. "General Foster will be pleased to hear this. Be sure his staff gets the latest figures. He may want to mention something about it in his speech tomorrow. Anything else?"

"Just one last thing, sir," Burke added, pulling a sheet of paper from his folder. "I've prepared our final press release. With your approval, this will go out later today once the end-of-mission has been formally announced."

"OK, let's hear it."

Effective immediately, Operation Righteous Protector (OPR), the US advisory support mission to the Democratic Republic of Gisawi (DRoG), is de-activated. The end of ORP marks the culmination of a highly successful campaign to neutralize the notorious warlord Daniel Odoki and his Gisawian Liberation Army (GLA). Last week Pentagon officials confirmed Odoki's death following a targeted strike operation against a high-level GLA leadership meeting in the remote western region of the country.

During three years of active operations, ORP validated a new conceptual model for "small-footprint, big-impact" military intervention designed to amplify American combat power through the tailored application of ground-based forward presence focused on empowering local partners. This dynamic, collaborative model produced unprecedented synergistic effects and seamless interoperability between US and Gisawian forces, enabling robust, multi-dimensional, full-spectrum joint maneuvers against a highly adaptable and unconventional adversarial force.

To achieve this outcome, the overall mission commander, Major General William G. Foster, devised and implemented an innovative public-private partnership arrangement allowing indigenous forces to leverage cutting-edge military technologies and precision targeting capabilities without placing undue demands on finite US resources. This unique commercial sector partnership has redefined the doctrinal template for future stability and support operations throughout the region.

With the formal de-activation of ORP, remaining US forces will transition to a sustained forward presence posture, assisting local partners with consolidation activities and long-term stabilization. The center of gravity for this effort will be the new joint counter-terrorism operating base and training center hosted by the Democratic Republic of Gisawi. This regional Center of Excellence will provide training and advisory support enabling long-term cooperative counter-terrorism efforts. A recently completed infrastructure upgrade to the international airport will offer US forces with access to a modernized forward logistical base and state-of-the-art facilities from which to project American influence and provide tangible reassurance of the enduring US commitment to peace and stability throughout the region.

"Good. It strikes the right tone," Kittredge said thoughtfully. "Be sure to get it out before General Foster arrives for the dedication ceremony. What's next on the agenda?" he asked, looking around the room.

"Sir, I have a few last administrative items to cover," Carson said.

"OK, go ahead."

"The deactivation of the camp is on schedule," Carson began. "Moving crews from ESP are hauling out the last of the office furniture later today. They'll start pulling all the computer equipment out of the conference room as soon as this meeting ends. By next week there should be no sign we were ever here."

"What about the gym equipment?" Kittredge asked.

"I spoke with Slyker. He promised to have his guys take it over to the new base."

"Good," Kittredge nodded. "That's top-end gear. It would have been a shame just leaving it here to rust. Anything else?"

"Yes, sir. Sid has our last intelligence update. Once that's done, we should be finished."

The colonel looked across the table at Sid, who was staring down into his notes, lost in thought.

"Sid, what have you got?"

"What?" Sid stammered, glancing up in surprise.

"The intelligence update…," the colonel reminded. "Don't check out on us yet. We're not done until we're done."

Sid blinked and looked around the room, suddenly aware that everyone was staring at him.

"Sorry, sir, I was thinking about something else," he muttered.

"So, what have you got?" Kittredge asked again, trying to keep things moving along.

"Quite a bit, I guess. Operation Brushfire continues to make steady gains. According to the latest report from MoD, Gisawian troops have seized over twenty underground sites and detained hundreds of GLA fighters over the last two weeks. The offensive has reestablished government control over most of the western region and largely dismantled the GLA's logistical network. So far government forces have encountered only sporadic resistance from the last remnants of the GLA."

"That's all good news," Kittredge said. "But why do you think there hasn't been more resistance from Odoki's fighters? I expected the GLA to hit back hard once they started losing territory, but it seems like they're just fading away into the jungle. Is there a chance they're laying low, waiting to hit back when conditions are more favorable?"

"I suppose that's a possibility," Sid said somewhat indifferently. "MoD is claiming that the one-two punch of the leadership strike on Odoki, combined with ground offensive, has paralyzed the movement. They think the remaining fighters have dispersed and are no longer able to mount an organized defense."

"I gather from your tone that you're skeptical," Kittredge said.

Sid shrugged. "To be honest, sir, I don't know what to believe."

Everyone waited for Sid to elaborate, but he said nothing more.

"Anything else?" Kittredge prodded.

"Just one last thing," Sid said, tapping a manila envelope laying in front of him on the table. "Last night, I received the final post-strike assessment."

"And?"

"It's highly compartmented. Only three of us have the clearance to see it. You, me, and Carson. Nobody else."

"Is it really that important? I think we all know the bottom line, don't we?" Kittredge said.

"Sir, I still think we should run through it before turning out the lights."

"OK," Kittredge relented, glancing down at his watch. "But let's make it quick. Everybody out of the room except for Sid and Carson," the colonel ordered. "Hurry up! We don't have all day," he prodded as the stragglers shuffled dutifully toward the door.

Once the room was empty, Sid broke the seal on the envelope and then pulled out several sheets of paper with bold red classification markings written across the top.

"Sid, we already know we got Odoki. How much more can there be?" Kittredge asked impatiently.

"Yes, sir, strictly speaking, you're correct. The forensics team confirmed a positive match between the DNA sample for Odoki and some of the remains found at the attack site."

"OK then, what's the rub? This is all old news, Sid. The president already announced all this on TV. We got him. End of story."

"Sir, there were just a few discrepancies that came up in the classified annex of the report."

"Such as?"

"For starters, it seems that the remains found at the site predated the strike."

"What do you mean, predated?" Carson interrupted.

"I mean that the bodies were already highly decomposed. There were no signs of soft tissue trauma that one would expect from a missile strike. It was basically just a bunch of old bones."

"But it wasn't just a missile strike," Kittredge reminded him. "The explosives buried under that building set off a huge secondary blast. It's hard to believe there were even any pieces left to analyze."

"All I can tell you is what was in the report," Sid continued. "The forensics team estimated that the recovered remains had been decomposing for at least a few years."

"How is that even possible?" Carson asked. "We saw guys on the ground moving into the building just a few minutes before the strike. It doesn't make any sense."

"I saw the same thing you did. But the site exploitation team said that the compound was sitting on top of a massive tunnel network where the explosives were stored. Who's to say that the guys we saw going into the building didn't escape out through those same tunnels before the strike happened? The operation wasn't exactly a well-kept secret. Someone here on base could have easily tipped them off when the drone was coming overhead."

"Sid, that's a completely crazy theory. Besides, where would they have gone?"

"Sir, looking through that drone camera is like seeing the world through a soda straw. We were all focused on the main target, but nobody was looking at anything beyond a few hundred meters from the impact point. Honestly, none of us have any idea what was really happening down there before or after the strike."

"Wait a second, Sid," Kittredge said. "Are you really suggesting that we bombed a bunch of old bones that were purposely buried underneath the building? And that some of those bones just happened to have DNA matching what we had on file for Odoki?"

"I know it sounds crazy, but I don't know how else to interpret what's in this report," Sid insisted. "That's what it says right here in black and white. There was no evidence that live human beings were inside that building when the missile hit."

"Jesus," Kittredge said. "This is not the news I wanted to hear on the day before I fly home. Does General Foster know?"

"He must," Sid confirmed. "He has access to the same report. I'm sure his staff must have briefed him on it this morning."

"Sid, let me ask you this," Carson said. "Does this really change anything? Nothing you've told us so far contradicts what the president said last week on TV. Either way, Odoki is still dead, right?"

"I suppose you can look at that way," Sid conceded. "There's no denying a positive match with DNA supposedly belonging to Odoki. But don't forget, that original sample came from Police Intelligence almost three years ago. They told us it was from Odoki, but how do we really know that for sure?"

"Sid, that's not our problem," Kittredge insisted. "We were sent here to neutralize Odoki. The Gisawians gave us what they said was his DNA. If that matches something that was blown up inside that building, in my book, that qualifies as mission accomplished. If that report doesn't say something disproving that fact, then I think this meeting is just about over. Anything else before we wrap things up?"

"Just one item, sir."

"Sid, you've got two minutes," Kittredge said, tapping at his watch to emphasize the point.

"According to the site exploitation report, the chemical residue from the secondary explosion was an exact match with the bombs that went off outside the camp gate and Police Intelligence headquarters a few months ago."

"What do you mean a match?"

"I mean that the explosives most likely came from the same source batch. If you remember, there was something a bit unusual about those first two attacks."

"Please, remind me…," Kittredge said, on the edge of losing patience.

"They weren't your typical home-cooked terrorist bombs. The explosives were commercial grade. Like the kind used for mining or engineering."

"OK, what the hell does that prove?"

"Nothing definitively, except that whoever planted those first two bombs were probably the same people who packed those tunnels full of explosives."

"Sounds like GLA to me," Kittredge declared, clearly ready to end the conversation. "I'd say, case closed."

"But sir, since the very beginning MoD has been insisting that Hezbollah bombed us! Police Intelligence has been busy cracking down on Lebanese storekeepers all over the country. If it was the GLA, then somebody better tell the Gisawians that their witch hunt has been misdirected."

"Damn it, Sid!" Kittredge said. "You're opening up a big fucking can of worms five hours before we announce the end of this mission. General Foster will be here in the morning to dedicate the new counter-terrorism operating base. This is not exactly the time to be turning over the apple cart. Especially for something like this. Nothing you've told me so far changes any of the relevant facts. Odoki is dead. Unless there is something in the report saying otherwise, then this conversation has come to an end. Am I clear on that?"

Sid looked at Carson and then back to Kittredge. "Yes, sir. Understood."

"OK then. Is that report going anywhere beyond this room?"

"No, sir. No one else is authorized to read it. It will be destroyed before we leave."

"Who else has access to it?"

"A few people at the Pentagon are cleared, but I doubt anyone will bother reading it."

"In that case, Sid, I feel comfortable in saying that our work here is done. By this time tomorrow General Foster will be at the airport dedicating the new training center and the three of us will be on our way home."

"Then that's it?" Sid asked. "Just like that?"

"Sid, do you really think digging deeper into this is going to change anything for the better?"

"Honestly, sir. I don't know."

"Well, then let me answer that question for you. It won't. We did what we were sent here to do. Now we're leaving. It's as simple as that. Hopefully, you can be proud of what you accomplished and just go on home to your family," Kittredge said. "Are you with me?"

Sid looked down at the report on the table, then picked it up and put it back into the envelope, carefully sealing the top.

"Yes, sir. I'm with you," he whispered.

"Good. The thing is, Sid, you just can't beat yourself up for not having all the answers. You're doing the right thing by letting this go. Here's what I want you to do. Go home to your wife and get some rest. A few weeks from now when you're sitting in your backyard, sipping a cold beer and putting some burgers on the grill, you're not going to be thinking about any of this. I guarantee it. You did a good job here. Just leave it at that."

Then Kittredge rose from his seat and moved toward the door. Before leaving, he turned and looked back at Sid and Carson one last time.

"Have a safe trip back. It was an honor serving with you," he said, before closing the door behind him.

The two of them sat there in silence until Carson finally spoke.

"So, what do you think?"

"About what? The report or the colonel's reaction to it?"

"Either one," Carson clarified.

"I guess the colonel was right about one thing. It doesn't really change anything. It's just a bunch of questions without any answers," Sid conceded.

"Yeah, but I can tell you're not happy about leaving it like this?" Carson hinted.

"Should I be?" Sid sighed. "Plus, there was one other thing. Not part of the final report. Something I didn't show the colonel," he added.

Sid opened up a different folder, pulled out a satellite photo, and pushed it across the table toward Carson. He studied it for a moment before looking back at Sid with a shrug.

"OK, I give up. What am I supposed to see here?" he said.

"It's a picture of the village where the church massacre happened a few years ago."

"The spot where Anna visited and talked to those women?"

"Yup."

"So, what am I supposed to be seeing that's so interesting?"

"Look to the northeast corner of the picture. Just beyond the edge of the village. What do you see?" Sid asked.

Carson strained his eyes, trying to decipher the grainy image. "You know, this isn't really my thing," he said.

"Come on. It's not rocket science. Just tell me what you think you see in the picture," Sid said.

"OK, I guess I see a big patch of ground where the vegetation has been cut back. It kind of looks like a small garden or farmer's field."

"Yeah, that's what I saw too."

"Well, so what? There must be thousands of little farms scattered all over the place. It's rural Africa. How else do people eat in the middle of nowhere?"

"Actually, there aren't any farms around that area. The village has been abandoned since the massacre. I went back into the imagery database and checked. No one has been farming near there for the last three years. But that shot was taken ten days ago. Meaning that the dirt was probably overturned sometime during the last few weeks."

"Sid, I still don't see where you're going with this. Maybe somebody moved back into the area and planted some crops. It could be a million things."

Sid shook his head. "Unlikely. There were no other changes in the area except that one spot of freshly overturned earth."

"I'm sorry, Sid, but I'm still not following you. What's your theory?" Carson said.

"Two weeks ago, we helped the Gisawians launch a drone strike against a target we knew almost nothing about. All based on MoD's claim that it was some high-level GLA meeting. Then after the strike, the exploitation team turns up a bunch of old body parts blown to smithereens by several tons of explosives buried in a tunnel network underneath the compound. Conveniently, some of those remains happened to match a DNA profile for Daniel Odoki."

Carson rubbed his chin as he mulled over Sid's story. "OK, so far, I'm following. But what about the satellite photo from the village? What's the link back to that?"

Sid pointed the tip of his pencil to the area on the imagery. "This coloration suggests a patch of freshly tilled earth, but from this resolution, it's almost impossible to tell how deeply the soil has been turned. It could be six inches or six feet."

"What are you getting at?"

"It could be someone planting a garden, or maybe digging up a mass grave."

Carson's eyes widened as he studied the picture more closely. "So, you think that Odoki has been there all along, lying in a grave next to the village that he supposedly razed?"

"I know it sounds crazy, but why not?" Sid asked.

"What's the motive? Why would someone go to all the trouble to fabricate such an elaborate story?"

"I can't answer that," Sid said. "All I know is that something doesn't add up. You remember when Anna told us about how the women from the village said there were soldiers in the area around the same time the church was attacked?"

"Hmm, yeah. I guess so."

"What if it was some kind of botched government raid? Think about it. If you're a Gisawian army commander, out there on the ground, about to get blamed for ordering a massacre. Wouldn't you rather find someone else to be the fall guy?"

"Like a notorious but rarely seen warlord?"

"Sure. Even better if you can convince a gullible super-power to join in the manhunt for the supposed perpetrator."

Carson shook his head, seeming unconvinced by the argument.

"Sid, I understand why you're suspicious. I agree, none of this makes much sense. But at this point, what's to gain by chasing after ghosts? This is all just speculation. You can't really prove any of it. Maybe you just need to go home, get some rest, and push it out of your head for a while. Like the colonel said."

"Carson, you really think that walking away from this is going to make me feel any better?" he said, holding up the envelope containing the report.

"Sid, I'm not saying that. But listen to yourself. Why would someone go to all the trouble of resurrecting a phantom warlord just to cover up an inadvertent massacre? There have got to be easier ways of fixing things like that. But even if it was true, I just don't see where this theory goes. Like the colonel said, it doesn't change anything."

"But what if this war wasn't even about Odoki to begin with?" Sid speculated.

"OK, man, now you're really losing it. You're suggesting that the entire thing was just a red herring? Are you crazy?" Carson exclaimed, waving his hands manically in the air. "If that's the case, then what the hell have we been here helping them do for the last three years?"

"That's a damn good question. How about seizing control over a valuable mining concession and eliminating a bunch of low-level freelancers who've been out there for years digging up all the profits? And maybe smuggling the minerals out of the country with the help of Lebanese shopkeepers?"

"Are you kidding me, Sid? You really expect me to believe that President Namono concocted a major military offensive just to cut out his business competition?"

"Carson, I know you think this is nuts, but that's probably the easiest part of the story to believe. In fact, no one is even trying to hide it. Think about it. A week after the start of the offensive President Namono announces a major economic development program aiming to exploit the entire region. Did you happen to look at the list of partners who signed on to the project?"

"Somehow it escaped my attention," Carson said.

"It was all Chinese mining and engineering firms. The economic development program was basically a mineral rights auction for the entire western part of the country. And conveniently, the Gisawian army is now sitting on top of the entire investment portfolio, keeping it nice and safe."

"Listen, Sid, maybe there's something to this story. But at this point, there's nothing you can do about it. You're getting on a plane in about eight hours and going home. And that report in your hands, in case you forgot, is classified top secret. Once this operation is over, no one is ever going to read it," Carson said, pointing at the envelope on the table.

"Here's the bottom line, Sid," he continued. "No one is interested in opening up this can of worms. Not on our side. Not on the Gisawian side. Nobody. What's done is done. And tomorrow morning General Foster is going to be standing over at the airport celebrating our little victory and cutting the ribbon on a new counter-terrorism training center. Do you really think anyone wants to be asking a bunch of questions about how we got here? As far as everyone outside this room is concerned, this has been one great big fucking success. Now they just want to tie it up in a bow and get on with business. Sid, I'm telling you as a friend. It's too late to be digging around in the ashes of this thing. You'll only end up getting your fingers burned."

Sid stared down at the satellite photo on the table, lost in thought. Finally, he gathered up the pages and slid them back into the envelope.

"I'm sorry, Sid," Carson said. "I know this is not how you wanted to leave things. But you did a great job here. No one can take that away from you."

"I did a great job at what? For who?" Sid asked, nodding at the envelope on the table.

Carson glanced at this watch. "Listen, Sid. I'm going to miss my flight. Let's get out of here."

Sid got up and followed Carson through the door. Out in the yard, they saw the local workers busy tearing down everything that could possibly be moved, sold, or otherwise scavenged from the camp. Soon there would be nothing left but a bare carcass of empty cinder-block huts and a naked flagpole.

"I guess this is it," Sid said, as Carson swung a duffel bag over his shoulder.

"Yup. I guess so. But it's a small army. I'm sure I'll be seeing you somewhere down the road," Carson said, reaching out for Sid's hand.

As they shook hands, a horn blared from across the compound. Sid looked over and saw Don Slyker sitting in the passenger seat of a flatbed truck filled with an assortment of old equipment from the camp. Slyker waved at Carson and pointed to his watch, signaling for him to hurry up.

"Skyler's giving me a lift over to the airport," Carson explained. "I figured he owed me one last favor."

"At least," Sid said, barely able to conceal his disgust.

"Believe it or not, the guy has actually grown on me a bit," Carson said. "Make no mistake, he's an asshole. But at least he doesn't pretend to be anything other than that. There's a certain kind of integrity to it."

"Just the same, I think I'll find a different ride over to the airport," Sid said.

"I guess I don't blame you. Anyway, good luck, Sid. It's been nice working with you," Carson said.

"Likewise. Hey, before you go. Can I ask one last favor?"

Carson took a deep breath. "Only if it has absolutely nothing to do with Odoki, the GLA, or the rest of this mess," he begged.

"Nope. I promise."

"OK then. What do you need?"

"Do you still have the screenshots of the underground blog that Burke was doing?"

"You mean his 'Black Ops' thing?"

Sid nodded.

"Maybe," Carson said evasively.

"Yeah, I figured you did," Sid said with a knowing smile.

"What do you want with it?"

"Nothing. Just burn a copy to a CD and send it to this address," Sid said, handing Carson a slip of paper.

"That's it?"

"Yup."

"Is this something I should be worried about?" Carson asked suspiciously.

"Trust me on this one. It's just a guy who will know how to handle it."

"Is this something that Burke will be happy about?"

"Nope. Just consider it a little nudge for karmic realignment."

"OK then, no problem. I'll get it done as soon as I'm back stateside," Carson said, smiling as he slipped the paper into his pocket. The horn blasted again as Slyker motioned that he was leaving, with or without Carson.

"Now I really gotta run."

"Safe travels," Sid said, watching as Carson jogged across the yard toward the truck.

+++

Carson threw his bag into the back of the truck and climbed up into the cab next to Slyker. As soon as the door was closed, the driver put the truck in gear and headed toward the front gate.

"What's the hurry?" Carson asked. "I've still got three hours until my flight leaves."

"We're on my schedule, not yours," Slyker said, staring down the road through mirrored sunglasses. "Time is money, my friend."

"Shouldn't you be taking it easy for a while, basking in the glory of your big victory?" Carson asked.

"My victory?" Slyker said, sneering at Carson through his sunglasses. "The way I see it, things turned out pretty well for everyone. You guys are going home heroes. And I'm guessing you won't have any problems on that next promotion board."

Carson simply shrugged, not entirely comfortable conceding the point. "So, you're sticking around here a bit longer?" he asked.

"Yeah. Unlike you, my job doesn't end when the war does."

"What's the new angle?"

"Same as the old, just bigger. ESP won the support

contract for the new counter-terrorism training center so I've been scrambling to get things set up."

"What a surprise," Carson said, shaking his head in disbelief.

"Hey, it pays to be prepared. We were the only firm ready to go with a proposal when the bid went out. It turned out to be a win-win for everyone. We were closing down this operation anyway, so it was easy enough to transition right over to the new location. But now it's crunch time. I've got a million things to get done before the dedication ceremony tomorrow morning."

"Putting on a big show, I assume?"

"President Namono wouldn't have it any other way," Skyler chuckled.

"Sorry I'm going to miss it."

"No worries. I'm sure you've got better places to be."

They drove for a while in silence as the truck bounced over the potholed road in the direction of the airport.

"So, is running the new base going to be a permanent gig for you?" Carson asked.

"Hell no! DRoG is a little provincial for my taste. But I promised my boss that I'd stay on through the transition. Long enough to get things set up and running smoothly. After that, he agreed to bring on some fresh talent to manage the contract for the long term."

"You really think it's going to be around for a while?"

"Are you kidding me?" Slyker laughed. "It's always easier to create these monsters than to kill them. That's Government Bureaucracy 101. Once the money starts trickling down, these things take on a life of their own. Trust me, people will find plenty of excuses to keep it alive for a long, long time."

"How reassuring."

"Hey, they don't call it the military-industrial complex for nothing," Slyker said with a shrug.

"So, if this is just a temporary gig, what's next for Don Slyker?"

"Well, between you and me, the home office was very pleased with the way things went down with the proof of concept. We got a green light to spin it off as an entirely new division, and they've asked me to take lead on the project," Slyker said, passing Carson a new business card.

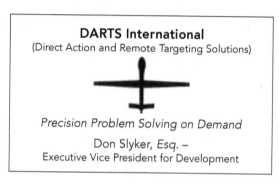

DARTS International
(Direct Action and Remote Targeting Solutions)

Precision Problem Solving on Demand

Don Slyker, Esq. –
Executive Vice President for Development

"Jesus, Slyker, you're not shying away from the merchant of death thing, are you?"

"Hey, it's just a concept card!" he blurted out defensively. "I'm playing with a few ideas before I pitch it to headquarters. Besides, the business card is the least of my worries. I'm going to be building this thing from the ground up. Lots of autonomy to chart the way ahead. This thing is going to be very high-vis inside the firm. I'll be answering straight to the top with nowhere to hide if things go wrong. This is a once-in-a-career opportunity."

"So, should I expect to see Don Slyker as the pitchman for worldwide rent-a-drone?"

"Not exactly. I'm kind of the guy behind the curtain making the magic happen. That's more my comfort zone. I've got someone else in mind to play frontman."

"Anyone I would know?"

Slyker smiled, shaking his head. "I'm not at liberty to discuss ESP's executive hiring decisions. However, I expect something will be announced very soon. Let's just say it will be a familiar face."

"I'm the edge of my seat," Carson said dryly.

A few minutes later the truck circled into the roundabout of the passenger terminal, pulling into the same parking spot where Carson had picked up Slyker several months before.

"I guess we've come full circle," he said, reaching out for Carson's hand. "No hard feelings, I hope. I know you thought I was playing you, but in the end, we're all on the same team, right?"

"I used to think that," Carson said. "But I'm not so sure anymore."

"Listen, man. The world is a complicated place. If you're searching for black and white answers or tidy endings, you're probably not going to find them around here."

"Wow, deep words of wisdom from Don Slyker. I guess I'll chalk this up as a learning experience. In any case, no hard feelings."

"Good. Of course, I wasn't going to feel bad either way," Slyker said, grinning.

"Yeah, I know. Regrets are not your style."

"True. But in all seriousness, stay in touch. I plan on keeping that B&B venture up in Ethiopia. It's going to be a real gem someday once I get the upgrades done. A perfect romantic getaway if you and the misses are ever in the mood for a little coffee-themed gastro-tourism. The VIP suite is on me if you ever make it over."

"Yeah, I'll keep that in mind," Carson said, shaking his head in amused disbelief as he climbed down from the cab and grabbed his duffel bag.

"Take care," Slyker called out, waving as the driver put the truck in gear and drove off toward the training center.

Carson stood watching until they disappeared into a cloud of dust, then turned and started walking toward the departure terminal.

+++

Back at the camp, Sid decided to take one last walk around the compound. The place was nearly empty except for a handful of local workers busily clearing away the detritus of empire. In the yard was a small mountain of broken furniture, unused office supplies, empty cans of energy drink, muscle magazines, soft-core porn videos, discarded containers of chewing tobacco, and half-empty packs of cigarettes. Sprinkled in amid the refuse pile was an assortment of local trinkets and tourist souvenirs that apparently had not made the cut from impulse purchase to treasured memento as bags were hastily packed.

Sid stood there a moment watching the hillock of garbage expand bin by bin, wondering how much of it would end up in the local markets by the end of the week, redistributed to the cosmos via secondhand junk dealers.

As he continued his farewell tour around the camp, Sid turned the corner and noticed to his surprise that the Sujah

Bean was still open. He spotted Sammy on a stepladder underneath the mango tree, taking down the Chinese lanterns from the branches. A few chairs and tables were still left in the garden. Sitting alone at their usual table was Anna, reading a magazine and nursing one last coffee. Beside her were two overstuffed travel bags. As Sid crossed the yard, she looked up and waved.

"Can I join you for one last round?" he asked.

"I can't think of a better send-off," Anna said, smiling as she put down her magazine.

Sammy appeared at the table a moment later.

"Coffee Mr. Sid?" the barista asked with a tired smile.

"That would be great, Sammy. Thank you."

"And some fried dough too, sir? The last order is on the house. No charge for my good friends," Sammy insisted.

Sid shook his head with a laugh. "No, thank you, Sammy. I would love to, but I'm back on my diet. Only water and coffee until I get home."

"Of course, sir. As you please."

"So, Sammy. Is this the last day for the café?" Sid inquired.

"Yes, sir. After your coffee, I'm closing down the hut."

"Then what?" Sid asked, genuinely concerned over his fate.

"After that, I am very busy, Mr. Sid. Very, very busy."

"That's great news, Sammy. I was worried this might be the end of Sujah Bean."

"No, sir. We have big plans ahead."

"We?" Sid questioned.

"Me and Mr. Slyker," Sammy explained. "I have the café concession at the new terrorism base."

"*Counter*-terrorism," Sid corrected.

"Yes, sir, pardon me," Sammy said with a smile. "But the new café will be much better," he added, waving his hand dismissively at the cozy little garden. "Not just coffee. Full hot menu! With wood-oven pizza!" he exclaimed.

"Wow, big league!" Sid said, genuinely happy for Sammy's good fortune.

"Yes, sir. The grand opening is tomorrow, after the dedication ceremony. We have Sammy's premium signature blend for all the VIPs. Mr. Slyker sent down ten kilos of Yirgacheffe from his plantation."

"That's great, Sammy. I'm really happy for you."

"Thank you, sir," the barista nodded excitedly. "All because of Mr. Slyker. He is a good man. A very good man."

Sid glanced over at Anna, catching an eye-roll behind her sunglasses.

"I'm going to miss you, Sammy," Sid said, reaching out to shake his hand.

"I will miss you too, Mr. Sid. Please be safe, and God bless you," Sammy said before turning back to the hut and brewing one last coffee.

"Seems like Sammy found his golden parachute," Sid said after the barista was out of earshot. "Just when I think things can't get weirder, something always proves me wrong."

"I will say this, it has all been an eye-opening experience," Anna offered with a sigh of resignation.

"So, when are you heading out?" Sid asked, nodding at her bags under the table.

"Soon. How about you?"

"Right after this coffee. Sergeant Goodwin is still here. He's driving me over to the airport. You need a ride?"

Anna shook her head. "I'm not heading to the airport."

"What do you mean? Are you swimming back to Rhode Island?"

"Nope. I'm staying here."

Sid sat back in his chair with a baffled expression on his face. "What do you mean you're staying? Don't tell me Skyler offered you a job too."

"For Christ's sake, Sid! Give me a little credit," she said. "I've had my fill of Don Slyker for one lifetime."

"Well, at least that's a relief. Then why on earth are you sticking around here? Especially after everything that's happened."

"The truth is, I didn't plan to. As of two days ago, I had tickets back to Providence and had notified my department that I was restarting work on the dissertation."

"Something changed since then?"

"Yeah, I guess you could say that. I asked Louie to come back with me to the states," she said, waiting for Sid's reaction. "This whole thing has been hard on him."

"I can imagine," Sid nodded.

"He was feeling pretty discouraged when it started becoming clear what had happened."

"Clear? Exactly what part of this do you consider clear?" Sid said.

"OK, wrong choice of words, but you know what I mean. Once he realized that nothing was quite as it seemed, I just think he had a hard time facing it. He still wanted to believe that he was on the right side of things. I guess we all did…"

Sid nodded but said nothing.

"Anyway, he was pretty conflicted about what to do next. It just seemed like he needed some time to get away and think it through. To make a long story short, I told him he could stay with me until he figured things out."

"And what did he say?"

"He thought about it for a few days, then decided he couldn't leave. But then, out of the blue, he asked me to stay," Anna chuckled, almost disbelieving her own story.

"And you agreed?"

Anna shrugged. "At least for the time being."

"Why, Anna? After everything we've seen? Do you really think you can change anything by staying here?"

"No. Probably not. But Louie does. After thinking it through, he decided that he didn't want to just give up on his country. He may not be able to fix everything from the inside, but he knows there's no way he can do it from the outside. Not by running away."

"And you believe that?"

"I'm not sure. But I admire him for believing it. I'm willing to take a chance that he's right. And maybe I can try to help him where I can."

"And what about school? What on earth will you do here?"

"I'll make it work, somehow. Louie's mom has an extra room at her house. I'll stay with her until I can find a place of my own. Louie thinks I can pick up some part-time work. Maybe teaching at one of the local schools or working with an NGO. In the meantime, I'll keep chiseling away at the dissertation. In a funny way, I'm sort of looking forward to the change of pace. Hopefully, it will inspire me just to get it done. And maybe cleanse my soul a bit after all the shit we've covered ourselves in."

"And Louie? What about him?"

Anna shook her head. "It's all kind of hard to believe. Things have been so crazy for him since the operation. They're treating him like a hero. Louie is disgusted by it all, of course, but there's not much he can do about it. When your uncle is the deputy minister of defense and the president mentions you by name in a televised speech to the country, it's hard not to play along. At least until he's in a position where he can change things for the better."

"So, what's next for him?"

"You're not going to believe it."

"Try me."

"He's been appointed the commander of the new counter-terrorism training center."

"Like I said, just when things couldn't get crazier, they do," Sid sighed.

"I know. He was shocked when his uncle told him. Apparently, it's considered a plum assignment for a rising star. It came with a promotion as well. By direct order of the minister of defense. A reward for loyalty, I suppose."

"Is he conflicted?"

"Of course, Sid! Louie's not an idiot. He realizes now that he was played by his uncle. We were all played!"

"But he still took the position? Why?"

"I know it seems counterintuitive, but Louie's convinced that the only way to fight this is from the inside. Otherwise, it is all just too opaque. Nothing is what it seems. Unfortunately, I guess we all got a taste of that."

Sid was quiet for a moment, thinking about what Anna had said.

"He's probably right," Sid finally agreed. "I just hope he can take it on without getting sucked in. It's not going to be easy. But if anyone can do it, Louie can."

"I hope that's true. I just worry that he's underestimating what he's up against. There are just too many secrets, too many people protecting their interests."

"And not just on his side," Sid lamented.

Just then Sammy appeared at the table with Sid's coffee.

"Enjoy, sir. Please have a safe trip home," Sammy said, bowing slightly before scurrying off to finish dismantling the café.

Anna and Sid sat quietly for a moment, sipping their coffees and staring up into the branches of the mango tree. Suddenly, Anna glanced across the table with a surprised look.

"Listen, Sid. I know it's our last day and we've been through a lot together, but now is not the time to try some kind of lame-o pass at me," she said, smiling mischievously. "Please stop pawing at my leg under the table like some pathetic schoolboy."

"Fuck off, Anna," Sid whispered. "Don't move. Look normal. Just pretend like we're talking."

"Sid, we are talking," she chided.

"Listen to me!" he said nervously. "Don't look down. Keep your eyes on mine. Now, very slowly, reach down under the table and grab the envelope."

Anna's eyes dropped involuntarily to the table.

"Jesus, Anna. I said, 'don't look!'" Sid scolded her.

"I'm sorry!" she whispered defensively. "I haven't practiced passing secret notes under the table since grade school. My skills are a little rusty."

"Just take it. Quickly," Sid begged. "Keep looking at me while you slip it into your bag."

Anna followed his instructions as Sid held his breath, sighing with relief once she had zipped closed the flap on her bag. Then he glanced nervously around the yard, trying to ascertain if anyone had observed the inelegant hand-off.

"What do you want me to do with it?" Anna asked, attempting to act nonchalant.

"Give it to Louie," Sid instructed.

"Why are you doing this? I don't know what's in that envelope, but I'm guessing it's something that could get you into a lot of trouble."

"Just give it to Louie. Tell him to read through it carefully. Then burn it."

"Sid, I don't understand."

"If Louie is going to stay here and fight this fight, he needs to know what he's up against. Someone besides me needs to see it."

Anna took one last sip of her coffee and then looked back across the table.

"Sid, you don't need to do this," she whispered.

"Yes, I do," he said, finishing off his drink and getting up from the table.

"You're a good egg, Sid. I'm going to miss you."

"I'll miss you too. Please be careful. And be sure to look me up if you and Louie ever get back to the states."

"Will do," she said, smiling as Sid turned and went off to find his ride.

ABOUT THE AUTHOR

Glenn Voelz served in the Army as an intelligence officer. He now lives in Oregon with his family. *War Under the Mango Tree* is his first novel; he is currently working on a sequel.